Praise for THE MATCH

"[*The Match*] shows off [Coben's] expert plotting and storytelling, which is fully on display here and makes for one heck of a good read." —Bookreporter.com

"Harlan Coben's puzzle-box mysteries have inspired numerous Netflix series, and his latest book, *The Match*, seems poised to follow suit." —PopSugar

"2022 is the year of Harlan Coben's adrenaline-pumping thrillers." —BuzzFeed

Praise for Harlan Coben

"*The Boy from the Woods* is as much an action as a psychological thriller, as much a riveting read as a superb character study in which Coben challenges himself by taking his story outside his suburban comfort zone. A must-read for any mystery or thriller fan." —*Providence Journal*

"The crafty Coben knows how to weave a compelling story with intriguing characters, and Wilde is one of his best." —Associated Press

"The modern master of the hook and twist." —Dan Brown

"Coben never, ever lets you down." —Lee Child

"The beauty of Coben's craftsmanship...is how often he can lure us into not perceiving what's clearly right in front of our eyes." —*Washington Post*

"I liked [*The Boy from the Woods*] a lot!" —Stephen King

"Harlan's a great thriller writer...one of my favorites."

—John Grisham

"Every time you think Harlan Coben couldn't get any better at uncoiling a whip snake of a page-turner, he comes along with a new novel that somehow surpasses its predecessor."

—*San Francisco Chronicle*

"Coben is simply one of the all-time greats."   —Gillian Flynn

"Harlan Coben is one of my favorite authors, and he's a fantastic thriller writer...I gobbled *Win* in literally a couple of days."

—Rachael Ray

"[Coben] has revealed himself as a master at shaping elaborate plots, and [*Win*] is no exception...Keep[s] the reader guessing."

—*Toronto Star*

"Coben, as is his wont, raises moral dilemmas readers will enjoy chewing on and pulse-pounding action scenes will keep the pages at least semifrantically turning."

—*BookPage* (Starred Review on *Win*)

"Harlan Coben's books are full of the thrilling, the unexpected, the twisty, and the memorable."   —*CrimeReads*

"There are lots of levels to [*The Boy from the Woods*]...Wilde is wild in a believable way and we want to know just what it is that keeps him going. As always, the women are great."

—*Globe and Mail*

"[Harlan Coben is] one of the world's finest thriller writers."

—Peter James

"Twisty—and we'd expect no less from the author of hot thrillers like *Tell No One* and *Missing You*."   —AARP

"Coben is the undisputed king of suspense."　　—Real Book Spy

"Harlan Coben's addictive crime novels keep readers on the edge of their seat. Get ready for twists, turns, reversals, and you'd-never-guess-it plot twists. His thrillers are virtuoso mysteries that expose the dark side of familiar settings. Prepare yourself for relatable characters, crackling prose, and shocking endings."
　　　　　　　　　　　　　　　　　　　　—*Reader's Digest*

"Fun to read...with some tricky twists."
　　　　　　　　　　　　—*Pittsburgh Post-Gazette* on *Win*

"*The Boy from the Woods* is a one-sit read. The characters and plotlines are so well drawn out that it is easy to find yourself caught up inside them."　　　　　　　—Bookreporter.com

"Harlan Coben is one of the best suspense novelists on the scene today."　　　　　　　　　　　—*Huffington Post*

"Harlan Coben is a master at writing spellbinding thrillers, and his latest, *The Boy from the Woods*, is no exception...a wild ride."
　　　　　　　　　　　　　　　　　—*Orange County Register*

"There may be no other thriller writer alive today who has mastered that fundamental trick of the genre. When you start a new Coben novel, or just pick one up and read the jacket copy, you know that nothing will unfold as it seems. You can be assured that surprises will keep appearing until the final page."　　　—*BookTrib*

"Coben never lets the pace stall."　　　　　—*Detroit News*

"I read [Harlan Coben's] new book *Run Away* straight through without moving. It's RIVETING."　　　—Ann Patchett

"A thriller laced with plot twists and bombshells."
　　　　　　　　　　　　　　　　　—*USA Today* on *Run Away*

"Coben keeps you in suspense from beginning to end."
—*Newark Tribune*

"[A] greased-lightning domestic thriller." —*Kirkus* on *Run Away*

"[Harlan Coben is the] master of 'the hook.'"
—*Charlotte Observer*

"Solid Coben, with clever plotting and dead-on character sketches."
—*Booklist* on *Run Away*

"A master at creating a page-turner that will keep you up reading until the wee hours and keep you guessing right up until the end." —Joan Lunden

"Coben is like a skilled magician saving the best, most stunning trick for the very end." —*Publishers Weekly*

"Another Coben classic—you'll tear through it—and wish it could last."
—George Stephanopoulos, *Good Morning America* on *Run Away*

"[Harlan Coben is the] master of the suburban thriller."
—Associated Press

"Harlan Coben has long been the master of the jaw-dropping twist."
—*Providence Journal*

"Being a master, Coben knows how to hook readers from the opening line...readers are lucky to go along for the ride."
—*Star-Ledger*

"Coben's unique imagination has made him a past master of fast and witty dialogue, and architect of memorable characters."
—*New York Journal of Books*

"A twisty, edge-of-your-seat thriller...to say more would ruin the sheer genius of...an absolutely brilliant, taut thriller that begs to be read in one sitting."

—*Library Journal* (Starred Review on *Run Away*)

"Coben stands on the accelerator and never lets up."   —*People*

"I'm a huge Harlan Coben fan, and I just finished *Run Away*— maybe my all-time favorite of his! In addition to the incredible twists and surprises that he is famous for, the book is a powerful and emotional portrait of a father's anguish at losing his daughter, and the limitless lengths that parents will go in order to save their child from danger. Impossible to put down!"

—S. A. Lelchuk, *Entertainment Weekly*

"A propulsive thriller about a man whose quest to enact vigilante justice takes him down a dangerous path."   —PopSugar on *Win*

"*Run Away* by Harlan Coben proves once again he is a master storyteller...exciting and riveting. Readers will be unable to put the book down."   —*Crimespree Magazine*

"Yet another fantastic thriller from the master."

—Bookstr.com on *Run Away*

"Harlan Coben has been keeping me awake at night."

—*Orlando Sentinel*

"Few of Harlan Coben's thrillers are anything less than gripping, but every now and again he writes one that exceeds his own high standards. *Run Away* is one."   —*The Times Online*

ALSO BY HARLAN COBEN

THE
MATCH

HARLAN COBEN

GRAND
CENTRAL

New York Boston

This book is a work of fiction. Names, characters, places, and incidents are the product of the author's imagination or are used fictitiously. Any resemblance to actual events, locales, or persons, living or dead, is coincidental.

Copyright © 2022 by Harlan Coben

Cover design by Philip Pascuzzo
Cover art from Getty Images
Cover copyright © 2022 by Hachette Book Group, Inc.

Hachette Book Group supports the right to free expression and the value of copyright. The purpose of copyright is to encourage writers and artists to produce the creative works that enrich our culture.

The scanning, uploading, and distribution of this book without permission is a theft of the author's intellectual property. If you would like permission to use material from the book (other than for review purposes), please contact permissions@hbgusa.com. Thank you for your support of the author's rights.

Grand Central Publishing
Hachette Book Group
1290 Avenue of the Americas, New York, NY 10104
grandcentralpublishing.com
twitter.com/grandcentralpub

Originally published in hardcover and ebook by Grand Central Publishing in March 2022

First Trade Paperback Edition: February 2023

Grand Central Publishing is a division of Hachette Book Group, Inc. The Grand Central Publishing name and logo is a trademark of Hachette Book Group, Inc.

The publisher is not responsible for websites (or their content) that are not owned by the publisher.

The Hachette Speakers Bureau provides a wide range of authors for speaking events. To find out more, go to www.hachettespeakersbureau.com or call (866) 376-6591.

Library of Congress Control Number: 2021949901

ISBN: 9781538748282 (hardcover), 9781538748336 (ebook), 9781538710227 (large print), 9781538724453 (signed edition), 9781538724446 (special signed edition), 9781538723333 (international trade), 9781538748299 (trade paperback)

Printed in the United States of America

LSC-C

Printing 1, 2022

In loving memory of
Penny Hubbard
1966–2021

CHAPTER
ONE

At the age of somewhere between forty and forty-two—he didn't know exactly how old he was—Wilde finally found his father.

Wilde had never met his father. Or his mother. Or any family member. He didn't know their names or where he was born or when or how he, as a very young child, ended up living alone in the woods of the Ramapo Mountains, fending for himself. Now, more than three decades after being "rescued" as a little boy— "ABANDONED AND FERAL!" one headline had put it; "A MODERN-DAY MOWGLI!" shouted another—Wilde sat no more than twenty yards from a blood relative and the elusive answers to his mysterious origin.

His father's name, he had recently learned, was Daniel Carter. Carter was sixty-one years old and married to a woman named Sofia. They had three grown daughters—Wilde's half sisters, he assumed—Cheri, Alena, and Rosa. Carter lived in a four-bedroom ranch on Sundew Avenue in Henderson, Nevada. He worked as a residential general contractor for his own company, DC Dream House Construction.

Thirty-five years ago, when young Wilde was first discovered living alone in the woods, doctors estimated his age to be between six and eight years old. He had no memory of parents or caregivers or any life other than scrounging around to survive in those mountains alone. That little boy stayed alive by breaking into empty cabins and summer homes, raiding the refrigerators and pantries. Sometimes he slept in empty homes or in tents he'd stolen from garages; mostly, if the weather was cooperative, young Wilde liked to sleep outside under the stars.

He still did.

After he was located and "rescued" from this untamed existence, Child Services placed the little boy with a temporary foster family. With the onslaught of media attention, most speculated that someone would come forward immediately and claim "Little Tarzan." But days turned into weeks. Then months. Then years. Then decades.

Three decades.

No one ever came forward.

There were rumors, of course. Some believed that Wilde had been born into a mysterious and secretive local mountain tribe, that the little boy had run off or been handled in a somewhat negligent manner, and so the tribespeople feared admitting he was one of their own. Others theorized that the little boy's memories were faulty, that he couldn't really have survived on his own in the harsh woods for years, that he was too articulate and intelligent to have raised himself with no parents. Something awful had happened to little Wilde, these people surmised—something so traumatic that the boy's coping mechanism had blocked out all memory of the incident.

That wasn't true, Wilde knew, but whatever.

His only early memories came in incomprehensible snap-flash visions and dreams: a red banister, a dark house, a portrait of a man with a mustache, and sometimes, when the visions decided to be audible, a woman screaming.

Wilde—his foster father had come up with that apropos name—became something of an urban legend. He was the local boogeyman who lived alone in the mountains. If parents in the Mahwah area wanted to make sure that their offspring came home at sunset—if they wanted to discourage them from wandering through those miles of thicket and trees—they'd remind their children that once darkness set in, the Boy from the Woods would come out of hiding—angry, feral, thirsting for blood.

Three decades had gone by and still no one, including Wilde, had a clue about his origin.

Until now.

From his rental car parked across the street, Wilde watched Daniel Carter open the front door and head toward his pickup truck. He zoomed in on his father's face with his iPhone camera and snapped a few photos. He knew that Daniel Carter was currently working on a new town house development—twelve units, each with three bedrooms, 2.5 baths, and according to the website, a kitchen with "charcoal-colored cabinetry." Under the "about" section of DC Dream House Construction's website, it read, "For twenty-five years, DC Dream House Construction has designed, built, and sold top-quality, top-value homes that are personalized to meet your needs and dreams."

Wilde texted three of the photos to Hester Crimstein, a re-nowned New York City attorney and probably the closest thing he had to a mother figure. He wanted Hester's take on whether she thought there was any resemblance between himself and the man who was supposed to be his biological father.

Five seconds after hitting send, Hester called him.

Wilde answered and said, "Well?"

"Whoa."

"'Whoa' as in he looks like me?"

"If he looked any more like you, Wilde, I'd think you were using age-progression software."

"So you think—"

"It's your father, Wilde."

He just held the phone to his ear.

"You okay?" Hester asked.

"Fine."

"How long have you been watching him?"

"Four days."

"So what are you going to do?"

Wilde thought about that. "I could just leave well enough alone."

"Nah."

He said nothing.

"Wilde?"

"What?"

"You're being a candy-ass," Hester said.

"Candy-ass?"

"My grandson taught me that phrase. It means coward."

"Yeah, I got that."

"Go talk to him already. Ask him why he left a little boy alone in the woods. Oh, then call me immediately because I'm super curious."

Hester hung up.

Daniel Carter's hair was white, his skin sun-kissed, his forearms ropey probably from a lifetime of manual labor. His family, Wilde had observed, seemed pretty tight. Right now, his wife, Sofia, was smiling and waving goodbye as he got into his pickup truck.

The past Sunday, Daniel and Sofia had a family barbecue in their backyard. Their daughters Cheri and Alena and their families had been there. Daniel worked the grill wearing a chef's hat and an apron reading "Trophy Husband." Sofia served sangria and potato salad. When the sun dropped low, Daniel lit the firepit, and the entire family actually roasted marshmallows and played board games, like something out of a Rockwell painting. Wilde expected to feel a pang as he watched them, pondering on all he had missed, but in truth he felt very little.

It wasn't a better life than his. It was just different.

A big part of him wanted to drive to the airport and fly home. He had spent the last six months living something of a normal, domestic existence in Costa Rica with a mother and her daughter, but now it was time to return to his remote Ecocapsule deep in the heart of the Ramapo Mountains. That was where he belonged, where he felt most at home.

Alone. In the woods.

Hester Crimstein and the world at large may be "super curious" about the origin of "The Boy from the Woods," but the boy himself was not. He had never been. In his view, his parents were either dead or had abandoned him. What difference did it make who they were or what their reason was? It wouldn't change anything, at least not for the better.

Wilde was good, thank you very much. There was no reason to add unnecessary upheaval to his life.

Daniel Carter turned the ignition key of the pickup truck. He headed down Sundew Avenue and made a left on Sandhill Sage Street. Wilde followed. A few months back, Wilde had succumbed to the temptation and reluctantly put his DNA into one of those online genealogy databases that were all the rage. It didn't mean anything, he told himself. If a match came in, he could still ignore it if he chose to. It was a noncommittal first step, nothing more.

When the results came in, there was nothing earth-shattering. His closest match was someone with the initials PB, whom the site described as a second cousin. Big deal. PB reached out. Wilde was about to respond, but life ended up throwing him a massive curveball. Surprising even himself, Wilde ended up leaving the woods he had always called home for an unconventional attempt at family life in Costa Rica.

It hadn't gone as planned.

Two weeks ago, while packing to leave Costa Rica, the DNA genealogy site had sent him an email with the subject: "IMPORTANT UPDATE!" They'd matched him to "a relative sharing far more DNA" than "any other in your relative chain." This account went by the initials DC. At the bottom of the email, a hyperlink urged him to "LEARN MORE!" Against his better instincts, he clicked it.

DC was, according to the age, gender, and match percentile, Wilde's father.

Wilde had just stared at the screen.

Now what? The door to his past was right in front of him. All he had to do was turn the knob. Still, Wilde hesitated. Didn't this crazy, intrusive website work the other way too? If Wilde had received notification that his father was on the site, didn't it stand to reason that his father received one saying that his son was here too?

Why didn't DC reach out to him?

For two days, Wilde let it go. At one point, he almost deleted his entire genealogy profile. No good could come of this. He knew that. Over the years, he had gone through all the possible machinations that might explain how a little boy had ended up in the woods, left alone for years, left (if we want to be frank) to die.

When he'd called Hester about this paternal match and his reluctance to pursue it, she'd said, "You want my take?"

"Sure."

"You're a schmuck."

"Helpful."

"Listen to me closely, Wilde."

"Okay."

"I'm a lot older than you."

"True."

"Quiet. I'm about to drop some knowledge on you."

"Did you get that line from *Hamilton*?"

"I did."

He rubbed his eyes. "Continue."

"The ugliest truth is better than the prettiest lie."

Wilde frowned. "Is that from a fortune cookie?"

"Don't be a wiseass. You can't walk away from this. You know that. You need to know the truth."

Hester was, of course, right. He may not want to turn that knob, but he couldn't spend the rest of his life staring at the door either. He signed back onto the DNA site and wrote a message to DC. He kept it short and simple:

I may be your son. Could we speak?

When he hit send, an auto-reply bounced back. According to the website, DC was no longer in the database. That was both suspicious and odd—his father choosing to delete his account—but it suddenly hardened Wilde's resolve to get answers. Screw turning the doorknob; it was time to kick the damn door down. He called Hester back.

If Hester's name seems familiar, it could be because she's legendary television attorney Hester Crimstein, host of *Crimstein on Crime*. She made some calls, used her connections. Wilde worked some other sources from his own years in what is dubiously dubbed "freelance security." It took ten days, but eventually they got a name:

Daniel Carter, age sixty-one, of Henderson, Nevada.

Four days ago, Wilde flew from Liberia, Costa Rica, to Las Vegas, Nevada. Now here he was, in a blue Nissan Altima rental, following Daniel Carter's Ram pickup truck to a construction site. He had stalled long enough. When Daniel Carter pulled up to the town house development, Wilde parked on the street and got out of the car. The construction noise was in full throat, deafening. Wilde was about to make his move when he saw two workers approach Carter. Wilde waited. One man handed Carter a hard hat. The other handed him some sort of earplugs. Carter put them all on and led his cohorts into the heart of the development. Their work boots kicked up desert dust to the point where it was hard to see them. Wilde watched and waited. A sign put up with two-by-fours announced in too-ornate a font that VISTA MEWS—could you come up with a more generic name?—would feature "three-bedroom luxury town houses" with a starting price of $299,000. A red banner slashing left to right read: "COMING SOON!"

Daniel Carter might have been the foreman or general contractor or whatever you might call the boss, but the man clearly didn't mind getting his hands dirty. Wilde watched as he led his workers by example. He hammered in a beam. He threw on protective goggles and drilled. He inspected the work, nodding toward his employees when he was happy, pointing out deficiencies when he wasn't. The workers respected him. Wilde could tell. Or maybe Wilde was projecting. Hard to know.

Twice Wilde saw Daniel Carter alone and started to make his approach, but someone always got there first. The site was busy, in constant motion, loud. Wilde hated loud noises. Always had. He decided to wait and catch his father when he got back home.

At five p.m., the workers started to leave. Daniel Carter was one of the last. He waved goodbye and hopped into his pickup. Wilde followed him back to the ranch on Sundew Avenue.

When Daniel Carter turned off the ignition and stepped out of the truck, Wilde pulled up and parked in front of his house. Carter spotted Wilde and stopped moving. The front door of the ranch opened. His wife, Sofia, greeted him with an almost celestial smile.

Wilde slid out of the car and said, "Mr. Carter?"

His father stayed by the open truck door, almost as though he were debating getting back in and driving away. Carter took his time, staring warily at the interloper. Wilde wasn't sure what to say next, so he went with the simplest:

"Could I have a word with you?"

Daniel Carter glanced toward Sofia. Something passed between them, the unspoken language of a couple who had been together some three decades, Wilde assumed. Sofia stepped back inside and closed the door.

"Who are you?" Carter asked.

"My name is Wilde." He took a few steps closer so that he wouldn't have to shout. "I think you're my father."

CHAPTER

TWO

D aniel Carter didn't say much.

He listened quietly while Wilde explained about his past, about the DNA genealogy site, about reaching the conclusion that they were most likely father and son. Carter kept his expression neutral throughout, nodding every once in a while, wringing his hands maybe, losing a little color in his face. Carter's stoicism impressed Wilde, reminded him, oddly enough, of himself.

They were still in the front yard. Carter kept sneaking glances back at his house. Finally, he said, "Let's take a drive."

They got in the pickup truck and drove in silence, neither feeling the need to talk. Wilde assumed that his words had stunned Carter, that Carter was using the drive like a boxer uses the standing eight count. But maybe not. Hard to read people. He could be stunned. He could be cunning.

Ten minutes later, they slid into a booth at Mustang Sally's, a sixties-themed diner located inside a Ford car dealership. The booth had red vinyl seating and tried very hard to bring on nostalgia, but when you come from New Jersey, faux diners just don't cut it.

"You after money?" Carter asked him.

"No."

"I didn't think so." He let loose a long breath. "I guess I could start off by doubting your claim."

"You could," Wilde agreed.

"We could do a paternity test."

"We could."

"But I don't really see the need. There is a resemblance between us."

Wilde said nothing.

Carter ran his hand through his white mane of hair. "Man, this is weird. I have three daughters. Did you know that?"

Wilde nodded.

"Greatest blessings of my life, those girls." He shook his head. "You're going to have to give me a few minutes with this, okay?"

"Okay."

"I know you have a ton of questions. So do I."

A young waitress came over and said, "Hey, Mr. C."

Daniel Carter gave her a warm smile. "Hey, Nancy."

"How's Rosa?"

"She's doing great."

"Tell her I say hey."

"I sure will."

"What can I get you fellas?"

Daniel Carter ordered a club sandwich with fries. He gestured toward Wilde, who ordered the same. Nancy asked if they wanted anything to drink. Both men shook their heads at the same time. Nancy picked up the menus and left.

"Nancy Urban went to high school with my youngest," Carter said when she was out of earshot. "Great kid."

"Uh-huh."

"They both played on the same volleyball team."

"Uh-huh," Wilde said again.

Carter leaned in a little. "I really don't get this."

"That makes two of us."

"I can't believe what you're telling me. You're really that little boy they found in the woods all those years ago?"

"I am," Wilde said.

"I remember the news stories. They called you Little Tarzan or something. Hikers spotted you, right?"

"Yes."

"In the Appalachians?"

Wilde nodded. "The Ramapo Mountains."

"Where are those?"

"New Jersey."

"Seriously? The Appalachians reach New Jersey?"

"They do."

"I didn't realize that." Carter shook his head again. "I've never been to New Jersey."

So there you had it. His birth father had never been to the state Wilde had called home his whole life. Wilde wasn't sure what, if anything, to make of that.

"You don't think of New Jersey as having mountains," Carter said, trying to grasp at anything. "I think more about overcrowding and pollution and Springsteen and *The Sopranos.*"

"It's a complicated state," Wilde said.

"So's Nevada. You can't believe the changes I've seen."

"How long has Nevada been home for you?" Wilde asked, trying to gently steer the conversation.

"I was born near here, in a town called Searchlight. Ever heard of it?"

"No."

"It's about forty minutes south of here." He pointed with his finger, as though that was helpful, then he looked at the finger, shook his head, put his hand down. "I'm making small talk for no good reason. I'm sorry."

"It's fine," Wilde said.

"It's just...a son." His eyes may have been welling up. "I'm having trouble wrapping my head around that."

Wilde said nothing.

"Let me tell you one thing right off the top, okay, because I'm sure you're wondering." He dropped his voice. "I didn't know about you. I didn't know I had a son."

"When you said 'didn't know'—"

"I mean, never. Not until this very moment. This is all a complete shock to me."

Something cold coursed through Wilde. He had waited for answers like this his whole life. He had blocked on it, pretended that it didn't matter, and in many ways it didn't, but of course, the curiosity was there. At some point he'd decided that he wouldn't let the unknowable define him. He had been left in the woods to die and somehow survived. That obviously changed a person, molded them, was part of everything they did or became.

"Like I said, I have three daughters. To find out now, all these years later, that I had a son before any of them were even born . . ." He shook his head and blinked his eyes. "Oh boy, I have to get acclimated to this. Just give me a little time to catch my breath."

"Take your time."

"You said they call you Wilde?"

"Yes."

"Who named you that?"

"My foster father."

"Apropos," Carter said. Then: "Was he good to you? Your foster father?"

Wilde didn't like being on the answering end here, but he said "Yes," and left it at that.

Carter still wore his work shirt. There was a film of dust on it. He reached into the breast pocket and pulled out a pen and reading glasses. "Tell me again when you were found."

"April of 1986."

Carter wrote that down on the paper mat. "And they guessed you were how old?"

"Six, seven, something like that."

He wrote that down too. "So that means, give or take a year, you were born around 1980."

"Yes," Wilde said.

Daniel Carter nodded, his eyes on his writing. "My guess would be, Wilde, that you were conceived sometime in the summer of 1980 and born nine months later, so that would be, what, between March and May of 1981."

A small vibration shook the table. Carter picked up his mobile phone and squinted at the screen. "Sofia," he said out loud. "My wife. I better answer it."

Wilde managed to gesture for him to go ahead.

"Hey, hon...Yeah, I'm at Mustang Sally's." As he listened, Carter flicked his gaze toward Wilde. "A supplier. He's bidding to get the PVC pipe order. Right, yeah, I'll tell you about it later." Another pause before he added a very sincere, "Love you."

He hung up and put the phone back on the table. He stared at it for a long time.

"That woman is the best thing that ever happened to me," he said. Still staring at the phone, he added, "It must have been hard on you, Wilde. Not knowing about your past. I'm sorry."

Wilde said nothing.

"Can I trust you?" Carter asked. Before Wilde could respond, Daniel Carter waved him off. "Dumb question. Insulting even. I have no right to ask anything from you. And a man either keeps his word or he doesn't. Asking him isn't going to change anything. The biggest liars I've ever met are the best at making promises and holding eye contact."

Carter folded his hands and put them on the table. "I guess you're here for answers."

Wilde didn't trust his voice, so he nodded.

"I'll tell you what I can, okay? I'm just trying to think of where to start. I guess with..." He looked up in the air, blinked, dove in. "So Sofia and I started dating our senior year of high school. Fell in love pretty fast. We were kids though. You know how it is.

Anyway, Sofia is a lot smarter than me. When we graduated, she went to college. Out of state. In Utah. First in her family to attend college. I joined the air force. Did you serve?"

"Yes."

"What branch?"

"Army."

"Did you see action?" he asked.

Wilde didn't like to talk about it. "Yes."

"I didn't. My age, I was lucky. After Vietnam, I mean in the seventies and up until Reagan bombed Libya in 1986, it felt like we'd never go to war again. I know how weird that sounds now, but it's true. That's what Nam did to our psyche. Gave us a nation-wide case of PTSD, which maybe was a good thing. I was mostly stationed at Nellis, maybe half an hour from here, but I also did short stints overseas. Ramstein in Germany. Mildenhall in the UK. I didn't fly or anything. I worked Pavement and Construction Equipment, basically building bases. It's where I learned about construction."

Waitress Nancy interrupted. "The fries were ready, so I brought them out first. They're best when they're hot."

Carter snapped on the wide, charming smile. "Well, isn't that thoughtful of you? Thank you, Nancy."

Nancy Urban set down the big basket of fries between the two men and put small plates in front of them. There was already ketchup on the table, but Nancy moved the bottle to the center, as though to remind them it was there. When she left, Carter reached out and grabbed a single fry.

"Sofia and I got engaged right before I left for my summer assign-ment at Ramstein. We were still really young, and I was worried about losing her. She was meeting all these cool people at college. Every high school couple I knew had already broken up—or had a shotgun marriage because they were pregnant. Anyway, I bought an engagement ring from a pawnshop of all places." He narrowed his eyes. "Do you have any trouble with alcohol, Wilde?"

"No."

"Drugs? Any kind of addiction?"

Wilde shifted in the booth. "No."

Carter smiled. "I'm glad to hear that. I had a bout with alcohol, though I'm twenty-eight years sober. But I can't blame that. Not really. The long and short of it? I had a crazy summer in Europe. I figured it was my last chance as a single man, and stupidly I thought I should sow my wild oats or whatever nonsense we men used to justify acting out that way. That summer was the only time I cheated on Sofia, and sometimes, even after all these years, I look over at her sleeping and feel guilty. But I did it. One-night stands, we used to call it. Heck, I think people probably still call them one-night stands, don't they?"

He looked at Wilde as though he expected him to answer.

"I guess," Wilde said to keep the conversation going.

"Right. You married, Wilde?"

"No."

"Not my business, sorry."

"It's okay."

"Anyway, I slept with eight girls the summer of 1980. Yep, I know the exact number. How pathetic is that? Other than Sofia, they are the only women I've had sex with in my entire life. So the obvious conclusion here is that your mother is one of those eight women."

Conceived during a one-night stand, Wilde thought. Did that matter? Wilde couldn't see how. Perhaps there was some irony in the fact that Wilde was most comfortable in short-term situations or, more bluntly, one-night stands. He'd had girlfriends, women he tried to connect with, but somehow it never quite worked out.

"Those eight women," Wilde said.

"What about them?"

"Do you have their names or addresses?"

"No." Carter rubbed his chin, his eyes turning upward. "I only remember a few first names, sorry."

"Did any ever reach out to you?"

"You mean after? No. I never heard from any of them again. You have to remember. This was 1980. None of us had mobile phones or emails. I didn't know their last names, they didn't know mine. Do you ever listen to Bob Seger and the Silver Bullet Band?"

"Not really."

A wistful smile crossed his face. "Oh man, you're missing out. I bet you've heard 'Night Moves' or 'Turn the Page.' Anyway, in 'Night Moves,' Bob sings, 'I used her, she used me, but neither one cared.' That's what it was like for me that summer."

"So they were all one-night stands?"

"Well, one girl was a weekend fling, I guess. In Barcelona. So that was more like three nights."

"And they only knew you as Daniel," Wilde said.

"I go by Danny mostly, but yeah."

"No last names. No addresses."

"Right."

"Did you tell them you were a soldier or where you were stationed?"

He thought about that. "I may have."

"But even if you did," Wilde continued, "Ramstein is huge. Over fifty thousand Americans."

"You've been?"

Wilde nodded. He had spent three weeks there training for a secret mission in northern Iraq. "So if a young woman got pregnant and she wanted to find the father and came to the base looking for a Danny or Daniel—"

"Hold up," Carter interrupted. "Do you think your mother looked for me?"

"I don't know. It's 1980. She's pregnant. Maybe. Or maybe not. Maybe she was just one-night-standing too. Maybe she had one-night stands with a bunch of guys and didn't know or care who the father was. I don't know."

"But you're right," Carter said, his face seeming to drain of color. "Even if she tried to find me, she would never have been able to locate me at that base. And I was only there for eight weeks. I may have even been back stateside by the time she'd learned that she was pregnant."

Nancy came back with their sandwiches. She placed one platter in front of Carter, one in front of Wilde. Her eyes danced between the two. Sensing the mood, Nancy hurried away.

"Eight women," Wilde said. "How many of them were Americans?"

"What difference does that make?" Then: "Oh right, I see. You were left in the woods in New Jersey. It would stand to reason that your mother would be American."

Wilde waited.

"Only one. I mostly met the girls in Spain. It was like spring break for all kinds of Europeans back then."

Wilde tried to keep his breathing even. "What do you remember about her?"

Carter picked up a single french fry, held it between his thumb and forefinger. He stared down at it as though it might give him the answer. "I think her name was Susan."

"Okay," Wilde said. "Where did you meet Susan?"

"A discotheque in Fuengirola. That's a town on the Costa del Sol. I remember saying hi to her and being surprised when I heard her accent because there were so few Americans who vacationed down there."

"So you're at the disco," Wilde continued. "Try to think back. Who were you with?"

"Some guys from my regiment, I guess. I don't remember. Sorry. They may have been there. We'd bounce from disco to disco."

"Did Susan tell you where she was from?"

Carter shook his head. "In fact, I can't even say for sure she was American. Like I said, we rarely saw young American girls down there. It wasn't a spot for them back in 1980. But her accent was clearly American, so I'm guessing she was from here. I also had a lot to drink. I remember dancing with her. That's what you did. You danced hard and sweaty and then you left."

"Where did you two go?"

"A couple of us had chipped in for a room at a hotel."

"Do you remember the name of the hotel?"

"No, but it was right near the nightclub. A high-rise. I remember it was round."

"Round?"

"Yeah. It was a round high-rise. Distinctive. Our room had a balcony. Don't ask me how I remember that, but I do. If I looked at pictures of hotels online, I could probably figure it out. If it's still there."

Like that would make a difference, Wilde thought. Like he could fly over to Spain and visit some hotel and ask them whether a young American woman named Susan had a one-night stand in their hotel in 1980.

"Do you remember when exactly this happened?"

"You mean like the date?"

"Whatever, yes."

"I think she was later in my stay? Like the sixth or seventh girl, so probably August. But that's a guess."

"Was she staying at this round high-rise too?"

He made a face. "I don't know. I doubt it."

"Who was she traveling with?"

"I don't know."

"When you started talking to her, was she with anyone?"

He slowly shook his head. "I'm sorry, Wilde. I don't remember."

"What did she look like?"

"Brown hair. Pretty. But..." He shrugged and said that he was sorry again.

They talked about other possibilities. An Ingrid from Amsterdam. Rachel or Racquel from Manchester. Anna from Berlin. An hour passed. Then another. They eventually ate the sandwiches and the now-cold french fries. Daniel Carter's phone buzzed several times. He ignored it. They talked, though Carter did the majority of the speaking. Wilde wasn't one for opening up.

When the phone buzzed yet again, Daniel Carter signaled Nancy for the bill. Wilde said that he would pay it, but Carter shook him off. "I would say it's the least I could do, but that would be too insulting."

They got back into the pickup truck and started back toward the house on Sundew Avenue. Both men fell into a silence so thick you could reach out and touch it. Wilde looked out the front windshield at the night sky. He had spent his entire life looking up at the stars, but there was something about the color of the sky just past dusk, the turquoise tint that you only find in the American Southwest.

"Where are you staying tonight?" his father asked.

"The Holiday Inn Express."

"Nice."

"Yeah."

"I need to ask you a favor, Wilde."

Wilde looked over at his father's profile. There was no doubting the resemblance to his own. Carter was staring out the front windshield, his gnarled hands gripping the wheel at a perfect ten-and-two-o'clock.

"I'm listening," Wilde said.

"I got a really nice family," he said. "Loving wife, wonderful doting daughters, grandkids even."

Wilde said nothing.

"We are pretty simple people. We work hard. We try to do the right thing. I've owned my own business for a long time now. I never cheat anyone. I provide a solid service to my customers. Twice a year, me and Sofia, we take a vacation in an Airstream to a different national park. The girls used to come with us, but now, well, they've got families of their own."

Carter carefully put on his turn signal and steered hand over hand. Then he looked at Wilde.

"I don't want to drop a grenade on their lives," he said. "You can understand that, can't you?"

Wilde nodded. "I can," he said.

"When I got home from that summer, Sofia met me at the airbase. She asked me about what I'd done over there. I looked her straight in the eye, and I lied. It may seem like a long time ago—and it is, don't get me wrong—but if Sofia hears now that our marriage was built on that lie..."

"I understand," Wilde said.

"I just...can I have a little time? To think about it?"

"Think about what?"

"To think about telling them. If I should tell them. How I should tell them."

Wilde thought about that. He wasn't so sure that he wanted any of that either. Did he want three new sisters? No. Did he want or need a father? No. He was a loner. He chose to live by himself in the woods. He was best detached. The only person he felt any real responsibility toward was his godson, Matthew, a high school senior—and the only reason he did was because Matthew's father, David, Wilde's only friend, had died because of Wilde's negligence. He owed the kid. He would always owe him.

There were other people in his life. No man, not even Wilde, was an island.

But did he need this in his life?

When they pulled onto Sundew Avenue, Wilde felt his father stiffen. Sofia and his daughter Alena were on the front stoop.

"How about this?" Daniel Carter began. "We meet for breakfast tomorrow morning. Eight a.m. at the Holiday Inn Express. We discuss it then and make a plan."

Wilde nodded as Carter pulled into the driveway. Both men hopped out. Sofia hurried toward her husband. Her husband started peddling the PVC pipe supplier story again, but judging by the way she looked at him, Wilde was not convinced that Sofia was buying it. She never took her eyes off Wilde.

When it didn't seem to be overly rude, Wilde made a production of checking his watch and said that he had to go. He quickly headed toward his rental. He didn't look back, but he could feel their eyes on him. He slid into the driver's seat and hit the accelerator. He never, not once, looked over his shoulder. When he got back to the Holiday Inn Express, Wilde packed his bag. There wasn't much stuff. He checked out, drove to the airport, dropped the car off at the rental dealership.

Then he caught the last flight from Las Vegas back home to New Jersey.

He sat in a window seat and replayed the conversation. He didn't want to drop grenades on them. He didn't want to drop grenades on himself.

It's over, he thought.

But he was wrong.

THREE

C hris Taylor, formerly known as The Stranger, said, "Next up—Giraffe."

Giraffe cleared their throat. "I don't want to sound melodramatic."

"You always sound melodramatic." That was Panther. Everyone chuckled.

"Fair enough. But this time...I mean, this guy deserves a world of hurt."

"A Category 5 hurricane of hurt," Alpaca agreed.

"A Black Death plague of hurt," Kitten added.

"If anyone deserves our worst," Panther said, "it's this guy."

Chris Taylor sat back and looked at the faces on his giant wall monitor. To the layman, this looked like a Zoom call on steroids, but this meeting was taking place on a secure video conferencing program Chris himself had designed. There were six of them on the screen, stacked three on top, three on the bottom. Their true images were hidden by full-body digital Animoji of, you guessed it, a giraffe, a panther, an alpaca, a kitten, a polar bear, and The Stranger's own mask as the group leader, the lion. Chris, who now hid in plain sight in an upscale loft on Franklin Street overlooking the Tribeca Grill in Manhattan, had not wanted to be the lion. He felt the lion was too on-the-nose for the leader, separated him too much from, if you will, the pack.

"Let's not get ahead of ourselves," Chris said. "Please present the case, Giraffe."

"The application was filled out by a single mother—or should I say *was* a single mother—named Francine Courter," Giraffe began. Their giraffe Animoji always reminded Chris of his childhood toy store—Geoffrey the Giraffe had been the mascot for the chain Toys "R" Us. Chris remembered his parents taking him there on only the most special of occasions and being awestruck as he entered, the sheer magic and wonderment of the place. It was a happy memory, and he often wondered if Giraffe, whoever they (the pronoun for every member of the group) might be, had chosen this Animoji for this very reason.

"Francine's only child—her son Corey—was murdered in that school shooting in Northbridge last April. Corey was a fifteen-year-old sophomore. Theater kid. Talented musician. He'd been at a rehearsal for the spring concert when the gunman burst in and shot him in the head. There were eighteen kids shot in that rampage, if you remember. Twelve died." Giraffe stopped and took a breath. "Lion?"

"Yes?"

"Do I need to go into more details about that shooting?"

"I don't think so, Giraffe," Chris/Lion said. "We all remember the news stories. Unless someone objects?"

No one did.

"Okay, let me continue," Giraffe said. Even through the voice-altering app, Chris could hear the quake in Giraffe's tone. They all used voice-changing technology of one sort or another. Part of the security and anonymity. The Animoji didn't just cover their faces either—they replaced their entire appearance.

"After burying her only son, Francine fell into a terrible sadness. You can all imagine, of course. Her way out was to channel her grief, try to do something so that other parents wouldn't have to go through this hell. She became a vocal advocate for gun control laws."

"Giraffe?"

It was Polar Bear.

"Yes, Bear?"

"Maybe I shouldn't raise this, but I'm pro Second Amendment. If someone is disagreeing with this woman's viewpoint, even if she's a grieving mother—"

Giraffe cut them off with a snap. "That's not what this is."

"Okay, I just don't want to get political in here."

Chris spoke up. "We all agreed. Our mission is about punishing cruelty and abuse, not politics."

"This isn't about politics," Giraffe insisted. "Someone truly evil is attacking Francine Courter."

"Go on," Chris told them.

"Where was I?...Right, she takes up the cause. Naturally, like Bear said, people disagreed with Francine's viewpoint. She expected that. But what started as tough discourse quickly grew into a sweeping targeted campaign of terror against her. Francine received death threats. She was constantly hounded online by bots and harassed. Her residence was doxxed. She had to move in with her brother's family. But nothing prepared her for what really got the ball rolling."

"And that was?"

"A conspiracy wingnut posted a video claiming that the shooting never happened."

"Seriously?" Kitten said.

"Guess that CCTV footage of kids being slaughtered wasn't enough proof for these psychos," Panther added.

"A fake," Giraffe said. "That was what the conspiracy video

claimed. All staged by gun control advocates who want to take away your guns. Francine Courter was a 'crisis actor,' whatever that means, and—this is the truly awful part—the video claimed that her son Corey had never even existed."

"My God. How did they—?"

"Mostly they just made stuff up. Or they manipulated the narrative to the point of incredibility. For example, they found another Francine Courter who lives in Canada and lists herself as childless, and so they have an audio of the narrator calling her on the phone and 'Francine Courter' saying she never had a child named Corey and so, of course, no child of hers was shot or killed. Ergo it's all a hoax."

"I can't with these people," Alpaca said.

"Bad enough to lose a child," Kitten, who had an English accent, though again that could be from their voice-distortion app, added, "but to then be tormented by these lunatics."

"Who is dumb enough to believe this stuff?" Polar Bear asked.

"You'd be surprised," Giraffe said. "Or maybe you wouldn't be."

"What else did the conspiracy video show?" Chris asked.

"Nothing that makes sense. They ask weird suggestive questions like, 'Why are some of the school CCTV videos only in black and white and others in color?' as if that's proof it's all a fake. Then they doctor or make up evidence with photographs. So, for example—and wow, this is just so skeevy—a bot posted a photograph of someone who looks a little like Corey at a Mets game that took place *after* the shooting. Then they write, 'Here's the actor who played Corey Courter in the Northbridge High shooting at a ball game last week!'' and then others comment stuff like, 'Wow, this is proof it was all staged, he looks fine to me, it's a fraud, stupid sheeple, stop believing what the mainstream media tells you, do your own research, Francine Courter is a traitor,' whatever."

"Awful as this sounds," Polar Bear said, "it seems like we are talking about too many people to take meaningful action."

"That was my worry too," Giraffe said, "until I dug into the second video."

"Second video?"

"So the first video posted on YouTube claiming that the shooting was a hoax was created by an account called Bitter Truth. Eventually it was taken down, but as always with these things it was too late. By then, it had over three million views. It was duplicated and spread, you guys all know the drill. But a second video came out under the name Truth de Bitter."

"Not much of a nom de plume," Chris said.

"No, not much of one at all. He wanted us to know it was the same guy."

"You said 'he,'" Panther noted.

"Yes."

"So it's a man?"

"Yes."

None of them were surprised. Yes, women troll. But not like men. That wasn't sexism. That was simple data.

"His second video..." The Giraffe stopped, overcome.

Silence.

Panther broke it. Tenderly they said, "You okay, Giraffe?"

"Take your time," Chris said.

"Yeah, just give me a second. It was just hard to watch. The link will be in my report, but in sum, the guy goes to Corey's gravesite. To the tombstone of a fifteen-year-old boy. The guy is wearing all ninja black and a mask, so he can't be recognized. Anyway, he brings this device with him. It looks like a metal detector you see guys walking with at the beach. Heck, it probably is. He claims it's a 'BCD'—a Buried Corpse Detector. He demonstrates at other graves how when he hovers it over the ground, it gets a reading. A sound like static. That's how the device knows, he claims, that there is actually a dead body buried underneath the tombstone. Then he waves the device over Corey's tombstone. Guess what happens?"

"Oh my God," Alpaca said.

"Exactly. He claims the reading says that there is no body underneath."

"And people buy this?"

"If it fits their narrative," Chris said, "people buy anything. We all know this."

"Sadly, I'm not finished," Giraffe said, letting loose a deep breath. "At the end of the video, the guy urinates on Corey's grave."

Silence.

"He then posts the video of him doing that on every page associated with Francine Courter."

Silence.

Chris spoke first. "What's his name?" he asked between clenched teeth.

"Kenton Frauling. It took me a while, but I traced at least ten of the bots to the same account as Bitter Truth and Truth de Bitter."

"How did you track him down?"

"I sent an email pretending to be a member of the media who believed his story. He clicked the link, and well, you know the rest—"

"So not only did this Frauling guy create these awful videos—"

"He made most of the comments, yes. Carried on fake conversations with himself. Attacked in unison. He also hired a foreign bot farm to join him in the ceaseless barrage on Francine. Besides tons of posts on Twitter and Facebook and all that, he calls Francine's phone at all hours. He sends letters to her home with graphic pictures of Corey, even put flyers on her car."

"And what's Frauling's deal?"

"He's a thirty-six-year-old sales manager for a large insurance company. Makes six figures."

Chris felt his hands tighten into fists. This part, the fact that Kenton Frauling had a life, should have shocked him, but it didn't.

Most people assumed that the vast majority of destructive trolls harassing people were unemployed losers furiously posting from Mommy's basement, but more often than not, they were educated, employed, financially comfortable enough. What they did have in common was carrying some sort of perceived slight, some sort of imagined resentment, some unwarranted feeling of victimhood.

"Frauling has two kids. Recently separated. That's the outline of the case. I've sent you all a file with the videos and posts."

Chris said, "On behalf of the other members of Boomerang, I want to thank Giraffe for their tireless work on this case."

There were murmurs of agreement.

"Let's take the vote," Chris said. "All in favor of moving forward on Kenton Frauling?"

All voted "Aye." This was the sixth and final case presented to the Boomerangs today. The rule was, if two members voted nay, the troll was left alone. Of the six cases today, five had passed. The only one that had been rejected involved a pretty-boy reality star getting hounded online. Panther had presented, but the pretty boy was a fairly unsympathetic victim, so they chose to spend their energies on the more deserving.

The Boomerangs' motto was an obvious one: Karma is like a boomerang—whatever you give out will come back to you. The group carefully selected their targets after a thorough application and vetting process. In his previous guise as The Stranger, Chris had learned the hard way that you only seek justice when there is no question—no reasonable doubt at all—that the perpetrator deserves it. To be absolutely sure, Chris would now comb through Giraffe's full file to make sure all the details fit the presentation. Doubtful that there would be an issue. Giraffe was the most anally thorough of them all.

"Okay," Chris said, "let's talk response. Giraffe, what hurricane category do you want to go with?"

Giraffe did not hesitate. "If there was ever a monster crying out for a Category 5 . . ."

"Aye," Panther cut in. "Category 5."

The rest quickly agreed.

The Boomerangs did not go to Category 5 often. Most trolls came in more at a Category 2 or 3, in which case their punishment would involve hurting credit ratings or emptying a bank account or perhaps blackmail, something to teach the troll a lesson but not destroy them.

Category 5, on the other hand, was cataclysmic. Category 5 wasn't so much about damage as total annihilation.

God may offer mercy, but for Kenton Frauling, the Boomerangs would not.

CHAPTER
FOUR

Four months later

Hester Crimstein, celebrity defense attorney extraordinaire, watched her opponent, prosecutor Paul Hickory,
adjust his tie and begin his closing statement.

"Ladies and gentlemen of the jury, this is not only the most
obvious and clear-cut murder case that I've ever prosecuted—
it's the most obvious and clear-cut that anyone in my office has
ever seen."

Hester resisted the urge to roll her eyes. It wasn't time.

Let him have his moment.

Hickory lifted the remote with a flourish, pointed it at the
television, hit the on button with his thumb. The screen came
to life. He could have had the image already up on the monitor,
but no, Paul Hickory liked a little pizzazz, a little showmanship.
Hester put on her bored face, so that if any jury members sneaked
a glance at her, they would see how unimpressed she was.

Sitting next to Hester was her client, Richard Levine, the
defendant in this murder trial. She had discussed with Richard at
great length how he should behave, what his demeanor should be,
how he should react (or more importantly, not react) in front of
the jury. Right now, her client, who would spend the rest of his life

behind bars if Hickory got his way, had his hands neatly folded on the table, his gaze steady.

Good boy.

On the screen, there were maybe a dozen people crowded together near the famed arch in avant-garde Washington Square Park. Paul Hickory made a production of clicking the play button. Hester kept her breathing steady as the video started up.

Show nothing, she reminded herself.

Paul Hickory had, of course, played this video before. Several times. But wisely, he hadn't overexposed it, hadn't shown it ad nauseam until the jury became numb to the brutality of what they were witnessing.

He still wanted it to be a gut punch. He wanted it to be visceral.

On the tape, Richard Levine, Hester's client, wore a blue suit with no tie and Cole Haan black loafers. He walked up to a man named Lars Corbett, raised a hand that held a gun, and without the slightest hesitation, fired two shots into Corbett's head.

Screams.

Lars Corbett collapsed, dead before he hit the ground.

Paul Hickory hit the pause button and spread his hands.

"Do I really need to sum it up more than that?"

He gave his rhetorical question time to echo through the chamber as he strolled from one end of the jury box to the other, locking eyes with those who looked his way.

"This, ladies and gentlemen, is an execution. It's a cold-blooded murder on the streets of our city—in the heart of one of our most beloved parks. That's it. No one disputes these facts. We have our victim, Lars Corbett, right here." He points at the screen, at the fallen man lying in blood. "We have our defendant, Richard Levine, right here, firing a Glock 19 that ballistics confirmed was the murder weapon, a handgun Levine purchased only two weeks before the murder from a gun dealership in Paramus, New Jersey. We've put on the stand fourteen witnesses who saw the murder and identified Mr. Levine as the perpetrator. We presented two other videos from two independent sources that show this same murder from different angles."

Hickory shook his head. "I mean, my God, what else do you need?"

He sighed with perhaps, in Hester's viewpoint, a little too much melodrama. Paul Hickory was young, midthirties. Hester had gone to law school with Paul's father, a flamboyant defense attorney named Flair (yes, Flair Hickory was his real name), who was now one of her toughest competitors. The son was good, and he would get better—the apple not falling far from the tree—but he wasn't yet his father.

"No one, including Ms. Crimstein and the defense, has denied any of these key facts. No one has come forward to say that this"—he points hard at the paused video—"is not Richard Levine. No one has come forward to give Mr. Levine an alibi or claim in any way that he didn't brutally murder Mr. Corbett." He paused now, moving closer to the jury box.

"Nothing. Else. Matters."

He said it like that, three separate sentences. Hester couldn't resist. She met the eye of one of the jury members—a woman named Marti Vandevoort she felt was vulnerable—and did the smallest of conspiratorial eye rolls.

As if he knew what Hester was up to, Paul Hickory spun toward her. "Now, Ms. Crimstein will do everything she can to muddy this very simple narrative. But please, we're all too intelligent to fall for her shenanigans. The evidence is overwhelming. I can't imagine a case being more open and shut. Richard Levine bought a gun. He illegally carried it to Washington Square on March 18. We know from the testimony and computer forensic reports that Mr. Levine was destructively obsessed with Mr. Corbett. He planned this out, he stalked his victim, and then he executed Mr. Corbett on the street. That is the textbook definition of first-degree murder, ladies and gentlemen. And—I don't believe I even have to say this—murder is wrong. It's against the law. Put this killer behind bars. It's your duty and obligation as citizens. Thank you."

Paul Hickory collapsed into his chair.

The judge, her old friend David Greiner, cleared his throat and looked at Hester. "Ms. Crimstein?"

"In a second, your honor." Hester fanned herself with her hand. "I'm still breathless from that overwrought yet completely irrelevant closing from the prosecution."

Paul Hickory was on his feet. "Objection, your honor—"

"Ms. Crimstein," the judge half-heartedly admonished.

Hester waved away an apology and stood.

"The reason I say Mr. Hickory is being overwrought and completely irrelevant, ladies and gentlemen, is..." Then Hester stopped herself: "First, let me say good afternoon to you all." This was a small part of Hester's closing technique. She would give them a little tease, make them wonder where she was going, let them bathe in that for a moment. "Jury duty is solemn and important work, and we on the defense team thank you for being here, for participating, for being diligent and open-minded about a man being so obviously railroaded. Lord knows this isn't my first case"—Hester smiled, checking to see who smiled back, noting the three that did, including Marti Vandevoort—"but I don't think I've ever seen a jury that has adjudicated a case so seriously and intelligently."

This was nonsense, of course. All juries looked pretty much the same. They were bored at the same time. They were riveted at the same time. Her jury expert, Samantha Reiter, sitting three rows behind her, believed that this jury was more malleable than most, but Hester's defense was also more insane than most. The evidence, as Paul Hickory had laid out, was indeed overwhelming. She was starting the race miles behind the prosecution. She got that.

"Wait, where was I?" Hester asked.

This was a small reminder that Hester was not a young woman. She wasn't above playing your favorite aunt or grandmother when she could. Sharp, fair, strict, a little forgetful, lovable. Most of the jury members knew Hester from her cable news show *Crimstein on Crime*. The prosecution always tried to select jury members who didn't know who she was, but even if the juror claimed that they didn't watch the show—not many did on a regular basis—almost all had seen her as a television analyst at some point or another. If a potential juror said that they didn't know who Hester was, they were often lying, which made Hester want them because, for some reason, that meant they *wanted* to be on her jury and would probably be on her side. Over the years, the prosecution had picked up on that and so they stopped asking.

"Oh, that's right. I was characterizing Mr. Hickory's closing as 'overwrought yet completely irrelevant.' You probably want to know why."

Her voice was soft. She always tried to start the closing that way to get the jury to lean in a little. It also gave her voice space to grow, space for her narrative to build.

"Mr. Hickory kept blabbing on about what we already knew, didn't he? In terms of evidence, that is. We don't dispute that the gun belonged to my client or any of that other stuff, so why waste our time with that?"

She gave a heartfelt shrug but didn't wait for Hickory to try to answer.

"But everything else Mr. Hickory claimed...well, I won't call them bald-faced lies because that would be rude. But the pros-ecutor's office is a political one, and like the worst politicians—don't we have too many of those nowadays?—Mr. Hickory slanted the story so that you only heard his biased and distorted narrative. Boy, I'm sick of that, aren't you? I'm sick of that with politicians. I'm sick of that with the media. I'm sick of that on social media, not that I'm on social media, but my grandson Matthew is and sometimes he shows me what's there, and I tell you, it's Crazyville, am I right? Stay away."

Brief laughter.

This was all a bit of rapport/showmanship on her part. Everyone dislikes politicians and the media in the same way they dislike attorneys, so this made Hester both self-deprecating and relatable. It was, however, an interesting dichotomy. If you ask someone what they think of lawyers, they will trash them. If you ask them what they think of *their* lawyer, they will speak glowingly.

"As you already know, most of what Mr. Hickory said doesn't add up. That's because life isn't, as much as Mr. Hickory wants it to be, black and white. We all know this, don't we? It is part of the human condition. We all think that we are uniquely complex, that no one can read our thoughts, but that we can read theirs. Are there black-and-whites in the world? Sure. We will get back to that in a moment. But mostly—and we all know this—life is lived in the grays."

Without turning to the screen, Hester hit the remote and a slide appeared on the television screen the defense had brought in. Her television was intentionally bigger than the prosecution's— seventy-two inches while Hickory's was a mere fifty. Subliminally, it told the jury that she had nothing to hide.

"For some reason, Mr. Hickory chose not to show you this."

The jury's eyes were naturally drawn to the image behind her. Hester didn't turn and look. She wanted to show them that she knew what it was; instead she watched their faces.

"I hate to state the obvious, but this is a closeup of a hand. More specifically, the right hand of Mr. Lars Corbett."

The image was blurry. That was part technology—it was an extreme closeup—and part intentional. If it had worked in her favor to improve the lighting or pixels, she would have done so. A trial is two competing stories. It didn't serve her interest to do anything but blow it up in this way, quality be damned.

"Do you see what's clutched in his hand?"

Some of the jury squinted.

"A little hard to make out, I know," Hester continued. "But we can see it's black. It's metal. Watch now."

Hester pressed play. The hand began to rise. Since this was

extreme closeup, the hand appeared to move fast. Again: intentional. She strolled over to the exhibit table and picked up a small gun. "This is a Remington RM380 pocket-size pistol. It's black. It's metal. Do you know why you buy a gun this size?"

She waited a beat, as though the jury would answer. They didn't, of course.

"Well, it's obvious, isn't it? It's in the gun's name. Pocket-size. So you can carry it. So you can conceal it and use it. And what else do we know? We know that Lars Corbett owns at least one Remington RM380."

Hester pointed again to the blurry image.

"Is that the gun right there in Lars Corbett's hand?"

Again she paused, shorter this time.

"Right, exactly, so we already have reasonable doubt, don't we? That's enough to end all of this. I could sit down right now and not say another word, and your vote not to convict is obvious. But let's continue, shall we? Because I do have more. Much more."

Hester motioned dismissively toward the defense table. "We heard testimony that Lars Corbett's Remington RM380 was 'found'"—Hester put the word in sarcastic air quotes—"in his basement, but really? Do we know that for certain? Corbett owned a lot of guns. You saw them during this trial. He had a fetish for all sorts of destructive weaponry—big scary assault rifles and machine guns and revolvers and Lord-knows-what. Here, let me show you."

She clicked the remote. The prosecution had tried to keep this photograph found on Corbett's Facebook page out of the case. It didn't matter, Paul Hickory had valiantly argued, what a victim looked like or wore or how he decorated his home. During voir dire, Hickory had asked Judge Greiner, "If this was a rape case, would you let Ms. Crimstein show the jury a photograph of the young woman in racy clothing? I thought we were beyond that." But Hester argued that there was probative value because a man who had made public his vast gun collection would conceivably be more likely to draw a weapon, or at least, Richard Levine's "state of mind"—his believing he was in real danger from Corbett—could thus be better explained.

But there was a bigger reason why Hester wanted the jury to see this photograph.

"Do you really think this man"—she pointed to Corbett—"only bought guns legally? Do we really think it's not possible he had several small handguns and that what we see in his hand"—now she enlarged the blurry black mass in Corbett's hand—"is one of them?"

The jury was paying attention.

Hester didn't want them looking at the black mass for too long, so she clicked her remote and moved the image back to the photograph of Corbett with the assault rifle. She slowly walked back to her table so that they could stare at the photograph a little longer. Lars Corbett sported a crewcut and smirk. But the backdrop was the key.

Behind Corbett was a red flag with a swastika in the middle.

The flag of Nazi Germany.

But Hester didn't say anything about it yet. She tried to keep her voice even, unemotional, detached, reasonable.

"Now Mr. Hickory has claimed, with very little proof, that this isn't a gun in Lars Corbett's hand but an iPhone." In truth, Paul Hickory had very solid evidence that it was an iPhone. He had blown away this he-saw-a-gun theory pretty conclusively during the trial. He had introduced other photographs of the hand and used several videos and eyewitness testimony to support his claim that it was indeed an iPhone, that Lars Corbett was raising it in order to film the encounter, that we could all see, after the bullet went through Corbett's head, his phone drop to the pavement.

Hickory had been convincing, so Hester didn't dwell on it. Instead she tried to spin it another way.

"Now maybe Mr. Hickory is correct," Hester allowed in her best conceding-the-point-aren't-I-fair? tone. "Perhaps it is an iPhone.

But I don't know for sure. And you don't know for sure. Think about that image of that hand I showed you. Now imagine you have a split second. Your blood is pumping. You are in fear for your life. You are standing in front of this man"—she points to the photograph of the smirking Lars Corbett in front of the Nazi flag—"who wants to kill you and your entire family."

She turned back to the jury. "Would you bet your life on it being an iPhone? Me neither."

Hester slowly circled so that she stood behind her client and put both hands on Richard Levine's shoulders. Warmly. Maternally.

"I want you to meet my friend Richard," she said with her kindest smile. She looked down at him. "Richard is a sixty-three-year-old grandfather. He has no criminal record. He has never been arrested before. Not once. He has no DUIs. Nothing. In his life, he has one speeding ticket. That's it. He is—and I'm not a fan of this term but I have to say it here—a model citizen. He's a father to three children: two sons—Ruben and Max—and a daughter, Julie. He had two grandchildren, twins Laura and Debra. His wife Rebecca died last year after a long battle with breast cancer. Mr. Levine took a long leave from his job just to care for his dying wife. He has worked for the past twenty-eight years in the corporate head office for a popular drugstore chain, running their accounting department for most of it. Richard was elected three times to the town council in his hometown of Livingston, New Jersey. He serves on the volunteer fire department and gives his time and money to a host of worthy causes. This, ladies and gentlemen, is a good man. No one has come forward and said otherwise. Everyone adores Richard Levine."

Hester smiled again, patted Levine's shoulders reassuringly, and strode back toward the photograph of Lars Corbett. "Lars Corbett's ex-wife Delilah divorced him because he was physically abusive. He beat her constantly. She had to be hospitalized three times in a year. Delilah, thank God, got custody of their three-year-old daughter and a restraining order against him. Lars Corbett has numerous arrests and convictions for assaults and disorderly conduct and—and we need to stress this—illegal possession of a handgun. Look at this photograph, ladies and gentlemen. What do you see? Let's not mince words. You see scum."

Paul Hickory's face reddened. He was about to rise, but Hester raised a hand.

"Maybe you don't see scum, Mr. Hickory, I don't know. That doesn't matter. Richard Levine probably didn't see scum either. He saw something much worse. Richard's grandfather was a Holocaust survivor. The Americans rescued him in Auschwitz. Half starved. Near dead. But they were too late to save his family. His mother, his father, even his baby sister—all died in Auschwitz. They were murdered. Gassed. I want you to think about that for a moment."

Hester moved toward the screen with Lars Corbett on it.

"Now I want you to imagine something. Imagine a man breaks into your home and kills your entire family. All of them. He tells you that's what he's going to do, and then he does it. He kills all those you hold dear and promises that he will come back and kill you too. He makes it clear that your death is his ultimate goal. A few years pass. You make a new family. And now that man is back in your house. He is coming up the stairs. He has something that looks like a gun in his hand."

Hester gave it a moment, letting the room fall totally silent, before adding: "Do you give that monster the benefit of the doubt?

"Mr. Hickory"—her point now is angry, accusing—"keeps saying that this isn't self-defense, that Lars Corbett made no threat of bodily harm. Is he joking? Is Mr. Hickory disingenuous or, well, dumb? Lars Corbett was the leader of a Nazi militia group in this country. His message of hate had thousands of social media followers. Nazis aren't subtle, ladies and gentlemen. They made the goal clear: Kill. Slaughter. Exterminate certain people, including my friend Richard. Is anyone naïve enough to believe otherwise? That's why Lars Corbett was marching that day—to rally his troops to murder and gas good people like Richard and his three children and his twin grandchildren."

Hester's voice was louder now, trembling.

"Now Mr. Hickory will tell you that Lars Corbett had the 'right'"—again the air quotation marks—"to talk about throwing you in the gas chamber and butchering your entire family, just as Corbett's Nazi forefathers did to my client's. But put yourself in Richard's shoes and ask yourself—what would you do? Do you sit at home and wait for Nazis to rise again and murder more? Do you have to wait until you're pushed into the gas chamber before you defend yourself? We know what Corbett's goal was. He and his filth state it very clearly. So you, as a concerned citizen, as an empathetic human being, as a loving father and doting grandfather leading an exemplary life, go to Washington Square Park to hear the hate these murderers are spewing. Of course, you're scared. Of course, your heart is thundering in your chest. And then this evil man, this man who has sworn to kill you, this man who everyone knows owns tons of guns and rifles, starts raising his hand with something black and metallic in it and . . ."

Hester's voice petered out now, broke down in a semi-sob, her eyes welling. She lowered her head and closed her eyes.

"Of course this is self-defense."

Hester let one tear slide down her cheek.

"It is the most clear-cut case of self-defense any of us could ever imagine. It is not only rooted in the moment, but the roots of his defense have traveled seventy years and across an ocean. The self-defense is in Mr. Levine's DNA. It is in your DNA and my DNA too. This . . ." Hester pointed again to Lars Corbett in front of the swastika flag. "This *man*," she said, spitting out the word, "wants to kill you and your loved ones. He has something black in his hand. He raises it toward you and all of that—all of the horrible past, the concentration camps, the gas chambers, all of the ugliness and blood and death Corbett wanted to resurrect—it reaches up from the grave to grab you and those you love."

Hester moved back to the defense table, back behind her client, and once again she put her hands on Richard Levine's shoulders. "I don't ask why Richard pulled the trigger."

Hester closed her eyes, let one more tear leak out—then she opened them and stared hard at the jury.

"I ask, 'Who wouldn't have?'"

———————

As the judge gave his final instructions, Hester spotted her grandson Matthew standing alone against the back wall. Hester felt a flutter in her heart. This couldn't be good news. The last time Matthew had surprised her at work, a classmate had gone missing and he'd come to her for help.

Why was he here this time?

Matthew was a freshman at the University of Michigan. Or at least, he had been. If he was back in the area, Hester assumed the school year was over. It was May. Was that when school ended? She didn't know. She didn't know that he was back either, which disturbed her. Neither Matthew nor his mother, Laila, had told her that her grandson was back. Laila was Hester's daughter-in-law. Or would the correct terminology be *former* daughter-in-law?

What do you call the woman who was widowed when your youngest son died?

"All rise."

Hester and Richard Levine stood as the jury headed out for deliberations. Richard Levine kept his eyes forward. "Thank you," he whispered to her.

Hester nodded as the guards took Levine back into custody. At this stage of momentous trials, most attorneys enjoy playing pundit, breaking down the case's strengths and weaknesses, trying to read the jury members' body language, predicting the outcome. Hester made her living—part of it anyway—doing just that on television. She was skilled at it. It was fun too, a mental exercise with no real-world implications, but when it came to her own cases—cases like this where so much of her heart and soul was invested—Hester let go. Juries were notoriously unpredictable, as, when you think about it, is most of life. Think about those "genius" talking heads you see on cable news. Do they ever get anything right? Who predicted a man in Tunisia would set himself on fire and start an Arab uprising? Who predicted we would be staring at smartphones for half our waking life? Who predicted Trump or Biden or COVID or any of that?

As the old Yiddish expression goes, "Man plans, God laughs."

Hester had done her best. The jury's decision was out of her hands. That was another key thing she had learned with age: Worry about what you can control. If you can't control it, let it go.

That was her serenity prayer without the serenity.

Hester hurried toward her grandson. It never got easier to see the echo of her dead son David in this handsome boy-cum-man. Matthew was eighteen, taller than her David had ever been, darker skinned since Laila was black and so her grandson was biracial. But the mannerisms, the way Matthew stood against the wall, the way he looked around and took in the whole room, the way he walked, the way he hesitated before he spoke, the way he looked to his left when he was mulling over a question—it was all David. Hester relished that and let it crush her all at the same time.

When she reached Matthew, Hester said, "So what's wrong?"

"Nothing."

Hester gave him the skeptical-grandma frown. "Your mom . . . ?"

"She's fine, Nana. Everyone is fine."

He had said that last time he'd surprised her like this. It hadn't proved accurate.

"When did you get back from Ann Arbor?" she asked.

"A week ago."

She tried not to sound hurt. "And you didn't call?"

"We know how you get at the end of a trial," Matthew said.

Hester wasn't sure how to counter that, so she skipped the

reprimands, opting to wrap her arms around her grandson and pull him close. Matthew, who had always been an affectionate boy, hugged her back. Hester closed her eyes and tried to make time stop. For a second or two, it almost did.

With her eyes still closed and her head pressed against his chest, Hester once again said, "So what's wrong?"

"I'm worried about Wilde."

CHAPTER
FIVE

I haven't heard from Wilde in a long time," Matthew said.

They sat in the backseat of Hester's Cadillac Escalade. Tim, Hester's longtime driver and quasi-bodyguard, veered the vehicle onto the lower level of the George Washington Bridge. They were heading to New Jersey, more specifically the town of Westville, a mountain suburb where many years ago, Hester and her late husband, Ira, had raised their three boys: Jeffrey, a dentist living in Los Angeles; Eric, a financial analyst of some kind residing in North Carolina; and the youngest, Matthew's father David, who was killed in a car crash when Matthew was seven years old.

"When was the last time you spoke?" Hester asked.

"When he called from the airport and said he'd be gone for a while."

Hester nodded. That would have been when Wilde left for Costa Rica. "So nearly a year."

"Yes."

"You know how Wilde is, Matthew."

"Right."

"I know he's your godfather." Wilde had been David's best

friend—in Wilde's case, David was probably his only friend. "And yes, he should be doing a better job of being there for you—"

"That's not it," Matthew interjected. "I'm eighteen."

"So?"

"So I'm an adult now."

"Again: So?"

"So Wilde was always there when I was growing up." Then Matthew added, "Other than Mom, he was around more than anyone."

Hester leaned away from him. "Other than Mom," she repeated. "Wow."

"I didn't mean—"

"Other than Mom." Hester shook her head. "Low blow, Matthew."

He lowered his head.

"Don't pull that passive-aggressive nonsense on your old grandma. It doesn't play with me, do you understand?"

"I'm sorry."

"I live and work in Manhattan," she continued. "You and your mom live in Westville. I came out as often as I could."

"I know."

"Low blow," she repeated.

"I know. I'm sorry. It's just..." Matthew looked her in the eyes and they were so like David's that she almost winced. "I don't want you to attack him, okay?"

Hester looked out the window. "Fair enough."

"I'm worried, that's all. He's off in a foreign country and—"

"Wilde came back months ago," Hester said.

"How do you know?"

"He was in touch. I got someone to take care of that metal tube he calls home while he was gone."

"Wait. So he's back in the woods?"

"I assume so."

"But you haven't spoken to him?"

"Not since he's been back. But before last year, I hadn't spoken to Wilde in six years. That's how it is with me and him."

Matthew nodded. "Now I'm really worried."

"Why?"

"Because I wasn't home six months ago. I'm home now. I've been home a week."

Hester saw where he was going with this. When Wilde lived in the mountain forest behind their home, he would watch over Matthew and Laila, mostly from a hidden perch in the hills, sometimes sitting in the backyard by himself in the dark, and sometimes—at least for a brief period—from Laila's bed.

"If he's back in the country and okay," Matthew continued, "he would have said hello to us."

"You don't know that for sure."

"Not for sure," Matthew agreed.

"And he's had a rough go of it."

"How so?"

Hester wondered how much to tell him and then figured what's the harm. "He found his birth father."

Matthew's eyes widened. "Whoa."

"Yes."

"Where was he? What happened?"

"I don't really know, and if I did, it wouldn't be my place to tell you. But I don't think it went well. Wilde came home, threw away the disposable phone I was using to reach him, and I haven't heard from him since."

Tim veered onto Route 17 North. For three decades, Hester had made this commute to and from Manhattan. She and Ira had been happy here. They had managed the balance of career and family as well as any couple she knew. When the boys moved out, Hester and Ira sold the Westville house and bought a place in Manhattan. This had been Hester and Ira's long-term plan: Work hard, do your best by your kids, spend your "golden years" in the city with your spouse. Alas. Not to be. Hester may like the

expression "Man plans, God laughs," but an offshoot translation—
"If you want to make God laugh, tell him your plans"—seemed
more apropos in her case.

"Nana?"

"Yes?"

"How did you reach Wilde last time?"

"You mean, when you asked me to find Naomi?"

Matthew nodded.

Hester let out a long breath and considered her options. "Is
your mother home?"

Matthew checked the clock on his phone. "Probably. Why?"

"I'm going to drop you off. If it's okay with her, I'll be back
in an hour."

"Why wouldn't it be okay with her?"

"Maybe she has plans," Hester said. "You know me. I'm not one
for prying."

Matthew burst out laughing.

"Nobody likes a wise mouth, Matthew."

"You're a wise mouth," he countered.

"Exactly."

Matthew smiled at her. The smile cleaved Hester's heart in
two. "Where are you going after you drop me off?"

"To see if I can find Wilde."

"Why can't I come?"

"Let's do it my way for now."

Matthew was not thrilled with that reply, but his grandmother's
tone made it clear that resistance would be futile. They headed off
the classic New Jersey highway near a bunch of car dealerships,
and two minutes later, it was like they'd entered another world. Tim
made a right, then a left, then two more rights. Hester knew the
route too well. The beautifully bloated log cabin was carved into the
foothills of the Ramapo Mountains section of the Appalachians.

There was a Mercedes SL 550 parked in the driveway. "Mom
get a new car?" Hester asked.

"No, that's Darryl's."

"Who is Darryl?"

Matthew just looked at her. Hester tried not to feel that deep, hard pang in her chest.

"Oh," she said.

Tim pulled to a stop behind Darryl's Mercedes.

"You'll let me know if you find him?" Matthew asked.

"I'll call."

"Don't call," Matthew said. "Just come back when you can. I know Mom wants you to meet him."

Hester nodded a little too slowly. "Do you like Darryl?"

Matthew's reply was to kiss his grandmother on the cheek and slide out.

Hester watched her grandson walk toward the front door with the same gait as his father. She and Ira had built this home forty-three years ago. The cliché holds—it felt like forever ago and like it was yesterday. They had sold the house to David and Laila. Hester had been hesitant about that. It seemed odd to raise your family in the same house in which you'd been raised. Still, it made a lot of sense for a lot of reasons. David and Laila loved the place. They completely transformed the interior and made it their own. Ira also loved keeping the house in the family and would come out often so he could still hike and fish and do all that outdoorsy stuff that Hester so didn't get.

But then again, even if you don't believe in the butterfly effect, what if she had insisted that David and Laila buy someplace else? It drives you nuts to think of such things, and intellectually she understood that none of this was her fault, but if she had done that, the world's timeline would have changed somewhat, right? David wouldn't have been on that mountain road when it was so slippery. The car wouldn't have gone off the edge. Ira wouldn't have died of a heart attack—heartbreak, in her eyes—soon after.

So much for letting go what you can't control, she thought.

"I guess Laila has a boyfriend," she said to her driver, Tim.

"Laila is a beautiful woman."

"I know."

"And it's been a long, long time."

"I know."

"Also, Matthew's at college. She's all alone now. You should want this for her."

Hester made a face. "I didn't hire you for your empathetic insights into my family dynamics."

"I won't charge you extra," Tim said. "Where to?"

"You know."

Tim nodded and circled through the cul-de-sac and back out. It took longer to find than she would have thought. Wilde always kept the hidden lane off Halifax Road camouflaged and hard to locate, but now it was overgrown to the point where Tim couldn't turn the Escalade onto it. He pulled the car onto the shoulder.

"I don't think Wilde uses this anymore."

If that was the case, Hester was out of ideas. She could talk to Oren, her beau, about having the park rangers comb the area for Wilde, but if he didn't want to be found, he wouldn't be—and if something bad had happened to him, then, coldly put, it would probably be too late.

"I'll take the path on foot," Hester said.

"Not alone you won't," Tim replied, rolling out of the driver's side with a speed that defied his bulk. Tim was a big slab of a man in an ill-fitted suit and military-style crewcut. He buttoned his suit coat—he always insisted on wearing a suit to work—and opened the back door for her.

"Stay here," Hester said.

Tim squinted and scanned the surroundings. "It could be dangerous."

"You have your gun, right?"

He patted his side. "Of course."

"Wonderful, so watch me from here. If someone tries to abduct me, shoot to kill. Wait, unless it's a hunky man, then bid me adieu."

"Isn't Wilde hunky?"

"An *age-appropriate* hunky man, Tim. Oh, and thanks for being a literalist."

"Also, do Americans still say 'hunky'?"

"This one does."

Hester headed toward an opening in the thicket. Last time she'd been here, there'd been enough room for the car to slide through. Tim had driven in, setting off whatever motion-detector sensors Wilde used. They'd waited and he soon appeared. That was how it worked most of the time with Wilde. He took living off the grid to an art form. Part of it was for reasons of personal safety. During his years of clandestine work in both military and then private security with his foster sister Rola, Wilde had made his share of enemies. Some would like to find him and see him dead. Good luck with that.

But most of it, Hester knew, stemmed from Wilde's childhood trauma. Somehow, as a small boy, going back as far as he could remember, Wilde had been alone, in these same woods, fending for himself. Think about that. According to the young boy himself, the only person he had spoken directly to in all those years was another about his age, a little boy Wilde had spotted playing alone in his backyard and so little Wilde approached and the two struck up a strange and clandestine friendship. When the little boy's mom overheard her son talking out loud, the boy would claim it was his imaginary friend, and the mother, naïve in so many ways, would believe him. It was not until Wilde was found that the truth came out.

The little boy—spoiler alert—was Hester's youngest son, David.

The perimeter was indeed overgrown and neglected, but the clearing inside of it—where Tim had parked the car last time—was still there. Hester wasn't sure what to do. She looked for motion detectors or cameras, but of course, Wilde was too good to let any of them be visible. She debated calling out, but that wouldn't be how Wilde would set it up. Either he was okay and would appear soon, or he was in trouble. She would know one way or another.

After about fifteen minutes, Tim fought his way into the clearing and stood with her. Hester checked for messages on her phone. The Levine jury had finished for the day. No verdict, which was no surprise. Deliberations would resume in the morning. Matthew texted twice asking for updates and to reassure her that it would be good to stop by the house.

Another fifteen minutes passed.

Hester swung between worry (suppose Wilde wasn't okay?) and anger (if he was okay, why had he abandoned his godson?). On the one hand, she got it. The textbook diagnosis: Wilde had never gotten over his abandonment as a child and so he still couldn't form true attachments. That made sense, she guessed, except she also knew that Wilde would lay down his life in a moment for Matthew or Laila. Wilde loved those he cared about fiercely and protectively—and yet he couldn't live with them or be with them on a steady basis. It is a paradox, a contradiction, and yet that is what most of us are, when we think about it. We want to make people consistent and predictable and simple, but they never are.

Hester looked over at Tim. Tim shrugged and said, "Long enough?"

"Yeah, I guess so."

They headed back through the thicket. When they turned to the car, a bearded man with long hair was casually leaning against the hood with his arms crossed.

"So what's wrong?" Wilde asked.

———

Hester and Wilde stared for a few seconds. Tim broke the silence.

"I'll wait in the car," he said.

Seeing Wilde again opened the floodgates. The memories rushed at Hester, pouring toward her in unceasing waves, the kind of waves that hit you at the beach when you aren't looking and every time you manage to get up, another pulls you back under. She saw Wilde as the little boy found in the woods, as the teen in her kitchen with David, the high school sports star, the West Point cadet, the grooms-man looking so out of place in his tux at David and Laila's wedding (Wilde probably would have served as best man, but Hester more or less insisted that David choose his brothers for that role), the god-father holding baby Matthew after the birth, the man who kept his eyes down as he told her that David's death was his fault.

"You grew a beard," Hester said.

"You like it?"

"No."

He was still gorgeous, of course. When the little boy was found in the woods, the newspapers had called him a modern-day Tarzan, and physically it was almost as if he grew into that role. Wilde was all coiled muscles and stony angles. He had light brown hair, eyes with gold flecks, a sun-kissed complexion. He stood very still, panther-like, as though preternaturally ready to pounce, which, in his case, might be accurate.

"Has someone else gone missing?" Wilde asked.

That had been the case last time she'd come to him like this.

"Yes," Hester said. "You."

Wilde didn't reply.

"Guess who reported you missing," she continued. "Guess who was so worried about you that he asked me to find you."

Wilde nodded slowly. "Matthew."

"What the hell, Wilde?"

He said nothing.

"Why are you ignoring your own godson?"

"I'm not ignoring him."

"He loves you. You're the closest thing he has..." Hester just let the words peter out. She changed subjects for a moment. "I did everything you asked, right?"

"Yes," Wilde said. "Thank you."

"So what happened when you found your father?"

"Dead end."

"I'm sorry. So what's the next step?"

"There is no next step."

"You're giving up?"

"We've discussed this before. Finding out how I ended up in the woods won't matter."

"What about Matthew?"

"What about him?"

"Does he matter? I know we are all supposed to shrug off your eccentricities as 'Oh, you know how Wilde is,' but that's no excuse for ignoring Matthew."

Wilde thought about that. Then he nodded and said, "Fair."

"So what's the problem?"

"Matthew's in college."

"He's home on break."

"Yeah, I know."

Hester nodded. "You're still keeping an eye on them."

Wilde did not reply.

"So why . . . ?" Hester shook her head. "Never mind. Get in the car. We'll drive over together."

"Nah."

"Seriously?"

"I'll be in touch before the end of the day," Wilde said. "Tell Matthew."

He turned and started toward the woods.

"Wilde?"

He stopped.

Hester tried to keep her voice even. Hester hadn't planned on raising this, not yet anyway. She'd hoped to see him a few times, ease into it, but that wasn't her style and it wasn't his style, and part of her feared that confronting him on this now, the tragic event that bonded them forever, would just lead him to disappear deeper into the woods. "Right before you left the country"—she heard the crack in her tone, tried to stifle it—"I made Oren take me to that spot up Mountain Road. To the embankment."

Wilde didn't move, didn't turn and face her.

"A makeshift cross is still there. On the side of the road. All these years later. Weathered and faded, I guess, but it still marks the spot where David's car went off the road. You probably know that. That the cross is still there. I bet you visit sometimes, don't you?"

Wilde still wouldn't face her.

"I looked down that embankment. Where the car skidded off. I let myself picture it all—the whole thing. The icy road. The dark."

"Hester."

"Do you want to tell me what really happened that night?"

"I told you."

Her eyes filled with tears. "You always said it was your fault."

"It was."

"I don't believe that anymore."

Wilde did not move.

"I mean, I never fully believed it, I don't think. I was in shock for a very long time. And I didn't see a need to know the truth. Like you. With your past. What's the difference, you always tell me— you'll always be the boy left in the woods. What's the difference, I told myself—my son will always be dead."

"Please." Wilde slowly turned back to face her. Their eyes locked. "I'm sorry."

"You've said that before. But I never blamed you. And I don't want your apologies."

He stood there and looked very lost.

"Wilde?"

"Tell Matthew I'll be in touch," Wilde said, and then he disappeared into the thicket.

CHAPTER
SIX

H ester, Wilde knew, was right about Matthew. He should not have stayed away.

Things had changed. That had been his rationale. Matthew was grown and was at college. More to the point, Laila had a boyfriend now, the first guy she'd kept around since David's death eleven years ago. Wilde had no rights here. He had no standing. He wanted no part of it. In the past, his presence had been, he hoped, a comfort to her. There had been a role for him. Now that role was gone. He could only cause disruptions.

So he stayed away.

Of course, Wilde still kept a clandestine watch on Laila and Matthew from the woods—that was how he knew Matthew was back—but his vigils were becoming less and less frequent. There is a fine balance between being appropriately protective and creepily stalking.

Still, Laila was one thing. Matthew was another. So maybe he was just making excuses. Maybe he had simply been selfish. In the past year, he had taken too many risks in terms of personal entanglements. Now he wanted to take none.

Hester had also surprised him by bringing up the car crash. Why? And why now?

Wilde stopped by a specific tree and dug up one of his hidden stainless-steel lockboxes. He had six such all-weather storage containers throughout the forest, all with fake IDs, cash, passports, weaponry, and disposable smartphones.

Wilde tucked the box under his arm and hurried back to his microhome—a state-of-the-art, off-the-grid abode called an Ecocapsule. The cutting-edge habitat was tiny, under seventy square feet of habitable space, yet it had everything Wilde needed—a folding bed, a table, cabinets, kitchenette, a shower, an incinerator toilet that turned your waste into ash. The Ecocapsule incorporated both solar and wind power. The pill-shaped exterior not only minimized heat loss but facilitated collecting rainwater into water tanks where it could be filtered for immediate use. With the pod being both mobile and camouflage-skinned—not to mention the advanced security features he had set up—Wilde had made himself very difficult to locate.

He opened the box and took out a military-grade disposable phone. The safety features made it virtually impossible to track, but the key word here was "virtually." No matter what you're told, there is always a backdoor when it comes to technology, always a way to track and uncover, always, at the end of the line, a human who can see what you are doing if you're not careful. Wilde tried to mitigate that via various VPNs and internet masking technologies.

Once the protective protocols were in place, Wilde powered up the device and checked his texts and emails. For a second, Wilde wondered whether his father, better known as Daniel Carter, had reached out, but that would be impossible. Wilde hadn't given him any contact information. When his alarms had first sounded—when Hester had crossed into the woods from his overgrown path—he'd let the thought that it was indeed Daniel Carter enter his mind, that after Wilde had taken off without a warning or goodbye, his father had taken it upon himself to do some research and had either figured out where Wilde could be or had gone to Hester to help find him or . . .

Didn't matter.

Wilde checked his messages for the first time in months. He spotted a few from Matthew, always brief, basically asking him where he was. There were two from Rola, his foster sister, the first asking where he was, the second reading:

Sigh. Don't be like this, Wilde.

He should call her too.

Nothing from Ava. Nothing from Naomi. Nothing from Laila.

Then he saw a message that surprised him.

It was from PB, sent via the DNAYourStory messaging service. The email was dated September 10, eight months ago. Wilde hit the message link. It brought him to the full thread of messages between him and PB in ascending timeline order.

The first communication had come from PB to Wilde a year ago, before he left for Costa Rica:

To: WW

From: PB

Hi. Sorry about not giving my name, but there are reasons I don't feel comfortable letting people know my real identity. My background has too many holes in it and a lot of turmoil. You are the closest relative I've found on this site, and I wonder whether you have holes and turmoil too. If you do, I may have some answers.

Wilde hadn't replied until months later, not until he sat in Liberia Airport and waited to fly to Las Vegas to confront his father:

To: PB

From: WW

Sorry I didn't reply sooner. I found my father on here.

I'm going to attach a link to his profile. Could you let
me know if he also came up as a relative of yours?
If so, we will know whether we are related on my
mother's or father's side. Thank you.

But after Wilde's visit to Las Vegas, he'd chosen not to pursue
the matter anymore or check his emails. What was the point?
He realized now that it sounded as though he was wallowing in
his own pity party, but that wasn't it. He craved isolation. It was
just how he was built. The shrinks had a field day with how his
upbringing made him this way, how important the first five years of
life are, and to make no attachments during that era, no physical
or emotional contact, to be alone with no other human beings, all
of that made him become irreparably damaged.

Could be, Wilde thought.

He didn't know, and he wasn't sure he cared. He'd never really
hunted for his true identity because he could never see the point.
It wouldn't change those first five years, and while he understood
that he was "not normal," he wasn't unhappy this way either. Or
maybe he was and was fooling himself. Living in the woods didn't
make you any less prone to the same self-delusions the rest of
mankind conjures up.

Too much self-reflection today. That had to do with Matthew,
of course. And Laila.

Especially Laila.

The bright red lettering said CLICK HERE FOR NEW MESSAGE!
Wilde did so and the message popped up:

To: WW
From: PB
Your father's profile isn't related to me, so I guess
that we are related on your mother's side. I hope it all
works out with seeing your father. Let me know how
that goes.

Since my last message to you, my life has taken a dark turn. When you find out who I am, you will probably hate me like everybody else does. I was warned this would happen. What goes up has to come down. That's what they always say. The higher up you go, the harder it is when you crash. Well, I was up high without a care in the world, so you can imagine the crash.

Sorry if this seems all over the place. I don't know where to begin. There are so many lies out there about me. Please don't believe them.

I'm at the end of my rope. I don't see any way to survive. Then your message came in like someone had thrown a life preserver to a drowning man. Do you believe in fate? I never did. I don't have family I can trust. Everything I knew about myself and my upbringing turned out to be a lie. You're my cousin. I know that doesn't mean anything and yet maybe it does. Maybe it means everything. Maybe you messaging me back right now is meant to be.

I've never felt so lost and alone. The walls are closing in. I really can't escape it. I just want to sleep. I just want peace. I want it all to go away. You probably think I'm crazy, writing to you, a stranger, like this. Maybe I am. First, they lied to me. Now they're lying about me. They're relentless. I can't fight back anymore. I try but it only makes it worse.

Could you call me? Please? My private mobile is listed below. Don't give this out to anyone. Please. You'll understand when we talk.

Wilde looked up past the branches to the sky. The message had been sent almost four months ago. Whatever crisis PB had been dealing with had probably passed. Even if it hadn't, Wilde saw no way that he could help. It sounded like PB mostly needed a shoulder to cry upon. That was not Wilde's forte.

Hester would be with Matthew by now. It would be wrong to keep them waiting.

Then again, what was there to lose by making a phone call?

Wilde dreaded it, of course. Having to explain himself. Tell PB that he was the anonymous WW. Apologize for not replying sooner. And then what? Where would the conversation go?

Wilde started heading back down the other side of the mountain, toward David's house. He still thought of it that way, even though David had been dead for eleven years. When he'd walked two hundred yards, Wilde stopped, took out his phone, and dialed PB's phone number. He put the phone to his ear and felt a thud-thud in his chest as he listened to the ring. Somehow, he knew that this decision—the decision to reach out to the seemingly tormented PB—would change everything. He didn't believe in the supernatural or any of that, but when you live with the animals, you start to trust a certain buzzing in your body. The danger instinct is real. You have it too. If your bloodline has survived this long, it's because, unbeknownst to you, that primitive instinct has been a part of your DNA makeup.

And speaking of DNA...

PB's phone rang six times before a robotic voice pronounced that the owner of this mobile phone had not set up their mailbox. Interesting.

Wilde hung up. Now what?

He considered sending an anonymous text, but he was not sure what exactly he would say. Did he want to reveal that the message was from WW?

Or should he just let this be?

Not really an option. Not this time. Leaving out the possibility that following up could lead to his mother, PB had written to Wilde for help. PB had been desperate and had no one to turn to, and Wilde had ignored his cry for four months.

He sent a short text:

> This is WW. Sorry for the delay, PB. Text or call me back when you can.

He jammed the phone into his front pocket and started down the mountain.

CHAPTER

SEVEN

Fifteen minutes later, Wilde stood at the tree line separating the Ramapo Mountains from the Crimsteins' backyard. He saw movement in the second-floor window on the right. Laila's bedroom. Weird to think it, but the truth was the truth: Wilde had spent the best nights of his life there.

Wilde flashed back to the first time he had stood in this tree line, though the memory had faded. Six-year-old David had been playing in the yard with his two older brothers. There was a fairly elaborate cedarwood swing set in the yard with slides and a clubhouse and monkey bars. Wilde had been, he now realized after meeting his father, five years old. Up until that day, Wilde had never talked to another human being.

Or at least he had no memory of it.

Young Wilde did know how to speak. He'd spent most of that winter in a lake cabin near the New York–New Jersey border. Most people only used these homes in summer. Wilde remembered going from house to house, trying doors and windows, frustrated that they were all locked. He finally kicked in one small basement window, forming an opening barely big enough for the little boy to slide in. Luckily, the cabin had been winterized, and while that meant there was always the threat that someone could visit, it also meant that young Wilde had running water and electricity. The family that lived there either had children or grandchildren. There were toys to play with and, more important, VCR tapes from PBS television like *Sesame Street* and *Reading Rainbow*. Wilde spent hours watching them, talking out loud, so despite the comparisons to Tarzan and Mowgli, Wilde had educated himself enough to understand that there was a world out there, that the world was larger than him and the woods.

David's older brothers were supposed to watch their young sibling, but they were busy playing some kind of game involving capturing the clubhouse. Wilde watched them. This wasn't the first time he'd ventured near the tree line and watched his fellow man interact. He'd even been spotted a few times by various hikers, campers, and even homeowners, but Wilde just ran off. Some people probably reported him to the authorities, but really, what would they say? "I saw a boy in the woods." So what? It wasn't as though he ran around in a loincloth—he'd stolen clothes from the homes he'd broken into—so for all anyone knew, he was just a kid wandering on his own.

Stories had surfaced about the "feral boy," but most people dismissed them as the product of sun, exhaustion, drugs, dehydration, alcohol, whatever. The older Crimstein boys were now roughhousing on the lawn, laughing and wrestling and rolling around. Wilde watched, transfixed. The back door opened and their mother shouted, "Dinner in fifteen minutes, and I'm not giving a second warning."

That had been the first time Wilde heard Hester Crimstein's voice.

Wilde was still watching the brothers roll on the ground when he heard a voice near to him say, "Hello."

It was a boy around his own age.

Wilde was about to run. There was no way this kid, even if he tried, could keep up with him through the labyrinth of the forest.

But the same instinct that normally commanded him to flee told him to stay. It was that simple.

"Hello," he said back.

"I'm David. What's your name?"

"I don't have one," Wilde said.

And so their friendship began.

Now David was dead. His widow and his son lived in this house.

The back door opened. Matthew stepped into the yard and said, "Hey, Wilde."

The two men—yes, Wilde reluctantly admitted to himself, Matthew was more man than boy now—headed toward one another, meeting in the middle of the yard. When Matthew threw his arms around him, Wilde wondered how long it had been since he'd had physical contact with another person. Had he touched anyone since Vegas?

"I'm sorry," Wilde said.

"It's okay."

"No, it's not."

"You're right, it's not. I worry about you, Wilde."

Matthew was so much like his father that it hurt. Wilde decided to veer the conversation off this particular track. "How's college?"

Matthew's face lit up. "Beyond awesome."

The back door opened again. It was Laila. When her eyes met his, Wilde felt his heart somersault. Laila wore a white blouse open at the throat and a black pencil skirt. She had, he imagined, just come home from her law office, shed the suit coat, slipped out of the work heels and into the white sneakers. For a second or two, he stared, just stared, and didn't really care if anyone noticed.

Laila seemed to float down the steps and into the yard. She kissed Wilde's cheek.

"It's so good to see you," she said.

"Same," Wilde said.

She took his hand. Wilde felt his face flush. He had just left her. No call, no email, no text.

A few seconds later, Hester leaned out the door and shouted, "Pizza! Matthew, help me set up."

Matthew slapped Wilde on the back and trotted back to the house. When he was gone, Laila turned back to Wilde.

"You don't owe me any explanations," Laila said. "You can ignore me all you want."

"I wasn't—"

"Let me finish. You don't owe me—but you owe your godson."

Wilde nodded. "I know. I'm sorry."

She blinked and turned away. "How long have you been back?"

"A few months."

"So my guess is, you know about Darryl."

"You don't owe me any explanations," Wilde said.

"Damn right."

They headed back inside. The four of them—Wilde, Laila, Matthew, and Hester—sat around the kitchen table. There were two pizzas from Calabria's. One was split amongst the three older adults—the other was pretty much for Matthew. Between bites, Hester peppered Wilde with questions about his stay in Costa Rica. Wilde mostly deflected. Laila stayed quiet.

Matthew nudged Wilde. "The Nets are playing the Knicks."

"Are either of them any good this year?"

"Man, you really have been out of it."

They all grabbed a slice and moved into the family room with the big-screen television. Wilde and Matthew watched the game in comfortable silence. Wilde had never been a big fan of spectator sports. He liked to play sports. He didn't really get the joy of watching them. Matthew's father had been into all that stuff, into collecting cards and memorabilia, into going to the games with his older brothers, into keeping stats and watching games like this deep into the night.

Laila and Hester joined them, though both spent more time staring at their phones than the game. At halftime, Hester rose and said, "I better head back to the city."

"You're not staying out here with Oren?" Laila asked.

Oren Carmichael was the retiring police chief of Westville. He too had raised his family out here, been friends with Hester and Ira, even coached two of Hester's kids, including David. Now Hester was a widow and Oren was divorced and so they'd started dating.

"Not tonight. The Levine jury may come back in the morning."

"I'll walk you out to your car," Wilde said.

Hester frowned. When Wilde and Hester stepped onto the front pavement and fully out of earshot, Hester asked, "What do you want?"

"Nothing."

"You never walk me out."

"True," Wilde said.

"So?"

"So how hard was it to get my father's address from DNAYourStory?"

"Very. Why?"

"I need to find the details about another profile from that site."

"Another relative?"

"Yes. A second cousin."

"Can't you just answer them and meet up the regular way?"

"It's more complicated," Wilde said.

Hester sighed. "It always is with you."

Wilde waited.

"Fine, text me the details."

"You're the best."

"Yeah, yeah, I'm the balls," Hester said. She turned back to the house. "How are you holding up?"

"Meaning?"

"Meaning I see the way you look at Laila. I see the way she looks at you."

"There's nothing there."

"She's been seeing a guy."

"I know."

"I figured as much."

"I won't interfere."

Tim opened the car door for Hester. She hugged Wilde fiercely and whispered, "Don't disappear again, okay? You can live in the woods or whatever, but you need to stay in touch every once in a while." She pushed back and looked up into his face. "Do you understand?"

He nodded. Hester slipped into the backseat. Wilde watched the car pull down the cul-de-sac. He reached for his phone and dialed his foster sister. When she answered, he could hear the normal family cacophony. Rola Naser had five children.

"Hello?"

He knew that his name wouldn't pop up because he was calling from a disposable phone. "Can we skip the part where you give me shit for not staying in touch?"

"Hell no," she said.

"Rola—"

"What the eff—and I say 'eff' only because there are children present but I really *really* want to say the whole word—what the eff is wrong with you, Wilde? Wait. Don't answer. Who knows better than me?"

"No one."

"Exactly. No one. And you promised last time you wouldn't do this again."

"I know."

"It's like Lucy kicking the football with Charlie Brown."

"Lucy doesn't kick the football."

"What?"

"Lucy holds the football and then pulls it away when Charlie Brown is about to kick it."

"Are you kidding me? That's where you're going with this, Wilde?"

"You're smiling, Rola. I can hear it in your voice."

"I'm angry."

"Angry but smiling."

"It's been more than a year."

"I know. Are you pregnant again?"

"No."

"Did I miss anything big?"

"In the past year?" Rola sighed. "What do you want, Wilde?"

"I need you to trace a mobile number for me."

"Read it off to me."

"Now?"

"No, wait another year and then do it."

Wilde read her the number that PB had given to him. Ten seconds later, Rola said, "Interesting."

"What?"

"It's billed to a shell corporation called PB&J."

"Owners? Address?"

"No owners. Address is the Cayman Islands. Whose phone number is this?"

"My cousin's, I think."

"Say what?"

After young Wilde was found in the woods, he was taken in as a foster child by the kind and generous Brewer family. More than thirty foster kids had lived with the Brewers, and all had been made better by the experience. Most kids stayed only a few months. Some, like Wilde and Rola, had stayed for years.

"It's a long story," he said.

"You're looking for your birth parents?"

"No. I mean, I was."

"But you put your DNA into one of those genealogy sites?"

"Yes."

"Why?"

"What part of 'a long story' is confusing you?"

"You've never told a long story. I don't think you can. Just give me the broad strokes."

He told her about the communication with PB. He didn't tell her about his father.

"Read me the note," Rola said when he finished.

Wilde did.

"So this PB guy is famous?"

"Or thinks he is," Wilde said.

"I hope he's being melodramatic."

"Meaning?"

"Meaning that almost sounds like a suicide note," Rola said.

Wilde had certainly taken notice of the message's desperation and despair. "Can you see if you can get any information on the shell corporation?"

"Will you come by and see me and the kids?"

"Yes."

"This isn't a quid pro quo . I'll get you the info anyway."

"I know," Wilde said. "I love you, Rola."

"Yeah, I know. Are you back from Costa Rica?"

"Yes."

"By yourself?"

"Yes."

"Damn. I'm sorry to hear that. You back in the woods?"

"Yes."

"Damn."

"It's all good."

"I know," Rola said. "That's the problem. I'll see what I can dig up on PB&J, but I doubt it'll lead anywhere."

He hung up and headed back inside. Laila was gone from the room. Matthew was half watching the second half, half surfing or whatever on his laptop. Wilde collapsed onto the couch next to him.

"Where's your mother?" he asked.

"She's upstairs working. You know she's got a boyfriend?"

Wilde chose to answer the question with a question. "You okay with it?"

"Why wouldn't I be okay with it?"

"Just asking."

"Not up to me."

"True," Wilde said.

The game came out of commercial. Matthew folded his arms and focused on the screen. "Darryl's a little too polished."

Wilde gave a noncommittal "Oh."

"Like he never uses contractions. It's always 'I am' never 'I'm.' 'Do not' instead of 'don't.' Annoys the shit out of me."

Wilde said nothing.

"He's got matching silk pajamas. Black. Looks like a suit. Even his workout clothes match."

Wilde continued to say nothing.

"No thoughts?"

"He sounds like an ogre," Wilde said.

"Right?"

"Not right. We let your mom do what makes her happy."

"If you say so."

They fell into a comfortable silence the same way Wilde used to with Matthew's father.

A few minutes later, Matthew said, "Observation."

"What's that?"

"You're distracted, Wilde. Or if I was Darryl, I would say, 'You *are* distracted, Wilde.'"

Wilde couldn't help but smile. "I could see how that would be annoying."

"Right?"

"I met my biological father."

"Wait, what?"

Wilde nodded. Matthew sat up and turned all his attention to Wilde. His father used to do this too—one of those people who had the ability to make you feel like you're the most important person in the world. Spilling his guts was hardly Wilde's forte, but perhaps he owed Matthew at least that much after his stupid vanishing act.

"He lives in Las Vegas."

"Cool. Like in a casino?"

"No. He's in construction."

"How did you find him?"

"One of those ancestry DNA sites."

"Wow. So you went to Vegas?"

"Yep."

Matthew spread his hands. "And?"

"And he didn't know I existed and doesn't know who the mother is."

Matthew stayed quiet while Wilde elaborated. When he finished, Matthew frowned and said, "Odd."

"What?"

"He doesn't remember her name."

"Why is that odd?"

Matthew frowned again. "Okay, you, well, you sleep with a lot of women, so maybe you don't remember all their names. I get that. It's gross, Wilde. But I get it."

"Thanks."

"But your father? This Daniel Carter? He'd only slept with one girl before this. He only slept with one girl—the same girl—after this. You'd think that he'd remember the names of the girls in between."

"You think he lied to me?"

Matthew shrugged. "I just find it odd, that's all."

"You're young."

"So was your father at the time you were conceived."

Wilde nodded. "Good point."

"You should call and push him a little."

Wilde didn't reply.

"Don't just call it quits, Wilde."

"I haven't. Kind of the opposite, in fact."

"What do you mean?"

"It's why I raised this with you. I wanted your input on something."

A smile broke out on Matthew's face. "Sure."

"I heard from another relative on the site. He calls himself PB."

Wilde showed Matthew the most recent message from PB. Matthew read it twice and said, "Wait, this message came in when?"

"Four months ago."

"Is there an exact date?"

"It's right there. Why?"

Matthew kept staring at the message. "Why didn't you reply before now?"

"I didn't see it."

Matthew stared at the screen some more. "So that's it."

"What's it?"

"Why you are so distracted."

"I'm not following."

"You feel guilty." Matthew kept his eyes on the screen. "This blood relative cried out to you for help. You didn't even let yourself hear the cry."

Wilde looked at him. "Harsh."

"But?"

"But fair. He makes himself sound famous, don't you think?"

"Could be an exaggeration," Matthew said.

"Could be," Wilde agreed.

"I mean, that's the thing with social media. A kid in my class put out a song and got fifty thousand views on his YouTube channel. Now he thinks he's Drake or something."

Wilde didn't know who Drake was, so he kept silent.

"But something about this . . ." Matthew said.

"What?"

"Maybe Sutton would know."

"Sutton, the girl you've had a crush on since eighth grade?"

A smile toyed with Matthew's lips. "Seventh, actually."

"The one who's going out with Crash Maynard?"

"*Was* going out with." Matthew couldn't hold the smile back any longer. "You've been gone a long time, Wilde."

"Have I now?"

"Sutton and I have been dating for almost a year now."

Wilde smiled too. "Nice."

"Yeah." Matthew blushed. "Yeah, it's pretty great."

"Uh, we don't need to have that talk, do we?"

Matthew chuckled at that one. "I'm good."

"You sure?"

"Yeah, that ship has sailed, Wilde."

"Sorry."

"Mom handled it. It's all good."

When the game went to commercial break, Matthew said, "Speaking of which."

"What?"

"I'm going to grab a shower," Matthew said, standing. "Hate to eat and run, but I'm spending the night at Sutton's."

"Oh," Wilde said. Then he added, "Your mom's okay with that?"

Matthew made a face. "Really?"

"You're right. None of my business." Wilde rose. "I better get going too."

Matthew ran up the stairs, taking them two at a time, and vanished into his bedroom. Wilde was about to go up and say goodbye to Laila when his phone rang. It was Rola.

"What's up?"

"Pay dirt," Rola said.

"I'm listening."

"I got an address for PB&J. But it doesn't make much sense."

CHAPTER
EIGHT

The mailing address for PB&J was a luxury Manhattan condo on the seventy-eighth floor of a gleaming skyscraper simply called Sky, located on Central Park South near the Plaza Hotel. The high-rise was fourteen hundred feet tall, making it the second tallest residential building in New York City.

"Not just rich," Rola said. "*Stanky* rich."

"Stanky?"

"I learned that word on Urban Slang."

Wilde didn't even want to know. "Does PB&J own the condo?"

"Don't know. Right now, I just got it as a mailing address."

"You can't figure out who owns it?"

"No sales figures reported, but here's the thing: Apartments in that building start at ten million."

"Dollars?"

"No, pesetas," Rola countered. "Of course, dollars. The penthouse duplex on the top floor is on the market for seventy-five million."

Wilde rubbed his face and checked the time. "I bet I could drive there in an hour."

"Forty-six minutes if you leave now, according to Waze," Rola said.

"I'll see if I can borrow Laila's car."

"Oooooo," Rola said, mockingly drawing out the word in a singsong voice. "You're with Laila?"

"And Matthew," Wilde said. "And Hester was here too."

"Don't get defensive."

"I'm not."

"I like Laila," Rola said. "I like her a lot."

"She has a boyfriend."

"Yeah, but you know what you might have?"

"What?"

"An uber-wealthy relative who lives in Sky. Call me when you find out more."

Wilde headed for the stairs and called up. Matthew came crashing down, high-fived Wilde without breaking stride, and made his way to the door. "Later!" Matthew shouted before slamming the door behind him.

Wilde stood there for a moment. From the top of the stairs, Laila said, "He's grown up."

"Yep."

"Sucks."

"Yep."

"He's spending the night with his girlfriend."

"He told me."

"I swore I wouldn't be that mother, but ..."

"I get it." Wilde turned to face her. "Can I borrow your car?"

"Of course."

"I'll bring it back tonight."

"Don't bother. I won't need it until noon."

"Okay."

"You know where the key is."

Wilde nodded. "Thank you."

"Good night, Wilde."

"Good night, Laila."

She turned toward her home office. Wilde grabbed the key from

the basket by the door. Laila had traded in her BMW for a black
Mercedes-Benz SL 550—the same kind of car Darryl drove. He
frowned at that, flipped the radio onto a classic rock station, and
drove toward the city. The traffic across the George Washington
Bridge was shockingly light. Wilde took the upper level and slowed
in the right lane. Even from here, more than a hundred blocks north
of Central Park South, he could make out Sky jutting into the clouds.

He parked in the lot under the Park Lane Hotel. Sky was a pure,
emotionless glass tower. The lobby was all gleaming crystal and
white and chrome. During the ride, Wilde had wondered about
how to approach this, what he could really hope to accomplish by
coming here. He entered.

A male security guard looked at Wilde as though he'd been
phlegmed out of a vagrant's throat. "Food deliveries are in the
back."

Wilde held up his empty hands. "Do you see me carrying food?"

A well-dressed woman who'd been behind the front desk came
out and said, "May I help you?"

Nothing ventured, nothing gained. "Apartment seventy-eight,
please."

The receptionist shared a knowing glance with the security
guard.

"Your name?"

"WW."

"Pardon?"

"Tell them it's WW."

She flicked another look at the guard. Wilde tried to read their
expressions. A building like this would have tight security. That
was hardly a surprise. Even if he somehow got past this guard,
there were two others by the elevators. Their expressions and
mannerisms seemed born of something more akin to weariness
and resignation than alarm or worry. It was as though they had
been here before, played this role repeatedly, and were just going
through the motions.

The receptionist went back to the desk and picked up the phone. She held the receiver to her ear for maybe a minute and said nothing. Then she came back over and said, "No one is home."

"That's odd. PB told me to come over."

Both the guard and receptionist said nothing.

"PB is my cousin," Wilde tried.

"Uh-huh," the guard said, as though he'd heard the same thing a hundred times before. "Aren't you a little old for this?"

"For what?"

The receptionist said, "Frank."

Frank the Guard shook his head. "Perhaps it's time you left, uh"—small eye roll—"WW."

"Can I leave him a message?" Wilde asked.

"Who?"

"PB."

They both stared at him.

"You realize," the receptionist said, "we can neither confirm nor deny who lives in this building."

He tried to read their faces. Something odd was up.

"So can I leave a note or not?"

Wilde was not sure what he would write. The simple answer was to explain that he was the WW from the DNA website and put one of the untraceable phone numbers. But did he want to do that? Did he want to put himself on the radar like that? Now that he thought about it, what was he doing here? He didn't know PB. He wasn't responsible for him. Wilde had spent his entire life just fine not knowing all the answers to the mystery of who he was.

What was he doing here?

"Of course," the receptionist said and fetched a pen and paper. "May I see an ID please."

He had one under the alias of Jonathan Carlson, but that would just lead to questions about WW and his being a cousin, and really, what was the point? Did he want to kill a perfectly good alias for this?

He did not.

"I'll try his cell later," Wilde said.

"Yeah," Frank said, "you do that."

Wilde headed west on Central Park South. Some might think he would be uncomfortable on the streets of Manhattan, the so-called Boy from the Woods, but it was actually the opposite. He loved New York City. He loved the streets, the sounds, the lights, the life. Was that a contradiction? Perhaps. Or perhaps it was the change that won him over. Perhaps, in the same way you can't have an up without a down or a dark without a light, you couldn't appreciate the rural without the urban. Perhaps it was because this city, crowded and massive as it might be, left you alone, let you stroll and observe in solitude while surrounded by throngs.

Perhaps Wilde needed to shut down the philosophizing and grab a cup of coffee and a chocolate croissant at the Maison Kayser on Columbus Circle.

He stopped at an ATM on the way and picked up his daily max of eight hundred dollars. He had a plan of sorts: Wait for one of the employees, like the security guard or the receptionist, to get off work and bribe them for information on the occupant of the apartment. Did he think it would work? He did not. The guard seemed more likely to go for the bribe than the receptionist, but that could be sexism talking.

He crossed to the park side of the street and set up near the stone wall where he could keep a view for exiting employees. He drank his coffee. It was fantastic. He took a bite out of the chocolate croissant and wondered why he didn't leave the woods more often. He wondered what PB had wanted, what had made PB so desperate, what had led a man who lives in this gleaming tower to reach out to a total stranger, even if that stranger shared some DNA.

Wilde had been standing there for an hour when his phone rang.

It was Laila.

He picked up. "Hey."

"Hey."

There was silence.

"Matthew is gone for the night," she said.

"I know."

"Wilde?"

"Yes, Laila?"

"When you're done with whatever you're doing, come over."

He didn't have to be told twice.

When they were spent, Wilde fell into the deepest of sleeps. He woke a little before six a.m. Laila slept next to him. He watched her for a few moments, then he rolled onto his back, put his hands behind his head, stared at the ceiling. Laila liked luxuriant white bedsheets with an infinite thread count. The expense seemed obscene, but there were times, like right now, when Wilde got it.

Laila rolled and rested her hand on his chest. They were both naked.

"Hey," she said.

"Hey."

Laila moved in closer. He pulled her tight.

"So," she said, "Costa Rica."

"What about it?"

"It didn't work out?"

"It worked out," Wilde said. "It just didn't last."

Wilde loved her. Laila loved him. They'd tried to be more domestic in the beginning. It hadn't worked. That was his fault. Some blamed the ghost of David—that had been there initially, sure—or fear of commitment. It wasn't that. Not really. Wilde wasn't built for what most would consider a normal relationship. Laila needed more. The cycle went like this: Laila would start a new relationship with some guy. Wilde would leave her be and wish the relationship well. He wanted her happy. But the relationship would eventually peter out, not because Laila held some kind of candle for Wilde but because she still couldn't get over the death of her soulmate David. All other relationships came up short. So Laila would break up with the guy and then she'd get lonely, and there, alone in the woods waiting, was safe, convenient, can't-commit Wilde.

Rinse, repeat.

Wilde had given the "normal relationship" mode one last try in Costa Rica with another woman and her daughter. It had gone surprisingly well, this domesticity, until it didn't. All relationships die, he rationalized. His died faster, that's all.

"What time is it?" Laila asked.

"It's almost six."

"I doubt Matthew will be home before noon."

"But I should get going anyway."

"Yes."

Part of him wanted to ask about Darryl; most of him did not. He slipped out of the luxuriant silk sheets. He could feel her eyes on him as he padded for the shower. Being Mr. Eco-Living was all fine and good, but there were few luxuries he enjoyed as much as the strong water pressure and seemingly endless hot water of Laila's shower. He hoped that she would join him, but that didn't happen. When he got out, Laila was sitting on the edge of the bed in a robe.

"You okay?" he asked.

"Yes." Then: "I love you, Wilde."

"I love you too, Laila."

"Was I part of the reason you went to Costa Rica?"

He had never lied to her. "Part, yes."

"For my sake? Or your sake?"

"Yes."

Laila smiled. "You stayed with her a long time."

"With *them*," Wilde corrected. "Yes."

"It should all be simpler, shouldn't it?"

Wilde slipped into his clothes. He sat next to her on the bed and tied his sneakers. The silence was comfortable. There was more to say, but it could wait. He rose. She rose. They held on to each other for a long time. There was a lot of history here. David was in the room too. He had always been. Neither denied it, but neither minded his presence anymore. Their sleeping together had stopped feeling like a betrayal years ago.

Wilde didn't say he would call. He didn't say she should either. They both understood the situation. The next move would be up to her.

Wilde headed downstairs alone and crossed the family room. When he pushed open the kitchen door, he was surprised to see Matthew. He was sitting at the kitchen table with a bowl of cereal.

Matthew glared at Wilde. "Looks like it runs in the family."

"What?"

"Sleeping around, cheating, whatever."

Wilde did not reply to that. His mother would explain or not explain as she saw fit. It wasn't his place. He started for the back door. "I'll see you around."

"Don't you want to know what I mean by 'runs in the family'?"

"If you want to tell me."

"It's simple," Matthew said. "I know who PB is."

NINE

Wilde sat next to him. Matthew kept his eyes on the cold cereal in front of him.

"I thought you and Mom were done."

Wilde said nothing.

"I know you used to stay over. You don't think I'd hear you sneak out?"

"I'm not going to talk about this with you," Wilde said.

"Then maybe I don't want to talk about PB."

Wilde remained silent. He pulled over the box of cereal and emptied some into his palm. He ate a few pieces while he waited for Matthew to stop giving him the sullen.

"She's involved with someone right now," Matthew said. "I told you that."

"I'm not going to talk about this with you."

"Why the hell not? I'm not a kid anymore."

"You're acting like one."

"Hey, I'm not the one sneaking out of the house at six in the morning."

Matthew took a spoonful of cereal and jammed it in his mouth with ferocity.

Wilde said, "What did you mean by 'it runs in the family'?"

"You and PB."

"What about us?"

"Do you ever watch reality TV?"

Wilde kept his expression blank.

"Right," Matthew said. "Dumb question. But you've heard of it, right? Shows like *The Bachelor* and *Survivor*?"

Wilde continued to stare.

"PB's real name is Peter Bennett. He won a big reality show."

"Won?"

"Yes."

"Like a game show?"

"Not exactly. I mean this isn't *Jeopardy!* Have you heard of *Love Is a Battlefield*?"

"Sure," Wilde said. "Pat Benatar."

"Who?"

"She sang the song."

"What song? *Love Is a Battlefield* is a reality show."

"You win a show?"

"Of course. Sheesh, Wilde, where have you been? It's kind of like a contest. The show starts out with three women and twenty-one men all vying to find true love. But it's a hard road to get there. Fierce, the host always says. Love is like a war. Guess where they host it?"

"On a battlefield?" Wilde replied with his tongue firmly planted in his cheek.

"Right."

"You're serious?"

Matthew nodded. "In the end, there is only one woman who selects one man. Destined for each other. They're the only two standing. They get engaged right then and there. In the finale."

"On a battlefield?"

"Yes. Last season it was at Gettysburg."

"And this relative of mine, PB—"

"Peter Bennett."

"Right. He won?"

"He and Jenn Cassidy, his true love."

"Jenn?"

"Right."

Wilde said, "Please tell me you're joking."

"What?"

"Peter Bennett and Jenn," Wilde said. "Is that what PB&J stands for?"

"Clever, right?"

Wilde shook his head. "Maybe I don't want to meet him."

That made Matthew laugh. "They're pretty famous. Or they were. This was like a year or two ago."

"When he won this show?"

"Yes."

"I assume PB&J are no longer together," Wilde said.

"Why do you assume that?"

"Because One, I imagine—and this could just be me—that this probably isn't a great way to meet your lifelong soulmate. On TV during a contest."

"You're an expert on relationships now?"

"Fair," Wilde said again. "Harsh but fair."

"And what's Two?"

"Two, you got mad at me and said it 'runs in the family.' So I assume PB—Peanut Butter or whatever—cheated on this Jenn."

"You're good," Matthew said.

"How did you learn all this?" Wilde asked.

"I've seen an episode or two, but Sutton and her sorority sisters watch religiously. Before every episode, they down edibles and watch and laugh their asses off."

"So where is he now?"

"Peter Bennett?"

"Yes."

"That's the thing. No one knows. He's disappeared."

The kitchen door opened. Laila entered wearing a terry cloth robe and a frown.

"Damn," Laila said. "I thought I heard voices."

The two men looked at her. Matthew broke the silence.

"Do you want to tell me what's going on?"

Laila turned her gaze on him. "Do I answer to you now?"

"Maybe you should."

"No, I'll continue to be the mother, you continue to be the son."

"You broke up with Darryl?"

Laila flicked a glance at Wilde, then back to Matthew. "What are you doing home anyway? I thought you were spending the night at Sutton's."

"Nice deflection, Mom."

"I don't need to deflect. I'm the mother."

"Well, my plan *was* to stay at Sutton's, but I needed to tell Wilde something. So I came home to get the car keys and I heard noises upstairs."

Silence.

Laila gave Wilde a look that made his next move obvious.

Wilde rose and started for the door. "I'll leave you two alone."

Without so much as a backward glance, Wilde headed out the back door, closed his eyes, and sucked in a deep breath. He wondered for a moment or two about the fallout of last night. He wondered what Laila had wanted, why she had called him, where she would go from here. It might be smart for him to vanish again, to not complicate her life, but thinking like that was insulting to Laila. She wasn't a wallflower. She could figure out what she wanted or needed without him playing savior.

When Wilde hit the edge of the woods, he called Rola. It was early, but he figured that she'd be up or have her phone off. She answered on the first ring. He could hear the cacophony of morning breakfast with five kids in the background.

"What's up?" Rola asked.

He filled her in on what Matthew had told him about Peter Bennett.

"When you say he's missing," she began.

"I don't know. I need to do some research too."

"Well, we have his name now. That should be enough. I'll run his credit cards, phone bills, the usual. I'm sure it won't be that hard to track him down."

"Okay."

"We also got a new guy at CRAW named Tony, who is good at family tree stuff."

"Why would a security firm need 'family tree stuff'?"

"You think you're the only person looking for a biological parent?"

"Kids from closed adoptions?"

"Less and less. What happens is, a lot of people sign up for one of the DNA sites, mostly for the fun of it. To learn their ancestry or whatever. Ends up, they learn that their father—mostly it's the father, though it can be the mother or both parents—isn't really their father. Blows families apart."

"I can imagine."

"A lot of times, the father doesn't even know. He thought the kid was his and he raised them and now when the kid is grown up—twenty, thirty, forty years old—he finds out his wife slept with someone else and his whole life is a lie."

"That must get unpleasant."

"You have no idea. Anyway, I'll get Tony to start working up a genealogical breakdown on Peter Bennett. Someone on it may connect to you."

"Thanks."

"I'll call you back when I have something," she said before disconnecting.

Wilde retrieved his charged laptop from the Ecocapsule and found a spot two miles away where he could hook up to the internet without any chance of being tracked. He Googled "Peter Bennett" and "PB&J." The sheer amount of hits overwhelmed him. *Love Is a Battlefield* had fathered thousands if not millions of fan pages, social media hits, podcasts, Reddit boards, whatever.

Peter Bennett.

Wilde stared at a few of the many, many images online of his cousin's face. Did Wilde see some resemblance between his own face and Bennett's? He did. Or he thought he did. It could be projection or want, but the darker skin tone, the hooded eyes, the shape of the mouth...something was there. Peter Bennett's Instagram had 2.8 million followers. Wilde assumed that was a lot. There were over three thousand posts. Wilde scanned through them. Most featured a smiling Peter Bennett with a glowing Jenn Cassidy, the photographs' composition signaling that these two were in love and rich and, for many, probably crossed the line between aspirational and envy-inducing. Wilde clicked on Jenn Cassidy's profile link and saw that she had 6.3 million followers.

Interesting. Do women reality stars just have more fans?

He headed back to Peter Bennett's page for a deeper dive. Bennett's profile image featured him shirtless. His chest was waxed smooth. His stomach had the kind of chiseled six-pack that screamed show (as opposed to strength) muscles. For a couple of years, Peter Bennett had posted at least one photograph a day—him and Jenn on vacation in the Maldives, attending openings and premieres, trying on designer clothes, making extravagant meals, working out, dining in fancy restaurants, dancing in the clubs. But the posts had slowed down over the last year or so, petering out until the final one, four months ago, was a view of a large cliff with a cascading waterfall. The location was listed as the Adiona Cliffs in French Polynesia. The caption read:

I just want peace.

That was the exact same wording used in PB's desperate message. Little doubt now—Peter Bennett was PB.

Wilde clicked on that final posting and read the comments:

Jump already!
Buh, bye!

Can't wait for you to die.
Hope you land on a hard rock and survive in
agony and then an animal comes along and
starts eating your skin and then fire ants
crawl up your rectum and . . .

Wilde sat back. *What the hell . . . ?*

He skipped back. Bennett's photos over the previous few months were solo shots. No Jenn. Wilde traveled back. The last shot with the #PB&J hashtag featuring both of them was dated May 18. The #DreamCouple, as the frequent hashtag described them, sat in matching beach chairs in Cancun, both holding a frozen margarita in one hand and a bottle from a major tequila label in the other. Sponsorships, Wilde realized. Pretty much every photograph doubled as a paid advertisement.

After that last photo of the beautiful couple, no new post appeared on Bennett's page for three weeks—a lifetime, it seemed, in this social media world. Then there was a plain graphic with a quote inside of it:

Don't be so quick to believe
what you hear,
because lies spread quicker
than the truth.

The total likes on his last picture with Jenn in Cancun? 187,454.

Total likes for this quote? 743.

Wilde spent the next two hours finding out as much as he could online about his possible cousin. Wilde read boards, social media, and the cesspool of all cesspools, the comments. It all made Wilde want to shower and vanish even deeper into the woods.

Staying away from the details for now, here's what Wilde was able to glean:

Peter Bennett was a contestant on a reality program called *Love Is a Battlefield*. Good-looking, charming, kind, polite, modest, Bennett quickly became the season's most popular male contestant. The ratings for the season finale—when Jenn Cassidy picks Peter Bennett over bad-boy Bob "Big Bobbo" Jenkins at the Final Battle—were the network's highest in the past decade.

That was three years ago.

Unlike most couples who hook up on shows like this, Peter and Jenn—yes, PB&J—defied the odds by staying together. Their wedding—not to mention their engagement party, bachelor party, bachelorette party, couple's shower, bridesmaids' luncheon, groomsmen's cigar night, welcome party, Stag and Doe (whatever that was), rehearsal dinner, morning-after-wedding brunch, honeymoon—were major televised and social-media events. Their entire life, it seemed, was for public consumption and commercialized, and the happy couple didn't appear to mind that in the least.

Life was grand. All that was missing, it seemed, was a baby PB&J. The boards started speculating on when Jenn would get pregnant. There were surveys and even betting lines on whether she would have a boy or girl first. But when no pregnancy came in the next year, Peter and Jenn jointly announced, in a far more somber tone than anything Wilde had seen on their social media before, that the happy couple were having fertility issues and would deal with them the way they dealt with everything in their lives: with love and unity.

And publicity.

Peter and Jenn then began to document the medical procedures they had to endure—the shots, the treatments, the surgeries, the egg harvesting, even the sperm collection—but the first three rounds of IVF failed. Jenn did not get pregnant.

And then everything went kaboom.

It happened on the Reality Ralph video podcast in about as cruel a way as possible. Ralph had invited Jenn on his show purportedly to talk about her struggles with infertility so as to give others with the same problem some hope and support.

> **Ralph:**   *And how is Peter holding up under this stress?*
> **Jenn:**   *He's amazing. I'm the luckiest woman in the world.*
> **Ralph:**   *Are you, Jenn?*
> **Jenn:**   *Of course.*
> **Ralph:**   *Are you really?*
> **Jenn:**   (nervous laughter) *What are you trying to say?*
> **Ralph:**   *I'm saying that maybe Peter Bennett isn't who we all thought he was. I'm saying maybe you could take a look at these . . .*

Ralph showed a shocked Jenn text messages, screenshots, dick shots—all, Ralph claimed, sent by Peter Bennett. Jenn grabbed the water bottle with a shaking hand.

> **Ralph:**   *I'm sorry to show you these—*
> **Jenn:**   *You know how easy it is to fake this stuff?*
> **Ralph:**   *We hired forensic people to go over these. I'm sorry to tell you this, but they came from Peter's phone, Peter's computer. The, uh, more intimate photos—are you going to tell us that's not your husband?*

Dead air.

> **Ralph:**   *It gets worse, folks. We have one of the women here with us.*

Jenn removed her microphone and angrily rose from her chair.

> **Jenn:**   *I'm not going to sit here and—*
> **Ralph:**   *Guest, please go ahead.*
> **Guest/Marnie:**   *Jenn?*

Jenn froze.

Guest/Marnie: *Jenn?* (Sobs) *I'm so sorry...*

Jenn couldn't speak. Marnie, it turned out, was Jenn Cassidy's younger sister. Using some of those text messages and screenshots, Marnie told a story of Peter's steadily pursuing her until, one horrible night, Marnie had gotten drunk in Peter's presence, really drunk. Or perhaps—she couldn't say for sure—Marnie had been roofied.

Guest/Marnie: *When I woke up...* (sobs) *...I was naked and sore.*

The reaction was both swift and obvious. The hashtag #cancel peterbennett trended in the top ten on Twitter for almost a week. A potpourri of past *Love Is a Battlefield* contestants took to the various airwaves, podcasts, streamers, and social media platforms to let the indefatigable fans know that they always suspected something was "off" about Peter Bennett. Some anonymous leaks "confirmed" that Peter Bennett had conned the show's producer into thinking he was a nice guy; others claimed the producers had "created" a nice-guy Peter Bennett because they knew he was a sociopath who could play any part.

For his part, Peter Bennett proclaimed his innocence, but those proclamations got zero traction with the growing horde. For her part, Jenn Cassidy declined to speak at all, choosing instead to go into seclusion, though "sources close to her" revealed that Jenn was "devastated" and "seeking a divorce." Jenn issued a statement asking for "privacy during this private and painful time," but when you live your joys out loud, you don't get to go private for the tragedies.

Wilde felt his phone vibrate. It was Rola.

"Bad news," she said.

"What?"

"I think Peter Bennett is dead."

CHAPTER

TEN

H ave you had time to Google your cousin?" Rola asked.

"Yes."

"So you got the whole sordid PB&J story?"

"Enough of it," he said.

"Sheesh, am I right?"

"You are."

"Most people think he jumped off that suicide cliff."

"And you concur?"

"I do, yeah."

"Why?"

"Because Peter Bennett is either dead or he's really good at hiding—and most people aren't that good at hiding. I'm still combing through this stuff, but so far, there is no activity on his credit cards, on his bills, on his phone, no ATM withdrawals, nothing. So you take all that, you add in those social media posts, that cryptic message to you, the bullying deserved or not, the pain of getting canceled and, let's face it, hated by the entire world. You drop all of that in a blender and hit puree, and the outcome is probably something really bad."

Wilde considered that. "Anything on his family tree yet?" he asked.

"Peter Bennett's father died four years ago. Mother Shirley lives in a senior center in Albuquerque."

"One of those two is my blood relative."

"Right. He also has three older siblings. Your best bet? Peter's sister Vicky Chiba. Vicky is also his manager or handler or something. She lives with her husband, Jason Chiba, in West Orange."

"Got it."

"Wilde, do you know how close West Orange is to my place?"

"I do."

"I'm texting you Vicky Chiba's address right now. Maybe after you see her...?"

Rola didn't see a need to finish the sentence. West Orange was only half an hour away with no traffic. Wilde rented a car at the Hertz on Route 17 and found himself pulling up to the Chiba home before noon. He hit the doorbell. Vicky Chiba tentatively opened the wooden door but kept the screen door locked.

"May I help you?" Vicky asked.

Vicky Chiba's hair was white. Pure and blindingly white. Wite-Out white. The kind of white that had to come from a bottle rather than age. She had it cut in a tasseled fringe running straight above the eyeline. Her arms jangled with bracelets. Her earrings were long feathers.

"I'm looking for your brother, Peter."

Vicky Chiba didn't look surprised. "And you are?"

"My name is Wilde."

She sighed. "Are you a fan?"

"No, I'm your cousin."

Keeping the screen door locked, Vicky Chiba crossed her arms and looked him up and down as though he were a purchase she was considering.

Wilde said, "Your brother Peter—"

"What about him?"

"He signed up for a DNA ancestry site."

Her eyes flared for the briefest of moments.

"We were a match," Wilde continued. "As second cousins."

"Wait, why do you look familiar to me?"

Wilde said nothing. He had experienced this many times before. The story of the boy from the woods had made headlines more than three decades ago. Vicky probably would have been a young teen at the time, but once a year or so, some cable network, desperate for material, did a "where is he now" story on him, even though Wilde never cooperated.

"That means," Wilde said, hoping to just push on, "you and I are cousins too."

"I see," she said in a flat voice. "So what do you want from my brother? Money?"

"You said I look familiar."

"Yes."

"Do you remember the story of the boy from the woods?"

Vicky snapped her fingers and pointed at him. "That's how I know you."

Wilde waited.

"You never knew how you ended up in the woods, right?"

"Right."

"Wait"—her mouth formed an O as she got it—"so we're related?"

"It seems so, yes."

Vicky quickly unlocked the screen door. "Come in."

Her décor, like her look, was what one would likely label bohemian. Chaotic patterns and untidy textures and unruly layers, swirls of colors, everything seeming to somehow move and flow, even when nothing moved or flowed. There was something that looked like a crystal ball on the table along with tarot cards and books on numerology. One wall was covered by a gigantic tapestry with a silhouette of someone sitting lotus style with the seven chakra gemstones running from the crown of the head down to the root. Or was it the other way around? Wilde couldn't remember.

"You look skeptical," Vicky said.

He had no interest in getting into this, so Wilde said, "Not at all."

"It has helped a lot in my life."

"I'm sure."

"Your being here. It's not an accident."

"I know."

"But I have to say I'm surprised. Are you saying that my brother signed up for a DNA site?"

"Yes."

Vicky shook her head, the feathers on her earrings bouncing against her cheeks. "That's not like him. And he gave out his name?"

"No. He just used his initials."

"He didn't tell you his name?"

"That's right."

"So how did you find out who he was?"

Wilde didn't want to get into that, so he replied, "I understand your brother is missing."

"Peter is not missing," Vicky said. "Peter is dead."

CHAPTER

ELEVEN

Vicky wanted to hear Wilde's story first, so he told it.

"Whoa," Vicky said when Wilde finished. "Just so I have this straight: A female relative of ours traveled to Europe in 1980. While there, she met a soldier on leave, who got her pregnant. Am I right so far?"

Wilde nodded.

"Somehow, that baby, you, a boy, was abandoned in the woods at an age so young, the boy doesn't remember any time before he was fending for himself. Eventually you were rescued and raised and now, what, thirty-five or so years later, you *still* don't know how you ended up in those woods." Vicky looked over at him. "That sum it up?"

"Yes."

Vicky looked up as though in deep thought. "You'd think if it was someone related to me, I'd have heard about it."

"She might have kept the pregnancy secret," Wilde said.

"Could be," Vicky agreed. "Based on what you said, your mother would probably have been, what, eighteen at the youngest, and probably under twenty-five, when she met your biological father?"

"That's about right," Wilde said.

She chewed on that for a moment. "Well, my father is dead, and mom, well, she's in and out, if you know what I mean. But I can try to get you a family tree. Some relatives on my father's side are into genealogy. They can probably help you."

"I would appreciate that," Wilde said. Then he switched gears. "Why do you think your brother is dead?"

"Tell me the truth. Are you a viewer?"

"A viewer?"

"Of *Love Is a Battlefield* or any of that. Is that part of your interest here?"

"No," Wilde said. "I never heard of the show before this morning."

"But you did contact Peter via this genealogy site?"

"I didn't know who he was. He used his initials." Then Wilde added, "Peter wrote me first."

"Really?" Vicky gestured toward Wilde's phone. "May I see what he said?"

Wilde opened the messages app on the genealogy site and passed his phone to her. As Vicky read her brother's words, her eyes began to well up. "Wow," she said softly. "These are hard to read now."

Wilde said nothing.

"So much hurt, so much pain." She shook her head, still staring at the message. "Did you look at my brother's social media at all?"

"Yes."

"So you know what happened to him?"

"Some of it," Wilde said. "Do you think he jumped from that cliff in his last post?"

"Yes, of course. Don't you?"

Wilde chose not to answer. "Did Peter leave a suicide note?"

"No."

"Did he send you a message of any kind?"

"No."

"Did he send anyone else, maybe your mother or Jenn Cassidy, a suicide note?"

"Not that I'm aware of."

"And they never found a body."

"They rarely do with jumpers at Adiona Cliffs. That's part of the allure. You jump off the end of the earth."

"I raise all this," Wilde said, "because I'm wondering why you seem so sure he's dead."

Vicky thought about that for a moment. "A few reasons. One, well, you won't like this one because you simply won't understand."

Wilde said nothing.

"There's a life force in the universe. I won't go into details, especially with a skeptic who has blocked chakras. It isn't worth it. But I know my brother is dead. I could actually feel him leave this world."

Wilde bit back the sigh. He gave it a moment, and then let the moment land with a dull thud. "You said 'a few reasons.'"

"Yes."

"One is you *feel* Peter is dead. What are the others?"

Vicky spread her hands. "Where else would he be?"

"I don't know," Wilde said.

"If Peter were alive," she continued, "well, where is he? I mean, do you know something about the situation I don't?"

"No. But I'd like to look for him anyway, if that's okay."

"Why?" Then Vicky Chiba saw it. "Oh, wait, I get it." She held high Wilde's phone before passing it back to him. "You feel obligated. Peter sent you this distress message, and you didn't reply."

Vicky Chiba didn't say it accusingly, but then again, her tone didn't take him off the hook either.

"I blame myself too, if that helps. I mean, look at Peter's face." Vicky picked up a framed photograph of four people—Peter, Vicky, and what Wilde assumed were the other two siblings.

"Is that your other sister and brother?"

Vicky nodded. "The four Bennett children. I'm the oldest. That's my sister Kelly. The two of us were thick as thieves. Then came our brother Silas. Kelly and I spoiled him rotten until, well, until Peter came along. Look at this face. Just look at it."

Wilde did as she asked.

"You can sense it, can't you?"

Wilde said nothing.

"Peter's innocence, his naïveté, his fragility. The rest of us, well, we are attractive enough, I guess. But Peter? He had that intangible. These reality shows—sure, they're all fake and scripted, but the viewer still somehow sees through all that and finds the real you. And the real Peter was pure goodness. You know the expression 'too good for this world'?"

Wilde nodded. He debated asking why someone "too good" would have roofied his sister-in-law, but he imagined that Vicky Chiba would either deny it or shut down entirely, and neither of those results would be fruitful right now; instead, he asked, "You said you blame yourself for Peter."

"Yes."

"Could you tell me why?"

"Because I got him into this," Vicky said. "I knew he'd be a star, and then I did a tarot reading that encouraged me to be active, not reactive—that's what it said over and over, 'Be active, not reactive,' and I had always been so reactive, my whole life—so I filled out the application for Peter to be on the show. I didn't think anything would come of it. Or maybe I knew. I can't say anymore. But I didn't really comprehend the long-term impact on Peter's psyche."

"In what way?" Wilde asked.

"Fame changes everyone. I know that sounds like a cliché, but no one gets out unscathed. When that fame beacon hits you, it's warm and soothing and the most addictive drug in the world. Every celebrity denies it—they pretend to be above craving fame—but it's so much worse for reality stars."

"How so?"

"No reality star stays a star. There is always an expiration date. I worked for a while in Hollywood. I always heard, 'The bigger the star, the nicer they are.' And you know what? That's true—the big stars are often really nice—but do you know why?"

Wilde shook his head.

"It's because they can afford to be. Those big superstars are secure that the fame will always be in plentiful supply for them. But for reality stars? It's the opposite. Reality stars know that beacon is at its brightest when it first hits you and that it will only dim with time."

Wilde gestured to the family photograph in her hand. "And that's what happened to your brother?"

"I thought Peter handled it as well as anyone could. I thought he'd built a life with Jenn, a happy one, but when it all fell apart…" Her voice faded away. Her eyes grew moist. "Do you really think Peter is alive?"

"I don't know."

"It doesn't make sense," she said, trying to sound resolute. "If Peter was alive, he'd have contacted me."

Wilde waited. Vicky Chiba would get there soon enough.

"But then again, if Peter had decided to leave this world"—Vicky Chiba stopped, blinked back the tears, regained her composure—"I think he would have contacted me. To let me know. To say goodbye."

They both stood there for a moment. Then Wilde said, "Let's go back for a second. When did you last see Peter?"

"He was staying with me."

"Here?"

"Yes."

"When did he leave?"

"You saw Peter's social media profiles?"

"Some of them," Wilde said.

"He left three days before his last Instagram post."

"The one with the cliff?"

"Yes."

"How did that happen?"

"What do you mean?"

"You said he was staying with you."

"Yes."

"What precipitated him leaving? What did he tell you?"

Again her eyes welled up. "On the surface, Peter seemed to be getting better. There was that post about not being so quick to believe what you hear. Did you see that one?"

Wilde nodded.

"So I thought maybe Peter was turning a corner, but looking back on it, I see it was all kinds of forced. Like he was psyching himself up for a battle he knew he couldn't win." She headed toward a computer on a desk in the corner. "Did you read the comments under any of his posts?"

"I did," Wilde said.

"Vile, right?"

"Yes."

"The last few days he was here, Peter read them all. Every single one of them. I don't know why. I told him not to. They made him spiral. So on that last day, that's what he was doing. He read the comments. Then he went through hundreds of DMs."

"DMs?"

"Direct Messages. Think of it like the messaging service in your DNA website. Followers on Instagram can write to you directly. Most remain unread. I tried to keep up during the height of Peter's popularity—that was important to him, to be kind to his fans—but there were so many it was impossible. Anyway, he got a particularly awful one. And that, I don't know, that seemed like the last straw."

"When did he get this message?"

"A day or two before he left. Some toxic creep had been trolling him, but this particular message—it was the first time I saw a flash of anger from him. For the most part, Peter was just confused and baffled by all this, not angry. It was like the world punched him in the face, and he was just trying to get his bearings and figure out why. But with this message, he wanted to go after the guy."

"The guy who sent the toxic message?"

"Yes."

"What did the message say?"

"I don't know. Peter wouldn't let me see it. A few days later, he packed up and left."

"Did he tell you he was leaving or where he was going?"

Vicky shook her head. "I came home from work and he was gone."

"I assume you reached out to him?"

"Yes. But he didn't reply. I called Jenn. She said they hadn't spoken in weeks. I called some other friends. Nothing. After three days passed, I went to the police."

"What did the police say?"

"What could they say?" Vicky replied with a shrug. "Peter was a grown man. They took my statement and sent me on my way."

"Can you show me the message?" Wilde asked. "The one you said upset him."

"Why?" Vicky shook her head. "There's so much hate out there. After a while, it's hard to stomach."

"I'd like to see it, if that's okay."

Vicky hesitated, but not for very long. She brought up Instagram on her app and moved to her brother's profile. There was that cliff again and that caption:

I just want peace.

She shifted the cursor so that the post before it came up. Wilde again read the words in the photograph:

Don't be so quick to believe
what you hear,
because lies spread quicker
than the truth.

"So this one creep with the profile name DogLufegnev commented a lot," Vicky said. "Always saying something awful like 'You'll pay' or 'I know the truth about you,' 'I have proof,' 'You should die,' that kind of stuff. But here is what he wrote under this post."

She scrolled down to a comment made by DogLufegnev. DogLufegnev's profile picture was a big red button saying GUILTY. His comment read:

Check your DMs.

Vicky said, "Maybe DogLufegnev is a dog lover or something."

"No," Wilde said.

"No?"

"DogLufegnev," Wilde said, "is Vengeful God backward."

She shook her head. "Lunatic. A goddamn lunatic."

"Can we see his message to your brother?"

Vicky hesitated. "May I be honest?"

Wilde waited.

"I don't like it. Showing you the message, I mean."

"Why?"

"There is a certain flow in the universe, and this feels like the wrong kind of cosmic disruption."

Wilde bit back another sigh. "I don't want to disrupt the cosmos either, but what's more disruptive than unanswered questions? Don't these doubts disturb the life force or something?"

Vicky thought about that.

"I wouldn't ask if I didn't think it was important," Wilde added.

She nodded and started typing. A few seconds later, Vicky frowned, paused, muttered something under her breath, and then typed some more. "That's weird."

"What?"

"I can't get into Peter's Instagram account." She met Wilde's eye. "It says 'incorrect password.'"

Wilde took a step toward her. "When was the last time you signed in?"

"I don't remember. We just keep it logged on usually, I don't know. I'm not great with the technical stuff."

"Did Peter handle his own social media?"

"He did by then, yes. For a while, when he and Jenn were clearing six figures a month, they hired a professional firm that took care of the advertising and endorsements."

"Six figures a month?"

"Easily. The year Peter won the show? I'd say it was probably closer to seven figures."

Wilde was having trouble comprehending this. "Per month?"

"Sure." Vicky tried again and shook her head. "Maybe he changed the password. Maybe he didn't want us to see these messages." She blinked and turned away. "I know you mean well, Wilde, but maybe we shouldn't do this."

Vicky was shutting down. Wilde had an idea.

"Okay, let's forget that for now," he said. "Do you have access to his email?"

"Yes."

"Have you checked it?"

"Not recently. Why would I?"

"There could be something in there. If we see, for example, he's sent an email in the past few weeks—"

"He rarely emailed. He was more a text guy."

"But it's worth a check, don't you think? Maybe he reached out to someone. Maybe someone reached out to him."

Vicky reopened the browser and clicked the Gmail account icon. Her own email address popped up, so she clicked over it and typed in one beginning with PBennett447, and then she typed in his password. Her eyes scanned down the inbox.

"Anything stand out?" Wilde asked.

She shook her head. "The new stuff is all mailing lists or business related. Nothing's been opened since Peter vanished."

Wilde noticed that she said "vanished" this time, rather than "dead."

"Check the 'sent' tab," Wilde said, though that wasn't the real reason he'd had her sign in to her brother's email. This was just a diversion now—Wilde had already gotten what he wanted from Vicky Chiba. "See if he sent anything."

She clicked per his request. "Nothing new or relevant."

"Do we know if he spoke or communicated with anyone after he left?"

"I checked his phone. He didn't use it."

"How about your siblings?"

She shook her head. "Kelly lives down in Florida with her husband and three kids. She said she hasn't spoken to Peter in months. And Silas, well, they were the two babies, but Silas was always jealous of Peter. You know how it is. Peter was better looking, more popular, the better athlete. Anyway, I think the last time Peter and Silas talked was when we all appeared on the show."

"You were all on *Love Is a Battlefield*?"

Vicky nodded. "There's an episode toward the end called 'Homefront.' The finalists introduce Jenn to their families, so it was just Peter and Big Bobbo."

"Big Bobbo?"

"That was the other finalist. Bob Jenkins. He called himself Big Bobbo. Anyway, the producers want your entire family there and they want drama. We were supposed to be skeptical and interrogate Jenn, you know, make a commotion. The producers wanted all three siblings there. Silas didn't like it."

"But he still went?"

"Yes. The money was good, and they gave us a free stay at this cool resort in Utah, so he figured, Why not? But once he was there, Silas just sulked. I don't think he said two words. He became a pretty popular meme."

"A meme?"

"I think that's what they call it. People would post pictures of

Silas and call him Silent Silas or Sulking Silas, and then they'd add some comment about being grumpy, like 'Me before coffee.' Silas was upset about it. He wanted to sue the show."

"Where is Silas now?"

"I'm not sure. He drives a truck so he's on the road most of the year. I can give you his mobile number?"

"That would be great."

"I don't think Silas will be much help though."

"How about Jenn?"

"What about her?"

"Was Peter still in touch with her?"

Vicky shook her head. "Not toward the end, no."

"Do you and Jenn talk much?"

"We used to. I mean, before all this, we were all very close. She was devastated by the betrayal."

"So you believe Peter did it?"

Vicky hesitated. "He said he didn't."

Wilde waited.

"Does it matter anymore?"

"I'm not judging," Wilde said. "I just..."

"You just what?" Vicky said, and there was a little edge in her tone now. "This doesn't concern you. I told you I'd work on the family tree for you. That's why you're here, right? To find out why you were abandoned in the woods?"

It suddenly dawned on Wilde that for the second time in his conscious life—the first time was just a few months ago with his father—Wilde was conversing with a blood relative. He expected that it would mean nothing to him. He had spent his life convinced that the answers would provide no meaningful closure or change in his life, especially after his encounter with a father who clearly wanted nothing to do with him, and yet now, as he faced someone who shared his blood, there was an undeniable pull.

"Vicky?"

"What?"

"You talk about chakra and feelings and all that."

"Don't make fun of me."

"I'm not. But something about this whole thing isn't adding up."

"I still don't see how that concerns you."

"Maybe it doesn't. But I'm going to dig into this, with your blessing or not. At best, you'll get some answers. At worst, I've wasted some of your time."

"You're not wasting my time," Vicky Chiba said. Then she added, "You're our cousin. And you have my blessing."

TWELVE

R ola said, "Peter Bennett is most likely dead."

"I know."

"I don't get why you're looking for him."

Rola Naser, Wilde's foster sister, and her family lived in a classic 1970s split-level with a bloated addition on the back. A muddled mishmash of children's play equipment—bicycles, tricycles, pogo sticks, bright orange plastic baseball bats, a lacrosse goal, dolls, trucks—was scattered across the front yard as though someone had strewn them from a great height.

They sat at the kitchen table. One of Rola's kids was on Wilde's knee. Another was eating a jelly donut, wearing a lot of it on her face. The two oldest were in the corner working on a TikTok dance, which involved repeatedly playing a song that asked the musical question, "Why you so obsessed with me?"

Wilde bounced the kid on his knee to prevent him from crying. "You spent years pushing me to find out about my biological family."

"Truth."

"Nagged me ad nauseam about it."

"Truth."

"So?"

"So Peter Bennett's sister—what was her name again?"

"Vicky Chiba."

"Right. She said she would make up a family tree for you, right?"

"Yes."

Rola turned her palms toward the sky. "She's older than her brother, probably knows more about the family than he does. So that's all you need, right? I read about Peter Bennett online, and he sounds like a major-league douchenozzle. Why do we need to help him?"

Explaining would take too long and probably not make sense, even to him. "Can we just skip my motivations for now?"

"If you want. Can I fix you something to eat? And by 'fix' I mean, should I order more pizza?"

"I'm okay."

"Doesn't matter. I already ordered an extra pie. What can I do to help?"

Wilde gestured with his chin toward the laptop. "Mind if I use that?"

Rola hit a few keys and turned it to face him. Wilde snaked his hand around little Charlie's waist, so he could type and balance the kid at the same time. He brought up Gmail.

"What's up?"

"I watched Vicky Chiba type in Peter's email address and password."

"Let me guess. You memorized the password."

He nodded.

"Without her knowledge?"

He nodded again.

"What's the password?"

"LoveJenn447."

He typed that into the password field, hit return, and bingo, he was in. Wilde started scanning through the emails. It was just as Vicky had said—nothing useful, nothing personal. Wilde checked the trash folder. Again nothing. He would take a deeper dive later.

"Any idea what the 447 stands for?" Rola asked.

"Nope."

"Do you not trust the sister? Or should I say, your cousin?"

"It's not that," Wilde said.

He explained how Vicky had gotten a little queasy over the privacy invasion when she'd realized that her brother had changed his Instagram password. Using the LoveJenn447 password, Wilde tried to sign in to Peter's Instagram.

No. Incorrect password.

Wilde had expected that. Below the message was the common link asking him if he'd forgotten his password and would he like to reset it. He clicked on it. When he did, Instagram, like pretty much every website after a password reset request, sent a link to the email on file.

The email on file was, drum roll, the Gmail account Wilde had gotten access to by watching Vicky Chiba sign in.

"Clever," Rola said, when he explained it to her. "Primitive. But clever."

"My epitaph," Wilde said. He waited for the email to come in from Instagram. When it did, he changed the password to something benign. Then he signed back into Instagram with the new password. He hit the message icon. There were tons in the "All Request" messages, but Wilde clicked to the "primary" category.

The messages from DogLufegnev were right on top.

Rola was reading over his shoulder as Wilde clicked on the conversation.

> **DogLufegnev:** If you try a comeback, Peter, I'll destroy you. I know what you did. I have the proof.
> **Peter:** Who are you?
> **DogLufegnev:** You know.
> **Peter:** I don't.

DogLufegnev then sent a photo—a more graphic photo than the ones Marnie had produced for that podcast. Under the image was another message.

Dog Lufegnev: YOU KNOW.

There were no time stamps, so it was hard to say how fast Peter Bennett replied.

Peter: I want to meet. Here is my mobile. Please.

Rola was covering little Charlie's eyes. "Wow."

"Yes."

"Nice lighting on the dick pic too," she said.

"You want me to print it out for you?"

"Just send me a screenshot. So that's it? DogWhatever didn't reply to Peter's offer to meet?"

"Not on here. But Peter gave him or her his cell phone. He may have called or texted. Any way we can trace down DogLufegnev?"

Rola opened the refrigerator, grabbed an apple, tossed it to her son Elijah. "Our best hope is that this guy—or girl, we don't know, do we?—our best hope is that DogWhatever sent a text message or called Peter Bennett's phone."

"And if Dog didn't?"

Rola shrugged. "We can try to track them down via the Instagram account, but it's harder. We do this work a lot nowadays, mostly on a corporate level. So many fake accounts are created to slander and harass. Like, I mean, look at your cousin's account. People are making death threats. It's crazy. Why do these trolls care about people they don't know? Anyway, we get stuff like this all the time, though for more concrete reasons."

"But can you still find their real identities?"

"Sometimes. There are always digital footprints. We can often do metadata tracing or link analysis or advanced search tools, stuff like that. If the case is severe, like a real death threat, we can get a subpoena and try to provide the guy's IP address. I assume you want to find this DogWhatever guy."

"I do."

"Let me get my best people on it."

"Thank you."

"But Wilde?"

He waited.

"You don't owe Peter Bennett a thing."

THIRTEEN

Wilde checked his messages. Nothing from Laila. He'd wait and see how that played out. He returned the rental and hiked back up through the Ramapo Mountains to his Ecocapsule. The woods are serenity and solitude, but they are never silent. They brim with life, often hushed, and there is majesty and wonder in that. As he rambled through the trees, Wilde felt the muscles in his back and shoulders loosen. His breathing deepened. His stride became more languid. He let his relaxed brain view Peter Bennett with a somewhat renewed perspective.

Rola had said that Wilde didn't owe Peter Bennett anything. Perhaps. But did that matter? Do you have to owe someone to help them?

He took out his phone and called the number Vicky had given him for her brother—and Wilde's cousin—Silas. The phone was picked up on the third ring.

"Who's this?" the voice said.

Wilde could hear the dull roar of traffic and figured that Silas might be in his truck.

"My name is Wilde," he said. "I got your number from your sister Vicky."

"What do you want?"

"I'm your cousin."

Wilde explained about the DNA test, about Peter's messages, about searching for him.

"Damn," Silas said when Wilde had finished. "That's so messed up. So we are somehow related through your mom?"

"Seems so."

"And she never told your father about you and just left you in the woods?"

That wasn't entirely accurate, but Wilde saw no reason to correct him. "Something like that."

"Why are you calling me, Wilde?"

"I'm trying to find Peter."

"Why? You a cop?"

"No."

"A Battler?"

"A what?"

"That's what they call the *Love Is a Battlefield* groupies. Battlers. You a Battler?"

"No."

"Because the Battlers made a meme out of me. That stupid show, I mean. Almost every day—still!—some asshole walks up to me and says, 'Hey, you're that sulking guy!' Annoys the piss out of me, you know what I mean?"

"I can imagine."

"By the way, everyone thinks Peter's dead."

"Do you?"

"I don't know, Cuz." Silas snorted. "Cuz. That's weird, right?"

"A little."

"Look, I haven't spoken to Peter in a long time. Truth is, we weren't very close, but I'm sure Vicky told you that. You said you matched Peter on a DNA site?"

"Yes."

"Mind telling me which one?"

"Which site? DNAYourStory."

"Oh, that explains it," Silas said.

"Explains what?"

"Why you and I didn't match. I put my DNA into one called MeetYourFamily."

"Did you get any matches?"

"Got one that's twenty-three percent."

"What kind of relative is that?"

"Could be a lot of things. Most likely? A half sibling. My old man was a player. Don't tell Vicky. She thinks ol' Phil was a great dad. It would only break her heart."

"You don't think she'd want to know she has a half sibling?"

"Who knows? Maybe you're right. Maybe I should tell her. But I don't know what good it will do."

"Did you contact the relative?"

"I tried. I sent a message on the MeetYourFamily app, but they never replied."

"Could you text me the info?"

"On...? Oh, the match? Not sure what I could text you. The account was deleted."

Odd, Wilde thought. Just like with Daniel Carter's. "Did you get a name or initials or anything?"

"Nah, MeetYourFamily doesn't reveal identities until both sides agree, so I don't know anything about him. Or her. Or whoever. Just that we're a twenty-three percent match."

"That must be an odd feeling," Wilde said.

"What?" Silas asked.

"You may have a half sibling out there, and neither of you knows anything about it."

"I guess, maybe. Seems a lot of people are finding out odd stuff on those sites. I got a friend who found out his dad wasn't his real dad. Messed him up good. He didn't even tell his mom because he didn't want them getting a divorce."

"Did you get any other matches?"

"Nothing too interesting. I'll text you what I got when I get back to my home computer. By the way, Cuz, where do you live?"

"New Jersey."

"Near Vicky?"

"Not far," Wilde said. "How about you?"

"I got a place in Wyoming, but I'm never there. Right now, I'm carrying a load for Yellow Freight through Kentucky." He cleared his throat. "But I do go through New Jersey a fair amount. How close are we related?"

"We share a great-grandparent."

"That's not a lot," Silas said. "But it's not nothing either."

"It's not nothing."

"Especially for you, I guess. I mean, no offense or anything, but you don't have anyone but us. Might be nice to say hello or something. Have a coffee maybe."

"When do you come through New Jersey again?"

"Pretty soon. I usually stay with Vicky."

"Next time you're here," Wilde said, "give me a call."

"I'll do that, Cuz. And I'll try to think about our family and see what I can come up with."

"I'd appreciate that."

"You still going to look for Peter?"

"Yes."

"Good luck with that too. I'm not blaming anyone, but Vicky, she got him into this reality shit. I think she did it for the right reasons, but Peter wasn't made for that world. If I can help find him…"

"I'll let you know."

Silas hung up. Wilde put his phone into his back pocket and continued his hike. He took deep breaths, filling his lungs with the fresh mountain air. He slowly lifted his face toward the soothing sun and let his thoughts flow freely. They flowed, as they often did when he let them, to a familiar, comforting, beautiful face.

Laila's.

The buzz of his phone startled him. It was Hester.

"Hey," Wilde said, staying as much as he could in this pleasant semi-stupor.

"You okay?"

"Yes."

"You sound like you took an edible or something."

"High on life. What's up?"

"I got your message," Hester said. "So you already found your DNA website relative?"

"His identity, yes. Him, no."

"Explain."

"Have you ever watched a reality show called *Love Is a Battlefield*?"

"Every episode," Hester said.

"Really?"

"No, of course not. I don't even get the concept. Reality TV? I watch TV to *escape* reality. What about it?"

Wilde had time on the hike, so he filled Hester in on Peter Bennett and the ensuing saga of his scandal and disappearances. When he finished, Hester said, "What a mess."

"Yes."

"You found your family—and they're as dysfunctional as all the others."

"I was abandoned in the woods as a small child," Wilde said. "We didn't expect functional."

"Good point. So you're going to search for your missing cousin?"

"Yes."

"Maybe you'll just confirm that he committed suicide," Hester added.

"Maybe."

"And suppose that's the case."

"Then that's the answer."

"You just let it go?"

"What else can I do?"

"So next steps," Hester said, getting down to business. "Seems to me the person who might have some information is his wife or ex-wife or whatever she is, Jenn Whatshername."

"Cassidy."

"Like David? Man, I had a crush on him in the day."

"Who?"

"David Cassidy. *The Partridge Family*?"

"Right."

"Girls talked about his hair and smile, but he had some caboose too."

"Good to know," Wilde said. Then: "How should we approach Jenn Cassidy?"

"I know a lot of Hollywood agents," Hester said. "I can see if she'll talk to one of us."

"Good."

"I assume you got Rola working on the real identity of this Dog troll?"

"Yes."

"By the way," Hester began, her tone aiming for nonchalant and not coming close to hitting the mark, "did you shtup Laila last night?"

"Hester."

"Did you?"

"Did you shtup Oren?" he countered.

"Every chance I get. Oren has a better caboose than David Cassidy." Then: "Was that question supposed to stop me from asking about you and my former daughter-in-law?"

Wilde kept hiking up the mountain. "Where are you?"

"I'm in my office waiting on a verdict in the Levine case."

"Any idea when it will come in?"

"None." Then: "Was that question supposed to stop me from asking about you and my former daughter-in-law?"

Wilde stayed silent.

"Right, right, it's none of my business. Let me make some calls, see what I can learn. Hit you later."

Wilde did a little maintenance on the Ecocapsule. Rain had been in short supply since his return, so he took the water tank to the nearest brook to fill it. The Ecocapsule had wheels, so Wilde could move it every few weeks, just to be certain no one could track him, but he always stayed close to one of the mountain waterways for just such drought-like occurrences.

When Wilde finished, he headed over to the lookout spot that gave him a bird's-eye view of Laila's house on the end of the cul-de-sac. No cars. No movement.

His phone buzzed again. It was Rola.

"We got lucky. Sort of."

"Explain."

"We were able to trace the ISP for DogLufegnev. Seems he runs an extensive bot farm, several of which trolled your cousin pretending to be different people. So not only did 'Dog' post toxic stuff about Peter Bennett, he then amplified the posts as though a lot of other people agreed."

"Not uncommon," Wilde said.

"But still awful. What's wrong with people?"

"Did you get a name or address for DogLufegnev?"

"Sort of. Do you know how ISPs work?"

"Pretty much."

"What I have is the billing address that uses that particular ISP. It could be anybody in the household."

"Yeah, okay."

"The ISP is billed to the home of Henry and Donna McAndrews, 972 Wake Robin Lane in Harwinton, Connecticut. It's a two-hour drive from you."

"I'm on my way."

Wilde didn't use a rental this time. He had a place where he could "borrow" a car with a license plate that couldn't be matched or traced—the vehicular version of a burner phone. He figured that would be best. He also brought dark clothes, a mask, gloves, and an appropriate yet subtle disguise in case he felt it was needed. There was, Wilde had the self-awareness to realize, a fine line between caution and paranoia. Wilde may be flirting on the paranoia side of that line, but it seemed the more prudent way to behave.

He took Route 287 East and crossed what had once been the spot of the Tappan Zee Bridge, but that had been torn down and replaced with the newly minted "Governor Mario M. Cuomo Bridge," and while Wilde had no problem with Mario Cuomo, he still wondered why they'd change such a perfect name—"Tappan" for the Native American tribe, "Zee" as the Dutch word for sea— to honor any politician.

The ride grew more and more rural with each passing mile. Litchfield County had plenty of stunning wooded areas. Five years ago, when Wilde needed to escape the Ramapo Mountains but wanted to stay on the East Coast, he'd lived in these woods for two months.

It was nightfall by the time Wilde reached Wake Robin Lane. The road was still, quiet. He slowed the car. Every house had several acres of land. House lights twinkled through the thick foliage.

But there were no lights on at 972 Wake Robin Lane.

Wilde again felt that primitive tingle, that survival instinct most of us have long since smothered or let decay as we "progressed" and moved into sturdy homes with locked doors backed by trusted authority figures. He kept driving until the end of the street and turned right on Laurel Road. He passed Wilson Pond, found a secluded spot by the Kalmia Sanctuary, which, according to the sign, had been created by a local Audubon Society. Wilde was already clad in black. He put on his gloves, a black baseball cap, and pocketed a lightweight black ski mask in case he needed it. It was pitch dark now, but that didn't bother Wilde. He knew the skies and the stars well enough to hike the mile through wooded yards. He also carried a flashlight if need be—being a "survivalist" didn't give you the ability to see in the dark—but the skies were clear enough tonight.

Fifteen minutes later, Wilde stood in the McAndrews' backyard. Before heading out, he had looked up the house on Zillow. The McAndrews had bought it in January 2018 for $345,000. It was 2,600 square feet, three bedrooms, three baths, fairly new construction, and sat on two secluded acres.

As the old saw goes: It was quiet. Too quiet.

No lights on in the back.

Either the McAndrews family members were all in bed—it was only nine p.m.—or, more likely, no one was at home. Wilde felt his phone buzz. He had an AirPod in his left ear. He tapped it to answer. There was no need to say hello. Rola knew the drill.

"Henry McAndrews is sixty-one years old, his wife Donna is sixty," Rola said. "They have three children, all boys, ages twenty-eight, twenty-six, and nineteen. I'm still digging."

Rola hung up.

Wilde wasn't sure what to make of that. If one were to profile based on age and gender, the sons were more likely to be DogLufegnev than their parents. The question was, Do any of the sons still live at home?

Wilde slipped on the mask. None of his skin was showing. Most homes today have some kind of security system or camera setup. Not all. But enough. He stepped closer to the house. If he were to be spotted by camera or eyes, they would see a man dressed head to toe in black. That was it, and that, Wilde knew, was nothing.

When he got closer to the house, he ducked down in the flower bedding and grabbed a few pebbles. Staying low, Wilde threw the pebbles against the back sliding glass door and waited.

Nothing.

He did the same with the upstairs windows, throwing more pebbles, this time with a little more velocity. This was old-school—a crude yet effective way to see if anyone was home. If the lights came on, he could simply take off. No one would be able to track him before he disappeared back into the wooded area.

Wilde threw some more pebbles, slightly bigger ones, several at one time. They made plenty of noise. He wanted that, of course.

No reaction. No screams. No shouts. No lights. No silhouettes looking out the window.

Conclusion: No one home.

This conclusion, of course, was not definite. Someone could be a heavy sleeper, but again Wilde was not particularly worried. He would now search for an unlocked door or window. If that didn't work, he had the tools to break into any residence. Funny when he thought about it—he had been breaking into homes since he was too young to remember. In those days, of course, the little "boy from the woods" didn't use tools. He just tried windows and doors and if none opened, he would move on to the next house. Once—he was probably four or five—when he was super hungry and couldn't find an empty and unlocked house, he had thrown a rock through a basement window and crawled in that way. He flashed back to that, the hunger pains of that child, his fear and desperation winning out over caution. He'd cut his stomach on shards of glass when he crawled through that basement window. Up until right now, he'd forgotten that event completely. What had he done after he'd cut himself? Did that little boy have the wherewithal to locate a first aid kit in an upstairs bathroom? Did he just press his shirt against the wounds? Were the wounds deep or superficial?

He didn't remember. He just remembered cutting his flesh on the shards of glass. That was how the memories often came to him—in broken shards. His earliest memories: the red banister, dark woods, a portrait of a mustached man, and a woman's scream. He had dreamt about those images for his entire life, but he still didn't know what, if anything, they meant.

Wilde first tried the McAndrews' lower-level windows. Locked. He tried the back door. Locked. He tried the sliding glass door.

Bingo.

That surprised Wilde somewhat. Why lock all your windows but not the sliding glass door? Could have just forgotten or been careless, of course. It wasn't a big deal. And yet.

The tingle was back.

Wilde ducked low. He'd only slid the door open an inch. Now he slid it another inch. The door glided easily on the track. No sound. Wilde stayed low and slid it some more. Slowly. This could all be overkill, but overconfidence was often a bigger threat than any adversary. He waited and listened.

Nothing.

When he'd slid the door wide enough, Wilde crawled into the den. He debated closing the door behind him, but if he needed to make a quick exit, an open door would save time. For a full minute, Wilde stayed perfectly still, straining to hear any sound.

There was nothing.

Wilde spotted a mainframe computer on the desk in the corner.

Bingo again.

There was no one home. He was sure of it now. But he couldn't shake that tingle. He wasn't a woo-woo superstitious man. He didn't really believe in any of that. Yet there was an unmistakable crackle in the air.

What was he missing?

He didn't know. It could just be his imagination. He didn't dismiss that. Then again, there was no harm in being extra cautious. Wilde stayed low and crept toward the desk. This was his goal and reason for breaking into the McAndrews' home—to download everything he could off the McAndrews' computer and then get it to Rola's experts for a full analysis. He would at some point like to question the McAndrews family, though he was doubtful that could get him anywhere. The bigger key was to figure out how the troll DogLufegnev got those compromising photos that had sent Peter Bennett into a tailspin.

The computer was a PC with a Windows operating system and password protection. Wilde pulled out two USB flash drives. He stuck the first one into the USB port. The flash drive was an all-in-one hacker's tool. It was loaded with self-running programs like mailpv.exe and mspass.exe, and once plugged into the USB port, it would collect various passwords from Facebook, Outlook, your bank account, whatever.

Wilde didn't need all that.

He just needed the operating system password, so that he could back up the entire contents of the computer on the second flash drive. In the movies, this takes a relatively long time. In reality, the password is bypassed in seconds and the contents should be copied in no more than five minutes.

With the computer unlocked, Wilde opened up the web browser to check through the history. He knew that computers were hardly tell-alls anymore. People mostly used their phones to surf and search nowadays. You could spy on emails or texts, but the good stuff was often hidden in secure messaging apps like Signal or Threema.

First site bookmarked: Instagram.

Unusual. Instagram was normally a phone app, not something people did from their computer. Wilde quickly clicked on the link. Instagram came up. He expected to see DogLufegnev's handle in the profile box, but the screen name read NurseCaresLove24. The profile photo was of a woman who appeared to be Asian, no more than thirty. On the right, Wilde could see the option to switch profiles. He hit that link.

Dozens of accounts came up.

It was a vast potpourri of accounts—all creeds, genders, nation-alities, occupations, persuasions were represented. Wilde scrolled down the screen, counting as he went along. He took out his phone and snapped screenshots of the names just in case they didn't show up on the flash drive. He'd counted over thirty accounts when he finally located one with the name DogLufegnev.

He clicked on the profile and watched the page load. Dog-Lufegnev had posted only twelve photographs in total, all nature shots. His followers numbered forty-six, and from what Wilde could tell, they all seemed to be other accounts set up on this com-puter. Wilde hit the private messaging icon. He found the same correspondences between DogLufegnev and Peter Bennett he'd seen at Rola's house, but what was more curious, far more curious, was the message above it, the last one DogLufegnev received.

It was from someone named PantherStrike88. The message was chillingly simple:

Got you, McAndrews. You're going to pay.

Whoa, Wilde thought. This Panther account had found McAndrews out.

The flash drive blinked twice, indicating it was done with the download. Wilde pulled it out and put it in his pocket. He clicked on the profile for PantherStrike88, but it was gone. Whoever had created the account—and sent that threatening message—had deleted themselves.

What the hell was going on?

For the first time since Wilde had entered the premises, he heard a sound.

A car.

He quickly stepped toward the front window in time to see the car's taillights disappearing to the left. It was nothing. A car driving by. That's all. This street was silent again.

But the tingle was back.

Wilde padded back toward the computer room, debating whether he should stay and keep looking through the computer or leave now, when the first whiff hit him.

He froze.

Wilde's heart dropped into his stomach. He stood by a door he assumed led to the basement. He leaned toward it and inhaled deeper.

Oh no.

Wilde didn't want to open it. He wanted to flee. But he couldn't. Not now.

With his gloved hand he reached out and turned the knob. He

cracked the door open. That was it. That was all he needed. The awful stench of decay rushed out as though it had been pounding on the door demanding to be released.

Wilde flicked on the light and looked down the stairs.

There was blood.

Lots of it.

CHAPTER

FOURTEEN

When Wilde's call came in, Hester was on her back in bed, post flagrante delicto and still catching her breath. Lying next to her, staring up at the ceiling with a smile on his face, was her—was Hester too old to use the term "boyfriend"?—beau, Oren Carmichael.

"That," Oren said, right before the phone trilled, "was awesome."

They were in Hester's Manhattan duplex. Like Hester, Oren had sold the Westville home where he and his ex, Cheryl, had raised their now-grown kids. Oren had been on the periphery of Hester's life for a long time. He'd coached two of her sons in Little League. He had also been one of the policemen who'd found little Wilde in the woods.

Oren smiled at her.

"What?" Hester asked.

"Nothing," Oren said.

"So why the big smile?"

"What part of 'that was awesome' is confusing you?"

When Ira died, Hester had figured that she was done with men. It wasn't something she had concluded out of anger or bitterness or even heartbreak, though there was plenty of that. She'd loved

Ira. He was a dear, kind, intelligent, funny man. He had been a wonderful life partner. Hester could simply not see herself dating again. She had a busy career and full life, and the whole idea of getting ready for a date with a new someone made her shiver. It just seemed like too much of a hassle. The notion that she would ever one day get naked in front of a man other than Ira both terrified and exhausted her. Who needed it? Not her.

Westville Police Chief Oren Carmichael had been a surprise. Oren, an uber hunk with broad shoulders in a fitted uniform, would never be for Hester and vice versa. But she fell and he fell and now, here they were. Hester couldn't help but wonder what Ira would have made of this. She liked to think that he would be happy for her, the same way she would have been happy for Ira if he'd ended up with Cheryl, Oren's still-sumptuous ex-wife who even now posted pics of herself in bikinis—though on the other hand, maybe Hester would have haunted Ira like Fruma-Sarah in the dream sequence in *Fiddler on the Roof*.

She'd want Ira to be happy with someone new. Wouldn't Ira want the same for her? She hoped so. Ira could get so jealous, and Hester had been a bit of a flirt back in the day. Still, Hester was deliriously happy with Oren. They were ready to make more of a commitment, but at their ages, what did that mean? Kids? Hahaha. Marriage? Who needed it? Moving in together? Not really. She liked her own space. She didn't want a man around all the time, even a wonderful one like Oren. Did that mean on some level she loved him any less? Hard to say. Hester loved Oren as much as possible, but she didn't want to love him like she was eighteen years old, or even forty.

But there was one truth that constantly stung: The relationship with Oren was physical—more physical, though it would never be fair to compare, than with Ira. She felt guilty about that. Her and Ira's sex life had waned. That was normal, of course. You're building a life, two careers, you're pregnant, you're raising little kids, you're exhausted, you have no privacy. It was a story too often repeated. But it'd still upset Ira. "I miss the passion," he had said, and though she'd dismissed it as normal "man wants more sex" manipulation, she wondered about that.

One night, not long before David died in the car crash, Ira had been sitting in the dark with a glass of whiskey in his hand. He rarely drank and when he did, it went right to his head. She had come in the room and just stood behind him. She didn't think he even knew she was there.

"If I died and you start dating again," he'd said, "would you want your sex life with a new man to be what we have?"

She hadn't answered. But she hadn't forgotten either.

Maybe Ira wouldn't be happy about what was going on in his old bed. Or maybe he would understand. When you're young, you expect too much from a relationship; one day, you look back and understand that.

The phone trilled again.

Oren asked, "Verdict?"

Earlier, she and Oren had been discussing the Richard Levine murder case over dinner.

"Either you believe in the system," Oren, as a law enforcement officer, had commented, "or you don't."

"I believe in our system," she said.

"We both know what your client did wasn't self-defense."

"We don't know anything of the sort."

"If he gets off, does that mean our system doesn't work?"

"It may mean the opposite," she said.

"Meaning?"

"It may mean our system has the flexibility to work."

Oren considered that. "Levine had his reasons. Is that what you're saying?"

"In a sense."

"Every murderer thinks they have a reason to kill."

"True," Hester said.

"And you think it's okay to kill someone for that?"

"Only when it comes to Nazis," she said, kissing him lightly on the cheek. "When it comes to Nazis, I have no problem with it at all."

Hester sat up in bed now and looked at her phone. "Not the verdict," Hester said. She hit the answer button and put the phone to her ear. "Hello?"

"You alone?" Wilde asked.

She didn't like the quake in his tone. "No."

"Can you be?"

She mouthed to Oren that she was going into another room. Oren nodded that he understood. When she was in the living room with the bedroom door shut behind her, she said, "Okay, what's wrong?"

"I have a hypothetical for you."

"I'm not going to like this, am I?"

"Doubtful."

"Go on."

"Let's say hypothetically I found a dead body."

"I knew I wasn't going to like this. Where?"

"In a private home where I was not supposed to be."

Wilde explained about his search for his cousin and how it ended up on the doorstep of the McAndrews residence.

"Do you know whose body it is?"

"The father. Henry McAndrews."

"Are you still in the house?"

"No."

"Any chance the police could figure out that you were in the house?"

"No."

"You say that with a lot of confidence," Hester said.

Wilde didn't reply.

"How long would you say he's been dead?"

"I'm not a pathologist."

"But?"

"I'd guess at least a week."

"Interesting," Hester said. "You'd think his wife or kids would have called it in or something. I assume you called me for legal advice."

Wilde didn't reply.

"Two choices," she continued. "Choice One: Coming clean and calling it in."

"I broke into the house."

"We could work with that. You walked by. You smelled something funny."

"So dressed all in black with a black mask and gloves, I slid open the back door in a remote house on several acres of private property, nowhere near where anyone would be taking a casual stroll—"

"Could all be explained," Hester said.

"For real?"

"Might take some time. But they'd know you didn't kill him because the autopsy would show he was killed at least a week ago. I'll eventually get you off."

"Choice Two?" he said.

"Are you worried the police won't believe you?"

"If I come forward, they'll dig into me, my past, all of it. They might even relook at the Maynard case."

Hester hadn't thought of that. The Maynard case had seemed an "ordinary" kidnapping to the outside world; it was anything but. That had been kept quiet for a lot of good reasons. "I see," she said.

"And best scenario if I did come clean—who would be their main suspect?"

"I'm not following . . . oh, wait. Your cousin?"

"Who else?"

"Yeah, but come on, Wilde. Would you want to protect him if he murdered this guy?"

"No."

"Being trolled isn't a justification for murder," Hester said.

"Unless he's a Nazi."

"Are you making a joke?"

"Not a good one, but yes. I don't know if Peter Bennett was involved or not. We don't have a clue what's going on."

"You can't just leave a body to rot," Hester said. "My legal advice would be to call it in."

"What's Choice Two?"

"That is Choice Two. Choice One was to come clean. Choice Two is to call it in anonymously. I would advise Choice One, but I have a stubborn client."

"And you see his point," Wilde added.

"I do." Hester switched hands. "Tell you what. I'll call it in. They can't compel me to say a name. Attorney-client privilege, but this way they might keep me in the loop. I assume there is no way to trace our current call?"

"None."

"Okay, I'll let you know what I find out."

She hung up. When she got back to the bedroom, Oren was getting dressed. She didn't stop him. She had no trouble with him staying all night, but it was something neither encouraged.

"You okay?" Oren asked, pulling his T-shirt over those shoulders.

"Do you know any cops in Litchfield County?"

"I can find one, why?"

"I need to report a dead body."

FIFTEEN

Wilde got rid of the car back at Ernie's. Ernie would do whatever he needed to make sure the car could never be traced. When something like this went down, that usually entailed stripping down the vehicle for parts. Ernie wouldn't ask Wilde for details, and Wilde wouldn't ask Ernie. Safer for all parties.

Rola picked him up. He handed her the flash drive. Then he filled her in as she drove him away in a Honda minivan loaded up with child safety seats. Her face grew grim as he spoke.

"This flash drive," she said. "I better do the full analysis myself."

"You can do that?"

"If it's not too complicated, yeah. Don't get me wrong. I trust my experts. They understand discretion."

"But you don't want to put them in that position."

"Not when there's a dead body."

Wilde nodded. "Fair."

"Still, we can't be the bad guys here. If we find something that can help the police locate the killer, we turn it over to them, right?"

"Yes."

"Even if it's your cousin?"

"Especially if."

Rola veered toward the Route 17 exit. "You could sleep at my place tonight if you want. I have great internet."

"I'm good."

Ten minutes later, she put on her blinkers and pulled onto the shoulder in a pitch-black area. Wilde kissed her cheek, got out, and disappeared into the woods. There was nothing more to be done tonight. He would go back to his Ecocapsule and get some sleep. He was about a hundred yards from it when his phone buzzed. It was a text from Laila:

> **Laila:** Come over.

Wilde typed back a reply: Did you talk to Matthew?

> **Laila:** Losing it.
> **Wilde:** What?
> **Laila:** As in, If I have to text you 'Come Over' twice, I must be 'Losing It.'

He smiled in the dark and started in the direction of Laila's back-yard. He didn't really worry about Darryl. That was her concern, not his. He didn't worry about doing the right thing by Laila by staying away or any of that because, really, how patronizing would that be to Laila? He was transparent with her, and she understood the situation. Who was he to "rescue" her from making her own decisions, even when he questioned the wisdom of them?

Nice rationalization.

Laila met him at the back door. Matthew wasn't home. They headed straight upstairs. Wilde stripped down and stepped into the shower. Laila joined him. At seven in the morning, after the longest stretch of sleep he'd had in eons, Wilde blinked his eyes open and saw Laila sitting on the edge of the bed, looking out the window into the woods off the backyard. He stared at her profile and said nothing.

Without turning toward him, Laila said, "We will have to talk about this."

"Okay."

"But not today. I still need to figure out a few things."

Wilde sat up. "Do you want me to leave?"

"No." Laila faced him full-on, and when she did, he felt the thud in his chest. "Do you want to tell me about it?"

He didn't. Not really. Some people like to talk things out. It helps them find solutions to problems. For Wilde, it was the opposite. He found that he often learned more by keeping it internal, letting the pressure build until the answers rose to the top. To mix metaphors, when he started talking things out, it felt like a balloon losing air.

Still, he understood the value in bouncing off another human being, especially one as insightful as Laila, not to mention the fact that he could see it would bring her some measure of joy or satisfaction. He told her what he could about Peter Bennett, leaving out last night's corpse discovery.

"Occam's razor," Laila said when he finished.

He waited.

"The most likely answer is that your cousin was distraught over this scandal which cost him his marriage, his fame, his life in his eyes—and ended it."

Wilde nodded.

"But you don't buy that explanation."

"I don't know."

"Whatever happened to Peter Bennett, it probably relates to his being a reality star."

"Most likely."

"And I imagine your knowledge of that world is somewhat limited."

"You have a thought?"

"I do."

"And that is?"

"Let's get you educated on the subject."

"How?"

"Matthew and Sutton will be here in an hour."

"You want me to leave?"

"No, I want you to stay. They're the ones who are going to educate you."

———

All four of them—Wilde, Laila, Matthew, Sutton—spent the next several hours streaming episodes from the PB&J season of *Love Is a Battlefield*.

Sutton watched Wilde. "You hate this, right?"

He saw no reason to lie. "I do, yes."

It would be hackneyed for Wilde to note that the series was inane, repetitive, manipulative, dishonest, scripted, and even abusive—almost no contestant got out unscathed, without being mocked or ridiculed or made to look evil or heartbroken or deranged—but there was often too fine a line between hackneyed and truth. Wilde had tried to watch the show with an open mind and low expectations, understanding that he was far from the target audience, but *Love Is a Battlefield* was worse and even more destructive than he had imagined.

Matthew and Sutton held hands while they watched. Wilde sat in the chair to their right. Laila moved in and out of the room.

"My father thinks it marks the end of civilization," Sutton said. Wilde smiled at that.

"But the thing is, we get it," Sutton said. "Parents watch and think, 'Oh, these contestants are such horrible examples for our children, blah, blah, blah.' But it's the opposite. They're lessons."

"How so?" Wilde asked.

"No one wants to be like these car wrecks," Sutton said, gesturing toward the screen. "It would be like watching a crime show and worrying that you'll start wanting to murder someone. We mostly watch these people and think, 'Oh, I'd never want to be like them.'"

An interesting point, Wilde thought, though it hardly redeemed the awful voyeuristic appeal of the show. On the other hand, the contestants clearly knew what they'd signed up for, and Wilde was not in the judging business. If it didn't cause harm, who was he to turn up his nose at it?

Then again, were lives harmed?

Wasn't plucking unknown young people, often overly emotional and volatile people, and throwing their gas-soaked bodies into this fame tinderbox of a show asking for trouble?

Did this TV show destroy Peter Bennett?

Love Is a Battlefield's plot points were about what he'd expected, though ridiculously heightened, but it did help to watch a few episodes to get the full flavor. There were a lot of players (the show wisely put their names on a bottom scroll) and tons of manufactured drama, but in the end, it came down to a simple story we have seen many times. Jenn had to choose between two men. One was the dangerously sexy "Big Bobbo." That was what the blowhard Bob Jenkins called himself on the show—Big Bobbo—always referring to himself in the third person ("Big Bobbo digs a round ass, girls. None of that flat-ass stuff for Big Bobbo, 'kay?") during the inane "interviews" that were intercut into the drama. The other choice was the handsome, sweet, kind Peter Bennett, sculpted here as the perfect boy to bring home to meet Mom and Dad. Originally, Peter was portrayed as the "too safe" choice for Jenn, but eventually, based on the audience reaction too, the show lost any semblance of nuance: Big Bobbo was the evil, fauxcharming, smarmy villain, while hero-knight Peter was Jenn's path to true love and fulfillment, if only she could see the truth.

The endless teasers, especially as the series wore on, made it look so much like Jenn was going to select Big Bobbo that you knew there was no way she wouldn't end up with Peter. Still, the producers wrung every molecule of "suspense" out of the Final Battle, including a "fight" scene with tons of smoke in which it looked as though Big Bobbo had won, only for Jenn to cast him aside for the "winner of her heart," Peter Bennett.

Cue the strings.

"Big Bobbo's family was a total hoot, right?" Sutton said. "His mom got cast in Senior *Battlefield*."

"Senior? So that's...?"

"Pretty much the same show but with senior citizens. Those home visits are pretty wild. Did you see Peter's brother Silas? The guy didn't say a word the whole time. Just kept tugging down on that trucker hat. He became kinda famous as a grouch. Anyway, his sisters seemed nice, but none of them had any star potential. But Big Bobbo's mom? She's a hoot."

"How upset was Big Bobbo by his loss?" Wilde asked.

"Not very," Sutton said. "I can't believe you've never heard of Big Bobbo."

Wilde shrugged.

"Anyway, Big Bobbo was immediately cast on the spinoff show *Combat Zone*."

"A spinoff show?"

"It's basically all the most popular losing contestants thrown together on some island and they start hooking up. Lots of spilt tea and drama. Anyway, Big Bobbo was constantly on the Front Lines with various women. He made both Brittany and Delila fall in love with him, and then he slayed them at the Firing Squad—in the very first episode. Both of them. I think it was the first time the show ever had a double slay."

Wilde kept his face expressionless. "And Jenn and Peter?"

"They became PB&J," Sutton said, "maybe the most beloved couple in the show's history. I know you think the show is dumb and so do we, but we have watch parties where we sit around and comment and laugh and...we just get it, Wilde. Do you know what I mean?"

"I think so."

"There's one other thing. It may be a personal belief on my part, but I think it's true."

"What's that?"

"Yes, it's manipulative and edited to tell a specific story and all that, but the contestants can't deceive the audience forever."

"I'm not following."

"Your cousin Peter. I don't think it's just an act. He really is a good person—and Big Bobbo really is a douchebag. It isn't merely role-playing. After a while, no matter how much they try to hide who they really are, the camera somehow exposes their true self."

Wilde felt his phone buzz. It was a one-word text from Hester:

Call.

He excused himself and headed outside. He'd checked online to see if there had been any reports on a murder in Connecticut or anything on McAndrews. So far, there had been nothing. He called Hester back. She answered on the first ring.

"I'm going to give you the good news first," Hester said, "because the bad news is really bad."

"Okay."

"I reached Jenn Cassidy's agent. Jenn is in town for some promotional thingy and agreed to meet with me."

"How did you get her to agree to see you?"

"Honey, I work on television. That's all Jenn's agent needed to know. They think maybe I'll do a positive profile on her or something. Doesn't matter. I'm meeting her. I can ask her about your cousin Peter. That's the good news."

"And the bad news?"

"The murder victim in Connecticut was indeed Henry McAndrews."

"Okay."

"Henry McAndrews," Hester said again, "as in 'former assistant chief of the Hartford Police Department Henry McAndrews.'"

Wilde felt his stomach drop. "He's a cop?"

"Retired and well decorated."

Wilde said nothing.

"One of their own is dead, Wilde. You know how this is going to go."

"Like I said, I have no interest in protecting a killer."

"Correction: *cop* killer."

"So noted," Wilde said.

"Oren is really upset."

"Tell me what they know so far."

"McAndrews has been dead at least two weeks."

"Was he reported missing?"

"No. Henry and Donna were separated. He was using that house, and she stayed in Hartford. They've had no contact."

"Cause of death?"

"Three gunshots to the head."

"What else?"

"That's about it. The media will pick it up soon. Wilde?"

"What?"

"You can talk to Oren. Off the record."

"Not yet, but have him tell the cops to search McAndrews's computer." Something in Wilde's head clicked. "I'd also like to know what McAndrews was doing in retirement."

"What do you mean?"

"Like, was he working? Was he just living off his pension?"

"What does that have to do with anything?"

"If his murder is connected to my cousin—"

"Which seems likely, no?"

"Maybe, I don't know, whatever. But what was McAndrews doing? Was he just a typical anonymous trolling fan—or was he hired to troll?"

"Either way, you know who is going to be a prime suspect?"

He did. Peter Bennett.

CHAPTER

SIXTEEN

C hris Taylor was scrolling through Twitter when he stumbled across the headline:

CONNECTICUT MAN FOUND MURDERED

The story didn't really pique his interest. It was just a murder in another state, nothing to do with him, but Chris idly wondered why it was getting such significant social media play. He clicked the link and felt his blood go cold:

> Retired Hartford Police Assistant Chief Henry McAndrews was found shot gangland style in the basement of his Harwinton, CT, home.

Okay, he was a retired police chief. That explained why the story was making the rounds more than a normal slaying.

Henry McAndrews.

That name rang a bell. And not a good one.

Chris took off his hipster beanie. He'd also grown a hipster beard. He wore hipster slim jeans and ironic sneakers and basic T-shirts, all in a fairly successful attempt to change his look from that of the more nerdy Stranger. It worked well enough, especially when you rarely left your loft. In his previous incarnation, Chris had revealed secrets that he believed were detrimental to humanity. His own life had been blown apart by secrets. His philosophy had thus been a simple one: Drag those secrets into the light of day. Once exposed to sunlight, the secrets would wither and die.

But he had been wrong.

Sometimes, the secrets did indeed wither and die—but other times, they grew stronger, too strong, taking nourishment from the sunlight and wreaking destruction. The repercussions had caught Chris by surprise. He believed that you right wrongs with the truth, but in the end that often backfired. He'd learned that the hard way—in blood and violence. Innocent people had been hurt and even killed. And yet, when you have a setback doing good, do you just give up and say nothing can be done? Do you throw your hands up and surrender to malignant evils that infect us all? That would have been the easy route. Chris had gotten away safely from the mess he helped create. He had money from his exploits. He lived comfortably and could continue to do so without worrying about righting wrongs. But he wasn't built that way. He'd tried to let it all go, but that didn't hold.

So now Chris helps people in a different way.

He'd formed Boomerang in order to help those who were being attacked and couldn't fight back. He punished not only those who created secrets but those who lied, abused, bullied—and did so anonymously. He went after those who served no positive purpose whatsoever in society and only eroded and destroyed the good. He worked hard now to make sure that the mistakes he made as The Stranger were minimized. His old work had been a volatile compound. He couldn't control it.

With this—with Boomerang—he could ensure safety.

Not always. Not a hundred percent of the time. There was always the chance, despite his absolute best efforts, that an innocent person would be punished. He got that. He wasn't blind or dumb. It was why he double-checked and triple-checked. If Boomerang was going to go after you, Chris wanted to make sure you deserved what was coming. Sure, he could stop altogether, leave it to the authorities who were still lagging way behind in defending those being attacked in the new online world, but do we stop doing the right thing just because we fear mistakes? Our justice system is imperfect, yet no one suggests that we get rid of it because of the occasional error, do they? We don't just give up. We try to improve and make it better. We do our best and hope the balance sheet at the end of the day shows we did more good than bad.

Boomerang helps people. It protects the innocent and punishes the guilty.

But now he read the name again.

Henry McAndrews.

Chris looked up the name and found the file.

This was bad news. Very bad.

Chris—the Lion—grabbed hold of his burner phone. On it was a dark web communication device that was as untraceable as possible. He composed a message that no one other than Alpaca, Giraffe, Kitten, Panther, and Polar Bear would understand.

CATEGORY 10

The urgent signal. Then he added, just to be sure:

NOT A DRILL.

CHAPTER

SEVENTEEN

I t's so nice to meet you," Jenn Cassidy said to Hester. "I really love watching you analyze a court case on TV."

"Thank you."

"I've been a fan for years."

Jenn's voice was a little breathy. Hester was usually good at reading people, but it was hard to tell if the reality star was being authentic here or not. Jenn Cassidy was beautiful in a classic all-American way—blond hair, toothy smile, bright blue eyes. Her makeup, as was the wont these days, was a tad too heavy for Hester's taste. Jenn had those overtly fake eyelashes that looked like two tarantulas baking on their backs on hot asphalt. Still, she gave off a friendly, approachable, even trustworthy air, and Hester could see why she'd be cast as the perfect good-girl reality star. Nothing about her beauty felt intimidating.

The doorman held the door for them. Jenn led Hester across the lobby of the giant glass tower of the Sky building. Once inside, she pressed the button for the second floor.

"We used to be higher up," Jenn explained.

"I'm sorry?"

"I still say 'we'—meaning Peter and I. I have to stop doing

that. Anyway, when we—there I go again—when Peter and I were a couple, they had us up on the seventy-eighth floor in a four-bedroom duplex. Now I'm in apartment two. It's maybe a third of the size."

"You downgraded after the breakup?"

"Not me. They. In this case, the owners of the building. See, buildings like this always have unsold apartments. Since they're sitting empty anyway, they give them to influencers for free under the condition we post photographs."

"I see," Hester said. "You advertise the building?"

"Yes."

"Like a celebrity endorsement?"

"Exactly."

"And that's how you make your living," Hester continued. "Via endorsements. You wear a certain designer dress or you visit a new nightclub—and millions of people see you and so those businesses pay you."

"Yes. Or like in this case, we barter. When Peter and I were at our most popular, Sky gave us a two-year lease on suite seventy-eight, under the condition we put it on our social media accounts at least once a week. When it was time to re-up, they moved us—well, just me now—down here."

"Smaller celebrity, smaller room," Hester said bluntly.

"Don't get me wrong," Jenn said, putting her hand on Hester's arm. "I'm not complaining. It's still wonderful that I'm here." The elevator door dinged open. "I understand how this business works. Being an influencer has a short shelf life. You have to use it as a jumping-off point."

"So what are your future plans, Jenn?"

The apartment door opened with a fob-wave rather than a key.

"Oh," Jenn said, sounding somewhat crestfallen. "I thought that was why you wanted to see me. I was in the legal profession before *Love Is a Battlefield*."

"In what capacity?"

"A paralegal, but I'd been accepted to law school."

"Impressive."

Jenn's smile was both cute and endearingly shy. "Thank you."

"Do you plan to matriculate now that the show is over?"

"Actually, I was thinking of trying to be a television analyst who specialized in the law."

"Ah," Hester said. "I would love to discuss that with you at another time, but that's not why I'm here."

Jenn gestured for them to sit on an off-white couch. Mirrors and generic artwork hung on the walls. There were no photographs, nothing personal, the whole thing looking more like a tasteful, if not warm, chain hotel than a true home. Hester wondered whether this was a model unit.

"I'm here about Peter Bennett," Hester said.

Jenn blinked in surprise. "Peter?"

"Yes. I'm trying to locate him."

It took her a second or two to absorb that. "May I ask why?"

Hester debated how to play this. "It's for a client."

"One of your clients is looking for Peter?"

"Yes."

"Then it's a legal matter?"

"I can't really say more," Hester said. "As a trained legal professional, I'm sure you understand."

"I do, yes." Jenn still looked stunned. "I haven't heard from Peter in months."

"Can you be more specific?"

"I don't know where he is, Ms. Crimstein. I'm sorry."

"Call me Hester," she said, throwing up her most disarming smile. "You two were married."

Her voice was soft. "Yes."

"For real? Not just, like, a TV marriage?"

"Yes. Legally and in every way."

"Okay, and then, of course, we all know what happened on that Reality Ralph podcast. Was that what ended it with you guys?"

"This is all..." Jenn's eyes stayed on the blond hardwood floor. "I feel a little blindsided here."

"Why? You said you don't know where Peter is—"

"I don't."

"—but I'm sure you've heard the rumors about his fate, right?"

Jenn said nothing. Hester pushed through it.

"I'm talking about the ones where Peter was so distraught from the onslaught of hate that he killed himself."

Jenn's eyes closed.

"You've heard those rumors?"

Her voice grew even softer. "Of course."

"Do you think they're true?"

"That Peter killed himself?"

"Yes."

She swallowed hard. "I don't know."

"You were married. You knew him well."

"No, Ms. Crimstein, I *thought* I knew him well." There was steel in Jenn's voice now. She raised her gaze. "It made me realize something."

"What's that?"

"Maybe I never knew Peter," Jenn said. "Maybe we never know anyone."

Hester decided not to react to this dramatic albeit understandable declaration. "So I listened to the podcast, the one where your sister outed your husband."

"Ms. Crimstein?"

"Hester."

"Hester, I think I've said enough."

"But you haven't said anything yet. Were you angry with her?"

"Her?"

"With your sister. Were you angry with her?"

"What? No, why would I be angry with her? She was a victim too."

"How's that?"

"Peter may have roofied her."

"*May* have? Yeah, but even before that, your sister—what's her name again? I keep forgetting."

"Marnie."

"Thank you. Marnie. So here is what I find odd, Jenn, and maybe, as two legal minds, we can help each other out. Marnie said that your husband sent her nude pics *before* this may-have-been-roofied incident. Why didn't she say something to you right away?"

"It's not that simple."

"It is to me," Hester said. "Enlighten me."

"Marnie was a victim. You're victim shaming."

"No, sweetie, you'll know when I'm victim shaming. There will be no couching of language here. Here's what I don't get, so maybe you can explain: Let's say your name is Marnie Cassidy. You love your older, super-successful sister Jenn. She has this super-great new husband, Peter. One day, husband Peter sends you—may I be crude?—a dick pic. Do you, Marnie, say nothing to your beloved sister Jenn? Do you not warn her that she's married to a destructive, cheating pervert?" Hester shook her head. "Do you see my issue? Turn it around. Suppose Marnie had fallen in love and married some guy she met on a TV program. That guy sends you Schlong Selfies. Would you not tell Marnie?"

"I would tell," Jenn said slowly. "But again it's not that simple."

"Okay, make it complicated for me. Tell me what I'm missing."

"Marnie is not strong. She can be easily manipulated."

"Right, but how could she be manipulated into not telling her own loving sister?"

Jenn started to wring her hands. "I've wondered that myself."

"And?"

"I don't really want to talk about this."

"Tough. Tell me anyway."

"I think Marnie felt—or maybe Peter convinced her—that if she told me about the pics, I would blame her."

"Blame your sister?"

"Yes."

"Instead of your husband?"

"Yes."

"Oh, that's interesting," Hester said. "Like, for some reason, you'd think maybe Marnie had made the first move."

"Or, I don't know, encouraged it or asked for it or whatever."

"Between us girls, do you think that's what happened?"

"What?"

"Do you think Marnie made the first move?"

"What? No. That's not what I'm saying—"

"Sounds like it to me. And maybe not intentionally. Maybe your sister just flirted with Peter, and he took it the wrong way."

"That's an awful thing to say."

"Well, it was your theory, not mine. Either way, Marnie never told you about the dick pics. She never told you she'd had any illicit contact with your husband, isn't that correct?"

Jenn said nothing.

"In fact," Hester continued, "the first time you heard these terrible truths about your husband was when your sister Marnie made it public on that podcast. She didn't tell you first. She told the whole world. Didn't you find that odd?"

"What exactly are you insinuating?" Jenn asked.

"I think it's pretty obvious. Marnie is what we used to call—it's probably politically incorrect now—a 'fame whore.'"

"Now just wait—"

"Stop acting like you have no idea what I mean. It's insulting to both of us. Your sister auditioned for all kinds of reality shows, but she never got cast. No one noticed, no one cared. She did manage to get cast on a tiny network spinoff—only because she was the sister of Jenn Cassidy—and she was eliminated in week one. Her fame, whatever there was of it, plummeted. But lo and behold, ever since Marnie outed your husband and destroyed your marriage, well, now Marnie is a big star. She's got that judging gig on RuPaul and—"

"What is the point of all this?"

"Maybe Marnie lied. Maybe she made the whole thing up."

Jenn closed her eyes and shook her head. "No. Marnie didn't lie about Peter."

"How can you be so sure?"

She opened her eyes. "You don't think I was skeptical too?"

"Of your sister?"

"Of everything. Do you know how reality TV works?"

"No."

"It's all an illusion. It's a theater, sure, but it's more like a magic trick. You can't trust anything you see. I live with that every day. So yes, I trusted my sister. I still do and always will. But I wasn't about to throw away my marriage based on a podcast drama."

"You said your sister was easily manipulated. You thought that maybe—"

"I didn't think maybe anything," Jenn half snapped. "I wanted corroboration."

"And you got it?"

"Yes."

"From?"

Jenn took a deep breath. "Peter isn't a very good liar."

Hester usually kept the questions coming rat-tat-tat style, but she paused here to let Jenn elaborate.

"Peter admitted it. Right here. Right on this very couch."

"When?"

"An hour after the podcast."

Hester's voice was soft. "What did he say?"

"At first, he insisted that none of it was true. I just sat here and stared at him and stared at him and I tried to make eye contact and he couldn't. Oh, I wanted to believe him. I wanted to believe him so badly. But I could see it in his face. That's how stupid and naïve I was."

"Did he try to explain?"

"He said it wasn't what I thought. He said I wouldn't understand."

"What did he mean by that?"

Jenn threw her hands up in the air. "Isn't that what all men say in these situations? Maybe it was the stress of being on the show and living in the public eye. Then you add in our infertility issues. With Peter's background, that part was especially tricky, I think. He really wanted to have children of his own."

"What background?"

"What do you mean?"

"You said because of Peter's background, the infertility issues were trickier. What do you mean?"

"You don't know?"

Hester shrugged a no-idea at her.

"Well, of course," Jenn said. "How would you know? Peter kept it a secret. I didn't even know until we were married."

"Know what?"

"Peter was adopted. He has no idea who his birth parents were."

EIGHTEEN

When Katherine Frole comes to the door, I am dressed like a celebrity who pretends that they don't want to be recognized.

What does that entail?

Simple. A baseball cap. And sunglasses.

Every celebrity—okay, let's be fair and say *Most* instead of *Every*—does this, even though it's such an obvious move. Whenever you see someone indoors or in a place that isn't sunny and they are wearing a baseball cap and sunglasses, well, are they doing so to make sure that you don't recognize them—or are they signaling to the world in bright neon that they are important, that they are someone you *should* recognize?

Don't listen to their protests: Celebrities want to be recognized. Always. They don't exist without that.

I, however, have no interest in being recognized. Especially today.

Katherine is happy to see me. That is good. It means she doesn't know about Henry McAndrews yet. Interestingly enough, she points to me—at my cap and sunglasses, to be more specific—and asks, "What's with the disguise?"

"Oh, it's nothing," I say, ducking into her office. "You know how it is."

"I'm surprised to see you again. It's just that I already broke protocol for you—"

"And I'm grateful," I add quickly, smiling as widely as I can.

Katherine says nothing for a moment. I worry a bit because she works in law enforcement, more specifically, the FBI. That comes with its own set of problems, but I can't worry about it now. Katherine wears a fitted blouse and skinny jeans. In short, I can see she is not carrying.

I, on the other hand, sport an oversized yellow windbreaker. It hides my Glock 19 well.

I have only fired a gun once. Well, three times actually. But all three shots were fired back-to-back, bam, bam, bam, so I count it as once. I heard that aiming was difficult and tricky in real life, as opposed to what you see on television and in movies, that you need a lot of training and experience.

But in my case, all three shots hit the intended target.

Of course, I was at close range.

Katherine keeps smiling at me, almost giddy to be in my presence. This is what I find so remarkably odd about fame. Katherine Frole is an important woman. She works forensics for the Federal Bureau of Investigation. She has two thriving boys and a husband who is the primary stay-at-home caregiver, freeing her up to pursue her career. The two have been dating since they met sophomore year at Dartmouth College some twenty years ago. In short, Katherine Frole is highly educated and well-adjusted and successful—and yet she is a mad, mad, mad *Love Is a Battlefield* fangirl.

We are all contradictions, aren't we?

"I tried to stop by last week," I tell her, "but you were away."

"Yes." She clears her throat. "Barbados with the family."

"Nice."

"I'm just back."

Which, of course, is why I'm here now.

"So"—Katherine plops down at the desk chair—"what can I do for you?"

"When you were investigating my case," I begin.

"Let me stop you there," she says, raising her hand. "Like I said before, I violated protocol already because, well, you know why."

I do.

"But that's it. I can't give you more."

"I know." I make sure the smile reaches my eyes. "And I appreciate all you've done. Really. I was just curious about what else you might have learned."

For the first time, I see doubt color her face. "I don't know what you mean."

"You do this type of thing a lot," I say. "Don't you?"

"That's not relevant." Katherine's words come out now in nervous hitches. "I can't say any more. I broke protocol. I shouldn't have. But I can't do it again."

"I have a confession to make," I say.

"Oh?"

"You have to understand," I say. "I couldn't just sit on the name."

The smile drops from her face like an anvil. "What do you mean?"

"I had to go to him."

"Oh Christ.".

"For answers. I mean, how could I not?"

"But you promised—"

"Just having the name—that wasn't enough. You must understand that. I needed to confront him."

Katherine's voice is a low hush. "Oh no." She closes her eyes, takes a second, clears her throat. "Did you talk to McAndrews?"

"Yes."

"What did he say?"

"That he worked alone," I reply.

"That's it?"

"That's it. That's why I need to know more, Katherine. As someone who has been so supportive and did so much research for me, I have to ask: Did you find more?"

Katherine stays silent.

"You have a nice house and an office at FBI headquarters," I continue with the slightest head tilt. "And yet you keep this little dingy office that no one knows about. Why?"

"I'm going to have to ask you to leave."

"Do you keep the secrets here? Is that why? Are the secrets on that computer?"

Her mobile phone is on the desk. She reaches for it. At the same time, I unzip my yellow windbreaker and pull out the gun. I really haven't practiced, but I make the move smoothly. I've always been a pretty good athlete with good hand-eye coordination. Perhaps that's it.

"Put the phone down," I say.

Katherine's eyes are two dinner plates.

"Henry McAndrews is dead, Katherine."

"Oh God. You...?"

"Killed him, yes. Don't you think he deserved that?"

She is too smart to answer. "What do you want?"

"The rest of your names."

"But he was the main culprit here."

"Not just the ones involved in this."

She looks confused.

"I want all the names that you deemed not worthy of punishment."

"Why?"

I think it's pretty obvious, but I don't go there. "I'm not going to hurt you," I tell her in my most soothing voice. "Have you heard of mutually assured destruction? That's us, Katherine. That's you and me. If you try to pin McAndrews's murder on me, it will be bad for you. You gave me the name in the first place. You would be revealing yourself. So you see? You have something on me, I have something on you."

"Okay," she says with an overly dramatic nod. "Just go then. I promise I won't say anything."

She thinks I'm stupid. "I need the names first."

"I don't have them."

"Please," I say. "Lying to me is not in your best interest. Didn't you agree that McAndrews should have been punished?"

"Punished, yes, but—"

I raise the gun. Katherine stops talking and stares at the weapon in my hand. That's how it is. She barely has eyes for me. Her whole world has shrunk down to the size of the muzzle on my gun.

"Oh—okay," she stammers, "you're right. I'll give you the names. Just please put the gun down."

"If it's all the same, I'll hold on to it until we're done." I motion with the gun toward her computer screen. "Open up the files. I want to see what you have here."

We humans are such a melting pot of behaviors, aren't we? So I can't help but wonder: If it wasn't for Reality Ralph's podcast and the horror of that exposure, where would I be right now? My guess is, I would be living my "normal"—I think of that word in air quotes—life instead of preparing to commit my second murder. If it weren't for that podcast, I would never have sought the identity of the man who sent those awful messages and pictures. I would never have bought a gun. I never would have taken a life.

Of course, even so—and here is where it gets interesting—killing McAndrews could have been—*should* have been—the end of it. I'd gotten my revenge. His murder would never be linked back to me. It would all work out.

That had been my plan.

But then, when I was face-to-face with McAndrews, when I pulled that trigger the first time. Then a second time. Then a third...

Do you know what I discovered?

When I am completely honest with myself, do you know what I realized?

I liked it. A lot.

I liked killing him.

We've all read books and seen movies about psychotic killers, how they can't stop themselves, how they grow addicted to the adrenaline rush, how they start as children with small animals. You hear about a neighbor's cat going missing. Then a dog. That's how they say it works. A slow build. I used to believe that.

I don't anymore.

I believe that if I hadn't been forced to kill, I would have never discovered this high. I would have just lived my life. Like you. Like most people. This need, this hunger, would have stayed dormant.

But once I pulled that trigger...

Is "bliss" the right word? Or is it more like a compulsion?

I don't know.

Once I killed Henry McAndrews—once I got that taste—I knew that there was no going back.

It changed me. I couldn't sleep. I couldn't eat. Not out of guilt. I didn't care a lick about that. I was obsessed with thoughts of pulling the trigger and the way his head exploded in a mist of red. More than that, I was—I am—obsessed with when I can experience that again.

So I think to myself: If it wasn't for the Reality Ralph podcast, if it wasn't for the shame and abuse and betrayal, I would have lived my entire life not knowing this feeling, never experiencing this high—and low.

Would that have been a better or worse life? I'm not sure. For certain, it would have been an inauthentic life.

I'm smiling thinking about all this, and that is terrifying to Katherine. I've let go of the old ways, of life's niceties, of the daily masks we wear. It's so damn freeing—living life on its own terms.

I don't really want to kill Katherine. My future goal—the way I plan to justify what I'm doing—is to only kill those who deserve it. That's why I need the list of names. I will kill those who troll and get their jollies by anonymously hurting others.

That's not Katherine Frole. She means well.

But I also recognize that my "I have something on you, you have something on me" argument is extraordinarily weak. Odds are that she would eventually tell the authorities, even if it meant mild trouble for her.

Ergo, there is no way I can let her live.

Katherine is eager to please me now. She types on her computer and spins the monitor my way.

"Here are all the names," she says, her voice choking up. "I won't say a word. I promise. Please, I have a family, I have children—"

I pull the trigger three times.

Just like last time.

CHAPTER
NINETEEN

When Wilde arrived, Vicky Chiba, Peter Bennett's sister, was gardening in her backyard. She wore gardening gloves so thick they made her hands look like Mickey Mouse's. Her eyes were down, a hand trowel working on the loose dirt.

Wilde had decided on the direct approach. Before she could even turn around, he said, "You lied to me."

Vicky spun her head toward him. "Wilde?"

"You said you'd check your family tree for me."

"Yes, of course. I will, I promise. What's wrong?"

"My colleague met with Jenn."

"Right. So?"

"She said that Peter was adopted."

Her mouth went slack.

"Vicky?"

"Jenn said that?"

"Yes."

She closed her eyes. "So Peter told her. I didn't know."

"It's true?"

Vicky slowly nodded her head.

"So you're not genetically related to me. Your parents, your other two siblings, none of you share my blood."

Vicky just looked at him.

"Why did you lie to me?" Wilde asked.

"I didn't lie." She squirmed. "I just didn't think it was my place to tell you. Peter didn't want anyone to know."

"Do you know anything about his birth family?"

Vicky exhaled, stood, and brushed herself off. "Let's go inside. I'll tell you everything. But one thing first: Did you find Peter?"

"Weren't you sure he was dead?"

"I was, yes. But not anymore."

"What changed your mind?"

"I thought Peter killed himself because of the fallout with PB&J and that podcast."

"And now?"

"Now my brother is related to you by blood."

"So?"

"So now I'm thinking whatever happened to him," she said slowly, "maybe it isn't about Jenn and that show. Maybe there's something more."

"Like what?"

"Like *you*, Wilde. Like whatever happened to you as a child, I don't know, somehow years later, the echo of that came down to him."

Wilde stood there, not sure what to say.

"I need a second," she said. "This is very upsetting. But I'll tell you everything."

Vicky Chiba prepared a "healing herbal tea" she claimed was "magically medicinal." Wilde wanted her to get to the point, but there was a time to crowd in and a time to give space. He bided his time and watched her. Her focus on preparing the tea was total, her movements deliberate. Rather than store-bought tea bags, she used loose tea leaves and a strainer. Her kettle had a gray stone finish and a wood-pattern handle and whistled loudly when it was ready. One of the ceramic teacups read "Om Namaste" (she gave that one to him), while the other read "What We Think, We Become—Buddha."

She took a sip of tea. Wilde did likewise. There were hints of ginger and lilacs. She took another sip. He waited. She put the cup down then and pushed it away from her.

"One day nearly thirty years ago, my parents came home from what was supposed to be a Florida vacation. I don't remember how long they were gone. The three of us—me, Kelly, and Silas—stayed with Mrs. Tromans. That was our babysitter back then. She was a nice old woman." Vicky shook her head, reached for the tea, stopped, and put her hand back in her lap. "Anyway, we were living in Memphis at the time. I remember my dad picking the three of us up at Mrs. Tromans's. He was acting all weird and faking being excited. He said we were moving to a great big new home. Silas, he was only like two or three years old, but Kelly and I were old enough to get what was going on. I remember looking at Kelly. She started sobbing. She was worried because her friend Lilly was having her eleventh birthday party at a Chuck E. Cheese that Friday, and she really wanted to go. I asked where Mommy was. Dad said that she was at our new house and couldn't wait to see us. Anyway, we drove for a long time. Kelly cried for hours. When we finally arrived, Mom was there—with a baby boy. She told us this was our new brother, Peter."

Vicky held up a hand. "I know I should have told you, but you have to understand. We never talked about it. Even back then. Telling you would have been, I don't know, a family betrayal. I know this sounds crazy, but my mom and dad just said, 'This is your brother Peter.' No explanation—not at first anyway. I remember they were all smiles and acting excited, but even to me and Kelly, it felt forced. They were trying to sell it, you know, with 'Won't it be nice for Silas to have a little brother?' and 'Isn't this just the most wonderful surprise?' And I remember Kelly asking where the baby came from, and my father just said, 'Oh, honey, the same place you did.'"

She stopped and, with a shaking hand, took hold of the tea.

Wilde treaded carefully. "Your parents didn't tell you he was adopted?"

"No. Not then. Eventually, they had to."

"What did they say?"

"Just that. They said it was a private adoption, but part of the deal was that no one could ever know. My parents made us swear we would never tell anyone. And after a while—I know this sounds weird—but it just became what it was. We all loved Peter so much."

"Did Peter know he was adopted?"

She slowly shook her head. "My parents never told him. He was a little baby when they brought him home. He never knew that he was adopted."

"When did Peter find out?"

"Not until he went on *Love Is a Battlefield*."

"Who told him?"

"I probably should have. He was an adult. He had the right to know." She stared down at the cup of tea. "He found out from the producers."

"The producers from *Love Is a Battlefield*?"

Vicky nodded. "That's what he told me. They do a full medical workup on all the contestants. Something came back showing that he couldn't be our parents' biological son."

"That must have been a shock."

She didn't reply.

"How did Peter react?"

"He was angry, disoriented, confused, even depressed, which is something I'd never seen in him. But he also said that there was relief too. Knowing the truth at long last. He said that he always felt like he didn't belong, like he never fit in. I started listening to a bunch of podcasts on the stuff. There's one called *Family Secrets*; when the host was an adult, she found out the father who had raised her wasn't her biological father. I listened to a bunch of stories like hers and Peter's, people who found out, mostly through DNA tests, that they were adopted or the product of sperm donation or an affair or whatever. What they all seemed to share was a lifelong feeling of displacement, like they'd never truly belonged. I don't know if that's true or not."

"You don't think those feelings are real?"

"Do you have them, Wilde? Talk about displacement, anger, confusion. You were abandoned in the worst way as a child."

"We aren't talking about me."

"Aren't we? Look, I don't know if Peter's feelings were real or not. I don't know if he looked back after the fact and felt displacement—he always seemed pretty well-adjusted—or if he somehow on some kind of cellular DNA level always knew that something was off. It doesn't matter. It hit Peter hard, all the years of lies and deceit. So he put his name in a bunch of DNA sites. He wanted to find out the truth about his birth family."

"Do you know what he learned?"

"No. He never told me."

"Did Peter tell Kelly he knew?"

"No."

"Or Silas?"

"No."

"Wait. How old was Silas when your parents adopted Peter?"

"Not yet three."

"So..." Wilde wasn't sure where he was going with this. "Did Silas know Peter was adopted?"

Vicky shook her head slowly. "We never told him."

"When you say 'never'—"

"Still. To this day. It was Peter's secret to tell. He made me promise not to tell anyone."

"Not even his own brother?"

"Their relationship is complicated. Do you have any siblings? Wait, sorry, dumb thing to say, I'm sorry. Silas was two grades ahead of Peter, but Silas was still in his shadow. Peter was more popular, the better athlete, all that. Silas was jealous and maybe even bitter, and then what with the show and all that fame Peter got? That made it worse."

Wilde thought about that, but nothing came to mind. He switched tracks. "Does the name Henry McAndrews mean anything to you?"

"No." Vicky tilted her head. "Is that Peter's biological father?"

"No, I don't think so."

"Then who is he?"

"DogLufegnev."

Her eyes widened. "You located that maniac? How?"

"That's not important."

"Can he be arrested? I mean, I know the laws on cyberstalking and bullying aren't strict enough, but if there's evidence he targeted—"

"Henry McAndrews is dead. He was murdered."

Vicky's hand fluttered to her mouth. "Oh my God."

"The police will be on this now."

"On what?"

He gave it a second. She saw it. "Wait. Are you saying that Peter might be a suspect?"

Wilde said nothing.

"Of course, he would be," Vicky said, answering her own question. "But he didn't do it. You have to know that."

Wilde was thinking of all the things Peter Bennett was dealing with when he vanished. The huge rise to stardom, the discovery that he was adopted, the harsh revelations from his sister-in-law on that podcast, the merciless cancellation in the #metoo era, the destruction of his marriage, his fame, his career, his life really. How untethered Wilde's cousin must have felt. How desperate, so desperate that he reached out as PB to WW, and WW didn't even care enough to respond.

"What did your parents do for a living?"

"Dad was a custodial manager. After we moved, he worked

at Penn State managing the Pollock Housing Area. Mom worked part-time in the admissions department."

Wilde made a mental note of that. He would get Rola to look into their time at Penn State, but what would he hope to find? The bigger clue might be in tracing down Peter Bennett's birth certificate and papers. Even if the adoption was private, there should be some records of his birth parents.

Except the Bennetts chose to move.

Suddenly. Without any kind of warning. They leave their children with a sitter, the father comes home, he drags them to some remote spot where no one knows them, they now have a new baby boy.

Something was way off.

"You said your dad is dead and your mom is, I think your words were 'in and out.'"

"Dementia. Probably Alzheimer's."

"I think it may be worth talking to her."

Vicky shook her head. "What good would that do, Wilde?"

"We want answers."

"*You* want answers. I get that. But whatever happened all those years ago, however my family ended up with Peter, I mean, what good will it do to dredge that all up now? She's an old woman. Fragile. In a bad mental state. She would get so agitated whenever I asked about Peter's birth that I stopped."

Wilde saw no point in pushing this right now. Rola would be able to find out where the mother was staying. They could decide what to do then.

"Wilde?"

He looked at her.

"I don't know how to say this, but for me and my family, I think this is over."

"How do you mean?"

"You said Peter is a suspect in this McAndrews murder."

"He will be, I think, yes."

"So think about it. Peter has been destroyed in so many ways. He lost everything. Let's say what we both think is possible. Let's say he found this McAndrews and somehow ended up involved in the man's death. Accident. Self-defense. Or even, though I can't believe it, murder. That would be the last straw for any man, wouldn't it? That would be when a man would run away and find a cliff or waterfall and..."

Wilde shook his head. "But what about his last post?"

"What about it?"

"Peter said lies spread quicker than truth and not to be so quick to believe what you hear. He told me the same in his message to me—that people were lying about him."

"That was before."

"Before what?"

"I think you should leave."

"If there is something more—"

"There isn't, Wilde. It's just...it's over. Peter's dead."

"And if he's not?"

"Then he ran away and doesn't want to be found. Either way, I think you should leave."

TWENTY

C hris Taylor waited for the full Boomerang animal menagerie to log into the secure video conferencing. The Giraffe came in first, followed by the Kitten and the Alpaca. A minute later, Polar Bear appeared. That made up the quorum. When they began this venture, they all agreed to a number of rules to protect their identities, the group in general, and their work. They also made rules about a quorum—that is, five out of six of them had to be present to discuss anything. If two couldn't make it, you just postponed the meeting.

"Let's wait a second for Panther."

They waited far longer than a second. Chris sent out another reminder. Again for reasons of safety, no one in the group could directly message another member. All messages had to go to the entire Boomerang menagerie.

"Panther isn't responding," Giraffe said.

"They didn't respond to the earlier call," Kitten added.

The group all identified as they/them, not so much out of true gender or politics, but because it was one more layer of protection. Chris had no idea of the real genders. This could be a group of him and five females or him and five males or any other combination under the sun. He had no idea where they lived other than Kitten telling them they went by Central European Time, so as to facilitate scheduling meetings when they were all awake.

"No reason to panic," Polar Bear said. "We only got Lion's message today."

That was true, but Chris did not like this. He did not like this at all. It would be one thing if one of the others was missing. He'd be worried, yes, but of all people to be a no-show, the Panther?

"We have the quorum," Giraffe said. "Do you want to tell us what's up now or do you want to wait for Panther?"

Chris thought about it. "I would be happier if Panther especially was here."

"Why especially?"

"Because this involves them."

"How so?"

Then, thinking more about it, Chris said, "I'm going to screen share something with all of you."

He brought up an article from page one of the *Hartford Courant*. There was a large headshot of Henry McAndrews in his blue uniform. The headline above his smiling visage read:

RETIRED ASSISTANT POLICE CHIEF
MURDERED

Shot in his Harwinton Home Gangland Style

Polar Bear spoke first. "Henry McAndrews. Why do I know that name?"

"He was a case file," Chris said.

"Victim or perpetrator?" Giraffe asked.

Chris hit another button on his computer. "I just sent you all the file. Panther presented the case. McAndrews was a perpetrator."

"My God, what punishment level did we give?"

"None," Chris said.

"I don't get it," Giraffe said.

"Here's the quick refresher. Panther presented the case of a reality star being trolled online."

"Oh right," Polar Bear said. "The PB in PB&J. My daughter is a fan—" Polar Bear stopped, probably catching themselves giving something personal away. "I'm familiar with the show."

"Peter Bennett," Chris said. "He was involved in a reality-show scandal and as usual, the internet exploded with hate and vitriol to the point that the guy's life was ruined. There are rumors he committed suicide or maybe he faked it, whatever."

"I remember," Kitten said. "But hadn't Peter Bennett been a sleazebag too?"

"Probably," Chris said. "He was outed on a podcast for cheating and maybe even roofying women. No proof or anything. Just an accusation. But we all decided, correctly in my view, that we had more deserving victims who needed our attention."

"We passed on him?"

"Yes."

"And if I remember, Panther was unhappy about that," Kitten said. "The Panther suggested the lowest storm—just give the McAndrews guy a Category 1 even. Teach him not to be such an asshole."

"Did we know the troll was a cop?" Polar Bear asked.

"We didn't get that far because we decided not to go forward," Chris said. "Would it have mattered?"

"I guess not."

Silence.

"Hang on," Kitten said. "We've all had plenty of cases that didn't move ahead to the punishment stage. It's part of what we all signed up for. Are you suggesting now that the Panther went rogue?"

"I'm not suggesting anything," Chris said.

"McAndrews was a city cop," Polar Bear said. "I would imagine he made his share of enemies. So maybe his death is just a coincidence. Maybe it has nothing to do with us."

"Maybe," Chris agreed with zero enthusiasm.

"The headline says, a 'gangland' slaying. Maybe that's what this was. Or maybe, hell, this guy was a serious troll."

"So?"

"So maybe he trolled someone else and they went after him."

"Right," Giraffe added. "Or maybe it was a routine break-in. Or maybe, like Polar Bear and Kitten are implying, this McAndrews was just an asshole with a gun, a badge, and the kind of psycho inferiority complex that made him a troll."

"Right," Kitten chimed in. "We know Panther would never betray our trust."

"Do we?" Chris asked.

"What?"

"We don't know any of us," Chris said. "That's kind of the point. And I would agree with you normally. I would think that there was an excellent chance that the murder of Henry McAndrews had nothing to do with us. In fact, an hour ago, I figured there was a sixty-to-seventy-five-percent chance that Boomerang had zero involvement in his death."

"So what made you change your mind?" Giraffe asked.

"Come on, Giraffe." It was Kitten with their British accent. "It's pretty obvious."

"What?"

Chris handled it. "Panther isn't here. He's"—he stopped himself and went back to the neutral identification—"I mean, *they* are our only no-show."

"Panther has never missed a meeting before," Giraffe added.

"In all the times we've met," Polar Bear said, "the entire group has attended. Except that one time when Kitten let us know they wouldn't be there."

"Exactly," Chris said. "It was Panther's case. And now Panther isn't replying to our messages."

Silence.

"So what do we do?" Giraffe asked.

"We have a very specific protocol in place," Chris said.

Polar Bear: "Are you saying we break the glass?"

"Yes."

"I agree," Kitten said.

"It seems extreme," Giraffe said.

"That's my take too," Polar Bear said. "We promised to break the glass only in the direst of emergencies. All of us have to agree. It can't be four out of five."

"I know," Chris said.

This had been Boomerang's top-level security from the start. None of them knew the others. That was a huge part of it. If one was caught, they couldn't sell out the others, even if they wanted to, no matter how much pressure was put on them to turn. There was no way to track each other down.

Unless they "broke the glass."

All of their names were in a secure file with every protection known to man implemented. Each member of Boomerang had created their own unique twenty-seven-digit security code. If all five put in their codes within ten seconds of the others, the five animals could see the name of the sixth member of Boomerang. That was the only way. All five had to put in their individual codes at the same time—and even then, they would only get the identity of the sixth member.

"Let's go through this step-by-step for a second," Chris said. "We have a past target, Henry McAndrews, who has been murdered."

"He wasn't a past target," Polar Bear said. "He was a *potential* target. In the end, we chose not to proceed."

"I stand corrected. A potential target. His case was presented to us by Panther, who is currently not replying to our messages. There are several possibilities, including several possibilities which can be boiled down to this: It's a coincidence. We deal with a lot of people who are acting rashly. The fact that one is murdered is no guarantee it has a connection to us."

"That was the argument we half-heartedly made," Kitten said, "before we remembered that Henry McAndrews was brought to us by our one missing member."

"Correct. I think for the purposes of this discussion, let's put the coincidence possibility to the side. Let's say that Henry McAndrews's murder is directly connected to us. More to the point, let's say the murder is directly connected to Panther's disappearance."

"Whoa, that's a little strong," Polar Bear said. "Disappearance? We don't know that. Has it even been twenty-four hours? Look, we are all very engaged in the tech world. Otherwise, we wouldn't be here. I don't know about you, but when I need a break—and that happens—I go cold turkey. I go on a boat out on the water where I don't have any mobile service or internet. There is a chance, a decent chance, that Panther has done the same."

"Without telling us?" Kitten countered. "And by coincidence, they choose to do so at this very moment?"

"So you think what, Kitten? That Panther murdered a police chief because he bothered some pretty-boy reality winner?"

"I didn't say that."

"Then what are you saying?"

Chris stepped in. "I think what Kitten is saying—or at least, what I'm saying—is that we need to find out what happened here."

"By outing Panther?"

"By getting Panther's name, yes. This way, we can check on them and make sure they're okay."

"I agree," Kitten said.

"I'm against it," Polar Bear said. "For a lot of reasons."

"Let's hear them."

"First, sorry, it's still too early. If it were me, if I were Panther in this scenario, I would not want you to out me. So I'm hard-pressed to do it to Panther."

"What else?"

"If you're right, Lion, if this is directly connected to Panther, then I can only see two possibilities. One, Panther was so incensed by our decision not to punish this McAndrews that he took matters into his own hands. I know, I know, I'm supposed to say 'they.' For all I know, Panther is a woman. But I find it awkward so let me just speak this way, okay? So that's one possibility, right? That Panther lost his mind and killed McAndrews and now he's ghosting us."

"Okay."

"Except that's pretty damn unlikely. Sure, Panther pushed for us to okay a low-level hurricane on McAndrews, but he didn't seem super upset about it. If he had, if Panther really pleaded for us to punish McAndrews, I think we would have relented. But he didn't. So why would he go and kill him?"

"Fair point," Chris conceded.

"Then let me take it another step. If Panther did decide to kill McAndrews and ghost us, well, he knows that we might break the glass. We would get his real name. We would be able to track him down. So ghosting us makes no sense."

Chris nodded. On the screen, he could see the Lion's head nod too.

"So what does that leave us?" Polar Bear asked. "Well, one possibility, maybe the most obvious one, is that the Panther was careless. Maybe this Peter Bennett was able to trace down the Panther as their contact."

"Impossible," Chris said. "We have too many security layers in place."

"Yeah, but we aren't infallible. There is a reason we set up breaking the glass and all these protocols. Because we knew that there was a chance someone might come after us. We set this up so that if that happened—and maybe it has now—we could keep the rest of us safe. So let's say someone got to Panther. I don't know how or why. But they got to him. Let's say, worst-case scenario—Panther has flipped or he's hurt or he's dead. If so, by rushing to his aid we may be exposing ourselves to greater harm."

They all considered Polar Bear's argument.

"What you're saying makes sense," Chris said, "but a man has been murdered. I still vote for getting Panther's identity."

"I agree with Lion," Kitten said.

"Me three," Alpaca said.

"I'm still on the fence," Giraffe said.

"It doesn't matter," Polar Bear said. "It has to be unanimous, and sorry, gang, but I want to wait another day or two. Let's give Panther a chance to reply. Let's give the local police a chance to solve the murder. Waiting a few days won't matter. We aren't in danger if we don't act."

Chris was not so sure. "You're officially blocking us from breaking the glass, Polar Bear?"

"I am, yes."

"Okay," Chris said, "that's final then. Let's all stay in touch and keep an eye on the McAndrews case in the meantime. Alpaca, maybe take a look at what Panther came up with. Maybe there is someone in that file we think is good for the crime."

"On it."

"How long do you want to give this, Polar Bear?"

"Forty-eight hours," Polar Bear said. "If we don't hear anything from Panther by then, we break the glass."

TWENTY-ONE

O kay," Hester said to Wilde, "let's see where we are."
They sat in Tony's Pizza and Sub, which looked
pretty much exactly how you'd picture a place with that
name to look. Two guys with hairy arms flipped pizzas. The table-
cloth was vinyl and checkered red. Each table held a paper napkin
dispenser and shakers for parmesan, oregano, and red pepper.

"Where should we start?" Wilde asked.

"You don't want me to say 'at the beginning,' do you?"

"Please don't."

"I'll get us rolling," Hester said. "First off, Peter Bennett is
adopted, what, twenty-eight years ago. Did the sister—what's her
name again?"

"Vicky Chiba."

"Did Vicky tell you how old he was?"

"No, just that he was a baby."

"Okay, I don't think it matters if he was two months or ten
months. He's adopted. He grows up near Penn State. Do we
think it was in this rural area because they wanted to keep to
themselves?"

"Could be. They were in Memphis before that."

"Okay, so Peter grows up never knowing he's adopted. The whole family lies about it. That's a little sketchy, don't you think?"

"I do."

"But let's skip that for now. Peter grows up, yada yada yada. He applies for a reality TV show and learns he was adopted. He's upset, naturally. He puts his name in a bunch of DNA sites hoping for a match. One match he gets is you." Hester stopped. "Well, that leads to the obvious question."

"What's that?"

"You only put your DNA in that one data bank, right?"

"Right."

"Peter Bennett put his in several, the sister said. So maybe he got other hits. You need to investigate that, Wilde. Maybe he reached out to other blood relatives. Maybe they got in touch with him."

"Good point."

"Back to our timeline. Peter goes on the show. He wins. He gets married to the comely Jenn. He becomes famous. He becomes rich. He's riding high. We don't know what he's doing about the fact that he's adopted. Maybe he's forgotten it. Maybe he's hearing from more relatives. Whatever. Peter is flying high, living the good life, and then, boom, the podcast ends it all for him. He crashes to the ground. He's ostracized and canceled and loses everything. We know he was distraught, not just by what others say, but by the communication he sent you via that DNA site. So you add it all up—the high, then the low, the confusion, the displacement, the losing everything, including his marriage. He sinks lower and lower. He's drowning. He tries to swim up, but then McAndrews or that DogWhatyoucallit hits him over the head again. That's it. He's finished. So—and now we are just theorizing—Peter finds McAndrews, kills him in revenge, realizes what he's done, flies to that suicide cliff, jumps."

Wilde nodded. "Not an unlikely scenario," he said.

"But you don't buy it."

"I don't buy it."

"Because you see a flaw in the logic or because you don't want to buy it."

Wilde shrugged. "Doesn't matter."

"You're going to see this through to the end."

"Yes."

"Because that's what you do."

"Because I don't really know any other way. I don't see any point in stopping now, do you?"

"I don't. One other thing."

"What?"

"There is something strange about that Reality Ralph podcast."

"Like?"

"Like maybe Jenn's sister Marnie is lying."

"Didn't Peter confess?"

"If we can believe Jenn," Hester said.

"You don't?"

Hester made a maybe-yes, maybe-no face. "Either way, we need to talk to the sister. I may have burned my bridges on that by talking to Jenn."

Wilde nodded. "I can take a run at Marnie."

They both reached for another slice.

"It's odd though," Hester said, taking a dainty bite. "As a small child, you're found in the woods. You have no memory of how you got there. You were just, I don't know, abandoned or whatever. You honestly believe you were in those woods for years—"

"Let's not go through this again."

"Let me say this, okay? I know I've questioned your memory in the past. So did a lot of experts. The majority concluded that you couldn't have survived that long on your own, that you were abandoned only days or weeks, but the trauma made you think it was longer. I used to believe that too. It makes sense, when you think about it."

"And now?"

"Now, some thirty-plus years after you were found, we learn a blood relative of yours was secretly adopted in an adjoining state— another child who seemed to have no past. So we have two babies with no background just appearing out of nowhere. That's bizarre, Wilde. So yeah, this started out as a curiosity quest. I've always been dying to know your origin story even if you've been reticent. But now, well, now it might be something bigger. Something more monstrous."

Wilde sat back and took that in.

Hester took a far bigger bite of the pizza this time. Still chewing, she said, "Seriously, how good is this pizza?"

"Very."

"The secret is honey."

"There's honey?"

Hester nodded. "Honey, hot Calabrian soppressata, mozzarella."

"It works."

"Tony's has been in town forever. You know that."

Wilde nodded.

"And you've been before, right?"

"Of course."

"Even as a kid?"

Wilde had no idea where she was going with this. "Yes."

"But never with David."

Boom. Just like that. Wilde didn't reply.

"My son was your best friend. You hung out a lot. But you never came here with David, did you?"

"David didn't like pizza," Wilde said.

"Is that what he told you?" Hester made a face. "Come on, Wilde. Who doesn't love pizza?"

Wilde said nothing.

"When Ira and I first moved to town—I mean, the very first day—we brought the boys here for dinner. The place was crowded, and the waiter gave us a hard time because one of the boys— Jeffrey, I think—wanted just a slice of pizza and the waiter insisted he had to order a full dinner. One thing led to another. Ira started getting impatient. It had been a long day and we were all hungry and cranky, and then the manager told us we couldn't sit at the table because of the slice of pizza. Ira got furious. The details aren't important, but we left without eating. Ira went home and typed out a letter of complaint. It was like two pages long, single-space. He sent it, but he never heard back, and so Ira made it a family rule that we'd never order from them or go into Tony's again."

Wilde smiled. "Wow."

"I know."

"I remember when our team won the county championship in baseball," Wilde said. "David and I were in eighth grade. We came here to celebrate, but David made some excuse for not being able to attend."

"My David was a loyal boy."

Wilde nodded. "He was at that."

Hester grabbed a napkin from the dispenser and dabbed her eyes. Wilde waited.

"Still eating?" she asked.

"I'm done."

"Me too. You ready to go?"

He nodded. The tab had been paid already. Hester rose to leave. Wilde did the same. When they were outside, Tim started up Hester's car. Hester put her hand on Wilde's arm.

"I never blamed you for what happened," Hester said. "Never."

Wilde said nothing.

"Even though I know now you lied to me."

Wilde closed his eyes.

"When are you going to tell me what really happened to my son, Wilde?"

"I've told you."

"No. Oren took me up to the crash site. Did I tell you that? It was right before you ran off to Costa Rica. He showed me where David's car went off the road. He walked me through it. Oren, he's always known you didn't tell the truth."

Wilde said nothing.

"David was your best friend," she said softly, "but he was my son."

"I know." Wilde met her eye. "I would never compare."

Tim got out of the car and came around to open the door for Hester.

"We are not going to do this today," Hester whispered to Wilde. "But soon. Do you understand?"

Wilde said nothing. Hester kissed his cheek and slid into the backseat. When the car was out of sight, he turned and headed down the road. He texted Laila.

> **Wilde:** Hey

The dancing dots told him she was typing a reply.

> **Laila:** How is a woman supposed to resist a line like that?

Wilde couldn't help but smile as he typed another text.

> **Wilde:** Hey
> **Laila:** Smooth talker. Get over here.

He pocketed his phone and picked up the pace. Laila had been his best friend's wife. There was no way around that. She and David had been soulmates. Wilde and Laila had both spent years, probably too many of them, trying to push away the obvious ghost in the room instead of simply letting him be.

His phone did the text-buzz thing again. Wilde looked down at the message.

> **Laila:** In all seriousness, come over when you can. It's time we talked this out.

He was reading the message a second time, his head down, his face lit up by the phone's screen, when the two cars came screeching to a halt.

"Police! Get the fuck down on the ground now!"

Wilde tensed and debated his next move. He could make a run for it. He would likely get away too, but they'd charge him with running from the police and resisting arrest, even if he was innocent. He'd have to go into hiding right when the search for Peter Bennett was revving up.

Wilde didn't want that.

"NOW, ASSHOLE!"

Four men—two in uniform, two plainclothes—pointed their guns straight at him.

They all wore ski masks.

This was not good.

"NOW!"

Three ran toward him, one kept a gun trained on him. With his hand still on his phone, Wilde slowly lowered himself to the ground, not so much to surrender peacefully as to give himself time to turn off the phone's volume with his thumb and then hit call. There was no opportunity to scroll through and get the right number. Laila's number had been the last one on his screen. The call would go to her.

The three men continued their bull rush.

"I'm not resisting," Wilde said, trying like hell to hit the right buttons on his phone. "I'm surrendering—"

The three men didn't care. They crashed into Wilde hard, knocking him onto the asphalt. They flipped him over onto his stomach. One jumped up and smashed a knee into his kidney, shocking the liver and internal organs. The other two grabbed Wilde's arms and pulled them too hard behind his back. Wilde felt the rip in his shoulder cuffs, but it didn't register much through the waves of pain still emanating from the kidney blow. The men twisted his wrist and knocked the phone from his hand. They cuffed him, pressing down on the bracelets so that they cut off circulation.

One of the uniformed cops—it was hard to make out a badge number or anything else in the dim light—stomped on the phone, then stomped again. The phone shattered.

On his stomach, his face being pushed into hard asphalt, Wilde was able to make out that the first car, the one closest to him, had all the earmarks of an unmarked police car—a Ford Crown Vic with municipal plates, a cluster of antennas, tinted windows, out-of-place lights on the mirrors, and grill that hid their flashers. The second vehicle was a regulation police squad car. Painted on the side, Wilde could now make out two words:

Hartford Police.

Henry McAndrews's old force. Oh, Wilde thought, this was definitely not good.

The cop who had kneed him lowered his lips to Wilde's ear. "You know why we're here?"

"To serve and protect?"

The punch to the back of Wilde's skull stunned him, made him see stars.

"Guess again, cop killer."

They jammed a black bag over Wilde's head, bathing him in dark, and pushed him into the backseat, being sure to bang his head on the way in. One of the men said, "Drive," and they were gone.

"I'd like to know what I'm being charged with," Wilde said.

Silence.

"I'd also like to call my attorney," Wilde said.

"Later."

"I don't want to be questioned until I speak to my attorney."

More silence.

Wilde tried again. "I said, I don't—"

Someone silenced him with a hard punch deep in the stomach. Wilde doubled over, retching, the air gone from his lungs. If you've ever had the wind knocked out of you, you know what an awful feeling it is, as though you're suffocating and dying and there is nothing to be done about it. Wilde had enough experience to know that this feeling would pass, that it was caused by nothing more than a diaphragm spasm, that his best bet was to sit up and breathe slowly.

It took thirty seconds, maybe a minute, but he rode it out.

Wilde wanted to ask where they were headed, but the blow to his solar plexus still stung. Did it matter? If they were taking him to Hartford, it would be an uncomfortable two-plus hours. His handcuffs were still on. There was one cop in the back with him, another in the driver's seat obviously. Could be a third. No way to tell with the bag over his head. He weighed his options and saw none. Any move he would make would be foolhardy. Even if he could incapacitate the guy in the back—through the blindfold and cuffs—the back door wouldn't open from the inside.

There was just no way.

Ten minutes later, the car pulled to a stop. Not Hartford, Wilde knew. Not Connecticut. The car door opened. Strong hands reached in, grabbed him, and dragged him out. Wilde considered going weightless, flopping to the ground, but he figured that would only earn him a kick in the ribs. He stayed upright and kept pace, letting the men lead him.

Even with the bag over his head, his deep inhalation detected pine and lavender. Wilde listened. No traffic sounds. No street bustle or voices or mechanical whirs. Under his feet was dirt and the occasional root. There was no way to know a hundred percent, but Wilde felt pretty certain he was somewhere quiet and rural, probably in or near woods.

Not good.

They hauled him up three stairs—he dragged his feet, testing the surface, realizing it was made of wood—and then he heard the creak of a screen door. There was the smallest tinge of mildew in the air. This wasn't a police station. A cabin, maybe, somewhere remote. A hand on either shoulder pushed him onto a hard chair. No one spoke. He could hear the men moving around, whispering. Wilde waited, trying to keep his breathing even. The black bag was still on his head, making it impossible to see or identify his assailants.

The whispering stopped. Wilde braced himself.

"They call you Wilde," a gruff voice said. "Is that correct?"

He saw no reason not to reply. "Yes."

"Okay, good," the gruff voice said. "I'm going to skip good cop, Wilde, and move right to bad cop. There are four of us. You know that. We just want justice for our friend. That's all. If we get that, it's all good. But if we don't, you, Wilde, end up dying a very long and painful death and we bury you where no one will ever find you. Am I making myself clear?"

Wilde said nothing.

That was when he felt something cold and metallic rest against his neck. There was a moment's hesitation and then a zapping sound. An electric current surged into him. His eyes bulged. His body lurched. His legs straightened. The pain was all-consuming, a living breathing thing that shut down everything except your desire to make the pain stop.

"Am I making myself clear?" the gruff voice said again.

"Yes," Wilde managed to say.

And then he felt the cold metal rest against his neck again.

"Good, glad we see eye to eye. This is a cattle prod, by the way. Right now, I have it set on low. That's going to change. You understand?"

"Yes."

"Do you know who Henry McAndrews is?"

"Yes."

"How do you know him?"

"I read about his murder in the paper."

Silence. Wilde closed his eyes and bit down, waiting for the high-voltage jolt. But of course, they knew that he would be. They wouldn't want that. They wanted to mess around with his head.

"We know you were at his house, Wilde. You came in through the sliding glass door. You messed around with his computer. He had a sophisticated CCTV system. We know it all."

"If you know it all," Wilde said, "then you know I didn't kill him."

"Just the opposite," the gruff voice said. "We know you did it. We want to know why."

"I didn't kill him."

Without warning, the cattle prod zapped him again. Wilde felt every muscle involuntarily stiffen. He slid off the seat to the ground, flopping like a fish on a dock.

Two strong hands picked him up and dumped him back in the chair.

The gruff voice said, "Here's the thing, Wilde. We want to play this straight. We are going to give you a chance, not like what you did with Henry. We just want to know what happened. We will then locate the evidence to back up that truth. You'll get arrested. You'll get a fair trial. Sure, you'll tell people about this little meeting, but there will be zero evidence it occurred. It won't affect the trial. Still, this is your best bet. You tell us what happened to Henry. We free you and find the evidence. It's all straight and fair. Do you understand?"

Wilde knew better than to contradict Gruff Voice: "Yes."

"We aren't interested in pinning it on you, if you didn't do it."

"Good, because I didn't. And before you hit me with that zapper again, I know you don't have me on CCTV. If McAndrews had those kind of surveillance videos, then you'd have also seen the killer weeks earlier."

"You broke in."

The metal was against Wilde's neck again. He shuddered.

"Are you denying that?"

"No."

"Why did you break in?"

"He was anonymously harassing someone."

"Who?"

"A reality star. He used bots and fake accounts."

Another voice: "You really think you can talk shit about Henry?"

This blast from the cattle prod must have been set at the higher level because it felt to Wilde as though his skull had exploded into a thousand pieces. His body wouldn't stop convulsing. He dropped again to the floor, but this time whoever had the cattle prod kept it on him. The voltage kept coursing through him. His legs jerked. His arms spasmed. Wilde's eyes started rolling back. It felt as though his lungs and internal organs were being overloaded, as though his heart would burst like an overfilled balloon.

"You're going to kill him!"

Through the din, Wilde heard the buzz of a phone. The cattle prod went silent. Wilde kept convulsing. He flipped over and vomited.

From seemingly a great distance, Wilde heard a voice say, "What? But how?"

Everything stopped, except Wilde, who was still madly twitching, trying to ride out the agony, the hot electricity still scalding his veins. His ears rang. His eyes started to close. He let them. He wanted to pass out, anything for relief. Then he felt the strong hands picking him up again. Wilde tried to help, but his legs wouldn't obey any command.

Soon he was back in the car.

Fifteen minutes later, the car stopped suddenly. Someone uncuffed him. The car door opened again. The strong hands shoved him out. Wilde hit the asphalt and rolled away.

"If you tell anybody about this," the gruff voice said, "we'll come back and kill you."

CHAPTER
TWENTY-TWO

When Oren Carmichael answered Wilde's knock, his eyes went wide.

"My God, what the hell happened to you?"

Oren Carmichael had been there that day thirty-five years ago when little "feral" Wilde had been found in the woods. He'd been the first one to talk to him, lowering himself to the boy's level and, in the most comforting voice, telling him, *"Son, no one is going to harm you, I promise. Can you tell me your name?"* Oren Carmichael had driven Wilde to his first foster home, stayed in his room until he fell asleep, been there when he woke up the next morning. Oren Carmichael had both tirelessly investigated how Wilde had ended up in those woods and been a huge help in that lost boy's transition into this new world. Oren Carmichael had coached Wilde in various sports, chosen him to be on his teams, looked out for him, made sure that Wilde felt as much a part of the community as a boy like Wilde could. Oren Carmichael had offered advice when he felt Wilde needed it, and even helped a rebellious Wilde navigate teen trouble. Oren Carmichael had been the first officer to arrive at the car accident that killed David.

Oren had always been kind, compassionate, strong, measured,

professional, intelligent. Wilde admired the way he carried himself, and he'd been happy when Oren and Hester started dating. Hester had been the closest thing Wilde had to a mother, and while he wouldn't go so far as to call him a father figure, Oren Carmichael had been the closest thing Wilde had to a male role model.

"Wilde?" Oren asked now. "Are you okay?"

Just as it had happened to Wilde less than an hour earlier, Wilde struck Oren's solar plexus with the heel of his palm, temporarily paralyzing the diaphragm, knocking the wind out of him. Oren made an oof noise and stumbled back. Wilde stepped inside and closed the door behind him. His eyes took in everything. Oren was not in uniform and was not carrying his gun. There was no weapon in the nearby vicinity. Wilde scanned for nearby drawers or places where Oren might stow his gun. There was nothing.

Oren stared up at Wilde with a look so pained—from the physical or emotional Wilde couldn't say, but he had a guess—that Wilde had to turn away. The strike had been necessary; that was what Wilde told himself, even as he questioned the need and remembered that Oren Carmichael was seventy years old now.

Wilde reached out his hand to help. Still heaving, Oren slapped it away.

"Take deep breaths," Wilde said. "Try to stand upright."

It took another minute or two. Wilde waited. He had tried not to hit him too hard, just hard enough, but again he had never hit a man in his seventies. When Oren could speak again, he said, "You want to explain yourself?"

"You first," Wilde said.

"I don't know what the hell you're talking about."

"Four cops from Hartford just grabbed me off the street, threw a black bag over my head, and worked me over with a cattle prod."

The realization came to Oren's face slowly. "Oh Christ."

"You want to tell me what's going on?"

"What did they do to you, Wilde?"

"I just told you."

"But they let you go?"

"You think that makes it better?" Wilde shook his head. "I managed to call Laila before they took me. She called Hester, who called someone in Hartford and made threats neither one of us want to know about. That someone made a call and they let me go."

"Oh, shit." Oren's face dropped. "Hester? She knows about this?"

"She doesn't know I'm here."

"You figured it out," Oren said. "How long do you think it will be before she does?"

"Not my problem."

"You're right. It's mine." He rubbed his face with his hands. "I messed up, Wilde. I'm sorry."

Wilde waited. He didn't have to prompt Oren to come clean. He would now. Wilde was certain of it.

"I need a drink," Oren said. "You want one?"

That sounded pretty good to Wilde right now. Oren poured them a Macallan single malt scotch. "I'm really sorry," he said again. "I know that's not good enough, but a cop had been murdered."

"Tell me what happened."

"As you already know, Hester called in Henry McAndrews's body being found on behalf of"—Oren made quote marks in the air—"'an anonymous client who is protected under attorney-client privilege.' You can't imagine how much this pissed off the Hartford police. One of their own takes three bullets to the back of his head in his own home—and some loudmouth city lawyer won't tell them who found the body? They were enraged. Naturally. You can understand that."

Oren looked at Wilde. Wilde's expression gave him nothing.

"And then?" Wilde said.

"And then the cops, still furious, checked into Hester and—surprise, surprise—they learned that she was currently dating a fellow law enforcement officer."

"You," Wilde said.

Oren nodded.

"So they came to you."

"Yes."

"And you betrayed her attorney-client privilege."

"First off, you're not a client, Wilde. You don't pay her. You're a friend."

Wilde frowned. "For real?"

"Yes, for real. But second of all, and far more important, Hester didn't tell me it was you. I didn't ask her. I didn't overhear her. I didn't obtain the information that you were the client in question in an illegal way. I *surmised* that you were the client that Hester was unethically protecting independently of my private relationship with her."

Wilde just shook his head.

Oren leaned forward. "Let's say this happened before Hester and I started dating. The Hartford cops come to me and say, 'That slick New York attorney from your hometown is protecting someone who broke into the house of a murdered cop, do you have any guesses who that might be?' My educated guess, even back then, would have been you, Wilde."

"Nice," Wilde said.

"Nice what?"

"Self-rationalization. 'If I didn't know what I did know I might have known what I said I knew.'"

"I made a miscalculation," Oren said.

"You gave them my name, right?"

"I did, yes, but I also made it clear that you and I were close. I told them I'd sit down with you and ask you to cooperate because you weren't the type to want a killer to go free. I never imagined they'd go rogue."

"Really?"

"Really."

"Even when the victim is 'one of their own'?"

Oren nodded. "Fair enough. Look, Wilde, I want to know who did this to you. I want them to be punished."

"That won't happen," Wilde said. "They blacked out their license plates. They put a bag over my head, so I never saw their faces. They did it on a quiet part of the street with no cameras. Even if I could figure out who they were, it would be my word against theirs. They knew what they were doing." Wilde took a sip and stared at Oren over the glass. "And you know how cops stick together."

"Damn. I'm really sorry."

Wilde waited. He knew what was coming. He just needed to turn it in his favor.

"But you need to listen to me," Oren said.

And here it comes, Wilde thought.

"A cop, a father of three, has been murdered. You have pertinent information. You just can't hide from that. You have a responsibility to come forward."

Wilde considered his next move. Then he asked, "Did the cops search McAndrews's computer?"

"They're working on it," Oren replied. "It's pretty sophisticated security and there's a lot on it. What should they be looking for?"

"How about we share?"

"Share what?" Oren said.

"You tell me what the police know about McAndrews's murder," Wilde said. "Based on that, I tell you what I think you should do or look into."

"Are you serious?"

"You have other options," Wilde said. "For example, you could ask your colleagues to torture me again."

Oren closed his eyes.

Wilde was furious, but at the end of the day, he wanted who-ever killed Henry McAndrews caught. If Wilde had information that could help find the murderer, so be it. He wanted to find Peter Bennett, not protect him.

"I went to McAndrews's house," Wilde said, "because I was searching for someone."

"Who?" Oren asked.

"Peter Bennett. He's a missing reality star, assumed dead."

Oren made a face. "Why are you looking for him?"

Wilde saw no reason not to answer. "I put my name in a DNA genealogy site. He came back as related to me."

"Wait. As in . . . ?"

"Yeah, I'm trying to figure out how I ended up in the woods. I know you've been pushing me for a long time to do it. So I did."

"And?"

"And I found my dad. He lives outside of Las Vegas."

"What?" Oren's eyes widened. "What did he say?"

"It's a long story, but it's a dead end. So I tried again, this time with a relative on my biological mother's side."

"And this reality star—"

"Peter Bennett."

"He's related to your mother?"

"Yes. But after he contacted me, he went missing."

"What do you mean, missing?"

"You can Google his name and get all the details," Wilde said. "He's famous. If he's involved in this murder, I want him captured. There is no love or blood loyalty here. My only self-interest in locating him is to learn more about my birth mother."

"So you're searching for this Peter Bennett and somehow you end up on McAndrews?"

"Right."

"And that's why you broke into his house?"

"I thought it was empty."

"So if that's all true, why didn't you just come forward? Why have Hester make the call?"

Wilde just looked at him. "You can't be that dense."

"I know your breaking into the house might look bad—"

"*Might* look bad. Come on, Oren. You know how it would look."

Oren nodded, seeing it now. "I do. An eccentric loner—no offense, Wilde—"

Wilde gestured to indicate none was taken.

"—breaks into a cop's house and that cop ends up dead."

"I'd never get a fair shake."

"You could have come to me."

"No."

"Why not?"

"You're the most trustworthy cop I know," Wilde said, "and look at how you bent the rules when it came to finding a cop killer."

Oren winced. "I guess I deserve that."

Enough, Wilde thought. It was time to press ahead. "McAndrews was a cop, right?"

"Retired, yes."

"Most cops still work after they retire. What did he do?"

"He was a private investigator."

Just as Wilde had expected. "On his own or with a big firm?"

"What difference does it make?" Oren saw Wilde's face and sighed. "On his own."

"Did he specialize?"

"I don't feel comfortable talking about that," Oren said.

"And I still feel like vomiting from being shocked repeatedly with a cattle prod," Wilde said. "I'm assuming from your answer that McAndrews's work was on the sketchy side."

Oren thought about it. "You think his work life had something to do with his murder?"

"I do, yes. What did he specialize in?"

"Most of McAndrews's work would be charitably labeled 'corporate security.'"

"And uncharitably?"

"Trashing the competition online."

"Explain," Wilde said.

"You and Hester had dinner tonight at Tony's, right?"

"What does that—?"

"Let's say your town has an established favorite pizzeria. You, Wilde, decide to open a competing one nearby. Problem is, people are loyal to Tony's. So how do you cut into Tony's customer base in the modern era?"

Wilde said, "I assume the answer is you trash the competition."

"Exactly. You hire a guy like McAndrews. He creates fake accounts—bots—that post bad reviews of Tony's. They flood certain websites with rumors about bad sanitation or spoiled food or rude service. Whatever. That would, of course, lower Tony's ratings on Yelp and wherever else people check reviews. The bots might casually mention that a new pizzeria in town is much better—and then other fake accounts would join in and, 'Yeah, that new place is awesome' or 'They have the best thin crust.' Like I said, this example is small-time. But corporations are doing this on a large scale too."

"Is this legal?" Wilde asked.

"No, but it's nearly impossible to prosecute. Someone writes a fake bad review of you online. Do you know the odds of being able to track the real identity of the poster, especially with anonymity software and VPNs?"

"Zero," Wilde said.

"And even if you're somehow able to track down the identity behind one of the bots, so what? The person might say, 'Oh, that's how I really felt, but I was afraid if I put my real name, Tony would come after me.'"

Wilde considered that. "Did McAndrews do more than corporate work?"

"Meaning?"

"I assume some clients wanted to trash people rather than corporations."

"Since the beginning of time," Oren said. "Why do you ask?"

"When you look up Peter Bennett," Wilde said, "you will see how many trolls swarmed his social media site, destroying his reputation, enflaming his former fans. Whenever the scandal would die down, these trolls would return and reignite them. A lot of the hate being leveled at Bennett was amplified by Henry McAndrews's army of bots."

"So someone was targeting this Bennett?"

"Yes."

"And they hired McAndrews to do it?"

"Could be."

"How did you figure out it was McAndrews?"

"That's confidential. It won't help to find his killer."

"Sure, it will," Oren countered. "Clearly McAndrews wasn't as good at hiding his identity as he thought. You figured it out. Not to be obvious, but if you could track down McAndrews's identity, so could Peter Bennett. And who'd have more reason to be angry at McAndrews than him?"

"Maybe," Wilde allowed. "Look, Oren, I need the name of whoever hired McAndrews to trash Peter Bennett."

"Assuming someone did hire McAndrews for that purpose—and that's a somewhat big assumption—there may be an issue with getting you that information."

"What's the issue?" Wilde asked.

"One of McAndrews's sons is an attorney. For an extra layer of security, McAndrews claimed all that he did was legal work product, so it would fall under attorney-client privilege. The clients didn't pay him directly—they got billed by his son's law firm." Oren looked at him hard. "You see, some people take advantage of the rules surrounding attorney-client. Some people will twist the spirit of that clause in a way some may find unethical."

"One of us is the bad guy here, Oren. And it's not me."

That landed. The two men stayed there for a moment, not moving.

"Did anyone report Peter Bennett missing to the police?" Oren asked.

"His sister may have, but I don't think anyone looked into it. At the end of the day, he's an adult who took off. There was no hint of foul play."

"Until now," Oren said. Then: "Thank you, Wilde. I appreciate your cooperation. I'll look into all this. And I'll help you as much as I can. We both want to find Peter Bennett."

Oren's phone rang. He looked at the caller ID.

"Shit. It's Hester."

Wilde rose. There was more to say to Oren, about how Oren had let Wilde down, how Wilde had considered Oren one of the few people in this world he could trust, how that trust was now shattered for good. But now was not the time. He headed for the door.

"You better answer it."

TWENTY-THREE

Wilde grabbed another burner from one of his lockboxes and called Laila.

"You okay?" she asked.

"Yeah."

"If you hadn't managed to call me—"

"I'd be fine," Wilde said. "They just wanted to scare me."

"Please don't do that, Wilde."

"Do what?"

"I heard them tackle you and then, poof, the phone went dead. Don't insult me with platitudes."

"You're right. I'm sorry. Thank you for calling Hester."

"Of course."

Wilde said, "I know you wanted to have a talk tonight..."

"Are you serious? Not after what happened. I'm still shaking."

"If it's all the same, I think I'll just go to the capsule and get some sleep."

"No, Wilde."

"No?"

"We won't talk," Laila said. "We won't fuck either. But I need you here. I need to hold you tonight or I won't be able to sleep, okay?"

Wilde nodded, even though he knew no one was watching. He just needed that second. "I'm on my way, Laila."

————————

Early the next morning, Wilde stood on Amsterdam Avenue between 72nd and 73rd Street, watching Marnie Cassidy, Jenn's sister, the one who'd leveled the most serious allegations against Peter Bennett on the Reality Ralph podcast, sitting in the window booth at the Utopia Diner across the street. She was having breakfast with what Wilde assumed was a friend. Marnie was animated and smiley and gestured maniacally.

Rola said, "Marnie looks annoying as hell."

Wilde nodded.

"She looks like she thinks she's just so much fun and crazy and yells 'woo woo' on the dance floor."

Wilde nodded again.

"She looks like a buddy's irritating girlfriend who insists on joining the boys at the sports bar and she dresses in full football gear and puts on eye black and spends the entire game cheering too loudly until you want to punch her in the face."

Wilde turned and looked at Rola. Rola shrugged. "That kind pisses me off."

"I guess."

"Look at her," Rola said. "Tell me I'm wrong."

"You're not wrong."

"Wilde, I want to find those Hartford cops and make them pay."

"Let it go," he said.

Marnie and her friend stood up and walked to the register to pay their bill.

"You sure you want to handle this on your own?" Rola asked.

"Yes."

"We'll meet in Central Park afterward?"

"Yes."

Rola kissed his cheek. "I'm glad you're okay."

She headed down the block as Marnie stepped out onto the street. Marnie gave her breakfast companion a big hug and kiss and started on her way toward, Wilde knew from Rola's intel, the ABC studios on Columbus between 66th and 67th. Wilde had planned his route. He wanted to catch Marnie before the studios were in sight. He headed around the block, hurrying his step. When Marnie turned onto 67th Street, Wilde was heading toward her in the opposite direction.

He stopped short.

"Excuse me," Wilde said, throwing on his biggest smile and flaring his eyes, "but aren't you Marnie Cassidy?"

Marnie Cassidy could not have looked more pleased if he had handed her a giant check. "Why yes, I am!"

"Oh man, I'm so sorry to bother you. People must pester you on the street all the time."

"Oh," Marnie said, waving it away, "that's okay."

"It's just that I'm a huge fan."

"Really?"

When it came to stroking a celebrity ego, there was no such thing as too much or too heavy a pet. "My sister and I watch you all the time on…" The name of the show slipped Wilde's mind, so he just kept going. "Anyway, we both think you're hilarious."

"That's so kind of you!"

"Would I be able to trouble you for an autograph and maybe a selfie? Jane—that's my sister—Jane will freak when she sees it."

Jane. So okay, Wilde wasn't great at coming up with names under pressure.

Marnie beamed. "Of course! How would you like it made out?"

"Oh, let's do it, 'To Jane, my biggest fan,' something like that. She's going to positively freak out!" Wilde fumbled as though searching for a writing instrument. "Oh, shoot. I don't think I have a pen."

"No worries!" Marnie said. Every sentence with Marnie seemed to end in an exclamation mark. "I have one!"

Now that Marnie had come to a full stop and started rummaging through her purse, Wilde shifted his body so that he faced her head-on and subtly blocked her path forward. He wouldn't stop her if she wanted to get by. It was all about body language.

"Can I ask you one other thing?" Wilde asked.

"Of course!"

"Why did you lie about Peter Bennett?"

Boom. Just like that.

The smile stayed locked on Marnie's lips, but it fled her eyes and dimmed that inner beam. He didn't wait, didn't give her time to recover from the blow or take an eight count. He pressed on.

"I work for CRAW Securities. We know everything, Marnie. You have a choice. You can talk to me now and keep yourself out of it—or we can destroy you in every way possible. The choice is yours."

Marnie kept blinking. This was the calculated risk Wilde had decided to take. If he approached her in any reasonable manner, Marnie Cassidy would stick to the story she had told on the Reality Ralph podcast. The only way that talking to Marnie could be useful was if he threw her off her game and she changed her story in some way. Then Wilde might have something to work with. There was no downside to this direct approach. If he interviewed her in a straightforward manner, he would gain nothing. If she stormed off now, he also would gain nothing—same boat.

But if she reacted now in some way that hinted at deception, then he had a chance at learning something.

Marnie tried to stand up a little straighter. "I don't know what you mean."

"You know exactly what I mean," Wilde said with no hint of give in his tone. "Let me put this plainly. We are talking alone. No one is listening. It's just you and me. This is my promise. If you tell me the truth now, it goes no further. No one will ever know you said a word to me. It's a secret just between us. You continue on your way to hair and makeup at the studio, and you remain a star. And

I wasn't kidding before. I have seen you, Marnie. You've got talent. You've got that intangible *it*. People love you. Your star is rising. I'd put money on that. And if you help me now, your star will continue to soar like we never met, except, well, you'll have me as an ally for life. You want that, Marnie. You want me on your side."

Her mouth opened, but no sound came out.

Wilde pushed on, shifting from carrot back to stick. "But if you walk away from me now, I'll make sure you get canceled so harshly you'll wish you were Peter Bennett. I won't be your friend, Marnie. I'll make it my mission to ruin you."

A tear ran down Marnie's cheek. "Why are you being so mean?"

"I'm not being mean. I'm being honest."

"Why do you think I'm lying?"

Wilde held up a flash drive. There was nothing on it. It was just a prop, part of this charade. "I *know*, Marnie."

And then Marnie said it: "If you *know*, why do you need me?"

There it was. The admission. A person telling the truth has no need to say this or worry. She hadn't been totally honest on that podcast. Wilde was sure of it now.

"Because I need confirmation. Just for myself. Dotting the i's and crossing the t's. I don't do any of this lightly. I *know* you didn't tell the truth on the podcast. I have the proof. It's enough to ruin you."

"Stop saying that!"

Marnie had a point. Wilde was winging this now and not doing a great job of it. It also dawned on him that those Hartford cops had done something similar to him in terms of trying to bluff. He felt bad about that, using their techniques, but not bad enough to stop.

"And I did the right thing," Marnie said. "If you know everything, you know that."

The right thing? Oh boy. He had to tread lightly here.

"No, Marnie, I don't know that. I don't know that at all. From where I stand, you are guilty and I'm going to take you down for it." Wilde cut off her denials with a raised hand. "Now if there is another side that I'm not seeing, if there is something I'm missing, you need to come clean fast, Marnie. Because right now, without further explanation, I don't see how you can claim you did 'the right thing.'"

Marnie's green eyes darted everywhere as she considered her options. This, Wilde knew, was where he had to play it delicately. Push her too hard and she might just run. Stop peppering her with threats and she may gain enough composure to realize that his whole line of questioning was a load of bullshit.

"Never mind," Wilde said.

"What?"

Wilde shrugged. "I don't like any of this."

"What do you mean?"

"I'm releasing the info to the Reality Ralph podcast."

"Wait, what?"

"You're not worth saving, Marnie. You deserve to be canceled."

The tears started flowing again. "Why are you being so mean?"

Again with that. "You know why."

"I was only trying to help!"

"Help who?"

Marnie sobbed some more.

"Look, I gave you a chance to save yourself, Marnie. I shouldn't have. But because my sister and I are genuine fans"—shovel, shovel—"I did. My boss, he said you weren't worth it. I'm thinking he was right."

Wilde took the risk now of turning away from her. She cried harder.

A woman's voice said, "Honey, are you okay? Is that man harming you?"

Shit, Wilde thought.

Wilde spun back around. The woman was small, wizened, wheeling a shopping cart and staring daggers at Wilde.

"Hon, do you want to come with me? We can go someplace safe."

Wilde decided to push his luck a bit. "No worries. We were finished talking anyway."

"What?" Marnie turned to the wizened woman and offered her a big yet sad smile. "No, no, I'm fine. Really. This man is a dear friend."

The wizened woman wasn't buying it. "Dear friend, huh?"

"Yes. His sister Jane and I were college roommates. He just...I'm crying because he just gave me bad news about Jane's cancer. It's stage four."

An Oscar-worthy performance, just like that. The wizened woman looked at Wilde, then back to Marnie. A second later, this being New York City, the wizened woman shrugged and moved on.

"Enough," Wilde said when they were alone again. "Tell me."

"You'll keep your promise?"

"Yes."

"It won't get out?"

"Promise."

"I won't get canceled?"

Wilde had no idea what the fallout would be. "Promise."

Marnie took a deep breath and blinked back more tears. "He did it to someone else, not me. Peter, I mean."

"He did what to someone—?"

"Stop it," she snapped. "You know what I'm talking about. Peter harassed this girl. He sent her nudes and when the opportunity came, he roofied her and..." Her voice just faded away.

"What girl?"

"This is what I was told."

"Told by whom?"

"By the girl herself, for one. She didn't want to come forward. That was part of the arrangement we made. If she came forward herself with those accusations, her life would be changed forever. Millions of people would hear it—and she couldn't handle that kind of attention. She isn't a celebrity. They needed someone to tell her story for her."

Wilde saw it now. "You."

"Her story was so awful. Awful. What Peter—my own brother-in-law—did to her. I cried so hard. He had to be punished. We could all see that right away. This girl, she thought about going to the police, but she didn't want that either. So we came up with an idea."

"You'd go on the podcast," Wilde said, "and say it happened to you."

My God, Wilde thought. It was just awful enough to make sense.

"I wanted to help this girl—and I wanted my sister to know what kind of man she'd married."

"So who is she? This 'girl' Peter attacked?"

"I can't say. I promised."

"Marnie—"

"No, you can make all the threats you want to, but I'm not doxxing a victim."

Wilde decided not to press on that for now. "But why go on the podcast at all?"

"I just told you. To help the girl. To help Jenn."

"But you could have just told Jenn, couldn't you? You didn't have to go public like that."

"What, you think I wanted to do it this way?"

And here the answer was obvious, Wilde thought: Yes. Yes, she wanted to do it just that way. Had to. She wanted the attention and notoriety, and damn if it hadn't worked. Hester had been right. Marnie wanted fame, no matter who paid the price, and she got it.

"I didn't have a choice anyway," Marnie said. "I was under contract."

"To?"

"To the show. That's how reality TV works. You sign a contract. The producers give you an instruction and you follow it to enhance the story line."

"But you weren't a contestant on the show."

"Not yet. But I'd applied and made it far enough to sign. If I wanted to make the cut next season, it was important I showed them my best."

Wilde couldn't believe what he was hearing, and yet it all added up. "A producer told you to lie in exchange for a slot on the show?"

"Hey, I got that slot on my own," Marnie said, her tone thick with indignation. "With my talent. And it wasn't a lie. It happened, just as I said it did."

"But not to you."

"What difference does that make? It happened. I talked to this girl myself. She had proof."

"What kind of proof?"

"Photographs. Lots of them."

"Those could have been photoshopped."

"No." Marnie sighed, shook her head. "Look, Jenn and I used to be close. We'd get drunk and talk, you know, about Peter. This is embarrassing, but I knew what *it* looked like. This wasn't Peter's head photoshopped on another body."

"Used to be close," Wilde said.

"What?"

"You said 'Jenn and I used to be close.'"

"We still are. I mean, we are again now. Peter...he wasn't good for our relationship."

"Why not?"

Marnie shrugged. "I don't know. He just wasn't."

"Did you like him?"

"What? No." Her phone buzzed. She read it. "Damn, you made me late for makeup and hair. I have to go."

"One last thing."

Marnie sighed. "Okay, but remember your promise?"

"Did you ever tell Jenn the truth?"

"I told you. This is the truth—"

Wilde tried not to raise his voice. "Did you ever tell Jenn

that what you said about Peter happened to another woman, not you?"

Marnie said nothing but her face lost color.

Wilde couldn't believe it. "So your sister still thinks—"

"You can't tell her," Marnie said in a harsh hush. "I did it for Jenn. To protect her from that monster. And Peter confessed. Don't you get that? It was all true. Now leave me the hell alone."

Marnie wiped her eyes, spun, and hurried away.

TWENTY-FOUR

L et me tell you what kind of person Martin Spirow is.

When a twenty-six-year-old "fitness model" named Sandra Dubonay died in a car accident last year, her family posted an obituary on her social media page with a heartbreaking smiling-in-the-sun portrait of their daughter and the epitaph: *You Will Always Be In Our Hearts*. Under that obituary post, in the comment section, Martin Spirow, using a fake account, posted the following:

It's sad when hot pussy goes to waste.

I ask you: Do you need to know more?

Boomerang investigated the case and ended up giving Martin a slap on the wrist. On social media, Martin Spirow follows a lot of robustly built "fitness models"—an intriguing euphemism— but claims that he has no recollection of writing those awful and cruel words and must have posted while blackout drunk.

Yeah, right.

We are supposed to believe that in a drunken stupor, Martin

Spirow knew to sign in to his sock puppet account rather than the account that was in his own name? That he knew to maintain online anonymity while "lost" in his documented problems with alcohol?

I don't think so.

And even if I do, I don't really care, do I?

As Katherine Frole had said about Henry McAndrews, Martin Spirow's crime probably doesn't warrant a death sentence. I realize that. But he doesn't deserve to live either. I am still self-aware enough to realize that I am justifying what I want to do, but that doesn't mean my justifications are groundless.

I am not, by any means, an expert in committing murder. Most of my knowledge, like yours, comes from watching crime dramas on TV. I know that I should take time between these killings or use different weaponry. I know that I should spend days or weeks or months planning, that there are CCTV cameras everywhere, that the smallest fibers or tiniest bits of DNA (by the way, who knows more about how DNA can change your life than I?) can be traced back to the perpetrator. I'll be careful, but will I be careful enough?

I think so. I have a plan. I have an endgame. If I do this correctly, it will lead to a resurrection like none since . . .

Blasphemy to say it.

I bought a silencer (or "suppressor" as the gun store guy kept calling it) for $189.

Martin Spirow lives with his wife Katie in a small ranch house not far from Rehoboth Beach in Delaware. There is one car in the driveway. At 9:45 a.m., Katie heads out the door. She wears blue jeans and a Walmart employee vest. Her walk to work at the nearby Walmart is only a quarter mile. Her husband Martin is unemployed and attends AA meetings twice a day.

This was all in the Boomerang files.

Most shifts at Walmart last seven to nine hours. That gives me a lot of time. I don't want to waste it. When Katie is out of sight,

I approach the door. I wear all brown, including a brown cap. I don't have UPS stenciling anywhere, but I don't think I need it. I carry an empty package. It is a primitive yet effective disguise—package delivery—and I will not be in view long anyway.

For me, the biggest issue is my vehicle. I know that with modern technology, they have cameras at all the tollbooths and other means to locate you. I parked several blocks away, at a nondescript professional building that houses doctors and lawyers and the like. I didn't see any security cameras. I noticed a green dumpster on the way where I can dump these brown clothes for the blue dress shirt and jeans I'm wearing underneath.

In short, I have something of a plan. Foolproof? Hardly. But it should be enough for now.

I ring the bell. No answer. I ring it again. And again.

A cranky, tired voice says, "Who is it?"

I clear my throat. "Delivery."

"Jesus, isn't it early? Just leave it on the stoop."

"I need a signature."

"Oh, for crying out loud…"

Martin Spirow opens the door. I don't hesitate. I take out the gun and point it directly at him.

"Back up," I say.

Martin's eyes bulge, but he does as I ask. He even raises his hands, though I didn't say anything about doing that. I can smell the fear coming off him in waves as I step inside and close the door.

"If you're here to rob us—"

"I'm not," I say.

"Then what do you want?"

I aim the gun at his face. "It's sad when hot pussy goes to waste."

I wait a second to make sure my words register in his eyes.

When they do, I see no reason to waste time.

I pull the trigger three times.

TWENTY-FIVE

Wilde headed up to 72nd Street and walked east until he entered Central Park. Rola was buying a soft-serve vanilla in a waffle cone from an ice cream truck.

"Want one?" she asked him.

"It's ten in the morning."

"It's an ice cream, not tequila."

"Pass."

Rola shrugged a suit-yourself. They passed the aggressive onslaught of soliciting pedicabs and headed down the narrow path that led to Strawberry Fields.

"You don't look good," Rola said.

"Thanks."

"Those cops."

"Let it go."

"Fine. How did it go with Marnie Cassidy?"

He told her as they passed the tourists crowding the *Imagine* mosaic to pay homage to John Lennon. When he finished, Rola said, "You're shitting me."

"I shit you not."

"Someone put her up to it?"

"From what I gather," Wilde said, "reality TV takes real lives and makes them into compelling stories. They don't have to be true. They just need to make you tune in. Most of their stars understand that's the point. You need to feed the drama monster. But Peter the reality character had grown kind of bland. He'd been married for a while. No kids. My guess is, someone on the show set this up to stir the pot. Maximize viewer interest."

"Which it did," Rola said.

"Which it did."

"Plus the producers knew that Jenn's sister would do anything for a slice of fame."

"Yes."

"So the big question: Did Peter roofie or harass other women?"

"Is there any proof he did?"

"The stuff you downloaded off Henry McAndrews's computer," she said.

"What about it?"

"We found more photos of Peter."

"And?"

"I'm having an expert check, but they seem legit. They were also pretty graphic."

Wilde thought about that. "Any idea who sent McAndrews the photos?"

"Nope. You know about how he billed through his son's law firm?"

"Yes."

"So it looks like all the emails were sent to the law firm first, using a VPN and anonymous email account. That's not difficult, as you know. The law firm then forwarded the emails and attachments to Henry McAndrews."

They crossed past the bronze Daniel Webster monument. They both stopped and read the inscription on the base: "LIBERTY AND UNION, NOW AND FOREVER, ONE AND INSEPARABLE."

"Prophetic," Rola said.

"Yep."

"But I guess you'd expect that from the dictionary guy."

That was Noah Webster, not Daniel, but Wilde let it go.

"If I'm following what you're saying," Rola continued, "you think the producers decided to cancel Peter Bennett, and by 'cancel,' I mean it in two ways. Cancel in the modern vernacular of ruining him. Canceling in terms of getting him off the show."

"Maybe."

"It seems extreme. Playing with people's lives like this."

"That's all these shows do. Have you ever watched? You take easily manipulated young people who are thirsting for fame, and then you mess with them. It's open season. They get you drunk. They create destructive drama. Every already-insecure contestant is put through an emotional wringer, and they aren't equipped for it."

"I get manipulation," Rola said, "but they can't just make up stuff."

"They can, yes."

"No, you don't get what I'm saying. It's one thing to tell someone, 'Pick a fight with that contestant' or even 'Break up with that guy.' Whatever. It's another thing to set up a situation where you accuse a man of committing a crime like this and destroy his reputation entirely. I don't care what the release says—he'd be able to sue for damages."

That was a good point. "Unless," Wilde said, "it's true."

"That's what I'm trying to get at. Suppose a woman did come to the producers. Or whoever. She told her story about being roofied. She has some evidence. The photos, texts, whatever. So now the producers can reveal this and even claim it's not only to help the show, but it's safest for their other employees."

Wilde frowned.

"What?" Rola asked.

"You're making sense. Awful sense, but sense."

"Right? And then add in Marnie. She'll do anything to get on the show, and she's easy to manipulate. Like you said, all these contestants are. Your cousin sounds naïve as hell too. Suddenly the nice-guy Peter is transformed into the ultimate villain. Not only did he cheat and sexually assault—but he did so with the beloved Jenn's very own sister."

"It got a ton of attention."

"Yes."

Wilde shook his head. "Gross."

"Also, yes."

"So what's our next step? Confront the producers?"

"What are they going to tell you?" Rola countered. "It's not like they'll admit any of this. But more to the point, what difference does it make? How does any of this help us find Peter Bennett?" Rola stopped and stared up at him. "We're trying to find him, right?"

"Yes."

"Because this sounds more like you're trying to rehabilitate his image."

"Rehabilitate the image of a reality star," Wilde said. "Hard to care."

"Precisely. So let me move on to more important matters, because this is weird. Really weird. I got a copy of Peter Bennett's birth certificate. He was born April 12 twenty-eight years ago. His parents are listed as Philip and Shirley Bennett."

Wilde frowned. "But that's his adoptive parents."

"That's just it. There's no sign Peter was adopted. According to this, they gave birth at Lewistown Medical Center, which is maybe half an hour from Penn State. There is a doctor listed. Curtis Schenker. He's still alive. I contacted him myself."

"What did he say?"

"What do you think he said?"

"Patient confidentiality?"

"Pretty much. A HIPAA violation, plus he's delivered like a

hundred million babies and couldn't remember them all. But here is something: Two years after Peter Bennett's birthday, Dr. Schenker surrendered his medical license for five years because of health-care fraud."

"Meaning he's sketchy."

"Yes."

"Sketchy enough to take a bribe to sign a birth certificate?"

"Could be. But let's review this. The Bennett family is living in the Memphis area—Mom, Dad, two girls. They move near State College, Pennsylvania, and suddenly they have a baby boy named Peter."

That was when Wilde saw it.

"Listen to me closely," Wilde said.

"What?"

"Keep walking like nothing is different."

"Oh, shit, what? Is someone tailing us?"

"Just keep walking. And talk to me. Change nothing."

"Got it. So what's the deal?"

"I've spotted three of them. There are probably more."

"Where are they?"

"Not important. Do not look for them, even surreptitiously. I don't want them to know we're on to them."

"Got it," Rola said again. "Are they cops?"

"Not sure. Law enforcement for certain. Pretty good at this too."

"So probably not the Hartford police guys again."

"Probably not. Could be doing them a favor though."

"You have a plan?"

Wilde did. They continued to cross the park. On the left, a ton of tourists milled around the red brickwork of Bethesda Terrace on the edge of a lake that, in a pique of originality, was dubbed The Lake. There were plenty of selfies and selfie sticks and all manner of phone-cum-social-media photography. Wilde and Rola moved through the crowd, faux chatting all the way. It would be hard for the people following them to keep up and hidden amongst the throngs of tourists. Wilde was careful not to look back. Now that he knew they were there, there was no use risking a glance.

He picked up his phone and hit Hester's number. She answered on the third ring.

"Articulate."

"I'm in Central Park and being followed," Wilde said.

Wilde and Rola took the path to the left of the fountain and crossed Bow Bridge, heading into the thicker bush of the Ramble.

"You think they're going to make an arrest?"

"Yes."

"Pin me your location."

"Rola is with me."

"Have her pin me too. Let me do a little research. I'll call you right back."

He and Rola had entered via West 72nd Street, not far from the garage where Rola had parked. The police—or whoever this was— would have their greatest presence there because they would have figured that Wilde and Rola would talk while strolling through the park and then return to the garage. That assumption would have been correct if Wilde hadn't spotted them. So now, as they headed up the twisty paths of the Ramble and farther away from that epicenter, it would be harder for the tails to keep up.

"Has to be about the McAndrews murder, no?" Rola said.

"Don't know."

"Could they have found something else linking you to the crime?"

"Doubtful."

His phone buzzed. It was Hester.

"Don't surrender," Hester said.

"That bad?"

"Yes," Hester said. "Can you get to my office?"

"I think so."

"Do you have a plan?"

"Do you trust Tim?" Wilde asked.

"With my life."

He told her what he hoped to do. Rola listened too and nodded along. They picked up their pace. They didn't want to stay in the Ramble for too long. The police might circle them and grab them in there. The good news was the wooded area had a fair amount of people. They'd already passed two large bird-watching groups. Would the police risk an arrest with that many people around? Unlikely. They'd wait until he was more in a clearing, like near Rola's car.

Rola said, "Woman with gray hoodie and white Adidas?"

Wilde nodded as they both pin-dropped their location to Hester. Hester in turn pin-dropped Tim's. From what Wilde could see, it would take Tim approximately fifteen minutes to get to the rendezvous stop. Time to stall. He went over his plan with Rola. Like most decent plans, this one was frighteningly simple. He needed them to think that he and Rola were just talking. He made sure they stayed in places where there were plenty of pedestrians, so whoever was following them couldn't make a move. He also tried to duck in and out of tree-lined paths, figuring that they probably had someone watching him from long range and it would be hard to see him that way.

"Guy with blue baseball cap and sunglasses who keeps pretending to study his phone," Rola said.

Wilde nodded.

They headed north past the Delacorte Theater with its horseshoe-shaped seating, home of the famed Shakespeare in the Park and the spectacular stage backdrop of Turtle Pond.

Rola said, "Remember when we saw *The Tempest* here?"

He did. They'd been in high school then, and a foster-kid foundation had secured tickets for the "underserved" in north Bergen County. He'd sat in that very theater with Rola by his side. They were living in the Brewer house together at the time, and they'd both expected to be somewhat bored—Shakespeare in the Park?—but the production, with that Turtle Pond backdrop, mesmerized them.

"Young woman with the ponytail and North Face backpack."

"You're good," he said.

"So young. She must be new."

"Could be."

"Oh, and the businessman with the newspaper. Newspaper. That's old-school."

"I missed him, but don't point him out to me."

"Sheesh, Wilde, do you think I'm an amateur?"

"No."

"I've been doing this longer than you have."

"You're right," Wilde said. He stopped for a second and looked at the Delacorte Theater. He remembered *The Tempest* so well. Patrick Stewart of *Star Trek* fame had played Prospero. Carrie Preston had been Miranda, Bill Irwin and John Pankow had been hilarious as Trinculo and Stephano.

"Did you keep the program?" Wilde asked.

"From *The Tempest*? You know I did."

He nodded. Rola saved everything. "I'm really sorry," Wilde said.

"For what?"

"For not always being there," he said. "I love you. You're my sister. You'll always be my sister."

"Wilde?"

"What?"

"Are you dying?"

He smiled. It was an odd thing to be thinking about, in the vortex of all this weirdness, but perhaps that was the only time he could be honest with himself. In the quiet, it was easy to push away and bottle up. In a storm of chaos, it was sometimes easier for Wilde to put himself in the eye and see the obvious.

"I know that you love me," Rola said.

"I know that you know."

"Still," she said, "it's nice to hear. Do you plan on vanishing again?"

"I don't think so."

"If you do, send me a text once a week. That's all I ask. If you don't, I know you don't love me."

They started east toward the Metropolitan Museum of Art. As they did, the crowd increased. They were almost out of the park now. That would leave them on Fifth Avenue and exposed if the police were ready and had a presence there. Wilde doubted that they would be ready, but once on Fifth Avenue, they picked up the pace and zigzagged through the throngs. They ducked into the Met's street-level "members only" entrance. Rola bought a membership every year to support the museum. She took her kids a lot. They passed security. As they crossed the corridor, Rola said, "Bye," and got on the ticket line. Wilde didn't miss a beat. He hit the stairwell and headed down to the underground parking garage. No one was behind him.

A minute later, Wilde was lying on the back floor of Hester's limo. Tim pulled out.

Twenty minutes later, he pulled into the garage of Hester's building. Hester was waiting for them.

"You okay?"

"I'm fine."

"Good. Oren is upstairs in my office. He wants to talk to you."

TWENTY-SIX

Hester pointed to a chair. "Sit over there, please," she said to Oren Carmichael. "Wilde, you sit over here next to me."

Oren Carmichael moved to one side of the long conference table, Hester and Wilde on the other. They were in a glass-enclosed office atop the Manhattan skyline. This office was mostly used for legal depositions, and Hester had made sure that Oren sat where the deponent normally did. Wilde didn't think this adversarial positioning was by accident.

"I need you both to listen to me," Oren began. "We have a murdered cop—"

"Oren?" It was Hester.

"What?"

"Shh. Tell us why Wilde was being followed in the park."

"Wait," Wilde said, "he hasn't told you?"

"Not yet. He just said it was bad."

Wilde turned to Oren. "How bad?" he asked.

"*Bad* bad. But first I need you to tell me—"

"You don't need anything first," Hester snapped. "You broke my attorney-client privilege—"

"I told you, Hester. I didn't break—"

"You did, damn it." Wilde heard something different in Hester's tone. The usual defiance was there, of course, but there was also a deep sadness. "Do you really not know what you did?"

Oren winced at the tone too, but he pushed through it. "I need you to listen to me. Both of you. Because this is huge. We have a murdered cop—"

"You keep saying that," Hester interjected.

"What?"

"You keep saying 'murdered cop.' Murdered Cop. Why does it matter that he's a cop?"

"Are you serious?"

"Dead serious. Why is a cop's death more important than any citizen's?"

"Really, Hester? That's where you want to go with this?"

"Law enforcement should do their best for everyone, regardless of position or status. A murdered cop shouldn't be any more a priority than any other citizen."

Oren turned both palms to the ceiling. "Fine, cool, forget he's a cop. It's a murdered *man*. Happy? You"—he spun toward Wilde— "found the body."

"I told you what I knew last night," Wilde said.

"Correct," Hester added. "And when was that exactly? Oh right, now I remember—right after your cop buddies kidnapped and tortured my client"—she raised a hand to silence him—"and don't you dare tell me Wilde's a friend, not a client, or you'll regret it. By the way, I wouldn't get so comfortable, mister. You're an accomplice to what those men did to Wilde."

That stung and it showed on Oren's face.

"You are, Oren," Hester continued, not letting up, and she looked heartbroken. "You can make a bunch of excuses, just like any criminal, but you gave them the information that led to the kidnapping and the assault. By the way, how did they know we'd be at Tony's?"

"What?" Oren straightened up in his chair. "You don't think—"

"Did you tell them?"

"Of course not."

"So why were cops after Wilde in Central Park?"

"They weren't cops," Oren said.

"So who were they?" Wilde asked.

"FBI agents."

Silence.

Hester sat back and crossed her arms. "You better explain."

Oren let loose a long breath and nodded. "The ballistics came back on Henry McAndrews. He was shot with a nine-millimeter handgun. The Hartford tech guy put the report in the national database, and they got a hit. Another murder with the same gun. Check that, another *recent* murder."

"How recent?" Wilde asked.

"Very. In the last two days."

Wilde stayed on it. "So this would have been *after* Henry McAndrews?"

"Yes. The same gun that killed Henry McAndrews was used in another murder. But that's not the headline."

Hester gestured for him to continue. "We're listening."

"The victim," Oren said, "was an FBI agent named Katherine Frole." He looked at Hester. "So it's not just a 'murdered cop' anymore. It's also a murdered federal agent. In Fantasy Land, it might not make a difference that two law enforcement officers were gunned down, probably by the same killer. They should be treated the same as if two Average Joe Citizens were killed. But in the real world—"

"What connects them?" Wilde asked.

"As far as we know? Not a damn thing, except that both were shot in the head three times with the same gun."

"Their work didn't overlap?"

"Not as far as anyone can tell. McAndrews was a retired cop from Connecticut. Frole worked in the Trenton FBI forensic office. So far, the only anomaly is, well, you."

Hester asked the next question in her most lawyerly tone. "Do they have anything linking my client with either Henry McAndrews or Katherine Frole?"

"You mean besides the fact that he broke into McAndrews's house and found the body?"

Hester put her hand to her chest and faked a gasp. "How do they know that, Oren?"

He said nothing.

"Do they have his fingerprints? Do they have witnesses? What evidence do they have that my client—?"

"Can we drop this, please?" Oren asked. "Two people have been murdered."

Hester was about to counter, but Wilde put a hand on her arm. The pissing contest between the two of them was becoming a distraction. He wanted to move this forward.

"What about Peter Bennett?" Wilde asked.

"Ah," Oren said. "That's the other reason why I wanted to see you."

"How's that?" Hester asked.

Oren flicked his gaze in her direction. They made eye contact and for a few moments, it was just the two of them. Wilde could feel it. He almost wanted to leave the room. These two had found love and now there were fissures, and while they were all dealing with bigger issues right now, Wilde still wanted to make that all right.

Still holding Hester's gaze, Oren said, "I promised Wilde last night that I would look into Peter Bennett."

Hester nodded slowly. "Go on then," she said, her voice softer. "Tell us."

Oren blinked and turned his attention to Wilde. "From what you told me, Peter Bennett naturally became a person of interest in Henry McAndrews's murder. I reported what you said to the lead homicide detective on the case, a guy named Timothy Best. By the way, I don't think Best had anything to do with what happened to you last night. Hartford PD is not handling the case, and he's state. McAndrews's murder was out of their jurisdiction, plus conflict of interest."

Wilde nodded. He didn't care about any of that right now. "And Peter Bennett?"

"I was helping him dig into Peter Bennett, but when the ballistics came in with the match to Katherine Frole, the FBI stepped in big-time. So last night before we talked, only you were looking for Peter Bennett. Now so are the Federal Bureau of Investigation and Connecticut State's top law enforcement agency."

"Have they found anything yet?" Wilde asked.

"Yeah, a lot."

Hester snapped again. "Get to it already."

Oren put on his reading glasses and took out a small notebook. "You mentioned Peter Bennett's last Instagram photo at Adiona Cliffs."

"Yes."

Oren read in a monotone: "Three days before the photograph was taken, according to flight records and passport control, Peter Bennett flew from Newark Airport to French Polynesia. He stayed at a small hotel near the Adiona Cliffs for two nights. On the morning that photograph was taken, he gave his backpack and clothes to a hotel housekeeper and told her that they were hers. He paid his hotel bill, checked out of the hotel, and hired a taxi to take him to the base of the mountain. The taxi driver saw your cousin walk up the path toward the top of the cliffs."

Oren snapped his notebook shut. "And that's it."

"What do you mean, that's it?" Hester asked.

"No one has seen Peter Bennett since. There has been no sighting as far as we are aware. There is no indication that he ever came back down that path. His passport has not been used. His credit cards and ATM have not been used. He hasn't been on any flight manifest or border-cross list."

"Is there a working theory?" Wilde asked.

"In terms of Peter Bennett? The FBI believes that he did indeed commit suicide."

"Or he faked it," Hester said.

"The FBI doesn't think so," Oren said.

"Why not?" Hester asked.

"Besides what I already listed? Two more things: One, Peter Bennett settled his estate before departing. We spoke to his financial guy, an advisor named Jeff Eydenberg at Bank of USA. Eydenberg wouldn't talk at first because of confidentiality, but the feds rushed through a warrant. Once that was secured, he cooperated, in part because he was worried about his client too. According to Eydenberg, Peter Bennett came in on his own and split the estate between his two sisters. Right now, it's all held in escrow because his divorce to Jenn Cassidy isn't final. But this Jeff Eydenberg met with Peter Bennett in person. He said Peter looked down and depressed."

Hester thought about that. "Still could be the act of a man who is faking a suicide."

"Anything's possible, I guess."

"You said there were 'two more things.' What's the second?"

Wilde answered that one. "No suicide note."

Oren nodded. Hester looked confused.

"Hold up," Hester said. "Why would *no* suicide note make you think it *was* suicide?"

"If you wanted to fake a suicide," Wilde said, "you'd definitely leave a note. If Peter Bennett went to all the trouble of posting that picture and taking care of his estate and flying to that island all to fake a suicide, it would be logical that he would have left a note in his own handwriting to seal the deal."

"I see," Hester said. Then: "But then I have another question. Either way, if he faked it or if it was real, why isn't there a suicide note?"

Wilde had been wondering that himself.

"If you read his last post on Instagram," Oren said, "there kind of is one."

"What did he write?" Hester asked.

Wilde took that one. "'I just want peace.'"

They all sat there.

Hester said, "A friend of mine used to quote Sherlock Holmes a lot. I don't remember the exact words, but it warned that you shouldn't theorize before you have facts because then you twist facts to suit theories rather than the other way around. In short, we don't know enough."

"Exactly," Oren said. "Which is why you two need to cooperate with the FBI now and get ahead of this."

"You know everything now," Wilde said. "There is nothing I can add."

"I know. But they insist. They won't let go until you do."

Hester said, "In other words, they'll illegally harass my client."

"Maybe."

"What do you mean, maybe?"

"I'm a lowly small-town police chief," Oren said. "The FBI doesn't confide everything in me."

"I'm not sure what that's supposed to mean," Hester said.

"It means I think there's something else, something big, something they aren't telling me."

"And yet you're suggesting we just waltz right in there and talk to them?"

"I think you have two choices," Oren said, again turning his attention to Wilde. "The first is, you go in and cooperate with your attorney present."

"And the second?"

"You run."

CHAPTER
TWENTY-SEVEN

The Boomerang menagerie logged on in the following order: Alpaca, Giraffe, Kitten, Polar Bear. Chris Taylor's Lion hosted the meeting as always. After everyone was in place, they all sat in silence, looking suddenly very silly to Chris in their digital disguises, waiting, hoping that the Panther would join them.

The Panther did not.

Chris spoke first. "We need to doxx the Panther."

"You realize what that means?" Polar Bear asked.

"I do."

"It's the end of Boomerang," Kitten said. "That was part of our agreement. Once we break the emergency glass, it's over. We disband. We never communicate with one another."

Chris's Lion nodded. "Do you all remember another Panther case with an abusive troll named Martin Spirow?"

"Rings a bell," Alpaca said.

"I'm going to share the file summary on the screen."

Chris Taylor pressed the share button.

"Oh, I remember him," Polar Bear said.

"He was the creep who tormented the grieving family," Kitten added.

"Exactly," Chris said. "In the end it was only one post. We checked. There were no others. We found out that Spirow may have been blackout drunk when he posted that."

"Which I never bought," Kitten said. "If you post blackout drunk, you don't make sure that it's from a new anonymous account."

"Which was the argument Panther made. In the end, Spirow only got a Category 1 response."

"Lion, why are you raising this now?"

"Because Martin Spirow was murdered. Also shot in the head."

Silence.

Polar Bear finally said, "My God."

Kitten: "What the hell is happening?"

"I don't know," Chris said. "But I don't think we have a choice anymore. Polar Bear?"

"I now agree. We need to know Panther's identity."

"We can't fool ourselves," Alpaca added. "This is the end of Boomerang."

"I'm not so sure," Chris said.

Polar Bear cleared their throat. "Those are the rules we all agreed to. Once one identity is discovered by anyone—law enforcement, perps, victims, even us—we need to disappear for our own safety."

"I'm not sure we can just do that," Chris said. "Someone has murdered two people."

"Again," Polar Bear said, "that's a conclusion you are drawing without proof."

"What, you think it's a coincidence?"

"I don't, no. But I don't know if the same person committed both murders. Do you? For certain?"

"And what exactly are we saying here?" Giraffe asked. "Both

murder victims were bullies investigated by Panther. We all agreed that they were both guilty. One we decided wasn't worth our efforts to punish. The other got a slap on the wrist."

"Now Panther is ghosting us," Kitten added.

"Or incapacitated," Alpaca said.

"Or," Giraffe said, "and let's face it, this is becoming most likely, Panther has gone rogue and is meting out their own justice."

"Either way," Chris said, "we need to out Panther."

"Agree," Alpaca said.

"So do I," Kitten said.

"Me too," Giraffe said.

Polar Bear sighed. "It's the right move, so yeah, I'm with you all. But as soon as we do, we disband, so I'd like to just say what an honor—"

"Not yet," Chris said.

"But that—"

"If Panther is behind this, we need to stop them. Once we know Panther's identity, we have to reach out."

"Too dangerous," Polar Bear said.

"We can't just walk away," Chris said.

"That's what we all agreed to do," Polar Bear said. "We aren't cops. I'm not hunting down one of my own to stop them."

"So Boomerang goes after people who bully and harass online," Chris said, "but we don't go after killers?"

"Yes," Polar Bear said. "Our mission is very specific. Our protocols are to protect us. We aren't here to solve climate change or war or even murder. Boomerang was just that—throwing karma back in the face of those who bully, harass, and abuse online."

"We created this," Chris said. "We can't just walk away."

"Lion?" It was Kitten.

"Yes?"

"Let's get the identity. Then we can each choose to disband or not."

"No," Polar Bear said. "We don't go off on tangents. That's not what we agreed to in the beginning."

"Things have changed," Kitten said.

"Not for me," Polar Bear countered.

"Fair enough," Chris said. "Let's get the identity and figure out what to do. We didn't foresee this complication. That's our bad. Let's all get our codes ready to type in the prompt I'm sending now. Is everybody ready?"

They all replied that they were.

"Okay, we have ten seconds. When I say 'three' we all type in our codes and press Panther. On my count. One, two...three."

It took very little time. The name came up on Lion's screen. Chris hadn't told them this, but he'd put them on seven-second delay, so he got the name first:

Katherine Frole.

Panther had been a woman. Or identified as a woman. Or had a woman's name. Whatever. For some reason, probably sexism, Chris had always thought of Panther as a guy. Did it matter? Not in the least. He was already typing Katherine Frole's name into the computer, and an article came up.

Chris opened the microphone back up to the whole group.

"Oh no."

TWENTY-EIGHT

Before sitting down with the FBI, Hester made sure that Wilde had full immunity for breaking into the McAndrews residence and any subsequent crime other than the actual murder. Hester also insisted that the interview take place at her law office, not FBI headquarters, and that the entire interview would be recorded by her firm's court videographer and stenographer, but the tapes and stenography would not be provided or available to the FBI.

It took a few hours to iron out the details, but in the end, the FBI agreed to Hester's terms. Now Hester and Wilde sat in the same chairs as before while one FBI agent, a woman who'd introduced herself as Gail Betz, took the chair where Oren had sat, and the other, a man who introduced himself as George Kissell, stood and leaned against the wall.

Betz did the questioning while Kissell stayed silent and looked bored. Wilde didn't see much reason to hold back in terms of his search for Peter Bennett and how it led him to Henry McAndrews's house. Hester stopped him several times, especially when Betz pressed for details about his break-in. Betz then turned her focus to Katherine Frole. She asked whether Wilde knew Katherine

Frole. The answer was no. Betz searched for possible connections. Frole worked in Trenton—had Wilde ever visited Trenton? Not since a class trip to the New Jersey capital when he was in seventh grade. Frole lived in Ewing, New Jersey. Wilde had never been. Her body was found in an office she rented out in Hopewell. Had Wilde ever been?

"What kind of office?" Wilde asked.

Gail Betz looked up. "Excuse me?"

"Katherine Frole was an FBI agent who worked out of Trenton, right?"

"Yes."

"So why did she rent an office in Hopewell?"

Kissell spoke for the first time. "We're asking the questions here."

"Oh, look," Hester said. "It speaks. I was about to applaud the FBI for hiring a mute."

"You're not funny," Kissell said.

"Wow, that hurt my feelings. Really. But seriously, my client has been cooperative. He wants to see the murderer of Special Agent Frole brought to justice. So why not answer his question?"

Kissell sighed and peeled himself off the wall. He looked at Betz. "You finished, Special Agent Betz?"

Betz nodded. Kissell pulled out the chair next to her. He sat down heavily, as though he had the weight of the world on him, and wheeled the chair toward the table so that his belly pressed against it. He took his time folding his hands. Then he cleared his throat.

"Have you ever been to Las Vegas, Wilde?"

Warning bells sounded in Wilde's head. Hester's too. She put a hand on his forearm, signaling him not to answer.

"Why do you want to know that?" Hester asked.

"I was hoping to get hotel tips," Kissell replied. Then: "It's relevant to this investigation."

"Perhaps you could explain how."

"Your client knows how. You, Ms. Crimstein, probably know

how. But I'm not in the mood to play games, so let me be more direct. We know you were in Las Vegas four months ago. More to the point, we know you visited the home of Daniel and Sofia Carter. I would like to know why."

Wilde sat stunned.

Hester's hand was still on his arm. She gave him a little squeeze. "What's the connection?" she asked.

"Pardon?"

"What's the connection between this line of inquiry and the murders of McAndrews and Frole?"

"Why don't you tell me?"

"We don't know anything about it."

"Well, see, Ms. Crimstein, neither do I. Yet. That's why I am asking the question. I hope that if I get an answer, I may find a connection. Then I can ask more questions and find more connections. Or, try to stay with me here, I ask questions and find no connections and so I can move on. That's how investigations work. So perhaps you can direct your client to tell us why he was in Las Vegas talking to the Carters, and then we can all see if it is relevant or not."

"I don't like it," Hester said.

"That makes me sad," Kissell said. "I want you to like my questions."

Hester pointed to her chest. "Hey, pal, listen up. I'll be the snarky wiseass here, okay?"

"Didn't mean to usurp your role, Ms. Crimstein. Are you refusing to let your client answer?"

Hester said, "I'd like to confer with my client."

Kissell shrugged for her to go ahead.

Hester whispered in Wilde's ear. "Any idea what this is leading to?"

Wilde shook his head.

"I don't like you answering blind questions like this," she whispered.

Wilde did a quick calculation. If they'd known about his visit to Daniel Carter, then what was the harm in knowing why?

He signaled to Hester that he was okay to answer the question and said, "Daniel Carter is my biological father."

Kissell was a cagey veteran. He was used to hearing crazy answers and keeping a straight face. He glanced at Betz, who didn't bother hiding her surprise.

Kissell waited a beat and asked, "Can you walk us through that?"

"Walk you through what?" Hester asked.

"We all know Wilde's history," Kissell said. "It's public record. I was always under the impression that no one knew the identity of his parents."

"That was true," Wilde said.

"How did you find—?"

"The same DNA genealogy site."

"Hold the phone." Kissell pushed back against the table. "Are you telling me that Daniel Carter was a DNA match on a website?"

"Yes."

"Let me see if I'm following this. You put your DNA sample in this website, the website says 'Hey, we found a match for you—this is your father.'"

"They do it by percentages, but yes."

"So you contacted him and the two of you set up a visit?"

"No," Wilde said.

"No?"

"I tried to reach out to him when I saw the match, but my message bounced back."

Kissell leaned back and crossed his arms. "Any idea why?"

"The message said his account had been closed."

"I see. So you contacted him, but he clearly didn't want to hear back from you so he closed his account."

"My client didn't say that," Hester interjected. "He said the account was closed. He has no idea when or why."

"I stand corrected," Kissell said. "What did you do next?"

"I flew to Las Vegas."

"So you had his address?"

"I got it, yes."

"How?"

Hester took that one. "Not relevant."

"It sure as shit is relevant. I know these DNA databases. They don't give out addresses. If his account was closed down, I need to know how you located Daniel Carter."

Hester leaned forward. "Agent Kissell, do you have any idea how the internet works?"

"What's that supposed to mean?"

"It means," she said, "there are no secrets on the web. We delude ourselves if we think anything we do is anonymous. There are always ways if you're resourceful. I, Agent Kissell, am resourceful."

"You found the address, Ms. Crimstein?"

Hester just spread her hands.

"How?"

"Do I look tech savvy to you? Theoretically, let's say I have people. Theoretically, let's say the DNA database has people. At the end of the day, all of these websites are run by people. People are motivated by self-interest."

"In short, you bribed someone."

"In short, if you're naïve enough to think it's hard to get information like that," Hester countered, "you shouldn't be an FBI agent."

Kissell thought about that for a moment. "Okay, so you fly to Las Vegas?"

"Yes."

"You meet with your biological father?"

"Not right away. I waited a few days."

"Why?"

"It was opening a big door I had kept closed my entire life,"

Wilde said, surprised at how unguarded he sounded. "I wasn't sure I wanted to see what was behind it."

"And what was behind it?"

"What do you mean?"

"I assume at some point you introduced yourself to Daniel Carter?"

"Yes."

"What did he tell you?"

"That he didn't know of my existence. He said that he spent a summer in Europe while serving in the air force. He theorized that he got a girl pregnant during a one-night stand."

"Did he tell you who the girl might have been?"

"He said he slept with eight girls from a variety of countries. He only knew first names."

"I see. So no hint about your mother?"

"No."

"Which is why you then answered Peter Bennett's message."

"Yes."

Kissell rested his hands on his paunch. "How did Daniel Carter react to the news of having a son?"

"It seemed to throw him off-balance."

"Did he seem happy about it?"

Hester turned to watch Wilde's face.

"No. He said that that summer was the only time he cheated on Sofia and that they now had three daughters. He worried my appearance would drop a grenade on their lives."

"I guess I can understand that," Kissell said with a nod. "What happened next?"

"He said he wanted a day to think about it. He suggested that we meet the next morning for breakfast and discuss it further."

"And how did that breakfast go?"

"I never showed. I flew home."

"Why?"

"I didn't want to be a grenade."

"Admirable," Kissell said. He glanced at Betz and asked, "Have you and the Carter family had any contact since?"

"No."

"None whatsoever?"

"Asked and answered," Hester said. Then: "So what does all this have to do with the current murders?"

Kissell smiled and rose. Betz did the same.

"Thanks for your cooperation. We will be in touch."

TWENTY-NINE

K atherine Frole.

When Chris Taylor Googled the name, the information that came up was worse than he imagined.

First off, Katherine Frole—Panther—was with the FBI. Chris Taylor wasn't sure what to make of that. He had always worried that law enforcement might try to infiltrate his group, but at the same time, Chris had suspected that at least one member of the Boomerang menagerie would be in law enforcement, someone who saw the limitations in the traditional criminal justice system and realized that the law had not yet caught up with these aggressors. You didn't have to be a vigilante to see the holes in the system and want to correct them. Plus, from what he could see, Katherine Frole did not work out in the field, meaning she probably had a job that required tech know-how. That was, Chris figured, something the entire group shared. You didn't join Boomerang without being able to understand and navigate the blackest corners of the dark web.

But of course, this was, to use a journalistic term, burying the lede:

Katherine Frole had been murdered.

When Chris saw that, when he realized how big this really was, he did something that would probably shock Polar Bear, Alpaca, Kitten, and Giraffe—the remaining members of Boomerang.

He deleted Boomerang.

All of it. Every file. Every correspondence. Every connection between members.

Did he still trust the other animals? He was not sure. But it was irrelevant. One had been murdered. Any road that could possibly lead to another member had to be severed.

Could one of the other Boomerang members be the killer?

It was horrifying, but Chris had to consider the possibility.

What was certain, however, was that the FBI would be on this case fast and with their best people. Assuming that they had Katherine Frole's computer, the feds would comb through it with all of the resources at their disposal. Chris had put in a lot of safeguards. All the members followed a strict protocol. But obviously that hadn't worked out. Either Panther had broken protocol or someone had found a way in. That meant, of course, Boomerang could be exposed.

In short, severing all ties was mandatory.

Now that Chris was alone, what was his next step?

He realized that he might know more than the FBI. Would they have already tied Panther's murder to Henry McAndrews's or Martin Spirow's? Doubtful. The news and the internet had nothing about links amongst the three, but there was no way to know for certain.

That was another big complication.

Even with stakes this high, Chris couldn't go to law enforcement. That would be breaking protocol in the worst way. If the FBI got their hands on anyone involved in Boomerang, that member would end up in federal prison or worse. No doubt. And if Boomerang's victims found out who was behind the group, they would demand revenge in violent ways.

There was danger everywhere. But that didn't mean Chris would let a killer walk free.

He would have to handle it himself.

The question was, How?

After Betz and Kissell left and they were alone again in her law office, Hester said, "What the hell, Wilde?"

Wilde said nothing. He looked up the number on his phone and hit the call button.

"Your father?"

Wilde put the phone to his ear and heard the ring.

"Peter Bennett is related to you on your mother's side, right?"

Wilde nodded. The phone still rang. No one answered.

"So how does your father fit into this?"

Wilde hung up. "No one is answering at his place of business."

"Whose place of business?"

"My father's. Daniel Carter's. DC Dream House Construction."

"Do you have his mobile?"

"No."

"His home?"

Wilde shook his head. "I'll ask Rola to track him down."

"Any clue why the feds would be interested in him?"

"None."

"Or why they'd find your visit to him suspicious?"

"Only one possibility," Wilde said.

"And that is?"

"Daniel Carter lied to me."

"About?"

Wilde had no idea. He called Rola and filled her in. In his mind's eye, Wilde could see young Rola, the serious student, taking notes in that room she shared with three other rotating foster girls. Rola was detail-oriented and industrious and dogged. It was what made her such a great investigator. You wanted Rola in your corner.

When he finished, she said, "Holy shit, Wilde."

"I know."

"I got someone in Vegas. I'll report back what I find."

Wilde hung up. Hester had moved to the window. She stared out at the awe-inspiring view of the Manhattan skyline. "Two people murdered," she said.

"I know."

"The FBI seemed convinced that your cousin is dead too," Hester said. She turned away from the window. "What do you think?"

"I don't know."

"Your gut isn't telling you anything?"

"I never go by my gut," Wilde said.

"Not even in the woods?"

"That's survival instinct. That's climbing out of the primordial muck and learning to stay alive. That, yes, I listen to. But if you are deluded and narcissistic enough to believe you should obey your gut rather than looking coldly at the facts, that's your bias, not your gut."

"Interesting."

"And right now, like you said with Sherlock, we don't know enough to theorize."

"Agree, but we really can't investigate the murders. The FBI will be digging into these cases with everything they have. But right now, only you and I know that Marnie Cassidy lied about what Peter Bennett did to her. That gives us one distinct advantage."

"What are you suggesting?"

"You up for rocking the boat?"

"I am. How do we start?"

Hester was already heading to the door. "We tell Jenn what her sister did."

CHAPTER
THIRTY

The receptionist at Sky buzzed up to the condo where Jenn Cassidy was staying. "Hester Crimstein is here to see you." The receptionist looked over at Wilde. "And your name?"

"Wilde."

"And a Mr. Wilde too."

The receptionist listened for a moment. She turned away as though to be discreet. Hester could see how this was going. She yelled out loud enough for Jenn to hear, "You'll want to see us before this story breaks, believe me."

The receptionist stiffened. A moment later, she hung up and said, "The elevator will bring you up to Miss Cassidy's home. Enjoy your visit."

The elevator door opened. The button for the second floor was already lit. When the door slid open, Jenn Cassidy, dressed in Versace, was waiting by the door to apartment two. She did not look happy to see Hester again. Hester didn't care.

Jenn squinted at Wilde. "How do I know you? Wait. You're that Tarzan kid. I saw a documentary on you a few years ago."

He stuck out his hand. "My name is Wilde."

She shook it, albeit reluctantly. "Look," Jenn said, blocking access to her apartment and meeting Hester's gaze, "I don't know what you want, but I think we said everything last time."

"We didn't," Hester said.

Jenn motioned toward Wilde. "And he's here because..."

"Wilde is related to Peter."

"My Peter?"

"Well, he's not yours anymore, is he? That's why we're here, in fact."

"I don't understand."

Wilde took that one. "Marnie lied. Peter never attacked her."

Jenn smiled at that. Actually smiled. "That's not possible."

"I spoke to her," Wilde said. "She admitted it."

The smile started to falter. "Marnie told you—"

"Do we really want to continue to have this discussion in the hallway?" Hester asked.

Jenn still smiled, but there was nothing behind it. It was a defense mechanism, a reflex, nothing more. She stumbled back into her apartment. Hester pushed in first, followed by Wilde.

"Let's all sit down," Hester said. "It's been a long day, and I'm pooped."

They did. Jenn staggered and collapsed onto the couch. The smile was gone now. Her entire expression had caved in, like a house with the support beams giving way. She cleared her throat and said, "Please tell me what happened."

Wilde told her about stopping Marnie in the street. She listened attentively, but every once in a while, she closed her eyes as if someone had struck her. When Wilde finished, Jenn asked, "Why would I believe you?"

"Call Marnie," Hester said.

Jenn chuckled without an iota of humor. "No need."

"What do you mean?"

"Marnie's on her way here now. We're heading to a new burger place in Tribeca."

It took ten more minutes before the receptionist buzzed up and announced Marnie's arrival. Hester spent the time talking to her office. The Richard Levine jury had still not come back, and the judge seemed prepared to call a mistrial. Wilde replayed his Las Vegas visit with Daniel Carter. How could his birth father possibly fit into what was happening with Peter Bennett? How did it relate to the murders of Henry McAndrews and Katherine Frole?

For her part, Jenn simply stared straight ahead.

When they heard the knock, all three of them stood. Jenn moved in a haze toward the front door. When she opened it, Marnie was in mid-blather. "You should just give me a key, Jenn. It's ridiculous not to. I mean, suppose you need someone to come by when you're away or what's the point in you having to get up and open the door, oh and this burger place, my friend Terry, remember him, he's that tall guy with the weird Adam's apple? He said it's great and they pay top dollar for influencer photos..."

That was when she spotted Wilde.

Marnie's eyes flew open. "No!" she screamed at him. "You promised! You promised you wouldn't tell anyone!"

Wilde said nothing.

Tears sprang from her eyes. "Why are you so mean?"

Jenn's voice was too quiet: "What did you do, Marnie?"

"What? You believe him?"

Jenn said, "Marnie."

"I didn't do anything!" Then: "I did it for you! To protect you!"

Jenn's eyes closed.

"And it was all true! Don't you see? Peter was a monster! He confessed! That's what you told me, right?"

Jenn sounded so exhausted as she repeated the question. "What did you do, Marnie?"

"I did the right thing!"

With more steel in the tone: "What. Did. You. Do?"

Marnie opened her mouth, probably to protest more, but when she saw her sister's face, she realized that more denials would be futile or worse.

Her voice was suddenly very soft, like a little girl crouching in a corner. "I'm so sorry, Jenn. I'm so so sorry."

———————

Marnie came clean.

It took time, of course. There were a lot of *I did this for you*'s and *Peter was a monster*'s, but through that smoke, the story came out. As Marnie recounted the events that led her to make those accusations on that podcast, Jenn just sat in silence and continued to stare straight ahead.

"I was out in LA going on a ton of auditions. But nothing was happening for me. Not that that matters. Oh, shoot, I'm not telling this right, am I? Anyway, you know I was a finalist for *Love Is a Battlefield*, but there were issues finding the right story line to fit my talents. They said I had a ton of star potential, but because I was your sister, it would be weird to launch a separate subplot for me, but if they could tie our story lines together, that could be gold."

"Who is they?" Hester asked.

"I was mostly talking to Jake."

Hester looked at Jenn. Jenn closed her eyes and said, "Junior producer."

Marnie recounted what she'd told Wilde about being called in, listening to a woman's tearful story (a woman, she now confessed, she hadn't known before that day or seen since), agreeing to go on the podcast to "help" the woman tell her story. Somewhere around then, Jenn stood up and said, "I have to reach him."

"Who?" Marnie asked.

"Who do you think?" Jenn snapped.

"But Peter admitted it!"

Jenn dialed Peter's phone number. The phone had been disconnected. Her texts bounced back. Wilde watched Jenn's agitation grow. She dialed another number, and when someone picked up,

Jenn said, "Vicky? Where is he? I need to talk to him." She closed
her eyes and listened, no doubt hearing Vicky tell her that she too
didn't know where her brother was.

Marnie's cheeks were coated in tears. "Jenn, he confessed! You
told me that! You said he admitted it!"

"No," Jenn said.

"Hold up," Hester said to her. "You told me the same thing—
that Peter came clean to you, that he confessed right here on
this couch."

"But don't you see?"

"See what?"

"What I saw on Peter's face...it wasn't guilt. It was betrayal.
My betrayal. I broke our trust when I didn't believe him. It's all
my fault."

"But those awful pics!" Marnie shouted. "Those were him!
They weren't photoshopped!"

"I have to talk to him." Jenn started plucking at her trembling
lower lip. "We need to get this out there."

"Get what out there?" Marnie started sobbing. "You can't tell
anyone!"

"We have to, Marnie."

"Are you insane?"

"I'll also need to post on Instagram right away."

"What? No!"

"We need to make sure Peter sees the message and comes
home."

"Comes home?" Marnie repeated. "He's probably dead."

Jenn's body went stiff. "We don't know that."

"Please, Jenn, just take a breath, okay? You can't just blame me
for all this! I spoke to that woman, the one Peter roofied—"

"Oh, come on, Marnie," Jenn snapped, "you're not that stupid.
She was a plant. Probably another junior producer playacting."

Marnie put her hands together in prayer position. "Please,
Jenn, I'm begging you. You can't—"

"Marnie?"

Marnie stopped talking, as though the word had slapped her across the face.

"I love you. You're my sister. But you've done enough harm, don't you think? Your best chance—your only chance now—is to do some good."

Marnie just sat there, hands folded in her lap, looking lost.

Wilde turned to Jenn and said, "Peter told you he was adopted."

The change of subject threw Jenn. It took her a second, but then she said, "Yeah, so? What does that have to do with this? For that matter, no offense, but what do *you* have to do with any of this?"

"Do you know Peter put his DNA into a genealogy website?"

"What does that...? Yes, I knew. When he found out he was adopted, he naturally wanted to learn about his birth family. He signed up for a bunch of those DNA sites, but I thought he deleted them all once he found out the truth."

Wilde glanced at Hester. Hester gestured for him to ask the obvious. "Are you saying Peter found his birth family?"

"Yes."

"Who were they?"

"He never told me."

"But he found them? You're certain?"

Jenn nodded. "He found the truth. That's what he said. And that was enough for him, I guess. Once he found the truth about his family, he didn't want anything to do with them."

THIRTY-ONE

Hester had been called back into court. There were rumors of a decision in the Richard Levine murder trial. Wilde headed back to New Jersey. As he passed the Sheridan Avenue exit on Route 17, his mobile rang. The caller ID told him it was Matthew.

"Holy shit," Matthew said.

"What?"

"You didn't hear about Jenn Cassidy's post? Sutton is freaking out. Did Marnie just make up all that stuff about Peter Bennett?"

Wilde sighed. "What does Jenn's post say?"

"Just something about the Peter stuff not being true and asking everyone to bring him home. Dude, the whole world is looking for Peter now. Did you have something to do with this?"

"Tangentially, I guess."

"I knew it! Sutton is going crazy. The Battler boards are blowing up. Your name hasn't gotten out yet."

"Good. Where are you?"

"Hanging at the house."

Wilde had an idea. "Do you mind if I come over and use the computer?"

"Sure. We got my laptop or the Mac in the family room—"

"Both if you can."

"No worries. Sutton isn't coming over until later."

"What about your mom?"

"Why don't you ask her, Wilde?" When Wilde didn't reply, Matthew sighed and said, "I'm not sure when she'll be home. Why? You avoiding her?"

"I'll be there in fifteen minutes. Can I ask you to do me a favor in the meantime?"

"What?"

"Search for DNA database websites."

"You mean like 23andMe?"

"Exactly. Find as many of the top ones as you can."

Fifteen minutes later, Matthew met Wilde at the door and led him to the Mac in the family room. He'd set up his own laptop on the other side of the table. Wilde sat in front of the Mac, Matthew in front of the laptop.

"Okay," Matthew said, "what are we doing?"

"You got the list of the DNA databases?"

"Yep."

"We need to try to sign in to all of them."

Wilde gave him Peter's email address and the LoveJenn447 password he'd picked up from his first visit to Vicky Chiba's.

Matthew tried the first. "Can't get in. It says incorrect password." He tried another. "Same. Are you sure about the password?"

"No." Wilde remembered how he'd gotten into the Instagram account via Peter Bennett's email address. "Here, let's try this. Hit the forgot password link so we can reset it."

While Matthew did that, Wilde signed in to Peter Bennett's email. He checked through it and saw nothing new. He moved from the tab labeled "Primary" to the one called "Promotions." As soon as he did, a new message popped up from MeetYourFamily with instructions on how to get a new password if you'd forgotten your current one. Wilde followed the directions. Matthew kept working. Another email popped up in Peter's inbox from yet another DNA database site with instructions on how to get a new password. Wilde again clicked the link.

When they tried to log in with the new passwords, an even bigger issue arose. The DNA site BloodTies23 sent them to a page that read:

> ERROR: You confirmed your request to permanently delete your data. Once confirmed, per our policy, this process cannot be undone, canceled, reversed, or withdrawn. We apologize for any inconvenience. If you wish, you can sign up again and send us another DNA sample.

"Damn," Wilde said.

"What?"

"Peter deleted all his accounts."

"So click backup."

"It says the deletion is permanent."

Matthew shook his head. "There must be a way to get them back."

"It says there's not."

They found ten major websites that did DNA testing for the purposes of genetic genealogy, including 23andMe, DNAYourStory, MyHeritage, BloodTies23, Family Tree DNA, MeetYourFamily, and Ancestry. According to what Wilde and Matthew could put together, Peter Bennett had signed up for all of them—and deleted his account at all of them. Seven of the ten made it clear that the deletions were permanent. Two others offered a way to "request" that your material, which had been "erased but kept in an archive," whatever that meant, be put back "live online." In order to do this, Wilde had to fill out forms and reply to emails with codes and, of course, pay a "processing fee."

Sutton arrived while they worked. She pulled up a chair and sat right next to Wilde.

"The Battler fan boards are blowing up," Sutton said to Wilde. "Spill the tea."

Wilde arched an eyebrow. "Spill the what?"

"Give us the dirt," Matthew said, typing away. "Did Marnie lie? Did she try to seduce Peter and he rejected her?"

"Is that what the statement says?"

"What statement?" Sutton replied. "The only thing is Jenn's Instagram post where she says it wasn't true and she just wants Peter found. Battlers are going crazy trying to figure out what really happened, but so far, no word from the show or Marnie."

Wilde got the authorization for the first site, BloodTies23. He signed back in as Peter Bennett and clicked the link to relatives. No one closer than two percent. No help.

Sutton said, "Do you want to hear the strangest theory that's gaining ground?"

Wilde continued to type. "Sure."

"A growing number of Battlers on the fan boards," Sutton continued, "think that Peter is behind all this."

Wilde stopped and looked up. "How's that?"

"It goes something like this." Sutton tucked a strand of hair behind her ear. Wilde glanced over at Matthew, who was smiling like a doofus or, to say the same thing in a different way, a normal college freshman with his first serious girlfriend. "Peter Bennett's star had seriously dimmed. He had a good run. Great even. But after a while, nice guys get so boring—not that you should learn anything from that, Matthew—"

Matthew blushed.

"—and when that happens," she continued, "the fans tune out. So the theory is, Peter saw the writing on the wall. He got tired of playing the dull good guy, so he set this all up to make himself the villain."

Wilde frowned. "Not a very good plan. Isn't he hated now?"

"Yeah, some people are replying with that, but maybe, I don't know, Peter didn't count on how bad the backlash would be. He took it too far, some say. It's one thing to be a funny villain like Big Bobbo. Even a cheater might have been, I don't know, interesting drama, though Jenn is pretty beloved. But a rapist who roofied his own sister-in-law?"

"Way too much," Matthew added.

"Exactly."

"So where is Peter now, according to this theory?" Wilde asked.

"In hiding someplace. There was so much heat on him that he faked his own death. Now that enough time has passed, Peter is making it look like he was wronged. That'll build huge anticipation for his return. Then when he does come back—probably in some cool way—Peter Bennett will be the biggest star reality TV has ever seen."

It was easy for Wilde to dismiss this theory as outlandish, but then again, look at what Marnie had done to become famous. Yet there were several problems with the theory that those who spent their time ruminating on fan boards couldn't take into account because they wouldn't know about them—like the murders of McAndrews and Frole or Peter's genetic connection to Wilde or Peter's murky adoption as a baby or...

Still. Could there be something to all this? Could Peter Bennett be behind it all in some way? Did that add up at all?

Wilde was missing something.

His phone rang. It was Oren Carmichael. There was a little quake in his voice.

"Do you know anyone named Martin Spirow?"

"No," Wilde said.

"Lives in Delaware. Thirty-one years old. Married to a woman named Katie."

"Still no. Why are you asking?"

"He's our third victim. Shot with the same gun that killed Henry McAndrews and Katherine Frole."

"When?"

"This morning."

Wilde said nothing.

"Wilde?"

"Is he in law enforcement?"

"Unemployed. Never been a cop or fed or even a mall security guard."

"So what's the connection to the others?"

"None as far as the feds can tell, but they just got the ballistics back. Some are starting to speculate that this may be a serial killer unrelated to all this."

Wilde said nothing.

"Yeah," Oren continued, "I'm not buying that either."

"Tell me about the Spirow murder."

"Shot three times in his home near his front door. Probably early in the morning. His wife found him when she came home for lunch from work. It's a fairly quiet street, but they're checking nearby CCTV and Ring doorbells right now."

"Shot three times."

"Yes."

"Just like the other victims," Wilde said.

"Right. That's the kind of thing that makes the feds look at a possible serial killer."

Again, Wilde tried to put it together. The reality-TV world. Peter's mysterious adoption. Wilde's abandonment. Three murders whose only link was a weapon.

He still couldn't see the overlap.

His phone buzzed again. Unusual for Wilde to be getting more than one call at a time, but this was not a usual day. "Got another call coming in," Wilde said.

"I'll update you if I hear anything else," Oren said before disconnecting.

When Wilde answered the new call, Vicky Chiba was sobbing. "Oh my God."

"Vicky—"

"Marnie lied? She made it all up?"

"Apparently. How did you hear?"

"My phone won't stop ringing. Silas heard about it on the radio."

"It made the radio?"

"An entertainment segment or something." Vicky sobbed again. "Why? Why would Marnie do that?"

Wilde didn't reply.

"Does she know what she's done? She killed an innocent man. Murdered him in cold blood. Same as if she stabbed him in the heart with a knife. She should go to jail, Wilde."

"Where are you?" he asked.

"I'm home."

"I'll come by soon and we can talk."

"Silas will be here in a few hours."

"He's in town?"

"He's making a delivery in Newark. Then he'll sleep here before starting another job in the morning. Wilde?"

"Yes."

"I have to tell Silas now, don't I? About Peter being adopted."

Wilde remembered that Silas had been a toddler when the family had moved to the middle of Pennsylvania and the mysterious baby arrived. "That's up to you."

"There have been too many secrets for too long. He needs to know."

"Okay."

"Silas thinks of you as his cousin."

"But I'm not."

"We can tell him that too, if you want."

Wilde did not like her use of the term "we."

"Would you please be here when I tell Silas the truth?"

Wilde said nothing.

"I think it would help. Having a third person here."

Wilde still said nothing.

"I'd also...It would mean a lot to me—to us, I imagine, Silas and me—if you could tell us what really happened to Peter. The truth of all this. We shouldn't have to just hear rumors on fan sites."

That much was true. He owed her that.

"Okay," he said. "I'll be there."

"And thank you, Wilde." Vicky started crying again. "Not just for agreeing to come tonight, but for believing in Peter. It may be too late, but at least now the world might learn what kind of a man he really was."

When Wilde hung up, both Matthew and Sutton were staring wide-eyed at the laptop.

Matthew said, "Holy shit."

Sutton added, "Whoa."

"What?" Wilde asked.

"We found a Peter Bennett relative. A close one."

CHAPTER
THIRTY-TWO

I raise the gun—yes, the same gun—and, once again, I fire three times.

I close my eyes and let the mist of blood spray my face. Some lands on my tongue. I'm not a cannibal or anything like that, but there is something about the metallic taste of her blood that arouses me. It isn't a sexual thing. Or maybe it is. I don't know. You hear that though, don't you? "A taste for blood." I get that now. I get that on so many levels.

Her dead body is slumped in the backseat. Her eyes are still open.

Marnie Cassidy's eyes.

I had lured her to this spot by sending her the message on a burner line via a private app many "celebrities" (mostly those in the reality world) use. How did I lure her? By offering salvation. By offering a life preserver when she was slipping under the choppiest of waters. I knew that Marnie would not be able to resist, that she would find a way to sneak out to meet me. Her world was collapsing in on her. The truth of what she had done had started to leak out into the world.

We are in my car. I again stole a license plate and then marked it up so that it would be nearly unreadable. I'm wearing a disguise. So had Marnie. Fans and even some press had gathered around her building after Jenn's post, so she sneaked out a back exit. If the police decided to do a hardcore investigation, I assume that they would still be able to pick her up on various street cams until the subway car. Would they be able to see her get on the 1 train at 72nd Street and head downtown? Probably. Would they eventually spot her getting off on Christopher Street, walking three blocks, jumping into the back of this car?

I don't know.

It would take time. We have been brainwashed by television into thinking that law enforcement is nearly infallible. That is, I've learned, nonsense. They make mistakes. They take time to get and sift through information. They only have so many man-hours, and technology has its limits.

Murders still go unsolved.

That said, I realize that I only have a limited shelf life with all this. If I continue, I will get caught. To deny that would be foolish. I am parked in Manhattan near the West Side Highway. I found a quiet spot—quiet enough anyway. It was near a construction site and right now, no one is working. It didn't take long.

She gets in. I turn. I fire three times into Marnie's pathetic, lying face.

Daring? Sure. But sometimes the best places to hide are in plain sight.

Marnie's phone was in her hand when I shot her. From the driver's seat, I stretch back and pick it up off the floor. I try to unlock it via facial recognition by holding it up to her face, but with the damage done to it, the phone won't open. Too bad. I had hoped to perhaps text Jenn a message pretending to be Marnie and stating that I was going away for a few weeks until things cooled down. That doesn't look possible now.

Could they trace her phone to this spot?

I'm not sure. I will destroy it—but does the technology exist so that they can see when and where she headed out of her apartment? My guess is, the answer is yes. Okay, fine. I have a plan for that too.

I throw a blanket over her body, though I don't really think CCTV or a bystander could look into the back window and see much. The blood did not reach the windows, so I don't have to bother wiping them down. I drive now through the Lincoln Tunnel and take the Boulevard East exit toward Weehawken. I can't resist the small detour and make the almost hidden right turn onto Hamilton Avenue. The view of Manhattan from this side of the river—the New Jersey side—is breathtaking. The skyline is laid out in all its glory. There is no view of New York City like the ones across the river in New Jersey.

But that's not why I like to drive by here.

There, on this unassuming street with unassuming homes, is an unassuming stone bust atop a column. The bust is of Alexander Hamilton. A plaque next to it commemorates the famous Alexander Hamilton–Aaron Burr duel that resulted in Hamilton's death. The plaque also notes that Hamilton's son Philip died on these same dueling grounds three years earlier. Even before this tale became well-known due to the musical, I loved to walk these grounds. I never understood why. I thought back then it was the skyline view, but of course, that wasn't it. It was the ghosts. It was the blood. It was the death. Men came here to "defend their honor" and often died in the duels. Blood was spilled here, maybe right here, maybe right where you are enjoying a leisurely stroll along the boulevard and perchance happen upon this display.

But creepier still, behind the bust of Alexander Hamilton, almost hidden by the marble column, is a large brown-red boulder. An inscription carved into the Manhattan-facing side reads:

UPON THIS STONE RESTED

THE HEAD OF THE PATRIOT

SOLDIER, STATESMAN, AND

JURIST ALEXANDER HAMILTON

AFTER THE DUEL WITH

AARON BURR.

I was always drawn to that. Then again, who isn't? The rock is enclosed by a jail-bar fence, but the separation between the bars is wide. It is easy to reach your hand through the bars and touch the rock. Think about that. You can place your hand on the very rock where, if you believe the legend, Alexander Hamilton lay mortally wounded more than two centuries ago.

It is morbid and macabre, but I find this fascinating. I have always found this fascinating. And the truth is, a truth that is both obvious and unspoken, you do too.

We all do.

That is why we have memorials like this, no? It isn't really a warning of a more dangerous time, though that's what we tell ourselves. It appeals to us on a much more primitive level. It turns us on. Perhaps, in hindsight, it was my gateway drug. You hear this often enough. One drug is a gateway to the next and the next until you're a strung-out heroin junkie.

Maybe it's the same with murder?

I don't slow down. I just want to drive past this modest monument and the duel grounds. To soak in this feeling. That's all. Bonus: If the police can somehow trace the exact movements of Marnie's phone, this small detour, though only minutes out of my way, will make them wonder about Marnie's mental state. That could help me.

I make the turn back onto Boulevard East and drive to Newark Airport. The quietest terminal today is Terminal B. When I get to the drop-off area, I take out my hammer and smash Marnie's phone to pieces. When her movements are traced, it will lead to an airport. That will help. I realize that there are probably cameras watching. Eventually they may reach the stage where they look to see whether she got out. But again, that will take time.

With the phone now rendered untraceable, I circle the airport and visit the other terminals, again just to confuse. I head onto Route 78 and take it west. I've rented a garage storage unit in Chatham. With my disguise in place, I keep my head down, get out of the car, pull open the roll-up door. I get back in my car, drive it into the unit, and then I shut the door. The storage facility has a powerful air-conditioning system. I made sure already that it was turned up full blast. I've read more than my share about rotting corpses and odors. I have time. Days at least. Probably more. Then I can find a way to get rid of the body. I do a light cleanup now and leave Marnie in the backseat. If I had dumped her body, the police would surely and immediately link her to the other murders. Ah, but if poor, beleaguered Marnie is just missing, with all the turmoil in her life, it will be more than plausible that she has decided to run away and hide for a little while. I wasn't sure how long that would last, but I knew the old credo: No body, no murder.

These moves should buy me days, if not weeks. That's all I need, really.

There is still work to be done.

THIRTY-THREE

Wilde looked over Matthew's shoulder at User32894, a twenty-three percent DNA match with Peter Bennett on the MeetYourFamily website.

"Did you check to see if User32894 and Peter had any communication?" Wilde asked.

"No messages at all. According to the website protocols, when you delete your account, all messaging is irretrievably gone. But in case you're wondering what twenty-three percent means..." Matthew clicked on the link and an explanation came up:

> If you are approximately a 25% match (between a 17%-34%), it means you are genetically related in the following ways:
> Grandparent/Grandchild
> Aunt/Uncle
> Niece/Nephew
> Half Sibling

"Weird they don't give you more of a breakdown than that," Matthew said.

"That's how DNA works," Sutton told him. "We learned all

this in Biology with Mr. Richardson, don't you remember? One hundred percent meant an identical twin. Fifty percent would be a sibling or a mother—your father has a little less, like forty-eight percent or something. I don't remember why."

"Still weird," Matthew said. "If Wilde here gets, say, a fifty percent match, he won't know if it's his mother, father, full sibling...Wait, when you found your father in Vegas, how did you know? I mean, when you first saw it on the DNA site, how did you know it wasn't your mother or a brother or something?"

"I didn't at first," Wilde said. "But then I found out he was a male more than twenty years older."

"Could still be a sibling."

Wilde hadn't really considered that. "I guess that's true."

"It's not likely," Sutton said. "If you're fifty percent, it means full sibling, not half. I mean, sure, mothers give birth over a twenty-year span, but the numbers are probably low. The far higher likelihood is that it's your father."

"Okay, true," Matthew countered, "but let's face it. Nothing about Wilde falls into the normal spectrum. He was abandoned in the woods when he was too young to remember. What do you think, Wilde? Could that guy you met be your brother instead?"

"I never really thought about it," Wilde said.

And he hadn't. Of course, Sutton was right. Odds were strong that Daniel Carter, matching at approximately fifty percent, was his father. But women can give birth at awfully young ages—whenever ovulation starts. Let's say his mother had been sixteen or seventeen when Daniel Carter was born, even in her early twenties, she could still have easily birthed Wilde too.

He picked up the phone and called Rola.

"Anything on Daniel Carter?"

"Nothing yet."

"When you say 'nothing'—"

"I mean just that. Nothing, nada, niente, nichts, nic, bubkes, so here's the headline: Daniel Carter is not his real name, Wilde."

"The man has a family, a business."

"DC Dream House Construction. It's owned by a shell corporation. No one is answering his home phone. No one at the business will talk about where he is. No one is answering the door at the house."

"He has daughters."

"We don't want a local PI I don't know well barging into their lives yet. Not until we know more. It's early, Wilde."

"Get your best people on it, Rola."

"I got my absolute best."

"Thanks."

"Me."

"What?"

"I'm flying to Vegas."

"You don't have to do that."

"I want to. The kids are driving me crazy anyway. I need a break. A little blackjack. A little discovering who abandoned a child in the woods. A little one-armed bandit. Maybe a magic show. And Wilde?"

"Yep."

"Whatever is going on with your bio-dad and the feds? It's seriously messed up."

"Daniel Carter might not be my dad."

Wilde quickly explained about the DNA percentages. Something about genetic-relationship discussions kept niggling at the base of his brain. He was missing something. But other things were starting to click. He remembered his phone call with Silas Bennett. Silas had said that someone matched him at twenty-three percent on MeetYourFamily.com. Now that Wilde could see that Peter Bennett had also gotten a twenty-three percent match, it seemed somewhat logical to assume that the two "brothers," one of whom was supposedly adopted, were genetically related, most probably half siblings. It wasn't definite, but there were ways Wilde could confirm that hypothesis.

He called Vicky Chiba. "Is Silas there yet?"

"No."

"When do you expect him?"

"He got delayed. Probably another hour, hour and a half."

"You still plan on telling him about Peter being adopted?"

"Yes. You'll be here for that, right?"

"Yes."

"Oh, thank you. I'm so grateful. Did you learn any more about Peter?"

"I'll fill you in when I see you."

"Okay, I'll text you if I get any updates from Silas."

Wilde hung up. They were still waiting on two more approvals from the DNA websites. He tried to put it together. Peter Bennett finds out that he was adopted. He signs up for a bunch of DNA sites to see whether he can find matches. Okay, fine. That all makes sense. He gets one close match—his own brother, Silas. Is that when he realizes he knows enough? That doesn't seem possible. Did he find someone else? Why did he close it all down once he found the truth? Did he learn something he wanted no one else to know about?

Wilde's phone double-buzzed for an incoming phone call. Odd. The double buzz indicated someone not in his rather small contact list. No one else had this number. No one else knew this number. He was about to send the call to his voicemail when he spotted the caller ID:

PETER BENNETT.

Wilde stood and walked toward a corner as he brought the phone to his ear.

"Hello?"

"We need to meet."

THIRTY-FOUR

When Hester got back to her apartment, Oren was there and waiting. He greeted her with a hug. Hester loved his hugs. He was a big man and he hugged big. It made her feel small and safe and comforted. Who doesn't love that? She closed her eyes and inhaled. He smelled like a man, whatever nonsense that meant, and even that made her feel happy and protected.

"How did it go?" Oren asked.

"The jury remains deadlocked. Judge Greiner wants to give it another day or two."

They ended the hug and headed into the living room. Hester's decorating style could best be described as Early American Frenetic. When she and Ira had first moved into Manhattan, they had "temporarily" filled the apartment with too many knickknacks and furniture from the house in Westville. The furniture didn't go, of course, not in size, shape, color, anything, but there would be plenty of time to change it.

Hester never had.

"If the jury comes back deadlocked," Oren said, "do you think they'll prosecute him again?"

"Who knows."

She sat on the couch. Oren poured her some wine. She was tired. That never happened to her before, but more and more, she could feel a certain heaviness in her bones.

"When this is over," she said, "I want to take a vacation."

Oren lifted an eyebrow. "You?"

"Where should we go?"

"Wherever you want, my love."

"I used to hate vacations," Hester said.

"I know."

"Work never tired me. It energized me. The more I was in the mix, the more alive I felt. When Ira and I would go away, I'd end up feeling more exhausted. I'd get antsy. If I sat on a beach chair, I wouldn't get energized—I'd want a nap."

"An object at rest," Oren said, "stays at rest."

"Exactly. If you slow me down, I slow down. If you keep me moving..."

"And now?"

"Now I want to go away with you. I'm tired."

"Any clue why?"

"I don't even want to think about it, but it might be age."

Oren didn't reply to that right away. He took a sip of the wine and said, "Maybe it's the Levine case."

"How's that?"

"Historically you've never been a fan of self-defense cases. I know it's your job to offer the best defense possible, truth be damned—"

"Whoa, slow down. Truth be damned?"

"That's not what I meant. I mean you have to leave your personal feelings out of it. You need to provide the best defense possible, no matter what your personal feelings."

"What makes you think I'm not doing that with Richard Levine?"

"He executed a man," Oren said. "We both know that."

"He shot a Nazi."

"Who was not an imminent threat."

"Nazis are always an imminent threat."

"So you're okay with what he did?"

"Yes, of course."

"It's okay to shoot a Nazi," Oren said.

"Yes."

"How about a Klansman?"

"Also okay."

"Where are you drawing the line at who you get to shoot?"

"At Nazis and Klansmen."

"No one else?"

"I'd prefer they get punched. I'm a big fan of punching Nazis in the face."

"Your client didn't punch the Nazi in the face."

"No, but if he had, he'd have been arrested too, and I'd still be defending him. If your sicko-psycho personal beliefs include exterminating those who are not of your race, I'm okay with someone putting you down like the horrid creature you are."

"You can't be serious."

"I am."

"So maybe we should change the laws, make it clear that it's open season on Nazis and Klansmen."

"You're cute when you try to debate me," Hester said. "But no, that's not what I'm suggesting. I'm okay with how the laws are written now."

"But the laws don't allow for what Richard Levine did."

Hester tilted her head to the right. "But don't they? We'll see, I guess. The current system may indeed work and set my client free. The current system may have the elasticity to stretch and make this right."

"And if it doesn't? If the jury comes back with a guilty verdict?"

Hester shrugged. "Then the system has spoken."

"So the system is always right?"

"No, the system may not be as elastic as I think it should be. At least, not with this jury. Not with the defense I made. I believe in the system. I also believe it's okay to kill Nazis. Why do you keep thinking those are contradictory?"

He smiled. "I love your brain, you know."

"I love yours too, though not as much as your bod."

"As it should be," Oren said.

She rested her head on his chest. "So where should we go on vacation?"

"The Caribbean," Oren said.

"You like the warm weather?"

"I like the idea of you in a bikini."

"Fresh." Hester couldn't help but blush. "I haven't worn a bikini since the end of the Carter Administration."

"Another victim of Reaganomics," Oren said.

Hester put her head on his shoulder. "I'm still mad at you."

"I know."

"Part of me was ready to end it," she said.

Oren said nothing.

"As much as I adore you, my job will always come first. Your telling other police officers that Wilde found the body..."

"Unconscionable," Oren said.

"So why did you do it?"

"Because I wanted to catch a cop killer. Because I'm stupid sometimes. Because I'm a small-town police chief who never worked on a homicide and maybe I let my pride get ahead of me."

"A chance to be a big man?"

Oren cringed. "Yes."

"You used your own justifications," she said.

"Doesn't make what I did right."

"No."

"So why are you forgiving me?"

Hester shrugged. "The system has elasticity. So do I."

"Makes sense."

"I also don't want to lose you. We all self-rationalize. You, me, Richard Levine. The question is, Is the system elastic enough to handle it?"

"And in this case?"

"With me, it's okay."

"Oh, good."

"With Wilde, I'm not so sure. He doesn't trust easily."

"I know," Oren said. "I'll try to make it up to him."

Hester did not think he could, but she kept that thought to herself.

"Another body has been found," Oren said. "Shot by the same gun."

"Whoa. Is Wilde a suspect?"

"No. The man was shot in Delaware at around the same time Wilde was under surveillance in New York City. He's totally in the clear."

"Good." Hester rose up and took a sip of wine. "In that case, is it okay if we don't talk about it tonight?"

"More than okay."

"I just want to rest."

"Okay."

"Or maybe neck," Hester said.

Oren smiled. "That might lead to other things."

She put down the glass and reached for him. "It might at that."

"I thought you just wanted to rest."

Hester shrugged. "The system may have elasticity."

CHAPTER

THIRTY-FIVE

The caller ID read "PETER BENNETT."

"My name is Chris," the voice said.

"That's not the name on here."

"I know. I wanted to get your attention."

"How did you get my number?"

"It's not relevant. We need to talk."

"About?"

"Peter Bennett, Katherine Frole, Henry McAndrews, Martin Spirow."

The man named Chris waited for a response. Wilde did not give him one.

"I hope that's all," Chris said, "though there will certainly be more if we don't act."

"Who are you?"

"I told you. My name is Chris."

"And why should I trust you?"

"The real question is, Why should I trust you? I'm the one with a lot to lose here. We need to meet."

"Where are you calling me from?"

"Look out the front window."

"What?"

"You're in the Crimstein house at the end of a cul-de-sac. Look at the front yard."

Wilde moved toward the picture window by the door. He gazed out into the night. A thin man stood silhouetted by the streetlamp. He lifted his arm and waved to Wilde.

"Come outside," Chris said. "Like I said, we need to talk."

Wilde hung up and turned to Matthew and Sutton.

Matthew said, "Who was that?"

"I'm going into the front yard. Lock all the doors. Both of you go upstairs. Watch us from your bedroom window. If anything happens to me, call 911, your mother, and Oren Carmichael. In that order. Then hide."

Sutton asked, "Who is he?"

"I don't know. Bolt the door behind me."

Chris was scrawny and pale with thinning blond hair. He didn't so much pace as stomp as though putting out small brush fires. He stopped when Wilde approached.

"What do you want?" Wilde asked.

Chris smiled. "Been a while since I did that."

He waited for Wilde to ask, *Did what?* When Wilde didn't, he continued.

"I used to drop bombs on people's lives. I don't mean literally. Well, maybe I do. I would reveal the worst secrets to unsuspecting, trusting people. I told one woman at her bachelorette party that her fiancé had posted a revenge porn video of her online. I told a husband with two sons that his wife had faked her third pregnancy to keep him from leaving her. Stuff like that. I thought they had the right to know. A secret revealed was a secret destroyed. I thought I was doing good."

He stopped and looked at Wilde.

"I know you have a lot of questions, so let me just get to it. I know enough about you to know that you're an outsider. You live on your own. You understand bucking the system. I would pretend this is all a hypothetical to protect myself, but there really isn't time. I have to trust you. But a quick reminder before I start: You saw how easily I traced you down. That's not a threat. That's a gentle warning, if you foolishly decide to go after me. You live off the grid in part out of fear of being found. Take your fears and raise them to the tenth power in my case. There are many who want me behind bars or dead. I don't want you for an enemy. You don't want me for one either."

"What do you want?" Wilde asked.

"Have you ever heard of an online organization called Boomerang?"

The name was not entirely unfamiliar. "Not really."

"It's a like-minded group of some of the best hackers on the planet."

"I assume you're a member."

"I was," Chris said, "the leader."

Chris waited again for Wilde to react. To move it along, Wilde said, "Okay."

"Boomerang's purpose was to find online trolls and harassers, awful ones, the worst of the worst—and both stop and punish them."

"You were vigilantes," Wilde said.

Chris tilted his head back and forth. "I look at it more like we were trying to maintain order on lawless land. Our system of justice hasn't caught up to the internet yet. The online world is still the Wild West. There are no laws, no rules, just chaos and despair. So we, a group of serious and ethical people, tried to bring some degree of law and order. Our hope was that laws and norms would eventually catch up and make us obsolete."

"Okay," Wilde said, "now that you've justified your vigilantism, what does it have to do with me?"

"You don't know?"

"Pretend I don't."

"It would help if you participated here, Wilde. I'm putting myself out here."

Wilde remembered the message sent to DogLufegnev: Got you, McAndrews. You're going to pay. "I'm guessing that your group stumbled across Henry McAndrews. He was a serial online bully, albeit for hire."

"We did, yes."

"Did you kill him?"

"Kill? My God, no. We never killed anyone. It never worked like that. Citizens—victims really—applied to Boomerang for help. Online. We have a website. If you wanted our help, you filled out forms—name, contact, how you were bullied, all the details. It's a fairly extensive process. That's on purpose. If someone hurt you to the point that you needed Boomerang to intercede, you should be willing to spend a few hours filling out an application. If, on the other hand, you gave up on the application, then your case wasn't serious enough to deserve our attention."

Chris stopped again. Wilde said, "Makes sense," again to keep it moving.

"The final applications were then divided amongst our members, where we each culled through them. Most were rejected. Only the most deserving got our full attention. Are you starting to put it together, Wilde?"

"Peter Bennett," Wilde said.

"Precisely. We got an application about the onslaught of bullying and harassment he'd been facing. I don't know if he filled it out or someone close to him, like his sister, or a devoted fan or someone posing as him."

"Did the application come to you directly?" Wilde asked.

"No. Panther handled it."

"Panther?"

"Everyone in Boomerang was anonymous. So we all had animal aliases."

Wilde remembered the name on the "Got you, McAndrews" post: PantherStrike88.

"Panther, Polar Bear, Giraffe, Kitten, Alpaca, and Lion. None of us knew the identities of the others. We had very strict security protocols in place. At the time, I only knew her as Panther. I didn't know her real name or even her gender. Anyway, Panther got the Bennett case. She then chose to present it to the group. There are six of us—five have to be on board in order to mete out retribution."

"And did you in this case?"

"No. We decided that it wasn't worth our effort."

"Why?"

"Like I said, we can't take them all on, and a lot of us felt that Peter Bennett wasn't a very sympathetic victim, what with the accusations of roofying and cheating leveled against him."

Added up, Wilde thought. "So you dropped it?"

"Yes. And normally that's the end of it. Case closed. We move on to the next. That's what we all did. Except for Panther."

"What happened?"

"What I didn't know about Panther—what I couldn't even imagine—was that she was a huge *Love Is a Battlefield* fangirl. Like she was really into the show. That was why she pushed to bring the case forward. Hard to predict who likes what, right? Panther was a hardened FBI technician, incredible at her job—but her head got turned by celebrity."

Wilde saw it now. "Panther was Katherine Frole."

Chris nodded. "I'm still putting it together, but once I had Katherine's name, I was able to hack into some of her accounts. Not all. Not even most. She was an expert too, remember? But she was openly a massive fan of this insipid reality show. So when Boomerang nixed the Bennett case, my theory is Katherine couldn't resist breaking protocol and reaching out personally to the applicant."

"To Peter," Wilde said.

"This is all speculation, but maybe Katherine called him and said how sorry she was that Boomerang rejected his application. Maybe she took it a step further. Maybe she met with him. Maybe she gave him the name of his biggest stalker."

"Henry McAndrews," Wilde said.

Chris nodded. "You can guess the rest. Not long after that, someone murders Henry McAndrews. When the body is discovered, maybe Katherine Frole realizes what she has done. Maybe she confronts Peter. Or maybe Peter realizes that he has to silence her."

"A lot of maybes," Wilde said.

"Either way, Katherine Frole ends up dead."

"So that might explain Henry McAndrews and Katherine Frole," Wilde said. "But how does Martin Spirow figure in?"

"Spirow was another troll presented to Boomerang."

"Did he harass Peter Bennett?"

"No. He posted something truly vile under a dead woman's obituary. The dead woman's family applied to us."

"Did you accept or reject the application?"

"Not me," Chris corrected. "Boomerang. We do everything as a group. But in this case, we accepted it. But see, Boomerang had various levels of punishment. His was mild. Let me cut to it, Wilde. I think someone—it could be Peter Bennett, it could be whoever filled out his application, it could be someone close to him or even a crazed fan—decided to take matters into their own hands because Boomerang did not act."

"By killing Henry McAndrews?"

"Yes. Then they killed Katherine Frole to either cover their tracks or, I don't know, as punishment to her. Her body was found in a small office she kept near her house. Very secretive. It's where she did her Boomerang work. I think whoever killed Panther forced her to give them names and files, and now they are on a killing spree."

"Do you know which names?" Wilde asked.

He shook his head. "Panther handled over a hundred cases."

"Why are you coming to me?"

"There's no one else," Chris said.

"Why not the authorities?"

Chris chuckled at that. "You're joking, right?"

"Do I look like I'm joking?"

"The entire Boomerang menagerie is a top-priority target of the FBI, Homeland Security, the CIA, National Security..." Chris spotted Wilde's skeptical expression and said, "Yeah, I know. I sound full of myself. But this is why we had all those protocols in place. You called us vigilantes. To the government, we are worse. We've hacked into law enforcement databases, private government websites, secure military mainframes, you name it. Some of the cyberbullies we've punished? They are very powerful people. The top echelons of society. They want revenge. The government wants us too. You may think black sites have all been closed down. They haven't. They'll drag us there in a heartbeat. Best-case scenario? We spend years in a federal penitentiary."

Wilde knew that Chris was probably right—the feds would arrest them at a minimum.

"But at the same time," Chris said, and tears formed in his eyes, "I caused this. I can't just walk away now, can I? I need to stop it before more people end up dead. So I'm pulling out all the stops and marshaling all my knowledge and resources. I have trackers, interception software, and most of all, the hacker's main tool—people. Everyone thinks that what we hackers do is magic, but here is what they all forget: Behind every firewall, password, security package—whatever—are human beings. You can trade favors with them."

Funny, Wilde thought. Hester Crimstein, who knows nothing about technology, had arrived at a similar conclusion when she talked about people's self-interest. Everything changes, nothing changes.

"When I searched through this entire situation, one weird name kept popping up. Yours, Wilde. When you called Vicky Chiba half an hour ago, I listened in. I know why you're involved. You're a skilled outsider. You get what I'm trying to do. I can't go to law enforcement. I can't put the other members of Boomerang at risk. I can't betray them or those who filled out applications and entrusted us to help them. Any kind of exposure could be catastrophic."

"So what are you suggesting?"

"We pool our resources. I tell you what I know. You tell me what you know. We keep each other in the loop. We catch this killer before they kill again. And maybe, as a bonus, you and I figure out what really happened to you when you were a little boy in those woods."

Wilde said nothing.

"Neither one of us trusts people, Wilde. That's part of how we ended up where we are. But that doesn't matter right now. I can't betray you. I mean, what would I say?"

"But I can betray you."

"True," Chris said. "But one, that wouldn't work well for you. I'm too dangerous. I have safeguards in place. You wouldn't want to see what I could unleash."

"And two?"

"You know every word I'm saying is true. So why would you?"

Wilde nodded. "Okay," he said, "let's see what we can do."

THIRTY-SIX

On the drive to Vicky Chiba's house, Wilde called Hester and filled her in on his conversation with Boomerang Chris. When he finished, Hester asked what Wilde wanted her to do with the information. Wilde told her to tell Oren about the Boomerang connections and decide what to tell the feds.

"You could have just told Oren yourself," Hester said.

"I could have."

"I get it," she said. "You're still mad at him."

"I'm not mad."

"Just not in the mood to trust."

Wilde said nothing.

"Is it okay if I still trust him?" she asked.

"You need my permission?"

"And your blessing, yes. I'm old-fashioned that way."

"You have both," Wilde said.

"Thank you. I used to be so unforgiving."

"And now?"

"Now I'm older and wiser," Hester said. "I also love him."

"I'm glad," Wilde said.

"Really?"

He assured her that he meant it, and they hung up.

When Wilde pulled into Vicky's driveway, she was pacing by her front door. "Silas should be here any minute," Vicky said to him. "Thank you for being here."

Wilde nodded. As Wilde joined her on the front stoop, a cargoless truck pulled up the street. A bearded man Wilde assumed was Silas Bennett stuck his head out the window, smiled, and hit a loud horn.

"I'm so nervous," Vicky said through a smile and a wave. "We've kept this secret from him since he was a baby."

Silas parked the truck in front of the house and jumped down from the driver's seat. He was a burly man with what one might describe as rugged good looks. The sleeves on his flannel shirt were rolled up over the Popeye forearms. He had a bit of a beer belly, but Wilde sensed strength with Silas. His muscles were not from a gym or for show. Silas's face split open in a grin as he rushed toward his sister and lifted her in the air with a big bear hug.

"Vicky!" he cried in the same deep voice Wilde remembered from their phone call.

Vicky closed her eyes and soaked up her brother's hug for a moment. When Silas put her down, he turned his full attention to Wilde. "I kinda want to hug you too, Cuz."

Wilde thought about it and then figured what the hell. The two men embraced briefly but with gusto. Wilde wondered when he'd last hugged another man. Matthew was too young to count. Thinking back on it, the last "manly" hug he shared must have been more than a decade ago with Matthew's father, Laila's husband, Hester's son.

David.

"It's great to meet you, Cuz," Silas said.

Wilde glanced at Vicky, who had her eyes on the ground. "Same," Wilde said.

Silas turned to his sister. "So what's wrong?"

Vicky's smile faltered. "Who said anything was wrong?"

"Well, you told me *not* to come over right away. I assume you were stalling until Wilde showed up. Am I wrong?"

"You're not wrong."

"So?"

Vicky started to fiddle with the ring on her index finger. "Should we go inside?"

"You're worrying me, Sis. Someone sick?"

"No."

"Dying?"

"No, not that." She put her hands on his broad shoulders and looked up into his face. "I want you to just listen, okay? Don't react right away. Just hear me out. In some ways, it's not a big deal. It doesn't change anything."

Silas shot a glance at Wilde before returning his gaze to his sister. "Man, you are scaring the piss out of me right now."

"I don't mean to...I don't..." She looked toward Wilde.

"Start with when you left Memphis," Wilde suggested.

"Right, good, thanks." Vicky turned back to her brother. "You don't remember when we moved to Pennsylvania, right?"

"'Course not." Silas chuckled. "I was like two."

"Right. Anyway, Dad drove us. He picked us up from Mrs. Tromans's. You don't remember her, of course. Sweet old lady. She adored you, Silas. I'm stalling, sorry. This is hard for me. Dad picked us up. When we got to our new home, Peter was already there with Mom."

Vicky stopped.

"Right," Silas said. "So?"

"Mom didn't give birth to him."

Silas frowned. "What do you mean?"

"She hadn't been pregnant. Mom and Dad left for like a week. On vacation, they said. Then they moved us from our home in Memphis to the middle of nowhere and suddenly we had a new baby brother."

Silas started to shake his head. "You don't remember it right. You were young."

"We weren't that young. Kelly and I—I should tell her I'm telling you this. How could I forget to do that? I should have Kelly here. I can call her maybe. Put her on FaceTime. She can verify—"

"Just," Silas interrupted, raising both his hands, "just tell me what happened."

"Like I said, we had a new baby brother. Suddenly. Out of nowhere. When we asked Mom and Dad about it at first, they just pretended he was ours. They finally admitted Peter was adopted, but they said we had to keep it a secret."

Vicky told Silas the rest of the story, the same way she'd told it to Wilde inside this very house not all that long ago.

"That makes no sense," Silas said when she finished. He'd started pacing in the exact same way his sister had a few minutes earlier. Genetics. His big hands formed fists. "If Peter was adopted, why not just say so? Why would our parents pretend he's their own?"

"I don't know."

"It makes no sense," he repeated.

Wilde, who had stayed silent, finally asked a question. "Did you suspect, Silas?"

"Huh?" He frowned. "No."

"Even a little? Even subconsciously?"

Silas shook his head. "I'd have believed the opposite more than this."

"What do you mean?" Vicky asked.

"That I was the one adopted, not Peter." Silas's voice was soft. "Peter, he was the favorite." He held up a hand to stop Vicky from speaking. "Don't pretend otherwise, Vicky. We both know. He was the golden child. In your eyes too. He could do no wrong." He shook his head again. A tear ran down his cheek. "I don't know why I'm upset. It doesn't change anything. Peter is...or he was...still my brother. It doesn't change how I feel about him." He looked toward Vicky. "Or you. It was all so hard on you. Dad was absent so much. Working late at the school, taking trips with friends. Mom was half in the bag most of the time. You got us ready for school. You made us school lunches."

Vicky was crying now too.

"I don't get it," Silas continued. "They had three kids they barely wanted. Why would they adopt another?"

No one had the answer. The three stood there for a moment in silence. Then Silas turned to Wilde and said, "Hold up. If Peter was adopted and you matched Peter, then, well, we aren't related, are we?"

"That's right," Vicky said. "He has no obligation to us. We aren't blood."

"Except," Wilde said, "we are related."

That surprised them. Then Vicky said, "You mean, like, because an adoption still counts as family? I guess in that case, but genetically—"

"Genetically," Wilde said, "we are related."

Silence.

Vicky said, "Do you want to explain what you mean?"

"Silas, you said you signed up for MeetYourFamily-dot-com, right?"

"Right."

"And they gave you a user number?"

"Yes."

"Do you remember it?"

"Not off the top of my head. It began with a three-two. But I can look—"

"Was it 32894?"

He looked surprised. "That sounds right."

"And you said you matched someone at twenty-three percent?"

"Wilde," Vicky said, "what's going on here?"

"That's right," Silas said.

"And when you reached out to the match, did you give your name?"

"Sure. Why not? I have nothing to hide."

"And the person you matched didn't reply?"

"No."

"The person you matched," Wilde said, "was your brother Peter."

Neither spoke. They both just stared at him.

"Aren't siblings like fifty percent?" Vicky asked.

"Yes," Wilde said.

"Oh my God," Silas said. "Now it all makes sense."

Vicky turned to him. "It does?"

"Perfect sense. It's what I suspected when I first saw the match. I just didn't think it was Peter."

"Could you explain to me?" Vicky asked.

"Twenty-three percent," Silas replied. "That's a half sibling."

Vicky still looked confused.

"Come on, Vicky," Silas said. "It's Dad. Dad messed around. He knocked someone up. Don't you see? DNA doesn't lie. Dad got a woman pregnant. With Peter. Mom and Dad decided to raise him on their own."

Vicky started to nod slowly. "Dad got a woman pregnant," she repeated. "Mom took him in. It explains so much."

"Peter looked like us for one thing," Silas said. "Better looking. No doubt about it. I bet his real mom was hot."

"Silas!"

"What? I'm trying to have fun with this because otherwise..." Silas stopped. "My whole childhood feels like a lie now." He turned his gaze toward Wilde. "You asked me before if I ever suspected. No. But now that I think about it, something wasn't quite right. I guess that's true of all families. I haven't met one that wasn't messed up in one way or the other. But now, I mean, what the hell, Vicky? Why did we move? I guess Mom would have been ashamed. There'd have been whispers. Our parents were pretty religious." Silas spread his hands. "So who is going to ask the million-dollar question?"

No one spoke.

"Okay," Silas said, "I'll do it: Who was Peter's mother?"

"She," Vicky added, turning to Wilde, "has to be the connection to you."

"Wait," Silas said. He faced his sister. "Did Peter know that he was adopted?"

"Yes."

"When he was a kid?"

"No." Vicky explained how Peter learned the truth via *Love Is a Battlefield*.

"I don't get it," Silas said. "Peter learns he's adopted. He puts his name in DNA sites. He stays anonymous because, I don't know, he's a big fancy star and people are lunatics with big fancy stars. You are a match, Wilde. He reaches out to you. Anonymously. Okay, I get that. But what about me? I matched him as a half brother. I wrote to him. I put my name."

"So he knew it was you," Vicky said.

"Right. So why wouldn't he reach out and tell me? Why would he close down his account and never reply?"

Vicky looked older now, wearied and pained. "I think it was all just too much for him."

"What do you mean?"

"Everything was taken away from him. His family was a lie. His life with Jenn was a lie. He'd been betrayed by Marnie and the fans he loved. The abuse he took. The betrayals from all sides. They added up. Peter was a gentle soul. You know this. It was all too much for him."

Silence.

"You think he killed himself," Silas said.

"Don't you?"

"Yeah," Silas said. "I guess I do."

Vicky turned to Wilde. "You promised to tell us more about what Marnie did to him," she said, her tone tinged with both sadness and anger. "All we know are the rumors, that Marnie lied about Peter, that he never roofied her or sent her photos. Did she lie, Wilde?"

"Yes."

"Why? Why on earth would Marnie lie?"

Wilde debated going into the long rationale Marnie had offered up about meeting another woman who claimed it really happened to her, but that didn't feel right. He simplified it instead:

"It was what you told me the first time we met," Wilde said. "Some people will do anything to be famous."

"My God," Vicky said. "What's wrong with people?"

Silas just stood there. His face reddened.

"So that's it?" Vicky asked. "Marnie lied about Peter. Jenn believed her. They ruined his life. Then you add on about his being adopted and..."

"There's another theory out there," Wilde said.

"Out where?" Silas asked.

"Fan boards, I guess. I should warn you. You won't like it."

"We're listening," Silas said.

Wilde turned to Vicky. "How much had Peter's popularity dropped recently? I mean, the last year, say. Before Marnie went on that podcast."

"I don't understand."

"I can see his Instagram posts," Wilde continued. "The likes in the last year—they were way down, maybe ten or fifteen percent of what they used to be. A friend ran a social media marketing report for me. Anyone can do that. There are free sites, but I paid ten dollars for a more extensive one. On all the major platforms, Peter's numbers had plummeted."

"That's normal," Vicky said, taking a step back. "I told you that too. I still don't see what you're suggesting."

"I'm not suggesting anything," Wilde said. "Some of the fans are posting a theory."

"What theory?"

"That Peter is behind it all."

Silas's mouth dropped open. Vicky looked as though Wilde had slapped her across the face. "That's insane."

"What," Silas said, "you mean, like, he told Marnie to lie about him?"

"Something like that."

"And say he roofied her?" Vicky added. "Are you listening to yourself? Peter is hated now. He's been completely canceled."

"Peter may have miscalculated," Wilde said. "That's the theory anyway. You know how reality shows operate. Controversy sells. Peter may have been tired of his nice-guy image. It's almost like when the hero pro wrestler suddenly turns into the villain."

"This is crazy," Vicky said, waving her hands in the air. "You didn't see him. The heartbreak. The depression. He'd never do something like that."

Wilde nodded. "I don't buy the theory either. But I wanted to run it by you. I wanted to see if there was any merit to it."

"There isn't," Vicky said firmly.

Silas looked up into the sky for a few moments. He blinked and said, "I hope it's true."

Vicky gasped. "What?"

"If it's true," Silas said, "if Peter planned all this, that means he's not dead. It means he wants everyone to *think* he's dead. It means now that he's been exonerated, even if he faked it all, maybe he can come back. Think about it, Vicky. Suppose tomorrow Peter shows up. With the way he's been unfairly treated, he would be bigger than ever—maybe the biggest thing in reality TV history. If he and Jenn got back together, wow: The return of PB&J—what do you think the ratings would be on their televised second marriage?"

Vicky shook her head. "He didn't do that. He wouldn't do that. It doesn't make any sense."

"So what does make sense?" Silas asked.

Her eyes were wet. "That Marnie lied, and then everyone turned against him. On top of that, his own family—me, really—lied to him his whole life about his birth. He felt abused and betrayed by everyone around him. Maybe Marnie was the final straw that broke him. Maybe it was Jenn not believing him. Maybe it was this McAndrews guy threatening to reveal more pictures or whatever. Or maybe..." She started to sob. "Maybe he found his real mother and couldn't handle that."

They stood there in silence.

"Wilde," Vicky finally said, "I want you to stop looking for him now. It's enough."

"I can't."

"Peter doesn't have the answers you're looking for."

"Maybe not," Wilde said, "but someone is out there killing people. We need to stop them."

———

Wilde started back toward the Ramapo Mountains. He figured a night under the stars near the Ecocapsule would do him good, but he also wanted to see Laila.

Laila.

She hadn't invited him over, and he never made assumptions where that was concerned. That wouldn't be fair to her. If she wanted him there, cool. If she didn't, who was he to get in her way with Darryl or anyone else? Wilde was chewing that over when his phone vibrated. The caller ID read "PETER BENNETT" again. Wilde answered and said hello.

"I have something for you."

It was Boomerang Chris.

"I'm listening."

"You asked me to look into the compromising photos of Peter Bennett—the ones already out there and the ones McAndrews threatened to release."

"Yes."

"First off, from what I can tell, McAndrews was intending to double-dip."

"How?"

"You already know that someone hired McAndrews to ruin Peter Bennett via online innuendo and bullying."

"Any idea who?"

"Not yet, no. That'll be trickier. Like you said, they paid McAndrews through his son's law firm to protect themselves via attorney-client privilege. This isn't an uncommon move, but it adds an extra layer. All I can tell you is that whoever hired McAndrews also emailed him those compromising photos."

"Okay."

"So that's the first thing. The second thing is more intriguing."

Wilde waited.

"The photos are real. For the most part. I mean, they aren't photoshopped."

"What do you mean, for the most part?"

"They're solid—no shadow errors, no warping. Even EXIF metadata is right for these images. But someone intentionally blurred the edges and cropped them in weird ways."

"Weird how?"

"Well, maybe not so weird. It's Peter. No doubt. But whoever sent the pictures? They didn't want to be seen."

"You mean whoever he's having sex with?"

"Yes."

"That would make sense. They wanted to be anonymous."

"Maybe," Chris said.

"You said McAndrews intended to double-dip," Wilde said.

"Yes."

"You mean sell the photos to Peter?"

"Exactly."

"Did they meet?"

"Peter Bennett and Henry McAndrews? I don't know yet. I'll keep digging."

They hung up. Wilde started into the woods. Night had fallen. He let his eyes adjust to the darkness. He started up the mountain toward the hidden Ecocapsule. It would be a two-mile hike. Not an issue. The tree branches were silhouetted by the moon tonight. The air was crisp and still. His footsteps echoed in the black. This was Wilde's kind of night. He had experienced thousands in his lifetime. A man could think in this stillness. He could relax his mind and ease his muscles. He could see and comprehend in a way that was impossible for those facing lit-up screens and noise and energy and even other humans.

So why didn't it feel right?

Why was he—he who had spent his life diving into the dark, he who loved to bathe in the solitude—suddenly unable to focus under the best of conditions?

When his phone rang again, the interruption, usually the most jarring of annoyances, felt like a reprieve, like a life preserver. He saw the call was from Matthew.

"Hello?"

"You coming back?"

"It was getting late so—"

"You need to get here."

"Why? What's up?"

"I got into the final DNA site. DNAYourStory."

That was the site that had matched Wilde and Peter in the first place. "You found a match?"

"Yes."

"It could be me," he said.

"No, it's not you. It's a parent, Wilde. It's either Peter Bennett's mother or his father."

CHAPTER

THIRTY-SEVEN

W ilde sat next to Matthew as he brought up the link in DNAYourStory.

"Okay, see, there it is," Matthew said. "A fifty percent share. Now we know that means either a full sibling or parent."

"Why are you so sure it's a parent?" Wilde asked.

"Here," Matthew said, pointing to the screen. "This account goes by the initials RJ, but the key thing is, they list their age. Sixty-eight. That seems a little old for a full sibling, right?"

"Right."

"So the most likely conclusion is that RJ is Peter Bennett's mother or his father."

Vicky and Silas had concluded that their father was Peter's, Wilde remembered. That would make the odds pretty strong that RJ would be Peter Bennett's mother.

"Something else," Wilde said.

"What?"

"I'm in DNAYourStory data banks," he said.

"So?"

"So this RJ didn't match me at all. PB does. So if it's PB's mother, I'm related on the father's side."

"Is that good or bad?"

"I'm not sure," Wilde said, leaning back and trying to sort through it. "Let's say this RJ is Peter Bennett's mother. Then the most likely scenario is that I'm related to the Bennett family—Vicky, Silas, Peter—on their father's side."

Matthew shook his head. "This stuff gets confusing."

"That's because we need more answers," Wilde said. "Let's message RJ."

Matthew nodded. "What do you want to say?"

They composed a message to RJ from PB, where PB noted that they were very closely related and that he—PB—had been searching for his parents, and it was urgent that they contact him. They stressed the urgent part, hinting that there could be a medical emergency, in the hopes that it would prompt a faster reply.

"Let's give RJ my phone number," Wilde said. "Tell them to call day or night, as soon as possible."

Matthew nodded, typing. "Got it."

When they both thought the message said everything that it needed to say, Matthew hit the send button. It was late now. Laila was still out. Wilde didn't want to ask where. It wasn't his business. He was going to head back into the woods, but Matthew asked him if he wanted to watch the Knicks game. He did, mostly because he wanted to spend more time with Matthew.

They both sprawled out and got lost in the back-and-forth of the game.

"I love basketball," Matthew said at one point.

"Me too."

"You were a great athlete, weren't you?"

Wilde arched an eyebrow. "Were?"

"I mean, like, when you were young."

"Were?"

Matthew smiled. "You still hold a bunch of our high school records."

"Your dad was pretty good too. He had a heck of a left hand."

Matthew shook his head. "You always do that."

"Do what?"

"Bring my father into it."

"He was the best man I ever knew."

"I know you think that."

"I don't *think* that. I *know* it. I want you to know it."

"Yeah, I get that. You kind of hammer it home without much sub-tlety." Matthew sat up a little. "Why is that so important to you?"

"To talk about your dad?"

"Yeah."

"Because I want you to know him. I want you to know what kind of man he was. I talk about your dad because I still want him to be alive for you."

"May I make an observation?" Matthew asked.

Wilde gestured for him to go ahead.

"I'm not casting aspersions here..."

"Uh-oh," Wilde said.

"...but I think you talk about him so much because you miss him."

"Of course I miss him."

"No, I mean, I think you talk about him so much not so he can still be alive for me—but so he can still be alive for you."

Wilde said nothing.

"I was just a kid when he died," Matthew said. "And don't get me wrong, Wilde. You were a good godfather before that. I know you love me. But I think after Dad died, you started hanging more, not just out of guilt or even responsibility. I think you were afraid to let go of him, and so when you're with me, it's the closest thing you have to still being with him."

Wilde thought about that. "You may have a point."

"Really?"

"When your father first died, yeah, I think what you're saying was true. You and I would go out. We'd go to a movie or a ball game, and when I dropped you back home, I'd start walking back into the woods and it was like..." Wilde swallowed. "I'd start thinking, 'I can't wait to tell David about this.' Does that make sense?"

Matthew nodded. "I think so."

"I would talk to your dad as I hiked back. I would tell him what we'd done and how much fun we had. I know that sounds weird—"

"It doesn't."

"So yeah, that's how it was—at first."

"But not now?"

"Not now, no. Now I just like hanging out with you. It may be because you're like your father. That could be it. But it's not because of your father. I don't talk to him when I leave you anymore. There is zero sense of obligation. I want to spend time with you. And I'm sorry if I keep talking about him. When I don't, that makes him feel more...gone."

"He won't ever be gone, Wilde. But he wouldn't want us to wallow, would he?"

"He would not," Wilde agreed.

Matthew grinned. "Wow."

"What?"

"That's the most you've ever opened up on that."

Wilde kicked back in the couch. "Yeah, well, I'm not myself lately."

They both settled back as the Knicks mounted a fourth quarter comeback. During a time-out, Matthew rolled over onto his stomach and looked at Wilde.

"What are you going to do about my mother?" Matthew asked.

"You're pushing your luck, kid."

"Hey, I'm not myself lately either. So what are you going to do?"

Wilde shrugged. "It's not up to me."

"You can't keep using that as an excuse."

"What?"

"Your whole bit, Wilde. We get it—you can't settle down, you have trust issues, you have difficulty with commitment, you can't attach, you need to be alone in the woods. But a relationship is a two-way street. You can't just keep saying it's up to her. She can't be working this all on her own."

Wilde shook his head. "Man, one year in college and you have all the answers."

"Do you know where Mom is tonight?"

"No."

"Right now, Mom is out with Darryl. You act like it doesn't matter. If it doesn't, you should let her know. If it does, you should let her know. Your 'silent man in the woods' thing? It's not fair to her."

"My relationship with your mother," Wilde said, "doesn't concern you."

"Like hell it doesn't. She's my mom. Her husband is dead. I'm all she has. Don't tell me it doesn't concern me. And stop hiding behind the 'it's up to her' bullshit. That's just a convenient out."

They stopped talking then. The Knicks called a time-out down by two with twelve seconds left. Wilde's phone rang. He didn't recognize the number.

"Hello?"

"Yes, uh, sorry. You asked me to call you. You said it was urgent."

The voice was male, gruff, sounded like someone a little older. Wilde sat up. "Is this RJ?"

There was a small hesitation. Then: "Yeah. I got your message."

"So," Wilde said, "we're related. Closely related."

"Looks like," the voice said. "What's your name?"

Wilde remembered that they'd written to RJ using the initials PB. "Paul," Wilde said.

"Paul what?"

"Baker. Paul Baker."

Wilde knew that Paul and Baker were always on the list of most common first and last names in the United States. It would make it harder to track down.

"Where do you live, Paul?"

"New York City. How about you?"

"I'm in that area too," the male voice said.

"Could we meet?" Wilde said.

"I'd like that, Paul. You said it was urgent, right?"

Something in his tone and readiness...Wilde didn't like this. "Right."

"Do you know Washington Square Park?"

"Yes."

"How about under the arch tomorrow morning at nine?"

"Sounds good," Wilde said. "Can I ask your name?"

"I'm Robert. Robert Johnson."

Another top-ten name. Wilde felt played.

"Robert, do you have any idea how we are related?"

"Isn't it obvious?" he said. "I'm your father."

He hung up before Wilde could say more. Wilde tried to hit the call back button, but the call didn't go through. He tried Chris next.

"You still have some kind of trace on my phone?"

"Yes."

"Who just called me?"

"Hold on. Hmm."

"What?"

"Burner number. Like yours. Hard to trace an owner. Give me a second." Wilde heard the clacking of fingers on a keyboard. "I don't know if this helps, but the call came from somewhere in Tennessee. Looks like Memphis."

Memphis. That was where the Bennett family had lived before their sudden move to the middle of Pennsylvania. He heard the sound of a car pulling into the driveway. It was nearly midnight. He moved to the window.

It was Laila.

He waited for her to get out of the car. She didn't. Not right away. Was someone with her? He couldn't see. Wilde watched for another few seconds. Then, feeling as though he were intruding on her privacy, he turned away.

"I better go," he told Matthew.

"Don't do that," Matthew said.

"What?"

"Run away."

"I'm trying to make it easier on her."

"You're not. You're just being a chickenshit." Matthew rose. He was taller than Wilde now. He looked like his father. He looked like a man too. When did that happen? Matthew put his hand on Wilde's shoulder. "No offense."

"None taken."

"I'm going upstairs," Matthew said. "You stay."

Matthew flicked off the television and trudged up, closing his bedroom door behind him. Wilde stayed. Five minutes later, Laila came in through the front door. She looked exhausted. Her eyes were red in a way that suggested recent tears. She also looked, as Laila always did, stunning. That was the thing with Laila. Every time Wilde saw her, he was still struck anew by how beautiful she was, like it was a surprise, like he could never quite comprehend or conjure it, and so every time he first laid eyes on her, there was a little catch in his throat.

"Hey," he said.

"Hey."

He wasn't sure what to do—hug her, kiss her—so not wanting to do the wrong thing, Wilde just stood there. "If you want to be alone . . ." he began.

"I don't."

"Okay."

"Do you want to be here?"

"I do."

"Good," Laila said. "Because I broke it off with Darryl tonight." Wilde said nothing.

"How does that make you feel?" Laila asked him.

"The truth?"

"Do you usually lie to me?"

"Never."

"So?"

"Happy," Wilde said. "Selfishly yet deliriously happy."

She nodded.

"Your eyes are red," he continued.

"So?"

"Were you crying?"

"Yes."

Wilde stepped toward her. "I don't want you to cry. I don't ever want you to cry again."

"You think you have that power?"

"No. But that doesn't mean I don't want to try."

Laila kicked off her heels. "Do you know what I realized tonight?"

"Tell me."

"I keep trying to force the round peg into the square hole. I've always bought into the belief that I needed a life partner, a man by my side, someone to share my life with and travel with and grow old with, all that stuff. I had that with David, but he's dead now. So I try to find that with someone else, but..." Laila stopped and shook her head. "It's not meant to be."

"I'm sorry."

"It's okay. That's the thing. Tonight I realized I'm okay with that."

Wilde stepped toward her. "I love you."

"But you can't be here all the time either."

"I can," he said. "I will."

"No, Wilde, that's not what I want. Not anymore. That would still be trying to put the round peg in a square hole." She sighed and sat on the couch. "So here is what I'm proposing. You listening?"

Wilde nodded.

"You and I continue to be together when we can. Come over when you want, stay at your Ecocapsule when you want."

"Isn't that what we have now?"

"Are you happy with what we have now?" she asked.

He almost said, *If you are*, but Matthew's words echoed in his ears. "I want more," he said.

Laila smiled, really smiled—and when she did, he felt his heart thump-thump and something rise up in his chest. "Do you want to hear the rest of my proposition?"

"More than you know."

"What's got into you, Wilde?"

"Just tell me what you're proposing."

"We become a couple. I'm not going to make a lot of demands, but if we are going to do this, I have a few."

"Go on."

"You can't just vanish on me like you've been doing."

"Okay."

"I'm tired of pretending that doesn't hurt. If you freak out or you need to run away—if you have to disappear into the woods or whatever—you have to tell me first."

"Deal. I'm sorry I hurt you. I didn't think—"

Laila held up her hand. "Apology accepted, but I'm not done."

Wilde nodded for her to continue.

"You and I are exclusive. Nobody else. If you still want to play around—"

"I don't."

"I know you like to go to that hotel bar—"

"No," Wilde said. "I don't want to do that."

"Also I want someone to take care of me when I need that. And I want someone I can take care of too."

Wilde swallowed. "I'd like that too. What else?"

"That's it for now." She looked at her watch. "It's late. I'm fried, you're fried. Maybe it's the exhaustion talking. Let's see how all this looks in the morning."

"Okay. Do you want me to stay or...?"

"Do you want to stay, Wilde?"

"Very much."

"Good answer," Laila said.

THIRTY-EIGHT

A t two in the morning, Wilde's phone rang.

He was awake, staring at the ceiling of Laila's bedroom, thinking about her and what they'd said tonight and realizing that they had talked more about their relationship in those three earlier minutes than they had in the previous decade.

With his fast reflexes, Wilde picked up the phone in mid-ring, throwing his feet onto the ground and rolling to a sit. The call was from Rola.

"You okay?" he asked her.

"I'm fine. Why are you whispering? Oh, wait, you're not alone, are you?"

He rose and started toward the bathroom. "You really are an ace detective."

"I'm in Vegas," she said. "Daniel Carter isn't home. The house is empty. No one has seen him and his wife lately. But I have a theory."

"I'm listening."

"The FBI agent who questioned you about your father. You said his name was George Kissell."

"Yes."

"Did he show you his badge?"

"No."

"That's because he's not an FBI agent."

"The other agent, Betz. She showed her ID."

"Right. But I looked into Kissell. Here's the kicker. George Kissell is not a fed. He's a US marshal."

Wilde froze.

"Yeah, I know. I'm out of here first thing in the morning. But that's not why I called you at two a.m. I mean, that could have waited for the morning."

"What, then?"

"The bug you planted? You were right. She just arrived at a hotel."

"Which one?"

"The Mandarin Oriental in the Time Warner building."

Wilde said nothing.

"Why would she be going to a hotel at two in the morning?" Rola asked.

"We both know," Wilde said.

"What are you going to do?"

"I'm going to head over there now."

The Mandarin Oriental is an Asian-fusion five-star high-rise luxury hotel on Columbus Circle. The hotel runs from the thirty-fifth to the fifty-fourth floor, so that all rooms have an enviable view of Manhattan. It is also, as Wilde found out, very expensive. To get past the various security apparatus, he'd booked the cheapest room available, which went for a thousand dollars per night when you added in whatever bizarre taxes and surcharges hotels seem to stick on your bill.

Wilde checked in at the lobby on the thirty-fifth floor. He

had requested a room on the forty-third floor because that was where she was staying and thus his card key would give him elevator access. His request was accepted and at almost four in the morning, Wilde politely turned down the receptionist's offer to personally escort Wilde to his room. He headed up in the elevator, found the right door, and knocked.

Wilde put his finger over the peephole, so no one could look out.

A male voice said, "Who is it?"

"Room service."

"I didn't order anything."

"Free champagne. Compliments of the manager."

"At this hour?"

"I messed up," Wilde said. "I was supposed to bring it up hours ago. Please don't tell. I'll get fired."

"Just leave it outside the door."

He debated faking that and waiting for them to open the door, but he didn't want to risk that they'd wait until morning. "I can't do that."

"Go away then."

"I could go away," Wilde said. "I could go away and call the press and tell them to camp outside this door. Or you can take your chances with me."

A few seconds later, the door was opened by a big man in a terry cloth robe. His chest was waxed.

Wilde said, "Hello, Big Bobbo."

"Who the hell are you?"

"My name is Wilde. Can I come in? I'd like to talk to your companion."

"What companion? I'm alone."

"No, you're not."

Big Bobbo narrowed his eyes. "Are you calling Big Bobbo a liar?"

"Did you really just refer to yourself in the third person?"

Big Bobbo scowled. Then he reached out to poke Wilde in the chest. Wilde grabbed the finger and swept the leg. Big Bobbo went down. Wilde stepped into the room and closed the door behind him. Standing in the far corner, wearing a matching terry-cloth Mandarin Oriental bathrobe, was Jenn Cassidy.

"Get out," Jenn shouted, tightening her robe. "Leave us alone."

"I don't think so," Wilde said.

Big Bobbo jumped back up off the floor in an almost comical fashion. "What the hell, bro? That was a cheap shot."

"What do you want?" Jenn asked.

"Yeah," Big Bobbo repeated. "What do you want? Wait, who is this guy?"

"He's a relative of Peter's."

Big Bobbo gave Wilde a sympathetic look. "Ah, bro, for real? Sorry, man. I liked the dude."

"It's none of your business who I spend my time with," Jenn said.

"That's true," Wilde said.

"I'm allowed a life."

"Also true."

"So get out," she said.

Big Bobbo stuck out his chest. "Hey, bro, you heard the lady."

Wilde ignored Bobbo and kept his gaze on Jenn. "I don't care who you date or about reality TV or your likes or your followers or any of that. But I need to know the truth."

"What truth?" Jenn asked. "Peter and I are over. I'm with Bob now."

"Yeah," Bob said. "We're in love."

"Wait," Jenn said, "how did you find me?"

Wilde wasn't about to tell her that when they were in her apartment earlier that day, he dropped one of Rola's tracking devices into her purse. It was that simple. Wilde had suspected this; something about Jenn's whole demeanor, about the whole story with her sister and the podcast and the photographs, had not felt right to him.

"Look, bro," Big Bobbo said, "I don't want any trouble, okay? Jenn and I, we're in love. We've been in love for a long time—"

"Bob."

"No, hon, let me just get this out, okay?" He turned to Wilde. "You care about Petey Boy. Cool, I get that. But he went too far."

"Went too far how?"

Jenn said, "Bob."

"You heard the podcast," Big Bobbo continued. "You saw the photos."

Wilde couldn't believe it. He shook his head and looked at Jenn. "Big Bobbo doesn't know?"

"Doesn't know what?" Bobbo said. "Oh, about Marnie lying? I heard about that today, and it sucks. Totally get that. But Petey Boy still did a lot wrong—those pics of him getting all nasty with other chicks and whatnot."

"Bob," Wilde said, still reeling from the fact that he didn't get it, "she made it all up."

"I know. Marnie—"

"Not Marnie," Wilde said. He turned and faced Jenn.

Big Bobbo looked confused. "What?"

"He's lying," Jenn said.

There was no reason to interrogate Jenn or ask pointed questions or try to trap her. There was no reason to let her continue to lie or watch her shed tears or whatever tactic she was going to use. Wilde just plowed full steam ahead. "Your popularity was plummeting. Yours and Peter's. You two had a great run. You were a lovable couple, and that was fun for a while, but really, you two had milked that for all you could. Bobbo, how long has she been stepping out on Peter with you?"

Big Bobbo glanced at Jenn.

"From the beginning?" Wilde asked. "Let's not pretend you only started up recently. But that doesn't matter." He turned back to her. "You and Peter tried to keep the viewers' attention. A baby might have helped, but you guys had trouble conceiving. Your social media engagements went way down. You got demoted down from the big penthouse to the smaller apartment—and you'd be kicked out of that soon. So at some point, you realized that staying with Peter would mean the death of your career."

"If that's all true," Jenn said, putting her hands on her hips, "why wouldn't I just break up with him?"

Wilde sighed. "Are we really going to play it that way? Okay, fine. If you broke up with Peter, the perceived nicest man in the world, you'd be the bad guy. You couldn't have that. But once you were the one wronged—pretty much the minute your sister went on the podcast—the fans flocked to social media to defend you and villainize Peter. Suddenly your social media engagements soared. You were bigger than ever. You set it all up, Jenn. You hired Henry McAndrews. You, of course, took the compromising photographs of Peter. Who else? It couldn't have been hard. You just hid a camera. You cut yourself out of the photographs. You were even smart enough to not do it in your own bedroom—someone might notice the background. But here you messed up a little. The EXIF data showed two of the photos were taken in Scottsdale. It wasn't hard to check. You and Peter were in Scottsdale on those dates. I'll be able to get someone to match up the background with your hotel room that night. There will be more proof. You paid Henry McAndrews via a law firm, but now he's been murdered, the cops will demand to know who his clients were."

Big Bobbo looked at her. "Babe?"

"Shut up, Bob," Jenn said. "This is all nonsense."

"We both know it's not. We both know it is all going to fall apart. I'm a little surprised though. I figured you"—Wilde turned to Big Bobbo—"were in on it. But of course, she couldn't trust you. Or anyone. Not even Marnie." He looked back at Jenn. "You knew Marnie would do anything for fame—she's just like you that way. So you set up Marnie's ambush with that producer. The woman who told Marnie the story about Peter roofing her—was she a producer too? Doesn't matter. But I do wonder why you didn't just ask Marnie to cooperate in your scheme. That part surprised me. But maybe even Marnie wouldn't have gone that far. Maybe you worried that if Marnie knew the truth, you were more vulnerable. I don't know. But tell me: When Peter swore up and down to you that he was innocent, what did you really say?"

Jenn smiled now. There was still denial, but there was also something akin to relief. "I told him I didn't believe him. I told him to get out."

Wilde nodded.

"And you're right for the most part," Jenn continued. "Peter and I had become boring TV. I thought about just breaking up with him, but like you said, how would I come across? I thought about asking him to manufacture a way to have us split up, but I couldn't think of a way, and Peter's game was to play it straight."

Big Bobbo said, "Babe?"

She sighed. "No, I didn't tell you, Bob. I didn't tell Marnie. Because neither of you are good enough actors to pull it off. This is a game, Wilde. *Survivor, The Bachelor, Big Brother, Love Is a Battlefield*—they are contests and entertainment. That's all. I used to watch *Survivor* and some pathetic contestant would get tricked and voted off and he would be throwing a hissy fit about betrayal, but of course, that's the whole game, isn't it? Someone has to come out on top. Someone gets the fame and the riches. Our life—Peter's, mine, heck Bob's—it's a game."

She moved closer to Big Bobbo and put her hand in his. "I wanted Bob from Day One on that show. Do you know what the producers told me?" Big Bobbo puffed out his chest. "They told me to keep both of them for now, but in the end, I had to pick Peter."

"So you never loved him? It was all a scam?"

"Not a scam," she said. "Our whole life is playacting. It's not a question of what's real and what's fake—there are no lines, no distinctions. Before I was on *Battlefield*, I was a filing secretary at a small law office. Do you know how boring that was? We all want to be famous. That's everyone's goal, if they're honest. Even the most pissant social media account wants more likes and followers.

Should I just let myself go back to that mundane life without a fight? No way. *Survivor, Bachelor, Love Is a Battlefield.* They're contests with winners and losers. In this case, I won. Peter lost. That's how it works. It was him or me, and guess what? It ended up being me. And what did I really do to him, huh? He wasn't thrown in jail. He wasn't being investigated or arrested. He just lost some fans—so what? He knew that the allegations against him weren't true. Shouldn't that have been enough? Anonymous losers online said mean things about him—big deal. Take yourself off social media if you can't handle that. Meet another girl. Live a simpler life. Peter could have chosen that, right?"

Big Bobbo just stood there.

Wilde said, "That's a hell of a rationalization."

"It's pure truth."

"Peter's sister thinks he committed suicide."

"And if that's true, that's terrible. But you can't blame me. Every week someone gets heartbroken on those shows. If one of them ends their life, is that another contestant's fault? Look, I didn't expect the hatred to get that out of control, but a healthy person doesn't commit suicide over mean tweets."

Wilde was awestruck by the passion in her self-justification. "In Peter's case, it may have been more than mean tweets."

"Like what?"

"Like maybe Peter was genuinely in love. Maybe the woman he loved wouldn't believe him when he denied roofying her sister. Or maybe, a few months later, he realized the truth—that his beloved wife had set him up. Did you ever love him?"

"That's beside the point," she said. "When you watch two people fall in love during a movie, does it matter if they're in love off-screen?"

"You weren't in a movie."

"Yeah, we are. Jenn Cassidy from Waynesville, Ohio, doesn't live in Manhattan's most expensive apartment building. She doesn't get invited to the Met Gala or hobnob with the rich and famous or endorse luxury brands or dine at the trendiest restaurants. People don't care where she's seen or what she's wearing. We in reality have chosen to make our life a movie. How do you not get that?"

Wilde was tired of listening to her. "Where is Peter?" he asked.

"I don't have a clue."

THIRTY-NINE

There was nothing more to learn from Jenn Cassidy, so Wilde left their room. He had paid a hefty price for a room of his own, so he figured that he might as well use it. He lay down on the hotel bed and stared at the ceiling. Shakespeare had written, "All the world's a stage, and all the men and women merely players." It was a bit of a stretch, but perhaps Jenn had a point. Peter had signed up for this life. Fame is a drug. Celebrity is what everyone wants—power and riches and the good life. Jenn was losing that. So was Peter. So she cut him loose in a way that would save herself.

But that didn't tell him where Peter Bennett was.

Wilde now knew that Peter hadn't cheated on Jenn or roofied Marnie—but he'd known that before he confronted Jenn. The fact that she'd orchestrated the whole thing didn't change the big picture much. It didn't tell Wilde who killed Henry McAndrews and Katherine Frole and Martin Spirow. It didn't tell Wilde who his mother was or why she'd ended up abandoning him in the woods.

In short, all he learned was that a reality star had lied. Hardly earth-shattering stuff.

Sleep wouldn't come, so Wilde headed out onto Columbus Circle and made his way south. He cut through Times Square, just because, and worked his way down to Washington Square Park. The walk was a little under three miles. Wilde took his time. He stopped for coffee and a croissant. He liked the city in the morning. He didn't know why. There was something about eight million souls getting ready for their day that appealed to him. Perhaps because his normal life—a life Jenn would undoubtedly find unworthy—had always been the opposite.

He couldn't stop thinking about Laila. He couldn't stop thinking of what this walk would be like with her by his side.

Wilde arrived at Washington Square Park. Central Park was his favorite, but this place was New York City in all its eccentric glory. The marble arch was done in the Roman triumphal style, designed by famed architect Stanford White, who was murdered in 1906 at the Madison Square Theatre by jealous and "mentally unstable" (according to his defense) millionaire Harry Kendall Thaw over Thaw's wife, Evelyn Nesbit. It was the first "Trial of the Century." The arch contained two marble figures of Washington in relief— Washington at War on one column, and Washington at Peace on the other. In both sculptures, Washington was flanked by two figures. In *Washington at War*, the two figures represented Fame and Valor, Fame seeming an ironic choice to Wilde, especially when he thought about Peter and Jenn, while the two figures flanking Washington at Peace were Wisdom and Justice.

As Wilde stood and stared up at the *Washington at Peace* sculpture, he sensed someone moving next to him. A female voice said, "Look closely at the figure on the far right."

The woman was in her early sixties. She was short, stocky, wearing a tan jacket, black turtleneck, blue jeans.

Wilde said, "Okay."

"See the inscribed book he's holding above Washington's head?"

Wilde nodded and read the inscription out loud. "EXITUS ACTA PROBAT."

"Latin," the woman said.

"Yeah, thanks."

"Sarcasm. I love it. Do you know what it means?"

"'The outcome justifies the means,'" Wilde said.

The woman nodded, adjusting her tortoise-framed glasses. "Amazing when you think about it. You build this giant monument to the father of our country. And what quote do you use to honor him and his work and his memory? Basically, 'The ends justify the means.' And even stranger, who is giving George Washington this somewhat amoral advice?" She pointed to the figure over Washington's left shoulder. "Justice. Justice isn't telling us to be fair or honest or truthful or law-abiding or impartial. Justice is telling our first president and all the park's millions of visitors that the ends justify the means."

Wilde turned to her. "Are you RJ?"

"Only if you are PB."

"I'm not PB," Wilde said. "But you know that already."

The woman nodded. "I do indeed."

"And you're not RJ."

"That's also correct."

"Do you want to tell me who you are?" Wilde asked.

"You first."

"My guess is," Wilde continued, "PB reached out to you— or should I say RJ?—before he closed down his account. Then he disappeared on RJ the same way he disappeared on everybody else. When I reached out last night, it made RJ curious."

"All true," the woman said.

"So who are you?"

"Let's just say I'm a colleague of RJ's. Do you know who PB really is?"

"Yes. You don't?"

"No," she said. "He insisted on anonymity. We told him the truth. I shouldn't say 'we.' I wasn't really involved. It was my colleague."

"RJ?"

"Yes."

"Who's your colleague from Memphis."

"How did you know that?"

Wilde did not reply.

"What do you say we cut to the chase?" the woman asked. "My colleague told PB what he wanted to know. In exchange, your friend PB promised to cooperate."

"But he didn't."

"That's right. Instead, he closed down his account. We never heard from him again."

"What did you tell him?" Wilde asked.

"Oh, I don't think we will play that game again," the woman said. "Fool me once, shame on you. Fool me twice..." She stopped. "What's your real name?"

"I'm Wilde."

The woman grinned. "I'm Danielle." She took out a police badge. "NYPD Detective Danielle Sheer, retired. Do you want to cooperate with us?"

"Is this an official investigation?"

Danielle Sheer shook her head. "I said I was retired, didn't I? I'm helping a colleague."

"The colleague from Memphis."

"That's right."

"And PB promised to help him too."

"I didn't say it was a him."

"Sorry. Is it a her?"

"No, it's a him. I'll tell you what, Wilde. You give me PB's real name, and I'll spill all. Believe me, you'll be interested."

"And if I don't give the name?"

"We say buh-bye."

"Peter Bennett."

"Hold on." Danielle typed something into her phone. "I'm just texting the name to my colleague."

"Do you want to tell me about RJ now?"

She finished texting and smiled up into the morning sun. "Do you know you can go inside this arch? There's a door on the east side of the other column. It's not open to the public, but when I was a cop, well, there were perks. You can actually go in and walk up these spiral stairs and stand on top of the arch. It's a one-of-a-kind view."

"Detective Sheer?"

"Retired. Call me Danielle."

"Danielle, what's going on?"

"What's your interest in this, Wilde?"

"It's a long story. But in short, I'm looking for Peter Bennett. We matched as relatives on the same site."

"Interesting. But you didn't match RJ?"

"No."

"So this is kind of a dead end for you. I mean, in terms of your search for relatives. And in truth, I'm here because my colleague doesn't need PB anymore. It's too late."

Wilde thought about it. "For some reason, RJ didn't want anyone to know his name—but he wanted possible matches to see his age."

"You have a theory on that, Wilde?"

"You're law enforcement."

"Retired."

"But your colleague isn't. I'm thinking your colleague is posing as someone else and using a DNA site to find relatives. Like in the Golden State Killer case. The killer left his DNA at a murder scene. The cops put it into DNA databases, like he was just any other guy searching for family. When the cops got matches—genetic relatives—they used that info to track down Joseph DeAngelo."

Danielle nodded. "That's pretty close. Have you heard of a man named Paul Sinclair?"

"No."

"How about Pastor Paul of the Church of True Christian Foundation?"

Wilde shook his head.

"He ran a religious community in the Memphis area for almost forty years before dying peacefully in his sleep last month. He lived ninety-two healthy years. Karma might be an actual thing, but it's not a thing down here on earth."

"Meaning?"

"He raped and impregnated a lot of his parishioners. Young parishioners. He denied it, of course, but a bunch of people online realized that they had the same father. So my colleague RJ from the Tennessee State Police got Pastor Paul's DNA and put it in online databases. He wanted to see how many people he'd fathered. In this database alone, he found seventeen. Of those, twelve had been put up for adoption. The other five had been told someone else was their father. Like your friend PB. None knew the truth."

"So PB's biological father is—"

"Pastor Paul. Does that help you in your search?"

Wilde thought about it. "I think it does."

Wilde walked back uptown toward Hester's place. When he arrived, Hester said, "Jenn Cassidy has been looking for you. She said it was important."

"Do you have her number?"

Hester did. Wilde called her back.

"You couldn't leave well enough alone," Jenn said when she answered.

"What's the matter?"

"Marnie is missing. Everyone thinks she just took off because of all the bad press, but we share locations with a phone app, you know, just in case. Her phone is off. It's never off."

"Maybe she really did—"

"No, Wilde, she didn't. There's no credit card activity, nothing. Marnie wouldn't run away. She's also not savvy enough."

Wilde closed his eyes. "When was the last time anyone saw her?"

"When she sneaked out of her apartment, I guess. No one's sure."

"Can you check her messages? Her texts? Her emails?"

"Don't you think I tried that? There's nothing."

"Where are you?"

"My apartment at Sky."

"Hold on a second."

Wilde beckoned for Hester to hand him her phone. When she did, he dialed Rola. "I need you to send your best person over to Jenn Cassidy's apartment at Sky. Her sister is missing."

"I'll do it."

"Aren't you still in Vegas?"

"I got a ride on a private flight to Teterboro. We touched down half an hour ago. I'll head there now."

Wilde put her on hold and clicked back to Jenn. "Stay in place," he told her. "My friend Rola Naser is on her way. Tell the front desk to let her up as soon as she arrives."

He hung up and called Vicky Chiba.

"Hello?"

"Is Silas there?"

"He just took off. He's picking up a load in Elizabeth and then he heads to Georgia. Why, what's up?"

"I wanted you both to know."

"Know what?"

"Jenn."

"What about her?"

"She set it all up."

Silence. Then: "What are you talking about?"

"Jenn set Peter up. She hired McAndrews."

"No..."

"She took the compromising photographs. She tricked Marnie into lying about him."

"No," Vicky said again, but her voice was weaker this time. So

Wilde kept talking. He told Vicky the whole story. He told her in his calmest, most detached voice.

Her cries turned into wails.

When they finally hung up, Wilde closed his eyes and leaned back. He took a deep breath.

Hester said, "Wilde?"

"I think I have it figured out."

CHAPTER
FORTY

C ould I pull it off?

One more. Just one more.

Then I could put it to rest.

Will they eventually figure it out? Maybe. Probably. But I don't have much fear. I would have accomplished what I set out to do.

One more.

And then what?

I have the list of cyberbullies from Katherine Frole's computer. Should I just keep going? They all deserve to die, don't they? The way I see it, I have two choices. One, I could run and hide after this next murder. Maybe get away with it. Who knows?

Or Two, I keep on killing.

There was a man named Lester Mulner who lived in Framingham, Massachusetts, who posed as a teenage girl to bully his own daughter's rival to the point where the poor girl committed suicide. I could kill him. I could then kill Thomas Kramer in Framingham and then maybe visit Ellis Stewart in Manchester, Vermont, and just keep going through Frole's list in what the press would one day undoubtedly label a "killing spree." I could keep going until I was locked up or killed or stopped in some other way, because the truth is, I won't stop on my own.

Someone else has to stop me.

I like this plan. Finish this up. Get justice or revenge or whatever you want to label it. And then, when I'm done with her, kill until I'm killed.

I have nothing left to live for anyway.

I've lost everything.

I am back at the storage garage. There is no smell yet. I have prepaid for six months in advance. I pull Marnie Cassidy out of the backseat of the car and wrap her body in black plastic garbage bags. I bought a box of fifty heavyweight ninety-five-gallon bags, and I use all fifty and a full roll of duct tape to seal Marnie up. I keep the AC on full blast.

When would they find her?

I don't know.

Would it be the smell eventually, or would it be that I hadn't paid my bill?

Again I don't know and don't much care. This will be long over by that time.

When I finish wrapping Marnie up, I drag her body to the corner of the storage space. I lay a few blankets on top of her. Then I get in the car and drive back into Manhattan via the Lincoln Tunnel. I don't bother changing license plates this time. I still have the altered one from when I killed Marnie, but the police aren't onto me yet. As I predicted, everyone thinks Marnie ran away.

Everyone except Jenn. Desperate Jenn.

I sent her a message not unlike what I did with Marnie.

I told her I could save her. I told her I could save Marnie too. I told her where to meet me.

I head there now to end this.

George Kissell worked out of the US Marshals Office on Walnut Street in Newark. Wilde had simply given his name and asked the receptionist to let Deputy US Marshal George Kissell know he was there and would like to see him. The receptionist asked Wilde to take a seat, but it didn't take long. George Kissell came out wearing a dirt-brown suit and scowl. He grumbled, "Come with me."

This Marshals office, like most, was in the federal courthouse. They took the wide stairwell down to the first floor, every sound echoing off the marble, and ended up back out on the streets of Newark. When they were near the curb and away from all possible prying ears, Kissell said, "What do you want?"

"Why did you pretend to be FBI?"

"I didn't pretend. You assumed. Why are you here?"

"We both know."

Kissell reached into his coat pocket and pulled out a pack of cigarettes. He stuck one in his mouth and lit it with a gold lighter. He took a deep inhale and let it out. "The FBI and US Marshals are both federal law enforcement agencies," he said, as though reading from a cue card. "We often cooperate on important cases."

"The US Marshals Office also runs the witness protection program."

Kissell was balding, but he had grown the side hairs long and plastered them down in a comb-over that would scream comb-over in pitch darkness. He continued: "The US Marshals is the oldest federal law enforcement agency in the United States. We protect judges, police courthouses, apprehend federal fugitives, house and transport federal prisoners, and yes, we run the Witness Security Program, known as WITSEC."

"You asked me about Daniel Carter, my biological father."

Kissell said nothing.

"I've been trying to reach him," Wilde continued.

"Have you now?"

"He's nowhere to be found."

"As my teenage daughter likes to say, 'Sounds like a *you* problem.'"

"I could keep looking," Wilde said.

"I guess you could."

"I could up the noise. Go public. Do you think that's a good idea, Deputy Marshal Kissell?"

"You mean do more than send private eyes to his residence and place of business and have your old partner Rola Naser knock on his door yesterday?" He shrugged. "Not sure what more you can do."

Their eyes met. Wilde felt the tingle in his veins.

"What do you want, Wilde?"

"I want to know my father better."

"Don't we all?" Kissell took another deep inhale, held it for a moment, and then let the smoke out with so much joyful release it almost felt like a sex act. "Tell you what. I'm not going to pretend I don't know who you're talking about because that's a waste of time. You already know too much. You also know I'm not going to confirm or deny."

"I didn't mean to put him or his family in danger," Wilde said. "I want you to know—I want him to know—that I get it now. It's okay. I really did find him via a DNA site. But I won't pursue it anymore."

Kissell took the cigarette out of his mouth and stared at it like it held some of the answers. "I have no idea what you're talking about."

"Did Daniel Carter—or whatever his real name is—lie to me?"

Nothing. Had Wilde expected more?

"Does he really not know who my mother is or why I ended up in the woods?"

Kissell made a production of checking his watch. "I better get going."

"I do have one request."

Wilde handed him a note.

Kissell said, "What's this?"

"It's for him. I'm going to stop by with sealed notes like this every once in a while. You and I can meet out here, if you want. You'll say, 'I have no idea what you're talking about,' but you'll take the notes from me. You'll deliver them. Maybe sometimes, he'll give you a sealed note to bring back to me. Or maybe not. Either way, we are going to do this."

Kissell looked out past him.

"Do we understand each other?" Wilde asked.

Kissell slapped Wilde on the back. "I have no idea what you're talking about."

CHAPTER
FORTY-ONE

I park. Just like last time. I just need to kill Jenn. If they catch me immediately after that, so be it. If they have the same car on tape parked in the same remote area, so be it. It'll be over by then. Any additional murders will be gravy.

I have the gun in my hand.

I keep it low and out of sight. Jenn will be here in approximately ten minutes. I wonder how to play it. Should I kill her fast? Three shots. My modus operandi. I bet the forensic serial-killer profilers will come up with some great theories on why I shot them three times. The truth is, of course, there is no rhyme or reason. Or at least not a very interesting reason. When I shot Henry McAndrews, my first kill, I fired three times. Why? I can't be sure, but I think that's when I eventually paused or wondered whether that was enough. Anyway, it was random. I could have shot him two times or four times. But it was three. So now I'm stuck with that number.

No great insight there, profilers. Sorry.

I close my eyes for a few seconds. I think about the gun in my hand.

I want to ease this pain.

That's how it started, isn't it? With pain. Pain is all-consuming. It robs you of reason. You just want it to end. I thought that killing those who had done such harm would ease the pain.

And, surprise alert, it did. Correction: It does.

But only for a little while.

That was the problem. Murder for me is a salve—but the salve works only for a little while. Its healing power starts to fade. So you throw more and more salve on the wound.

It is right then, while I'm thinking about salving a wound, that I see Jenn turn the corner.

I look down at the gun, then back up at Jenn, at those famed golden-blond locks framing the heartbreakingly gorgeous face.

Do I shoot her right away? Do I let her get in the car and see it is me and then, boom, boom, boom, end it immediately? I think that's the play. I want her to suffer. That's new. I only wanted the others dead. What they did was awful and hurtful. But what Jenn had done, the planning, the betrayal...

Jenn is only a few yards away.

I knew she'd come. Like her sister, she couldn't help but try to grab this life preserver.

She squints now, trying to see who is driving the car. But she can't make me out yet.

When Jenn is only a few yards away, I lift the gun.

I sit in the driver's seat and watch her reach out to the passenger side door. I hit the unlock switch so she can join me.

But that's not what happens.

The moment I hit the switch—as soon as I hear that little click indicating the car doors are unlocked—my car door swings open. I turn toward it, raising my gun, but a hand darts in and snatches the gun away from me.

I look up into Wilde's big blue eyes.

"It's over, Vicky."

———————

Wilde moved into the passenger seat, Vicky stayed on the driver's side.

She stared straight ahead out the window. "You set me up. You told me about Jenn to see if I'd act."

Wilde saw no reason to reply.

"How did you know it was me?"

"I didn't for certain."

"You should have let me kill her first, Wilde."

Wilde did not reply. He looked out the window too. Rola stood with Jenn by the chain-link gate to the construction site. She had two other people readied and in position, but Wilde hadn't needed them.

"What gave me away?" Vicky asked.

"What always gives people away? The lies."

"Specifically?"

Wilde still stared out the window. "For one thing, you lied about your relationship with Peter. You're not his sister. You're his mother."

She nodded slowly. "How did you find out?"

"The same way Peter did. From a DNA database."

"It wasn't my fault," she said in a small voice.

"That part? No, Vicky, that part wasn't your fault."

"He raped me, you know."

Wilde nodded. "Your family lived outside of Memphis."

"Yes."

"You were the oldest," Wilde said. "I didn't think about that at the time. But you told me your younger sister Kelly was upset about your moving because she'd miss a friend's eleventh birthday party at Chuck E. Cheese."

"That was true."

"I don't doubt it. But that got me thinking. Kelly was eleven. You were older. How much older?"

Vicky swallowed. "Three years."

Wilde nodded slowly. "You were only fourteen."

"Yes."

"I'm really sorry that happened to you," Wilde said.

"He started raping me when I was twelve."

"Pastor Paul?"

She nodded. "I didn't tell my parents. I mean not then. He was God to them. Then I tried, but they wouldn't listen. When I told them I was pregnant, they called me a whore. My own mother and father. They demanded to know what boy I had screwed around with. Can you believe that, Wilde? I told them the truth. I told them what Pastor Paul had done. My mom hit me. Slapped me across the face. She said I was a liar."

She stopped then, closed her eyes.

"So what happened next?" Wilde asked.

"Can't you guess?"

"You moved away."

"Something like that. My parents decided the only way to save the family name was for me and Mom to say we were going on a religious pilgrimage once I started showing. Mom would tell every-one she was pregnant. And when we came back to our community, we would just raise the baby as if it were hers."

"And you'd pretend to be the baby's sister."

"Yes."

"So how did you end up in Pennsylvania? I checked. Your father did work at Penn State. Your family did move to the area."

"They changed their minds. My parents."

"They believed you?"

"They never admitted it," she said. "But yes."

"Why?"

A tear came to her eye now. "Kelly."

"Your sister?"

"Pastor Paul started showing interest in her." She closed her eyes for a long moment. "That woke my parents up. They weren't bad people, my parents. They'd both been raised in brainwashing religions. They didn't know any better. The idea that the man they literally worshipped would defile their own daughters..." She took a deep breath. "I guess you found Pastor Paul through Peter's DNA."

"Yes."

"How did you know I was Peter's mother?"

"The same way Peter did. The match with Silas. Silas kept talking about sharing a quarter of his DNA with Peter as meaning you're a half sibling. He jumped to that conclusion. But that couldn't be anymore. Half siblings can only share one parent. Could Pastor Paul be both their fathers with two different, totally unrelated mothers? That seemed highly unlikely, especially since Silas found other matches on your father's side too. The key is, if you have a twenty-three percent DNA share, it doesn't just mean you could be a half sibling. The DNAYourStory website said as much. You could be a grandparent. Or, as in this case, an uncle. It was the only thing that made sense. You're Peter's mother, making Silas his uncle."

Vicky nodded. "Do you want to hear something odd?"

Wilde waited.

"Having Peter was the greatest thing that ever happened to me. After all the horror and abuse and cruelty, at the end for me, there was this perfect little baby boy—a golden child too good for this world. Nothing I told you about him was a lie. Peter was special."

Wilde pushed ahead. "Did Peter reach out to Boomerang, or was that you?"

"We both did. Peter still thought I was his sister back then. And he was devastated by what happened with Marnie and Jenn and the whole *Love Is a Battlefield* world. He was obsessed with proving his innocence. So when he saw that DogLufegnev account claiming he had more pics, worse ones, he wanted to know more. I pushed him to let Boomerang help us. Then one day, maybe a month later, someone from Boomerang emails me that our case had been rejected. I wrote back as Peter, saying how devastated I was and how we still needed their help. Eventually the person from Boomerang told me her name was Katherine Frole. She started going on about how big a Battler she was, how she loved Peter's season, all that. She said she still wanted to help."

"Katherine Frole gave you Henry McAndrews's name?"

"Yes, I got it out of her. But it was too late."

"What do you mean, too late?"

"Peter was already gone."

"So you went to McAndrews's house anyway."

"Yes."

"And you killed him."

She nodded. "I thought that would be the end of it."

"When I found McAndrews's body, when his murder went public, did Katherine Frole contact you?"

"Yes."

"She suspected you or Peter had something to do with it."

"We set up a meeting in her office at a time she knew no one would be there. I said Peter and I would explain everything."

"Were you afraid she'd talk?"

"That was what I told myself," Vicky said. "And I think she would have eventually. But Katherine Frole had a lot to lose too. She was an FBI agent working for an illegal vigilante group. I'm not going to go into detail on this part because it's not really important. But after shooting McAndrews, I realized—I know how this will sound—that I liked killing." She smiled again, but now that smile raised hackles. "You could chalk it up to my childhood, the trauma of rape, though that's a terrible cliché, isn't it? Or maybe it's an illness or some other life event or more likely just a chemical imbalance in my brain. Do you want to know my own theory, Wilde?"

He said nothing.

"A lot of people are potential serial killers. Not one in a million, like you read about it. I'd say more like one in twenty, maybe one in ten. But if you never do it, if you never kill for the first time, you don't ever get to experience that addictive high. Many of us *could* be, say, heroin addicts, but if we never try it, if we never get a taste for it..."

"And that explains Martin Spirow."

Vicky nodded. "There are so many terrible people, Wilde. Did you see what Martin Spirow put on that poor dead girl's obituary space? I got a Boomerang list of names from Katherine Frole—a list of people who were so pathetic and appalling that the only way they got through their day was saying cruel and vile and hurtful things anonymously to people they didn't know. I mean, think about it. Martin Spirow woke up one day and saw a heartbroken family grieving over the death of their young daughter, and what does he do? He writes, 'It's sad when hot pussy goes to waste.' What sort of awful life choices has a person made to end up doing something like that?" She shook her head in disgust. "I did the world a favor."

"So where is Peter?" Wilde asked.

"I told you the first time we met." She smiled. "You know, Wilde. You've always known. My son, my beautiful son, got his affairs in order. He bought a ticket and flew to that island. He went through passport control and checked into that hotel, and the next morning he checked out. He took a taxi to the path where you hike to the top of the cliff. He left a message for me on one of those apps that automatically deletes itself two minutes after you listen. He told me goodbye. I could hear the surf in the background. And then my son jumped to his death."

Wilde said nothing.

"You know how he was harassed and bullied, how he was shamed and disgraced, how no one would forgive him for something he didn't do. You know how he lost his wife, the supposed love of his life, and his career, and, yes, his celebrity. All of that and no one would believe him. Step into his shoes for a moment. The whole world believes you roofied your own sister-in-law and not even your own wife defends you. Everything you had is taken away from you. But don't stop there, Wilde. Add into that the fact that the person Peter loved the longest, the one who really raised him and took care of him and, as Silas pointed out, favored him above all else, the person he trusted most in the entire world, had lied to him his whole life, that in reality she wasn't his sister but his mother, that he was the product of a rape. Are you thinking about that, Wilde? Are you teetering yet? Good. Because now, after your call today, I can add one more. Peter was so cryptic toward the end, so suddenly quiet and sad. Now I know why. He'd figured it out. He'd figured it out that Jenn had set this all up. He loved that woman, Wilde. Imagine that pain. That final blow. So you tell me. Who do you blame? Was it Marnie? Was it reality TV? McAndrews? The cruel fans? Was it my fault? You tell me, Wilde. Who killed my boy?"

Wilde had no answer to that, so he opened the car window and nodded to Rola. She nodded back and made the call.

Five minutes later, the police came and took Vicky away.

FORTY-TWO

One month later, after Chris had vanished from his life, after Marnie's body was discovered in that storage facility, Wilde got a call from Deputy US Marshal George Kissell.

"They want to talk to you."

Wilde's grip on the phone tightened. "When?"

"Has to be now. Tell anyone about this, and they're gone. Take more than an hour to get there, and they're gone. I'm pin-dropping you the location right now."

Wilde felt his heart pick up apace. He checked his screen. The map showed a location just west of East Shore Road near Greenwood Lake in New York. Wilde could hike it, but it would probably take three or four hours.

Why there?

"You okay?" Laila asked.

They sat in the television room. It was Sunday, and they were watching pro football. Laila was a massive New York Giants fan and never missed a game. He almost said, "I think my father wants to see me," but a fly-through of good sense stopped him.

"Do you mind if I borrow the car?"

"You know you don't have to ask."

Wilde rose. "Thanks."

Laila studied his face. "You'll tell me about it later?"

He bent down and kissed her. He gave her the honest answer. "If I can."

He started up the car and headed west. Weeks ago, after it all ended, Silas had come to see him. "You and I," he said, "we're still family. Distantly, I know. But we kinda don't have anyone else." They met two weeks later. Silas volunteered to go through the family albums, back several generations, but Wilde didn't want that right now. Maybe he would again, but for now, he wanted to focus on the future, not the past. He asked Silas to leave it alone, and Silas respected his wishes.

That didn't mean Wilde had forgotten.

The drive took half an hour. He parked on the corner of East Shore Drive and Bluff Avenue. There were several black cars parked nearby. When Wilde got out of the car, Deputy Marshal George Kissell did likewise.

"You mind if I search you?"

Wilde raised his hands. The pat-down was thorough. Kissell nodded toward a house on the corner. It was a classic New Englandesque two-story saltbox with a center chimney and front door, overly symmetrical windows, flat front. Some of the colonial charm had been stripped away by an aluminum siding "upgrade" of too silvery a gray.

Wilde hesitated. He felt suddenly strange.

"The door is unlocked," Kissell said. "We have eyes on you. They'll take you out if you make a move."

Wilde just looked at him.

"I know, I know, but none of this is protocol. Everyone's on edge."

"Thank you," Wilde said.

He took his time walking up the front path. He didn't know why. He had waited for this moment his entire life. When he reached the door, Wilde stopped for a moment and considered turning around and just leaving. He didn't need the answers. Not anymore. He had never felt better about himself and his life. He was building something with Laila. He had stopped a serial killer. Life, he knew, was about balance, and right now he was standing on firm ground.

He turned the knob and entered.

He had expected to see Daniel Carter. Instead, standing in the front hallway next to the stairwell, looking at him with her head held high and her gaze steady, was Sofia Carter, Daniel's wife.

For a moment they both just stood there. Wilde noticed a quake in her lower lip.

"Is..." Wilde wasn't sure what to even call him. "Is your husband okay?"

"He's fine."

Relief flowed through him. Wilde hadn't expected that.

"Very little of what my Danny told you was true though," she said.

Wilde said nothing.

"He is your biological father. That's the most important thing for you to know. And he's a good man. The best I've ever known. He is kind and strong, a wonderful father and husband, and I hope for your sake that you take after him."

"Where is he?"

Sofia didn't reply. "You figured out that we were in witness protection."

"Are you guys safe?"

"We've changed identities."

"What about your daughters?"

"We finally had to tell them the truth. The partial truth anyway."

"They didn't know?"

Sofia shook her head. "We became Daniel and Sofia Carter before they were born. They are such good girls, your sisters. We are so blessed. They always wanted to know about our families, but of course, Danny and I had to lie about it. Pretend we didn't know anything. That's part of being in the program. So do you know what these wonderful girls did? These girls who loved their father so much? They surprised him by putting his DNA in a database, so he could learn all about his family and heritage. They used one of our home COVID tests to get his DNA and they sent it in to that site. Clever, our girls. Your sisters. When they gave Danny the gift, we both went pale. It was such a breach. Danny ran to the computer and deleted the profile. But, well, too late, of course."

"I'm sorry," Wilde said. "I didn't mean to cause you trouble. If I had any idea my father was in witness protection—"

"Danny isn't the reason we're in witness protection," Sofia said. "I am."

Wilde felt something icy slide down his back.

"Before I get into that," Sofia said, "do you mind if I ask you a question?"

Wilde nodded for her to go ahead.

Sofia Carter was a small woman, beautiful, with high cheekbones and steely eyes. She lifted her chin. "I read an old article on you. It said you sometimes have old memories from before..." Her voice petered out.

"Not really," Wilde said. His mouth felt dry. "I sometimes have dreams or like flashes."

"You see things like snapshots."

"Yes."

"Like a red banister, the article said. A dark room. A portrait of a man with a mustache."

Wilde couldn't move, but he was starting to feel it.

Sofia lifted her hand and rested it on the white banister heading up to the second level. "This used to be dark red," she said. "Blood red, really. The interior of this house? It used to be all dark woods. The new owners painted everything white." She pointed to the left where a blue-and-yellow tapestry now hung. "A portrait of a man with a mustache used to hang here."

Wilde felt dizzy. He closed his eyes for a moment, tried to regain his bearings. The woman's screams began in his head, and then those familiar images—banister, walls, portrait—came back to him, rapid-fire, quick flashes, like strobe lights. He opened his eyes.

It had been here. In this very foyer. He was back.

"The screams," Wilde managed to say. "I heard screams."

Their eyes met.

"They were mine," she said.

"So you're..."

She didn't bother nodding. "I'm your mother, Wilde."

So there it was. After all these years, Wilde's mother stood directly in front of him. He looked at her and felt his heart explode in his chest.

"This spot I'm standing on," Sofia said, her voice numb, "this exact spot, is where I stood the last time I saw you. I opened this little door"—she pointed now at the storage door under the stairwell—"and I made my little boy promise not to make a sound until I came back. Then I closed the door and never saw you again."

Wilde felt heady and faint.

"I can't tell you names. I can't tell you places or details. Like with your sisters. That's part of the deal we made to set up this meet. And we don't have much time. I'm scared because when you hear this story, you may end up hating me. I'll understand that. But it's time you knew the truth."

He waited, afraid to move, afraid to disturb the air. This all felt like one of those dreams, the good dreams, and midway through, you start to realize it's a dream and you're trying to do all you can to not yet wake up.

"When I was a teenager, I attracted the attention of a horrible, vile man. A truly deranged and damaged psychopath from a deranged and damaged crime family. The vile man became obsessed with me, and when a man like that decides that you are his, you either acquiesce or you die. There are no other options."

Her gaze wandered toward the stairs. Wilde had still not moved a muscle.

"You may wonder why my father and my mother didn't help me. My father was dead, my mother, well, she encouraged it. I won't go into my family or childhood. Suffice to say I knew no one who could help. I was a captive. The vile man put me through hell. I tried to escape once or twice. That made it worse. I was trapped in this big estate with three generations of the vile man's family—his grandparents, his father, his two brothers. Crime bosses of the crime bosses."

Sofia still looked up. "They had a furnace in the back of the estate. When I turned eighteen, the vile man took me up there and showed me the ashes. He said that's where his grandfather used to get rid of the bodies. His grandfather stopped burning them there because his grandmother complained about the smell. But the furnace still worked. And if I ever tried to leave him, he would shackle me to that furnace and set it on low and come back in two weeks, and by then, I'd be ashes too."

Sofia looked straight at Wilde. Wilde opened his mouth to say something—he wasn't sure what—but she stopped him with a shake of her head.

"Let me get through this, okay?"

Wilde may have nodded.

"One day I met your father. It's not important how or why. I fell in love with him. I was so scared. For me. For him. But"—she smiled now—"I was too selfish to give him up. I started to live a double life. God, we were both so young. I didn't tell your father the truth. I should have, of course. But he was leaving to serve overseas anyway. It couldn't last, and I was okay with that. We would only have two months together. That's more than I could ask for. After that, I could stay with the vile man and live off the memories." She smiled and shook her head. "That's the sort of nonsense you tell yourself when you're young. Can you guess what happened next?"

Wilde said, "You got pregnant."

"Yes. I didn't tell your father. You can understand that. Your father hadn't asked for any of this. I was afraid he'd want to do the right thing, get married, and then the vile man and his vile family would find out the truth. Your father was—is—a strong man, but he was no match for this kind of family. No one man is."

"So you pretended the vile man was the father?"

Sofia Carter nodded. "I told myself that was best. I would break it off with your father to protect him. I'd have his baby and say it was the vile man's, and this way I would always have a piece of your father." Sofia shook her head with a sad smile. "That was the young girl's foolish fantasy. So crazy when I look back on it now."

"So what happened?" Wilde asked.

"I tried to stick to my plan, but two years later, when your father finished serving, he came back for me. I tried to stay away, but the heart wants what the heart wants. I told him the truth. The whole truth this time. I thought that would repel him—when he knew who I really was, what I'd really done. But it didn't. He wanted us to run away. He wanted to confront the vile man. But we'd have no chance. You get that, right?"

Wilde nodded.

"The FBI was always trying to turn anyone close to this family. No one ever accepted because we all knew that the family would find out. Then they'd kill you slowly. But your father and I, we were crazy in love. I decided to risk it. What other choice did I have? So I went to the FBI. They promised your father and I witness relocation if I got them more information. They sent me back to live with the vile man. I wore a wire. I stole documents. I got them more info. But then something went wrong. Very wrong."

"They found out you'd turned?"

"Worse," Sofia said. "The vile man found out he was not your father."

The room seemed to hush. In the distance, Wilde heard the whir of a lawnmower.

"How?"

"Someone in the FBI leaked it to him."

"What did you do?"

"I got a heads-up, so I just jumped in the car with you and drove away. I called your father. A friend of his had a house by a lake we could use. No one would find us. That's what I thought. So you and I, we ran here. I was afraid to call the FBI. They'd been the leak. But we did know George Kissell by then. I called him when we got to this house. He said to sit tight. So I did. Except the vile man found us here first. He came with three other men. I saw them pull up right out there, right where George is parked now. The vile man came to the door and started pounding on it. He had a knife in his hand. He started screaming about how—"

She stopped, her chest hitching.

"—how he was going to slit you open right in front of me. I was so scared, desperate. You have no idea. I'm standing right here, right where I am now..."

Her eyes looked off as though she were back and seeing it.

"The vile man is coming in, trying to break the door down. What can I do? So I hide you under the stairs. I tell you to stay quiet. But that's not enough. The door gives away. The vile man bursts in. All I can think is that I need to get him away from you. I scream as loud as I can and I run upstairs. The vile man follows. That's good, I think. He's not downstairs. He's farther away from my son. I get to a bedroom window. He's right behind me. So I jump out into the hedges. I want to get them all away from you. You're safe in that closet. So I run across the street and into the woods. The vile man and his men run after me. That's good. They won't find you. Maybe they'll think you're with me. I run. It's dark. At times I think I can actually escape them. But then what? I can't lose them because then they might give up and go back to the house and find you. So I keep running and sometimes I'll even make a noise so they stay close to me. I barely care if I get caught. Because if I do, if they kill me, you'll still be alive. I don't know how long we do this. Hours. And then...then they catch me."

Wilde realized that he was holding his breath.

"The vile man starts to beat me. He broke my jaw. I can still feel it crack some days. He kept pounding on me and demanded to know where you were. I told him I lost you in the woods. I told him to keep looking for you because you ran ahead of me. Anything—*anything*—to keep them from going back to that house. I don't know how long they had me. I passed out. At some point, your father and the marshals showed up. The vile man and his henchmen ran. I remember your father wrapping his arms around me. The marshals wanted to take me to the hospital, but I said no, that I needed to get back to the house, to get back to you..."

Sofia Carter just shook her head. The tears started flowing.

"We searched for you. But you were gone. The vile man started burning the world down to find us. The marshals said we had to go now." She looked at Wilde, and his heart broke. "The marshals took us away. I let them in the end. We were given new identities and relocated. You know this. We had daughters of our own. It's the weird part of the human condition. We are forced to go on. What else can we do?"

Now the tears started coming down harder.

"But I abandoned my son. I should have stayed. I should have kept combing through the woods looking for you. I should have done it for weeks or months or years. My baby boy was alone, lost in the woods, and I gave up looking for him. I should have found you. I should have rescued—"

And then Wilde moved toward her, shaking his head, and let her fall into his arms.

"It's okay," he whispered.

Through her sobs, she kept repeating, "I should have saved you."

"It's okay," Wilde said, holding her closer to him. Then: "It's okay, Mom."

And when Sofia heard the word "Mom," she sobbed even louder.

FORTY-THREE

Oren worked the barbecue because that was the kind of guy he was. Laila was in the kitchen. Wilde sat on an Adirondack chair in the back with Hester. They looked out into the woods from the backyard of the house that Hester and Ira built over forty years ago.

Hester drank a white Chablis. Wilde had an Asbury Park Brewery ale.

"So now you know," she said.

"Most of it."

"What?"

"Some of what she said—there were holes."

"Like?"

He and his mother had talked more, but suddenly George Kissell was there telling them time was up. The danger, he said, was still real. Wilde wasn't sure how much he bought that, or if he bought that when that little boy was found in the woods, his parents didn't hear about it or put it together.

"It doesn't matter," Wilde said. "We know the important stuff."

"Your mother abandoned you to save you," Hester said.

"Yes."

"That's all that really matters."

Wilde nodded and handed her an old Polaroid. Hester took it, put on her reading glasses, studied it. The colors in the photo had saturated with age.

"Looks like a dance floor at an old wedding."

Wilde nodded. "Silas found tons of old photos his mother had stored in the basement. A lot were water damaged, but I went through them all. This one is from the early seventies."

"Okay."

"See the girl in the back by the drums?"

Hester squinted. "There are three girls in the back by the drums."

"The one with the green dress and ponytail."

Hester found her. "Yes." Then: "Wait, that's . . . ?"

"Mom, yep."

"Did Silas know who she was?"

Wilde shook his head. "No recollection of her. The wedding would have happened before he was even born."

Hester handed him the photograph. She closed her eyes and tilted her face toward the sun.

"You're spending more time here, aren't you?" Hester asked.

Laila came out back with a large empty platter. Oren started moving a tremendous amount of food off the grill and onto it.

Oren shouted, "Hope you're hungry."

Hester looked back at both of them and waved. "We both did good."

"Outkicked our coverage," Wilde agreed. "I love her."

"I know." She put her hand on his arm. "It's okay. He would be happy about it."

They sat back now. Wilde closed his eyes and worked up his courage.

"I have something I want to ask you," Wilde said.

But before he could go on, he heard Matthew from behind him. "Yo, Wilde, holy crap, you have to see this."

Matthew ran toward him with Sutton at his side. Sutton was holding up her cell phone.

"What's up?" Hester asked.

"It's the *Love Is a Battlefield* fan page," Matthew said. "It's been insane lately. Marnie is like a big-time hero-martyr now. They made that storage place where they found her body into like a giant shrine. And Jenn, she's still working on her excuses, but a lot of people are defending her. Some say she was just playing the game right. Others think she must have been abused or something so it's not her fault."

"But that's not the big news," Sutton said. She handed Wilde her phone. "Here, let me click this link."

Sutton hit the link, and the screen loaded an Instagram page.

Peter Bennett's Instagram page.

The last time Wilde had looked, the most recent post was the one of the suicide jump at Adiona Cliffs.

Now there was a video. It was dated twenty-two minutes ago. The location, listed in the upper right-hand corner, read simply FRENCH POLYNESIA.

Sutton hit the play button.

Peter Bennett appeared. He wore a long unkempt beard. He smiled for the camera.

"I'm alive, Battlers," he announced, smiling big for the camera, "and now that you know the truth, I'm coming home."

Sutton's phone rang in her hand. The video disappeared. She took the phone back and moved away, holding the phone to her ear. "I just saw it," she said excitedly to whoever was on the other end. "I know, incredible, right? He's alive!"

Matthew looked down at Wilde. "What do you think?"

"About?"

"Were the fan boards right? Was Peter behind it all the time?"

Wilde told the truth. "I don't know. Maybe."

Matthew looked over at Hester. Hester shrugged.

"But since you're here," Wilde said, his nerves returning, "I want to ask you both something."

Matthew moved closer. Hester sat up.

"What's up?" she asked.

"Do I have your permission to ask Laila to marry me?"

Hester and Matthew both smiled. Hester said, "You need our permission?"

"And your blessing," Wilde said. "I'm old-fashioned that way."

ACKNOWLEDGMENTS

Let's do this quickly because you don't want to read a long acknowledgment and I don't want to write one. I'll start with Ben Sevier, who has been my editor/publisher for over a dozen books now. The rest of the team includes Michael Pietsch, Wes Miller, Beth deGuzman, Karen Kosztolnyik, Autumn Oliver, Jonathan Valuckas, Matthew Ballast, Brian McLendon, Staci Burt, Andrew Duncan, Alexis Gilbert, Joseph Benincase, Albert Tang, Liz Connor, Flamur Tonuzi, Kristen Lemire, Mari Okuda, Rick Ball, Selina Walker (heading up the UK team), Charlotte Bush, Lisa Erbach Vance (agent extraordinaire), Diane Discepolo, Charlotte Coben, and Anne Armstrong-Coben.

A very special thanks to Person I'm Forgetting to Acknowledge Who Is Also Very Forgiving. You know who you are. You rock. Thank you for just being you.

I'd also like to give a quick shout-out to Timothy Best, Jeff Eydenberg, David Greiner, George Kissell, Nancy Urban, and Marti Vandevoort. These people (or their loved ones) made generous contributions to charities of my choosing in return for having their name appear in this novel. If you'd like to participate in the future, email giving@harlancoben.com for details.

The author photo was taken as part of JR's Inside Out Project. To learn more and participate, please visit insideoutproject.net.

ABOUT THE AUTHOR

Harlan Coben is a #1 *New York Times* bestselling author and one of the world's leading storytellers. His suspense novels are published in forty-five languages and have been number one bestsellers in more than a dozen countries, with seventy-five million books in print worldwide. His Myron Bolitar series has earned the Edgar, Shamus, and Anthony Awards, and five of his books have been developed into Netflix original series, including his adaptation of *The Stranger*, *The Innocent*, *Gone for Good*, *The Woods*, and *Stay Close*, which was released on December 31, 2021. He lives in New Jersey.

For more information you can visit:

HarlanCoben.com
Twitter: @HarlanCoben
Facebook.com/HarlanCobenBooks
Netflix.com/HarlanCoben